The Eye of the Octopus

The Eye of the Octopus

A NOVEL

Janice Miller

MOODY PRESS

CHICAGO

ISBN: 0-8024-2729-4

1 3 5 7 9 10 8 6 4 2

Printed in the United States of America

1

Monte Carlo, the Côte d'Azur

It was that brooding, silent hour before dawn. The black-sequined waters of Monaco Harbor rippled in a gathering seawind. Above the waterfront, the lights of the infamous green-domed casino twinkled feebly against the skyscraper-studded glitter of Monte Carlo.

Well behind the casino, on one wide serpentine bend of the Corniche—the coastal road—the Hotel de Mer rose like an ornate black antique, its twelve stories silhouetted against the steep, darker backdrop of Mont Charles hill. The hotel was hushed in that final hour of darkness. Its belle epoque facade was dimly illuminated by recessed lamps and ground-lit pathways through lush gardens. Several oblongs of hazed illumination were scattered across its looming forefront—windows swathed in satin damask draperies, rooms where troubled guests were unable to sleep.

Anyone familiar with the Côte d'Azur knew that dark secrets lay hidden behind this hotel's dead-eyed windows. The postage-stamp principality of Monaco was constantly awash in scandal. It had been from the very beginning of its infamous history. The notorious Hotel de Mer had seen more than its share of intrigues and conspiracies and trysts.

Now the hotel had become an anachronistic monument to another time. Most of Hotel de Mer's royal guests were has-beens whose titles were ancient relics.

Indeed, Hotel de Mer was a place where deposed royals now gathered to sulk about their dispossession, to dream of regaining their former glory, and to gamble in the hotel's gilded, green casino, squandering the fortunes their ancestors had accumulated over long and bloody centuries.

And so, in the hotel dining room and cocktail bar and even in the casino, a collective thread could be heard running through certain conversations. "Europe is not what it used to be."

And someone could always be counted upon to reply, "Certainly not, *cherie*. The problem is the European Union. Someone really should find a way to stop those pompous bureaucrats before they bankrupt every nation on the continent and take it all for themselves."

And then the conversation would turn perhaps to race cars or yachts or lovers or gambling, or even, if the tête-à-tête was of an intellectual bent, to further analysis of the newly consolidated European Union with its globalistic mind-set.

One point of special contention was the EU's presidency, which rotated yearly among all member nations. Most royals were intrigued with the fact that the office would soon be permanently filled—hopefully by a royal member of their own superior lineage.

Nowhere was the fact of Europe's so-called disintegration more obvious than in the guest register of the Hotel de Mer, where the occasional royal could now be seen sharing ink with all sorts of unroyal types, whose only right to admittance was that they had the hefty price of a room.

Sicily's Prince Dante di Veresi was in fact in residence at that moment, along with his aging, alcoholic mistress, a German-Italian *contessa.*

Or perhaps the common guest might share the musty perfumed air with an industrial giant or Greek shipping magnate; a film producer or sports icon; a movie star or oil tycoon; or possibly one of the many professional and polished Italian/Sicilian criminals who had invested heavily all along the Côte d'Azur for the past half century and who gleefully continued to plunder the area, even while using the region's real estate and casinos to launder vast soiled sums of cash.

One might, in fact, even share the Hotel de Mer's highly charged air with an occasional spy—perhaps even an elite member of the CIA's covert intelligence network, someone who was in Monte Carlo and staying at this pretentious old relic of a hotel precisely because it was a haven for those who favored an indulgent and dissipated lifestyle.

On the eighth floor of the Hotel de Mer, in a room facing the dark-spangled waterfront, just such a man lay sprawled in bed, the covers tangled about him. His tall, muscular frame nearly filled the four-poster. His thick black hair, cut short and neat, was disheveled from sleep. A square-cut jaw was covered by a dark, short-cropped beard with a gentle frosting of gray that aged him slightly beyond his thirty-eight years. The face was just shy of being handsome, for the clear brown eyes that brought it to life were closed, in that hour before dawn. He was asleep, haunted by his dream.

It was the same old dream. The tentacles of a sinuous black octopus, a massive beast with a chilling intelligence, searched relentlessly for him, searched and searched beneath a thick sea of boiling black water that was drowning him. His lungs were bursting even as the beast closed in, and behind it all was the threat of a world going up in icy black flames.

There was no secret to the symbolism. An octopus had the ability to inject poison into its prey and to spew out a blinding black ink within which to hide itself. The Italian press had therefore tacked the title "Octopus" onto the Sicilian Mafia decades ago, and Natale knew this monster well. He had watched it grow fat and bloated from the blood of its many victims. He had watched it entwine its prehensile arms with the growing tentacles of other global crime cartels.

Peter had in fact spent the past five years home-based at the CIA's Naples station, while he probed into the Italian/Sicilian black market, trying to curtail the double-headed scourge of arms and narcotics trafficking and now, especially, the emerging traffic in weapons-grade nuclear materials. These were enterprises that the Mafia controlled almost entirely in this part of the world.

The Octopus had developed a genius for manipulating its greed-spawned minions into strategic seats of power. It was helping usher in the most brutal fascist empire ever to enslave humanity. He could feel the corruption percolating to the surface all around him, and he had often awakened to the clammy awareness of this vast, many-tentacled beast.

He slept until a sudden noise penetrated his tormented dreams. Then Peter Natale shot wide awake.

He had heard a scratching, like a nail dragged lightly against stone. The afterimage of the sound was as acute as if he had heard it while fully awake. Every sculpted muscle in his body screamed for action, but Natale forced himself to remain motionless, feigning sleep, while his narrowed eyes ticked across the brooding darkness, searching for whatever or whoever had awakened him.

To his left, the balcony door was open to the inky Mediterranean night, just as he had left it. The moon etched gold on a dark bank of clouds scudding across the sky. Peter listened intently, but now the silence was broken only by the rhythmic whisper of the breakers touching the narrow shoreline eight stories beneath him, then receding with a soft throaty growl.

But something had broken this stillness. Something that had shot him through with the adrenaline of a well-disciplined fear so that he lay with muscles taut, listening.

His eyes quickly adjusted to the darkness. He examined the ghostlike shapes around him. Though this was only the second night he had spent in this palatial hotel room, the forms were familiar—the lush potted palms, the outline of the gold-brocaded sofa, the rococo finery of the gilded furniture, the carved perfection of the several marble sculptures.

The adrenaline rushing through his veins heightened every sense, making him keenly aware of his silk pajama pants and his bare chest, the soft rumpled sheets around him, the salty fragrance of the sea, the perfume of roses, the faint cold perspiration on his forehead, the clean powdery scent of his aftershave and soap. But he was even more aware of the lingering effect of some small trespass into this eerie stillness, that disturbance—ever-so-slight—that had awakened him.

He resisted an impulse to roll over and out of bed. His head was resting on his right arm, so he could see the luminous green dial of his watch without moving, and he registered the time: 4:15 A.M. It was ominously silent, as if the world held its breath.

Suddenly he remembered Judith Davies, and he was gripped with sudden panic. Again he halted an impulse to bolt upright, though he could feel his throat constrict. He kept his breathing steady, then shifted slowly, still feigning sleep, feeling invisible eyes on him that might have peered from his own tormented dreams.

Now he could see beyond the ornate stone pillars and carved nymphs of his balcony. He carefully scanned the wing of the hotel where Judith's room jutted out at an angle to his own. Her rounded stone balcony displayed the sightless, arched windowpanes of a closed door. He could see a faint light behind the heavy draperies. Perhaps she was still awake?

Or perhaps she was in trouble. A fleeting montage of images crowded up against his gnawing sense of danger. With dazzling speed he examined his situation and his options.

Earlier, he had tried to kiss Judith, standing beside the sea, as the lights of the yachts in the fairytale port made a gossamer backdrop to the night. Not a careful, respectful kiss, as he'd given her several times during this past shared week, but a real kiss, tender yet conveying passion.

She had stepped back and stared up at him, her flawless, waiflike face set into an expression of surprise. Her smoky-blue eyes had been wide with concern, and she had made the characteristic nervous gesture of pushing her shoulder-length, honey-colored hair away from her face. "No, Peter. Not now."

"Judith. I'm serious this time. I want to marry you." And he had never wanted anything so completely.

He had expected her to be pleased. At least that. He thought that at least he was building a new foundation.

But instead she gave him a sad smile that barely curled the corners of her mouth. "Thank you for saying that—if you really mean it. But it wouldn't work. Not yet."

"Why not?"

"Many reasons. Look, Peter, I'm suddenly very tired. Let's call it a day." And she turned back toward the hotel.

Natale knew better than to press her further.

Hurt and angry, he silently escorted her to her room, then came to his own room to brood. He had invested so much in this reunion, and now it was falling apart. He needed to understand what was happening between them so he could devise a plan that might pull it back together.

Finally, he fell asleep—to dream strangely alien dreams, to awaken with this urgent sense of danger that translated into a gnawing in his gut and a tightening in his throat until his racing thoughts and senses encapsulated the memory of the night and Judith into a split second's reflection.

He blinked hard, and once again his eyes ticked around the room, checking each ghoulish shape, probing every dark corner. Still nothing, no new noise, no visible enemy. And in that instant the dream that had held him captive slithered up out of his unconscious mind and into his awareness, fusing into his tangible fear and causing him to wonder if the dream had possessed him and caused him to imagine the noise.

But this sudden terror was different. It was a gripping, demonic panic that almost paralyzed him with its intensity. And he wasn't imagining things. Dream or reality, something new and immensely evil had invaded his sleep. Lying there, still motionless, he could almost hear its satanic heartbeat.

The icy fear filled him with a renewed vigilance, and he again eyed the dark shapes along Judith's balcony. Seeing nothing untoward, he then refocused on his own and minutely examined the ornate, curvaceous outline of the moon-glinted railing, the shadowed stone base with its inlay of tiny angels and nymphs and gargoyles.

Two chairs were pushed up to an umbrella table. The umbrella was folded against the night. Several ornate stone pots were filled with a silhouetted black filigree of palm ferns and the pale pink rosebushes that Judith had fallen in love with two nights ago, when they'd first arrived and had enjoyed a late dinner in his room.

Judith.

Natale forced his quickening breath to normalize, and in that split instant he summarized all they had done these past two days—the surveillance of the prince and his mistress, the ongoing investigation into the possible Mafia money laundering—all the possible dangers.

The sound came again, something scratching against stone, so faint that Peter couldn't place its direction, yet loud enough to flush him through with a new surge of adrenaline.

This time his reflexes forced him into action, and he flew off the bed, sweeping his loaded Czech-made CZ-75 automatic from the floor just beneath the bed in a motion that shot him through the inky darkness and toward the nearest light switch.

He sensed rather than heard the movement that came from behind him. He stopped short, captured for an instant between flight and fight, then braced his legs wide and whipped around to face the threat.

"Freeze." The strange male voice was a deep, low rasp. "Stop where you are."

But Natale had already lunged to one side, hitting the floor, coming up out of a roll in time to see the intruder standing uncertainly in the opened balcony door like a black marble sculpture frozen in time against the moonlight. Still moving, he registered a blurred snapshot of the man's appearance: slender, middle-height, black ski mask, black clothing, a sparkle of moonlight defining the leaden barrel of a weapon that was aimed dead at Natale, following his movement.

"I said freeze! I don't want to hurt you!" Desperation had entered the intruder's voice.

Peter braced himself for a full-on attack. But as he started to put some muscle into movement forward, the man remained motionless.

Natale stopped, confused by his visitor's failure to react. He was still facing the man, his own gun ready to fire, but the intruder simply stood there.

Natale was a fully trained professional and would shoot only to protect himself or others. And suddenly he felt no threat. Puzzled, he paused for an instant longer and tried to make sense of what was happening.

The man had been hidden in the small dark alcove just outside the balcony door and to Natale's right. As Peter realized this, he was suddenly angry with himself. How had he been so foolish as to let down his guard?

He had been consumed by his problems with Judith; he had deliberately left the balcony door open so he could watch the moon and the drifting clouds as he thought about his feelings for her—instead of his responsibility to provide their mutual safety. It had been a stupid thing to do, and now here he was, facing off with what appeared to be either a most unusual cat burglar or an exceptionally timid terrorist, but either way a man who should not have been able to gain admittance into this room.

Natale spoke. "If you don't want to hurt me, why don't you drop the gun?" He relaxed somewhat. If the man meant to kill him, he'd already be dead.

The gun barrel wavered a moment, then the figure deliberately aimed it downward.

"Forgive me for entering like this, Herr Natale." His voice was now a respectful whisper. The words were Italian, with a hint of German accent. "I have been followed this evening, and perhaps I am being overly cautious." His grip on the weapon loosened, and now it was fully pointed toward the floor.

Natale was startled to hear the intruder use his name. "Who are you?" he demanded.

"That doesn't matter. I just need to tell you—"

The words vanished in an explosion that buckled the man's knees.

Natale lunged aside, even as his visitor collapsed to the floor. A slight hissing sound escaped from the man's lips as the sound of gunfire came again. The intruder's weapon hit the carpet with a faint thud, and now he was moaning.

Natale had seen the flash of a gun muzzle on the balcony two stories above Judith's room. He rolled into a protective crouch, his gun aimed at the balcony. His mind was a turmoil of confused thoughts and possibilities. He wanted to crash out of the room and after the sniper. But if the murderer was a trained professional, he would already be gone, out and running, any mask stripped off in flight, his firearm abandoned, and no way to tell his identity. Even if Peter had known who to chase, it would be impossible to track anyone through the labyrinthine hallways and garden paths of Hotel de Mer. As he swiftly weighed the possibilities, another groan reminded him that his first responsibility was to the wounded man.

He stepped over to him. In the milky moonlight, he could see a large stain spreading dead center of the man's narrow chest. He knelt at an angle not visible from the balcony door, then bent over and gently pulled up the ski mask.

Natale had been working with the German secret service on a plutonium/uranium trafficking operation—"Kaleidoscope." He had finished up his end of the probe just before coming on this trip with Judith. Now, after hearing the young man's German accent, he expected to see someone connected to that probe or perhaps someone else from his past. He had made so many enemies through the years that he could no longer remember or count them all.

But the face was unfamiliar. The man was in his late twenties, tall and lanky, with pale corn-silk hair and a thin poet's face. The startled blue eyes were fixed like marbles, wide open and already glazing over with death. Though there was only a decade between them, a strange aura of innocence made the dying man seem, to Natale, a mere boy.

Sorrow welled up in him. And then anger. What had this fool been doing? Why had he surreptitiously entered this hotel room? He was angry at the youth for being here and angry at himself for not anticipating trouble.

The young man had apparently wanted to talk to him. That was all. To tell him—what?

But if he had merely wanted to talk, why the secretive entrance? Who had been following him? Why the ski mask? Why the cat burglar's clothing?

Natale had found the man's pulse by now. It still fluttered faintly. He pulled up the black knit shirt, looking for a place to apply pressure to stop the flow of blood. But the assassin's weapon must have been massive. The chest was a gaping wound, showing gray broken bone and the tangled red mass of damaged organs.

Peter offered up a fervent prayer for guidance, and even as he did so the man's eyes seemed to draw light and life from his own for an instant. He tried to speak.

Natale gripped the man's extended hand, trying to transfer some energy through contact.

The man squeezed back, exerting an effort that literally made the veins in his temples bulge, until finally his lips formed a raspy whisper. "They lied about everything. They have the Rhinegold. Warn her. Tell Gia that the dragon is coming, the reptiles . . ."

A sudden bubbling of blood drowned the words. The young man jackknifed and stiffened. Natale gripped the hand harder, prayed more fervently, this time out loud.

The pain seemed to pass quickly, and the intruder sighed deeply, then tried again to speak. But as the mouth formed a word, the throat made a death rattle. His eyelids twitched, and he went limp.

Peter knew, even before he touched the failed pulse, that the young man was dead. Yet he stayed there, letting tears well into his eyes. He had seen far too much death, far too much savagery, and now here, in the middle of the Mediterranean night, death came again, senselessly, suddenly, in the form of a bullet that had taken a man far too young to die.

He felt a sudden primeval urge to howl out his rage at the meaninglessness of this death, to break the earth apart in his fury, to claw down the sky.

But even as the emotions stabbed at him, he knew there was no time to mourn. Others would have heard the shots. He had to spin into action. Because if he couldn't get this straightened out, and fast, this death was going to be a mere foretaste of far darker things to come.

2

Monte Carlo

The dead man lay sprawled on the floor. Peter Natale leaned back on his heels and shook his head in an attempt to clear away the scalding grief and the lingering confusion, and he tried to understand. But as he replayed the incident in his mind, he only became more confused.

Swiftly and professionally he patted the dead man down. The pockets were completely empty, which told him the foray into his room had been planned. The intruder did not want to be identified.

He then moved to the desk beside the service table and carefully removed a sheet of hotel-embossed writing paper and an envelope from a drawer. He carefully pressed each of the man's fingertips onto the paper. Then he folded the paper, placed it inside the matching envelope, went to his closet, and stuffed the envelope into his overnight bag—in the side pocket beside his socks and shorts.

He knelt beside the man again, carefully studying the face, the clothing, the shoes—and the weapon.

The gun was a Beretta automatic, but there was no serial number, not even one that had been shaved off. This weapon was in truth a knock-off of the real thing—the type of counterfeit manufactured in several of the ex-Soviet satellites. The tag inside the black knit shirt was a common brand, perhaps also a counterfeit. The pants were black Levi's, available anywhere in the world. The man wore a pair of black sneakers, available at any department store or black-market shoe stall on the Continent.

There was nothing outstanding about him, nothing to grab onto, only those anguished blue eyes glazed over and the plea

"They lied . . . warn her . . . tell Gia . . ." And he'd muttered something about gold, about reptiles.

Natale stayed beside the man a moment longer, thinking hard about those words. Who was Gia? He probed his memory, but he knew no one by that name. He thought about this for what seemed like a long time, though in truth it was only a moment. Why would the dead man expect him to know "Gia"? He shook his head, bewildered. Perhaps the man had been hallucinating, as people sometimes did when taking their final breath.

Still, whether or not that was true, he was totally baffled by what had happened. And he also realized that the entire experience, from his leap out of bed until now, had taken less than three minutes.

With that thought, he was again faced with the realization that he had to move fast. He had landed dead center in a diplomatic minefield. He was a covert operative, working for the CIA in a region where he had no charter, no back-up, no fall-back position.

In recent years, anti-American sentiment had been growing throughout Europe. Most key members of the European Union were trying to diminish, if not destroy, the last traces of the American presence that had been stamped upon the face of Europe since the end of World War II. This meant getting the remaining American forces out of NATO and out of Europe. Natale and other CIA operatives walked on eggshells, trying to avoid any incident that might allow the EU bloc to turn something against them. Now he had landed smack-dab in a fiasco that would certainly be twisted to their advantage. They might even try to shut down a CIA station or two by hanging out Peter Natale as a lightning rod for all the anti-American sentiment that had permeated Europe over this past chaotic decade.

The urge to flee impacted him with the force of a blow, but logic instantly swept the urge away. The worst thing he could do was bolt. He needed to know what had happened and why, and in order to do that he was going to have to get a grip on himself and think about some serious damage control.

Carefully he peeled back a curtain and looked out. Lights were blinking on. Others had heard the gunfire. In Judith's room someone had turned on a brighter light. That was good news. She

16

was probably OK. But the room two floors above, where the killer had been stalking, waiting—that room was ominously dark.

Peter shut the balcony door and pulled the drapes—a precaution he should have taken earlier—then switched on the overhead lights. After that he went to the telephone and dialed Judith's room. He waited while the phone rang once, twice, a half-dozen times. His heart beat faster with every ring.

Finally he slammed down the receiver, then picked it up again and phoned hotel security. They had a guard station in Judith's wing and could reach her immediately.

When a man answered, Peter said, "Check on Judith Davies, room 810 in the east wing. It's an emergency."

"Yes, sir. And, sir, shots have been fired in the hotel." The man sounded excited. "The police are on their way. Please stay in your room."

"The trouble was *in* my room, 884. Send the police up. I'll explain when they get here. But first check on Ms. Davies."

"Yes, sir. Right away."

Natale dragged on the same gray slacks and matching gray knit shirt he'd worn yesterday, something loose so that he could holster his gun beneath it. He was just starting to strap on his waist holster, ready to go check on Judith himself, when a knock at the door stopped him.

He leaned into the door. "Yes?"

"It's Judith. Are you OK?"

He yanked open the door, flooded by a vast sense of relief, and started to embrace her. But something in her posture restrained him—a rigidity and distance. There was also a warning look in her eyes, so he stepped back and gave her room.

Her hair was brushed out but not mussed, as though she had prepared for bed but never slept. She was wearing a tailored sapphire-blue satin dressing gown with matching blue piping and belt in the resurgent 1930s style, with not a wrinkle in it. He could see the legs of matching pajamas beneath it and matching satin slippers with closed toes and small heels. She stepped forward, and he could smell the clean scent of heather soap.

"I heard a gunshot," she said. There was a husky tremor in

her voice. Her smoky-blue eyes were wide with apprehension and a faint trace of fear.

"Yes," Natale replied. He forced himself to sound in control. "I ran into some trouble."

He stepped aside so she could see the body sprawled on the floor behind him. It had become the focal point in the room. One dead hand was thrown across the handle of the firearm, where it had slipped during death. The black ski mask was still attached to the man's head, though the cloth was peeled back. The neck was twisted, so he faced the balcony, looking in the direction from which his death had come.

Natale could see Judith swallow hard. He reached out for her, but she stepped back and shook her head, holding out her hand to ward him off.

It took her a moment to compose herself. Then she straightened her back purposefully and stepped past him into the room. When she reached a position where she could fully see the dead man's face, she stopped short and blinked hard, her eyes widening. She swiftly drew one fist to her mouth, as if to stop any words that might erupt, and bit hard on her knuckle.

"You know him?" Peter already knew the answer. He had seen recognition flood her eyes.

She turned to stare at him, her eyes growing wider as some realization came, bringing with it a spate of terror.

"What?" Natale tried to prompt her to say something.

"It's—"

"Go on."

"I—Peter, I'm sorry." Her jaw clenched tightly. Her eyes became hooded as if she were storing away a secret. Then she turned her head slowly to look at the corpse again.

He saw stark, dazed sorrow come into her eyes. It was so intense that it trapped him too for a moment. But then she swiftly transformed her face into a brittle porcelain mask. She blinked coldly, turned to look defiantly at him, and said, "Why should I know him?"

Peter felt his eyes narrow with suspicion. "There's a dead man on my bedroom floor, Judith. Someone I've never seen before. If you know anything, I could use the help right now."

18

Her mask melted slightly. "I really am sorry, Peter. I—I just—" She looked at him as if she wanted to talk but truly couldn't speak.

"What's wrong?"

She swallowed. "Nothing. I—it's nothing." Her face was hard again.

Natale felt his jaw lock, felt his muscles tense up and his hands ball into fists. "Judith. Tell me what you know about this. We don't have time to fool around!"

It was the wrong approach to take. He saw that immediately.

She stared hotly at him, matching his growing rage, her lips pursed in stubborn silence, two spots of color rising in her pale cheeks.

He had never before felt so much as a twinge of desire to be violent toward Judith, but suddenly he had to stifle an impulse to grab her and shake the truth out of her. Forcibly he fought back the impulse, and then a fist slammed into the door, breaking his concentration. Then another, and another, and the banging turned into a full-on din.

Peter breathed deeply, quenching the anger. He stepped over and looked through the eyehole in the door.

He turned to Judith. "You ready for this?"

She nodded. There was a vestige of shame in her eyes now, and regret.

But Natale had no time to decipher her emotions or to deal with her secrecy. He braced himself and rolled his eyes heavenward. "Here we go."

He opened the door, and a small cluster of hotel security officers and Monte Carlo gendarmerie swooped in: five steely-jawed men with firearms drawn, though they did not immediately aim them at Peter or Judith.

A tall, spare man with a brown brush mustache, a sallow face, and clay-colored eyes led the pack. He immediately descended on Peter and fixed him with a long, penetrating stare. Then he broke his gaze to peer suspiciously around the room.

He was apparently satisfied with what he saw, for he nodded once, then stuck his firearm inside a waist holster and turned back to Peter and Judith. He was wearing civilian clothing, but it was apparent that he was one of the higher-ranking officers, even before he flipped open a small leather case to show Natale a badge.

"You are the resident of this room?"

"I am."

"You phoned hotel security that there had been a shooting, Monsieur?"

"I did."

"And your name?"

Natale introduced himself, then Judith. "We were vacationing above Nice and decided to finish up with a couple of days here," he said. No point in rushing the inevitable by telling too much of the truth.

"And I," the man said importantly, "am Chief Inspector Duvalier of the Monte Carlo police. Would you be so kind as to tell me why you have a dead body lying on your floor?"

Peter opened his arms in a gesture of bewildered resignation and tersely explained, leaving out only the man's dying words.

The look of disbelief grew deeper on Duvalier's face as the story developed. Finally the inspector said, "You think I am a fool."

"I'm sorry if you get that impression. I've told you what happened."

"Faugh! Why do you insult me with such a silly story? I would suggest, Monsieur Natale, that you think this over and decide to tell the truth. We will talk more later." He tossed his head, then turned and began barking orders to the other officers in an obnoxiously loud voice.

Natale and Judith were shunted to one side for the moment, which gave them a chance to finally put their heads together and talk. Peter explained in detail what had happened. He suspected that they were going to take him in for questioning, so he asked Judith to check the hotel room where the killer had lurked in waiting, and asked her to handle a few other things.

A uniformed gendarme with a narrow, impassive face and a nose worthy of de Gaulle himself stood guard over them and obviously tried to overhear what they were saying, while the others hovered over the body and talked excitedly. After a few moments of this, Duvalier and a second man descended upon Peter and Judith again with a full verbal assault, bombarding them both with questions, skewering them with baleful and disbelieving glares, skillfully bouncing them back and forth.

Natale did his best with the situation. He bore the brunt of the inquisition, because it was, after all, his room.

Judith spoke only when forced to and said next to nothing even then.

The investigation continued. The silent hour before dawn had been forever violated, and daylight arrived like thick, dark honey that had suddenly turned golden and hot to pour through the windows. The balcony doors were reopened as the policemen minutely examined the area. The Mediterranean was framed by the arched balcony doorsill and the fluted white railing, making a gleaming blue backdrop for the macabre scene.

Sometime around seven o'clock, a forensics expert arrived. Natale and Judith were asked to move out of the way into a small alcove, where they sat in high-backed chairs beside a small polished table holding an authentic classical Roman bust of Emperor Claudius.

The criminalist took their and the dead man's fingerprints, checked the room, officiated over the photographs being taken, and otherwise secured the crime scene.

As this took place, the chief inspector circled Judith and Natale like a shark from time to time, then returned to the others and talked quietly. Several times he used the telephone to talk portentously with the hotel's manager, then with the crime commissioner, finally with the governor himself. He appeared to make a point of speaking loud enough so that no one would miss how well-connected he was. He referred to Judith and Peter as Americans, in a tone so scathing that he might have been uttering obscenities.

When the forensics man was almost finished, Duvalier returned to Natale and Judith and began going over and over the same tedious questions yet again. Who were they really? What were they doing here? Why was the man here? Who shot him? Why was he armed? Most of all, who was he?

Natale couldn't identify the victim. If Judith could have, she didn't. She simply shook her head at the barrage of words.

Finally, well after 8:00 A.M., Chief Inspector Duvalier told Judith that they were letting her go. "But your friend Peter Natale will be required to tell his wild tale to our commissioner," he explained with a malicious smile.

A younger officer was already fumbling with a pair of handcuffs. He began to put them on Peter, who stood passively with his hands behind him, accepting the insult.

"Perhaps some miracle will occur to confirm Mr. Natale's bizarre story," the inspector said. "But since that seems unlikely, we will make certain that he remains in custody. He is, after all, a foreigner, and likely to leave the country if he is not detained."

Natale hid his anger and waited. He had already done everything he could to persuade Duvalier not to take him in.

The intruder's body was still sprawled on the floor but was covered now with a white sheet. The coroner's attendants were preparing to place it on a gurney for removal from the room.

Judith seemed drained of life, distracted, almost oblivious to the seriousness of what was happening around her. She looked hollowly at the chief inspector as he explained why he was taking Peter away.

She seemed to come awake only when Natale was fully handcuffed and they were pushing him toward the door.

He looked back and spoke sharply to her. "Get me out."

"Of course." She shot him a smoldering glare that said she was insulted he'd even have to mention it.

Natale was relieved to see that she was suddenly clear-eyed and focused on the moment. "You know what to do."

She shot him a questioning look.

He gave her a jabbing thumbs-down sign, meaning he preferred to be bailed out by his Mafia friend Carlo Ricaso rather than by his CIA connections in Rome or Naples. Peter didn't want to blow the cover he had carefully crafted over many years. And besides, revealing that he was CIA would almost certainly stir up an international incident. It was bad enough that they were Americans.

Judith nodded her understanding.

Carlo might or might not come through for him. There had been some strain in that relationship lately. Besides, even if Carlo wanted to help, things could go wrong. He might not be in. The Ricaso family's point man in Monaco might be unavailable. It was a truism of spy craft that whatever might go wrong did, so one must always be prepared for the worst, and at that moment he was prepared to spend a day or two behind bars.

Things had in fact already gone wrong with regard to Judith. Desperately wrong. He had been watching her carefully, ever since she'd recognized the dead man. She knew something, he was absolutely certain of it. Something vital, something that horrified her. Even in his anger, he realized this.

And he could see that the enormity of what she knew had catapulted her into a sort of shock, had absorbed the full mass of her brain as she tried to puzzle out the immensity of it all so she could come to terms with the emotional impact.

As the police guided Natale down the ornate hallway and into the elevator, these thoughts dissolved his anger and replaced it with growing trepidation.

He had to figure out what had happened here tonight—whether the bullet had been meant for him or for the stranger. And Judith had at least part of the answer to the puzzle. He was sure of that. But if he was going to learn what Judith knew about the polite young intruder who had stepped into his room to die, Natale was first of all going to have to get past the inconvenience of a Monte Carlo jail cell.

Then, if he knew Judith—and he did—he realized that he'd have to wait patiently until she had sorted this all out in her own mind and had fully come to terms with whatever terror was forcing her silence. Only then would she let him share her dark and frightening secret, and only then would he begin to understand the truth.

3

Berlin

Yuri Alexandr Lepkov shoved open the double plate-glass doors to his elegant suite of offices, stormed past his secretary, and said through clenched teeth, "I absolutely do not want to be disturbed until further notice."

The secretary, an exquisite middle-aged woman in a plum silk designer's dress and with silver highlights in her sleek platinum hair, made a prudent downward sweep of her eyelashes. "Of course, Herr Lepkov."

He entered his cherrywood office, locked the door behind him, then tossed his alligator briefcase toward the white divan. It landed beside his desk. In spite of his smoldering fury, he yielded to habit and stopped to check the combination fax machine, electronic message pad, and computer mail board.

Nothing important was waiting for him, certainly nothing as urgent as the problem that had arisen while he was attempting to meet with Prince Dante di Veresi.

Lepkov ran a multimillion dollar international corporation from these offices, laundering vast sums of money, brokering and overseeing delivery of Colombian cocaine, Sicilian heroin, Russian nuclear contraband, legitimate Middle Eastern oil, Liberian coal, stolen luxury cars, pilfered art—he didn't care what, so long as there was profit to be made. He had built his business up to include some thirty corporations in various countries, most of them dummies that facilitated his international movements.

His minions—a full dozen other KGB rogues among them—usually kept the day-to-day business operations under control. But for some reason ugly surprises seemed to be cropping up in his life these days. Take, for instance, the surprise that had just jolted him at Hotel de Mer. He certainly had not expected to find two CIA agents spying, almost openly, on the prince.

Lepkov was a thick-built man of sixty, unmistakably Slavic, with short gray-brown hair and a wide brow emphasized by a receding hairline. Today he was immaculate in a black pin-striped suit, white shirt and vest, all of him wrapped within a chilling aura of power.

He sat down on the silvery leather chair behind his enormous cherry desk and stared coldly out at the gray Berlin skyline. His hard-planed face was chiseled into stony anger, his eyes were glacial and flat as a reptile's. There had been a serious organizational breakdown somewhere. His CIA source had failed him, and at a most critical time.

He picked up a gold paperweight and toyed with it. It was a tsarist double eagle, the symbol of the new Russia. He resisted an impulse to fling it through the window. Why hadn't he been warned?

He set down the paperweight, grabbed up the telephone, and hit a button to speed-dial the CIA's Berlin station on the scrambled line.

When a colorless voice answered with an abrupt "Yes?" Lepkov forced civility into his voice, forced his Russian accent to disappear into fluent German, and said, "Please inform Herr Wolfe that Herr Carr needs to speak with him immediately."

He hung up before anyone could possibly have responded. Both Wolfe and Carr were code names. As soon as his CIA contact got the message, he would find a private phone and call back.

Lepkov was identified by the few workers at Berlin station only as one of their nameless assets, and he met on a regular basis with just one trusted ally, station chief Willie von Wolverton, who had been his adversary during the days when KINTEX was running strong. Things changed. Or rather, money changed things. Within the past five years he had made this man rich beyond words. Now, at the most critical juncture of his life, the man had failed him.

He cursed again, then leaned back in his chair to glare at the polished glass wall framing the city.

It should have been such a simple meeting. He had taken a

commercial jet so as not to be conspicuous. He even dragged his wife and her ancient father along as camouflage. Fortunately, he had also ordered up a contingent of handpicked hatchet men that Guappo flew in from Naples, just to guard against the unexpected.

Marco Guappo was a middle-aged thug. His father was now capo in the homegrown Neapolitan Mafia known as the Camorra. Marco had been in a state of idealistic rebellion when Lepkov recruited him into the terrorist Red Brigade many years ago.

Yuri Lepkov once held the top KGB spot in the Soviet satellite Bulgaria. He originated the idea of using Bulgaria's State Commerce Agency—KINTEX—as the primary clearinghouse for a good share of the morphine base that flowed out of Lebanon and Turkey and into other parts of Europe.

The system had been foolproof, since he ruled the KGB, which controlled Bulgarian Customs and the commercial attachés. He also controlled the camps where crack terrorists were trained. But when drug traffic surpassed terrorism as a way to destabilize societies, he turned his talents even more fervently toward that end. And there he had been when the Soviet Union collapsed, taking the Eastern Bloc with it and knocking him out of a job.

KINTEX had helped build underground corridors that riddled the destabilized West. Lepkov was capitalizing on those pipelines, and Marco Guappo was but one small example of the carry-over resources.

Marco had believed Communism would save his country from the stranglehold of the Mafia, including that of his own authoritarian and brutal father.

He finally realized, however, that Communism was just the other face of the coin of fascism and that both were systems of brutal totalitarian rule. He eventually went back to his father's organization to continue his training as a thug and killer, but he still made himself available to Lepkov when the price was right.

This time, the price had been hefty indeed: five million in US dollars, payable through Monaco's Banq de Mer, then wired on to Naples for dispersion to Marco's various reptiles.

Lepkov didn't begrudge the money. Marco's band of toughs was worth the price. Lepkov was now and had always been purely pragmatic. He preferred to use members of the Chechen Russian

Mafia to handle jobs both in Russia and across the Continent. But his KGB experience had taught him that sometimes outside teams were better. It was always wise to use Italians or Sicilians when operating on Italian soil, and his relationship with the criminal core of Italy/Sicily—the Ricaso crime family—was still sweet indeed.

And sometimes Marco proved his worth. As he had during the past two days at Hotel de Mer.

Lepkov cursed again as he thought about it. He hated person-to-person meetings. He refused to take such foolish risks unless he was absolutely certain he had to work on someone face to face. He had just checked into the hotel and notified the prince that he was ready to meet with him, when Marco knocked on his door unexpectedly, then entered the suite without invitation, eyeing Lepkov's wife like a hungry shark.

Lepkov sent her into the bedroom to tend to her decrepit father, then turned on Marco in fury. "What are you doing here?"

"Sorry to break rules, but we have a serious problem. The young man I recruited in Bonn?"

"Yes. What about him?"

"He was seen approaching a strange woman in the garden this afternoon."

Lepkov turned to granite. "Who is this woman?"

Marco handed him some Polaroid photographs. "I had a man follow her and take these. There." He jabbed a forefinger at the second photo. "This one is of her and the man who arrived with her yesterday. I learned this from a desk clerk."

Lepkov stared with hatred at the small blonde woman in the picture. "I know who she is." He had her photo in his data banks, along with most of the other 500 covert CIA operatives and administrators who still functioned in Europe. The computer files had been sold to him by his source at Berlin station.

He remembered the blonde woman because of her exceptional face, but he had forgotten her name. "Did the desk clerk ID them?"

"Peter Natale and Judith Davies."

Lepkov cursed. He remembered now. She was chief intelligence analyst at Moscow station, a recently converted Christian, anti-Mafia, antinarcotics, anti-everything he did. And the man,

Peter Natale? He had heard that name before too, though at the moment he had so much on his mind that he couldn't quite remember where.

"It gets worse," Marco said. "One of my soldiers also saw them watching the prince last night in the casino. They appeared to be gambling and socializing, but my man said they only had eyes for the prince."

Lepkov felt himself turn to stone. He swung slowly around to fix Marco with a chilling stare. "Cancel everything." He chiseled out every word from the depths of his anger. "Do not ask any more questions, do you understand? Do not mention this to even your soldiers."

The last thing he needed was for the CIA to suddenly start probing into his murky currency dealings or into his thus-far secretive association with Prince Veresi.

Most of all he was concerned that Judith Davies had been in Monte Carlo. All the way from Moscow. The whole thing could be unraveling. Why on earth else would a Moscow CIA analyst be in Monte Carlo?

Marco had nodded his understanding.

"I want you to personally handle this young man you recruited—what was his name?"

"Rudy. Rudy Brandenburg. He is the one whose family is old German aristocracy. They were former Nazis, members of the Black Nobility. That's the only reason I brought him in."

"Well, you have made a serious mistake, and I expect you to correct it immediately. Do you understand?"

Marco looked like a delicious treat had just been passed his way. "I'll take care of it tonight."

The hotel had erupted into chaos in the predawn hours. Rudy Brandenburg had been headed into Natale's hotel room via the eighth-floor balcony, which told Lepkov that Brandenburg was indeed trying to talk to the CIA. Disaster had narrowly been averted. This time.

But he was going to have to make sure that there were no more loose ends, for time was growing short—only two more weeks until the Italian EU president was selected. Everything depended on the success of his plan.

Lepkov had then notified the prince that a meeting would not be prudent, that he was returning to Berlin as soon as possible and would contact him later. He stayed in his room all day with his wife and her annoying father, waiting for a proper time to leave without attracting attention. Finally they'd flown commercially back to Berlin. He had the private limo drive his miserable family home. He took a rented car to the office.

And again, as Lepkov sat and thought about events, his hatred for all humanity surged up like boiling acid. He wanted to strangle someone—preferably someone American. All his life, every direction he turned, he seemed to meet with interference from the Americans. Without them the Soviet Union would still be strong. Without their interference, his present business would be so much simpler that he would probably live a good ten years longer.

He rifled through a stack of papers and brought out one of the memorandums that convinced him this was so. The Pentagon had budgeted some $2 billion for antinarcotics interdiction this year. The UN had been given an additional $2 billion to fight the narcotics traffic in Russia and Europe. The black budget of the CIA's Counternarcotics Division was secret, but it was apparent to anyone who cared to look that much of the energy that had once been spent on the Cold War was now being used to target the multinational narcotics cartels.

He cursed again. Why couldn't the Americans go home and take care of their disintegrating country and leave him and his colleagues to their own devices?

Most of Lepkov's countrymen were taking refuge in fantasies, waiting for the world to fulfill its promises to make Russia a part of the global economic community. He knew that only the elitist Russians would ever see any reward. He had faced reality. He had done the only thing possible within the situation. He had learned from none other than *don* Cesare Ricaso how to engineer situations and people so as to gain unbridled power and wealth.

And now the Americans had reared their ugly heads yet again.

His eyes glittered as he contemplated the CIA and the country it represented. He despised the Americans with their fading morality. He saw them as timidly dabbling in the dark areas of the world, flexing their atrophying muscles. Then when they got their fingers burned they ran safely home to the United States to whine about it to the United Nations and the global press.

But the EU was accomplishing what Communism could not. Americans were gradually being removed from their European power base. Their attempts to find a foothold in Russia were increasingly met with jeers. They were proving every day that they could no longer run their own country. How could they handle the far more difficult problems in Europe and Russia?

US military forces had left Germany several years after reunification. The northern NATO base in Europe's capital, Brussels, held only 1,000 remaining troops, mostly as a courtesy gesture allowed by the European Union. The only full military contingent the Americans still had in Europe was in Naples at NATO's southern headquarters, where the Sixth Fleet was still home-ported and where the US Air Force still kept a fleet of fighter jets and spy technology.

Lepkov smiled. There was hope. The Italians were beginning to press harder for an end to the American presence, and certain manipulations might make them press harder still. When the military went home, much of the intelligence-gathering apparatus would go with it, and so would the budget money to interdict drug traffickers. The CIA spies would be gone.

He sat back, shut his eyes, and forced himself to relax. He may have overreacted to the incident at the Hotel de Mer. After all, he had never been interested in the prince. He had merely used the evil old man to get to his lodge-mate Count Benito Jacovetti. Lepkov was backing the long-time Italian delegate to the EU's Council of Ministers to be the next president of the European Union.

In this he was at full odds with the Ricaso crime family, whose own choice, Volante Chicarelli, was totally under their thumb.

Either candidate could be relied upon to implement laws that would favor black market commerce. But Jacovetti's father had been deposed from his position as mayor of Palermo by a Ricaso replacement, and Jacovetti had never forgotten the betrayal. Therefore he had plighted his troth to Lepkov, whose resources would win him the appointment hands down so long as the massive amounts of stolen gold in Lepkov's reptile fund held out.

Money wasn't the point anyway. It was power, and the man who controlled the EU presidency—even and especially from behind the scenes—would be the most powerful man on the planet.

So what if he had to put up with a pack of fools who called themselves the Black Nobility and who believed that they were being ushered into political power by some occult force? Lepkov knew he was the true power behind their would-be thrones, and when it came time to collect what he had invested, he would be the true power indeed.

Still, the prince's Black Nobility mumbo jumbo could be quite disconcerting. Without Veresi around, Jacovetti seemed to be far more pliable. Perhaps in spite of his spiritism and astrological charts and gibberish, Jacovetti had been tamed.

Lepkov's eyes narrowed as he considered his options. The Black Nobility would still be needed, simply because Jacovetti was fully committed to their cause. But did he really need Prince Dante di Veresi now?

He felt the tightening in his head begin to melt, the tightness in his skin seem to dissolve. There would be problems. There were always problems. But his long years in Bulgaria running KINTEX had proved to him beyond doubt that he had the secret to controlling the pitiless narcotics monster to which the West had sold its very soul. The power of that knowledge suddenly coursed through his veins and assuaged the aching emptiness that gnawed at him almost constantly.

He looked out over the city. The lights were beginning to flicker on. The steely sky was stained over by a deep mauve sunset glossed in turn by a fine mist. He again picked up the scrambled phone. This time, he dialed a Naples number.

When the line was answered—always cryptically—he said to Marco, "What's happening with our Roman acquisition?"

"No problems. We'll ship to Naples as planned."

Lepkov hung up without another word and smiled darkly. Violence carried out within the framework of violence was seldom noticed, and in a country where the Mafia was everywhere, who was going to blame a Russian businessman for the kidnapping of an Italian politician's son?

Yet through this kidnapping he was going to cause a division between *don* Cesare Ricaso, his only true rival for power, and *don* Cesare's handpicked candidate for the president of the European Community. The rest would be easy.

He understood that the need certain men felt to enslave humanity was surpassed only by the desire of most people to be enslaved. Didn't the existence of so many brutal dictators—even the Mafia itself—prove that? Just look at the way people flocked to the drug dealers, like lemmings leaping off a cliff. There was some deep human need to self-destruct. He knew this craving had always existed. And he knew exactly how to exploit it.

He would be wealthy beyond belief, powerful beyond imagination. But he would also be part of history. A dark, surging wind was sweeping him along toward a future he'd never dreamed of. With this wind at his heels, he knew he could finally, fully succeed at anything—if only the infernal Americans would stay out of his way.

In that moment the anger left Lepkov, and he was staring into his tormented past. Now that he had the largest part of the stolen Red Gold and could buy up the very world, he wasn't sure he could purchase what he really wanted. Power was not the sum of it, either, though that was one component.

In that moment he faced the truth. His primary motive was revenge. He despised others' freedom, their lightness of being, their very lives. If he could not experience the joy of life, he would make certain that the light and pleasure was pillaged from others' lives, even as it had been from his own.

And so he wrapped himself in a cold, narcotic fury and contemplated the impending firestorm that his own crippled logic would soon create.

4

Rome

Late summer afternoon sunlight reflected gold in the windows of the high-rises towering behind the small, tile-roofed shops that lined Rome's Via Italica. The smell of roses wafted from the colorful baskets of the busy sidewalk vendors. A young, princely gladiator named Luciano Chicarelli strolled along the boulevard, a thoughtful smile on his face.

His blood quickened as he turned a corner and spotted the black-and-white striped awning in front of the fashionable Ristorante di Fontana at the end of the block. Gianalisa Lauro had promised to meet him there at 6:30 for a long, romantic dinner and a discussion of their respective—and perhaps mutual—futures.

Though Luciano was early he walked a bit faster, pushing his way through the teeming crowd. Brisk traffic moved both ways along the wide boulevard. The park across the street was bright with bougainvillea in bishop's purple, cardinal red, and virgin white. The filigree of the hanging gardens that decorated many of Rome's buildings was enhanced by growing shadows lush as episcopal velvet.

But Luciano barely saw this. Nor was he fully aware of the flirtatious glances from several of the women he passed, for he was a tall and handsome man in his early twenties, with dark hair and soulful brown eyes—a man who might have posed for one of Michelangelo's famous sculptures.

He edged past a cluster of people watching a sidewalk artist, stepped back into the flow of pedestrians, and at that moment a plain, brown-haired woman in a white T-shirt and denim slacks brushed suggestively into him.

Though the slight impact had been her fault, he graciously started to apologize. But the defiance in her posture told him the movement had been intentional. Embarrassed, he averted his eyes. He dug both hands into the pockets of his stylishly baggy linen slacks, as if to ensure their chastity, and made for the restaurant.

He was pleased that Gianalisa had come to Rome for the weekend. She had refused his invitation to stay at his father's elaborate palazzo. She even insisted on taking a taxi from the airport in order to freshen up at her hotel before meeting him.

Though he had known Gianalisa for only one short month, Luciano was already used to her unusual moods and her wild independence. He even knew about her problem with drugs—a not unusual problem among the children of nobility. She was a lost child and a misfit, like himself; a visionary and a poet and many other capricious things. But whatever she was, he adored her.

He thought about her with a sort of awe that he had captured such an uncommon treasure. Her novelty and fragility made her even more appealing to him. Sometimes a sort of madness welled up in her eyes and made them luminous. At other times the fear came, and she would let him hold her carefully in his arms, while she wept sad tears and talked about dreadful things, until she pulled him into that other dark world with her—a place that sometimes frightened even him.

Gianalisa had been born to wealth and position, for she was the only daughter of Prince Dante di Veresi. And though, at times, everything seemed to frighten her, nothing ever seemed to impress her—least of all the fortune of a politician and his scholarly son, vast though that fortune had become.

Luciano was just grateful that she had finally agreed to even meet his father—a man whom others stood in line for. For Gianalisa to engage in such a mundane social ritual as meeting his father was, in Luciano's mind, a true sign of her growing love and commitment.

Luciano had spent the past decade in boarding schools, then in college. He had been far removed from his father's milieu in the political conflagration that was Rome.

Luciano had paid scant attention to her father, the prince. The title was a relic. He hadn't even known that the prince had a beautiful daughter who had been ill for a time in a private hospital, then was safely tucked away at a Catholic girls' school until she emerged from her cocoon just this year, eighteen years old and beautiful.

Luciano had met Gianalisa by accident, in front of the nearest library. Even then, he hadn't known for a time who she really was. She used her dead mother's name, Lauro, because she did not want to be identified with her father, she later explained. Her mother had committed suicide when she was a child, and she wore the name defiantly, for there had been a scandal associated with the death—tales of spiritualist seances and dark rituals and a secret society that appeased certain jaded royals' long-standing fascination with the occult.

Luciano discounted the rumors as the clap-trap baggage of royalty. Certain royal antics still titillated the tabloids, and there was always an effort to unearth ever more sensational stories about them. But the suicide had left a mark on Gianalisa, who flaunted the fact of her mother's scandalous death as an act of rebellion against the world. At the same time, she minimized—even hid— her relationship to her princely father.

That fact impressed Luciano Chicarelli no end, for he had always wanted to be able to wrest his own life away from his father's dominant hand.

Aside from his own personal admiration of the tortured and beautiful Gianalisa, Luciano felt a certain mystique about royalty. And she was a true princess, moody and haunted, difficult and tormented. She was like someone who had stepped out of one of the darker fairy tales, and Luciano had never known anyone like her.

This beautiful and beguiling storehouse of singular royal blood had phoned him an hour ago, her voice a symphony of bemusement and promised delight, tinted with that enchanting tinge of sadness. She was ready for him, she said. She would be waiting at the Ristorante di Fontana with a surprise that would change his life. Luciano again quickened his step, for he believed he knew what the surprise would be. They would have a lingering dinner, then champagne.

In three more months he would have his doctorate from Rome University, then he would go to work for his famous father, managing the family's real estate from their family home in Palermo. Later he might even follow his father into politics and live here in Rome, the center of Italy's political inferno. But whatever he did, he was determined that he would make Gianalisa proud of him. For he was indeed deeply in love.

Her problem with drugs did not concern him, though it was a habit of which he strongly disapproved. But he was a patient man. He had known other girls who had grown up in rigidly authoritarian Catholic schools. It was natural that they should go wild for a season after their escape. It meant nothing. After their marriage, he'd give Gia many babies. That would calm her down. They would have a good life together.

Someone grabbed his sleeve, and he turned, startled.

It was the aggressive woman in the white blouse. *"Mi scusi,"* she said, smiling up at him. "Would you help me?"

Luciano frowned, irritated by the intrusion into his daydreams. He couldn't believe that this woman had followed him.

"I'm lost," the woman said. She spoke Italian, with a Neapolitan dialect. "Where can I find the Via Lampedusa?"

As she spoke she leaned toward him, so that he had to step backward to avoid a repeat of the suggestive physical contact. She moved forward again.

Though he was truly annoyed now, his excellent manners forced him to reply. "You must go three blocks, then turn left at the corner—"

At that precise moment the woman brought up her arms and with surprising strength shoved him off the curb into the path of an approaching black Volkswagen van. Luciano barely managed to keep his footing as brakes screeched, the van skidded to a stop, and the door slammed open.

Stunned, he looked in swift disbelief, back and forth, first at the van as two men leaped from it, then at the woman, who was now fleeing through the crowd.

One of the men shouted in fluent Italian, *"Pronto! Dai!"* Hurry up.

And then the other man had Luciano's arms pinned. Luciano's head swung around, and he stared at the man who was holding him. Only then did he notice the Skorpion machine guns. Both men were dressed in black from head to toe, complete with black mountaineer's masks. He got a brief glimpse of muddy eyes and predatory teeth, a hint of stale breath, then the taller man was prodding him with a gun muzzle, cursing him in a deep Neapolitan dialect, ordering him into the van.

Luciano was too surprised to be frightened, and he coiled tight, preparing to fight back. But his captors apparently sensed the motion, and a gun butt slammed into the back of his knees, toppling him forward. He heard someone screaming.

Then he was down, someone hit him in the face, blood streamed into his eyes, and he was distantly aware that people were running, shouting, a flood of collective fear holding sway now as a Skorpion chattered death into the sky, a warning to the people in the crowd to stay away.

"Quickly," said a third—familiar—voice, and Luciano was suddenly filled with hope. He tried to turn his head and look up, but something crashed into the back of his skull, and he felt himself sag. He was barely aware of the men grabbing his arms and dragging him into the van.

The calliope sound of sirens came from a distance.

"This is taking too long," the Neapolitan snarled. "Get going."

Luciano was still conscious, though just barely. He could tell that the two had climbed into the back of the van with him. Through a partition he could see a third black-clad figure slide behind the steering wheel, and then the door slammed shut.

He was aware that the police sirens were closer now but still too far away to offer hope. And then they were speeding along the boulevard through the colorful chaos of buses, cars, and motor bikes.

The men muttered excitedly for a time, though they kept their voices too low for Luciano to make full sense of what they were saying. He felt a pinprick and was vaguely aware that they had injected him with something.

Still, he managed to stay awake, though he was in some netherworld now, trapped between here and there, and an exquisitely silken feeling began to transport him to semiconsciousness. He felt someone binding his hands and feet and knew he should fight back, but when he tried to move, nothing happened.

Then for a long time there was silence except for the sound of traffic, a melodious background to a floating feeling, a lie of complete well-being.

Yet, a mild curiosity forced its way into the euphoria. Slowly he managed to angle his head until he could see telephone lines and the tops of buildings whizzing past. And then he saw an overhead highway sign: FIUMICINO, LEONARDO DA VINCI AIRPORT, 23 KM. They were south of the city, driving fast.

They were taking him toward Naples. The thought pierced through his drug-induced fog to alarm him. Without thinking he tried to sit up. Something hit him in the back of the head, shooting white bolts of light through his brain, though the pain was mercifully dulled by the drug.

"My father will pay you," he muttered. He tried to tell them they could have anything they wanted if they'd just let him go.

But the words came out in a jumble, and he realized that he could not talk coherently. Then he thought of Gianalisa, and in spite of the drug he felt a swift, stabbing pain. He stifled a sob.

"Give him another hit," a voice said. "He's still potential trouble."

After a moment, he felt another pinprick, then a sudden sagging as his body grew heavy, so heavy.

His last sensation was one of heartbreaking frustration at the thought of Gianalisa sitting in the restaurant alone, waiting for him, waiting and endlessly waiting, and he would never come.

5

Monte Carlo

The black, scabrous talons of the Sicilian Mafia had clawed deep into the glittering necklace of cities along the Côte d'Azur. From Marseilles to St. Tropez to Cannes to Nice to Monte Carlo to San Remo (and of course throughout all of Italy), the Mafia had untold millions invested in commercial real estate, opulent villas, banks, yacht brokerages, restaurants, casinos, luxury liners, and luxury hotels—the inevitable crown jewels in all Mafia portfolios—to mention but a few of their legitimate enterprises.

They had also bought up a politician here and there, a chief of police or a governor or mayor or other worthwhile asset.

That meant, of course, that once Judith phoned the special Sicilian phone number and asked to speak to Carlo Ricaso, this scion of the world's most powerful Mafia family had no trouble whatsoever getting Peter Natale off the hook—especially because he and his wily old uncle had recently purchased the Hotel de Mer, through a real estate syndicate with so many layered corporations that the ownership would never be traced to them.

As an added favor, Carlo directed the crime family's point man in Monte Carlo to pull the necessary strings to hush up Peter Natale's involvement in the shooting—all this carefully done behind the scenes, of course. And so the afternoon edition of the *Riviera Reporter* mentioned only that an unidentified young German man, distraught after losing more than he could afford at the casino, had taken his own life in Hotel de Mer, thoughtlessly disturbing other guests as he did so. This was a tragedy that everyone was more than eager to play down, since such events were bad for everybody's business.

Carlo would expect a favor in return for the bailout, naturally. Peter Natale's longstanding relationship with the young Mafioso was forged more in expediency than in corruption, but there were certain rules, and the Mafia always collected. Still, Natale wasn't concerned. Carlo knew exactly what Peter Natale would and would not do.

The alliance between the Mafia scion and the CIA operative was complicated and difficult to explain to anyone unfamiliar with the vast shadow government that the Mafia had become. Sometimes Natale believed that the dark dance that linked him to Carlo Ricaso was a waltz that led to certain ruin. He had even believed for a time that he was getting to be more like Carlo than like his own colleagues. Over the past three years the two men had shared a slice of reality that had given them a great deal in common with regard to their perception of life.

Their relationship was forged from mutual need. Carlo fed Peter information designed to help rid the criminal milieu of certain of his enemies. Natale gave up something from time to time as well, in order to put a good face on the game.

He was pleased with the arrangement. Most of Carlo's competitors were engaged in vile acts indeed, from heroin trafficking to contract killing to trading in nuclear materials. The information Carlo provided had helped the CIA take some very nasty players out of the game.

Not that Carlo was any better. Natale had recently seen him shoot a family enemy in brutal cold blood. However, though the risks to Peter Natale were substantial, the arrangement actually saved certain people's lives. His network offered Carlo an alternative to more permanent solutions. Often, those who needed to be expelled from the crime syndicate—and who were wise enough to keep their Mafia secrets—could be imprisoned and tucked away, which saved Carlo's underlings the trouble of administering the White Death, wherein enemies were assassinated and dropped in acid, or fed to the many Sicilian pigs, or otherwise made to disappear forever.

When Judith picked Peter up at the Monaco police headquarters at 4:45 P.M. that same day, there was no need for him to discuss his relationship with Carlo or the implementation of the favor. She had worked side by side with Peter for the better part of three years, based at Naples station. The final year had overlapped Carlo Ricaso's arrangement with Peter. So she knew Carlo, knew a great deal about the Ricaso crime family, and she had no illusions about the way things were done.

He was waiting at the curb and eagerly climbed into their rented black Lotus Elan S2 convertible.

Judith whipped it neatly away from the curb, then accelerated into the traffic. She was dressed in summer tweed slacks and a matching beige pullover with hand-tooled beige Italian leather sandals and bag. She looked cool and crisp in spite of the day's heat, but the expression on her face was steely.

Natale ignored the steel and dived in. "You get a chance to check the room above yours?"

"I did. It hadn't been rented out, but I found scratches where the lock had been picked. It was clean inside. No spent cartridges. Nothing."

"Anybody at the hotel see anything?"

She cut around a tour bus, then passed up two sight-seeing teenagers on Vesta motor scooters before she said, "If they did, they're not talking."

"So that's a dead end. How about the prince?"

"He and the *contessa* checked out this morning, shortly after the police took you away."

"Did they leave in a hurry?"

"They made a leisurely show of it. Half a dozen valets carrying her bags, a gold antique Rolls limo picking them up. She was staggering a bit—probably had her typical three-martini breakfast—but dressed to the teeth in a mauve Chanel sundress and wide-brimmed hat. I'd say they weren't trying to hide their departure. And I managed to look into the hotel computer during the reservationist's lunch break. They'd booked only the three days."

"So this thing last night could have been something else—nothing to do with them."

Judith moved her shoulders in the minimal shrug characteristic of the Sicilian underworld, a move she'd picked up while in Sicily. Then she yanked the steering wheel to bypass a white delivery truck. "Who knows?"

They turned, then angled north along the Boulevard Ranier III. Rocky, sun-glazed foothills jutted up to their right, and to their left the sea was blue-white in the late afternoon heat.

Natale was surprised at the direction they were taking. He turned to look at her. "I need to get back to the hotel, shower and clean up, change clothes."

"I already checked us out of the hotel. Your suitcase and overnighter are in the back."

He was surprised again. "We're going back to the villa?"

She shook her head, eyes straight ahead. "I contacted Frost to let him know what happened. He says our vacation is over."

"You agreed?"

"I think it was about over anyway."

Peter forced himself to hide the hurt he felt at her words. They'd agreed before coming to Monte Carlo to take at least another week when they were done with their surveillance. Nonchalantly he asked, "Frost is still in Rome?"

"Yes."

"What exactly did he say?"

"Not much. Sent his compliments on how you'd handled things. But he wants us there right away."

"Because of the shooting this morning?"

"Partly that. But he said he'd already planned to pull us out."

Natale thought he could actually feel the skin around his eyes growing tight, the sense of frustration hit him so hard. "You mind telling me why?"

Judith shrugged again. "He didn't say. Look, can we talk about this later? I have a splitting headache."

He offered to drive, but she tersely refused.

They remained more or less silent during the rest of the short drive up the coast to the airport.

Peter filled the time by thinking about everything that had happened and most of all by trying to understand this growing coldness in Judith. All during the drive, he could tell that she also was thinking hard. But she certainly wasn't sharing those thoughts with him.

6

Nice, the Côte d'Azur

By 5:30 P.M. Peter and Judith were sitting at a small, green-tiled table, facing one another, in the impersonal, chromed cafe at the Nice-Côte d'Azur airport.

Judith still looked crisp and elegant in spite of the heat and the wind-whipped drive up the coast. But she hadn't bothered applying make-up. Her honey-blonde hair was drawn severely back, and her sculpted face was unnaturally pale. When she removed her oversized sunglasses, Natale saw dark smudges under her eyes.

"Did you sleep at all?"

She shook her head. "Not really."

"And we have to go straight to Rome?"

"So Frost said."

"What's he doing in Rome anyway?" Nobody had really bothered to explain.

"He's en route to Washington. I suppose he decided to work in a quick visit with Tyler along the way."

Natale thought about that. Theodore "Teddy" Frost had served as chief of Rome station until being promoted to Moscow station during the last tumultuous days of the Cold War. He had watched Russia change from a mass totalitarian prison into a bloody free-for-all. This new Russia burned out good men at a fearsome rate, and Peter wondered if Teddy Frost had finally had enough.

Judith was also stationed in Moscow, as Moscow station's chief intelligence analyst. She had been there only three short years, after an equal amount of time working in Italy/Sicily with him. But in spite of the chaos in Moscow, she seemed to like her work there. She had refused all of Peter's recent attempts to get her to come back to Naples.

He watched her. She had a flinty look on her face as she drifted in her own thoughts, and he forced his mind away from romantic inclinations and turned it to the subject of Clyde Tyler, Rome station chief.

Tyler had recently decided to retire. Frost had worked with the old spy off and on for many years. It would be natural for him to drop by and say a professional farewell.

But, Natale reflected, Frost might have reasons other than friendship for spending time with Clyde Tyler. Rome was CIA-Italy's operational hub, and there had been an increasing amount of interaction between CIA-Italy and CIA-Moscow, mostly because of the ever-growing link between the Sicilian mobsters and the Russian Mafia, with its attendant arms and narcotics trafficking, money laundering, nuclear black-marketing, and other conspiracies that permeated the whole of Europe and Russia. But something else was going on too, something that he did not yet understand.

He said, "You mentioned yesterday that Frost may be leaving Moscow for good?" He was leaning back comfortably, legs crossed, one arm draped across the back of the chromed chair beside him. He was trying to keep things casual, but there was an unwitting edge in his voice.

Judith said, "He's fed up with Agency politics."

"He's usually smart enough to stay out of most of it," Natale commented.

Judith smiled thinly. "I'm afraid Ted's not as surefooted as he used to be."

Natale cocked an eyebrow. "That right?"

"I believe he's been a little too honest with Langley lately."

"How so?"

"You know he's been spearheading the new mole hunt?"

"Yes. I'd heard."

But I didn't hear it from you, he thought.

During their short vacation, Judith had deliberately steered him away from any professional topics of conversation. She wanted to forget work, she said. Natale agreed wholeheartedly.

He had just finished working a six-month stint on Operation Kaleidoscope and was completely burned out. He and the German authorities pried open a heroin pipeline that was also being used to traffic small but sufficiently dangerous amounts of plutonium-239, uranium-235, and MOX, a mixed-oxide fuel used to trigger nuclear bombs.

There was no longer any doubt about it. Organized crime had declared war on humanity decades ago in the form of mass chemical warfare better known as drug trafficking. Now they'd extended their grasp to lock hands with the Russian Mafia to loot Russia's nuclear stockpiles and market a more immediate form of mass destruction to the highest bidder.

The Germans pulled in Kaleidoscope's targeted traffickers just a week ago, freeing Natale to take this short vacation with Judith. Twelve traffickers were picked up, though only a fraction of them were working the nuclear black market. Others were engaged in more mundane forms of destroying the human race. The sting also pulled in two dirty bankers and the top man, a German real estate broker and investor named Harald Rupert, whom the Germans had wanted a piece of for a very long time.

Natale stared out the window. A fine curtain of rain was moving in from across the sea, cooling the day and ushering in the evening. A ton of work was piled up, waiting for him at Naples station. He dreaded going back. And now this new event, a young man shot dead on his doorstep. He wondered once again if there was any connection to Kaleidoscope or if it had something to do with their surveillance of the prince.

Judith shifted her position.

Natale saw that his long silence had made her uncomfortable. He said, "Just thinking about work."

She nodded.

"So what's up with Frost?" he asked. "Why do you say he's been a little too honest with Langley?"

She chewed on her lip, then leaned forward, elbows on the table between them, and surprised him by explaining. "Teddy remains convinced that someone inside the Agency was working with Al Grimes and is still firmly in place. He worries it like a dog with a bone, and he's not going to let it go."

Natale felt a lurch of apprehension at the thought of a deep penetration agent secretly gnawing away at the Agency's foundations. He had heard this sensation called "mole phobia." Whatever you called it, the fear that someone exceedingly evil and clever might be burrowed deep inside the network's nerve center was enough to give you the cold night sweats. Any number of covert agents had been killed because of such betrayals. And everyone knew that these betrayals would happen again no matter how careful you were. That was the nature of the beast, and it was always just a matter of time.

Two years ago the ongoing hunt within the CIA had spaded up a monster mole, a man who had lived like a lethal virus in the center of the CIA's brain for nearly two decades and who had destroyed more people than the average serial killer. Al Grimes had run the CIA's Soviet/East European division at Langley HQ for ten years during the height of the Cold War. He had wreaked havoc with American networks behind the Iron Curtain.

Teddy Frost played a key part in nailing Grimes. When Frost took over as Moscow station chief eight years ago, he realized the networks and agents had been compromised. He duked it out with CIA brass all the way, but he succeeded in overhauling Moscow station's security. He gradually transferred out all possibly compromised employees. The purge had been so complete that the press believed for a time that CIA-Moscow was actually being shut down as a result of the end of the Cold War.

Al Grimes weathered two years of Frost's housecleaning. But finally he realized that his hands were permanently tied with regard to Moscow station, and he transferred to Langley's newly developed Counternarcotics Division (CND). He remained there throughout the final breakup of the USSR and right up until he was finally unmasked two years ago—largely because of Frost's bulldog tenacity. He was tried, convicted, and was now serving life in a maximum security prison, alongside other mass murderers.

It finally came out that Grimes had blown twenty networks during the ten years preceding Frost's arrival at Moscow station. The KGB executed at least ten Soviet doubles during the peak years of the Cold War, maybe more, all of them sold out by Grimes. Nobody knew exactly what chaos he'd caused after leaving the Moscow desk, when he'd been buried within the Counternarcotics Division. This especially worried Peter, for the CND interlocked into many of his own missions, and wherever drug money was involved, the opportunities for corruption were infinite.

Furthermore, if a second mole was still operational—someone who had helped Grimes get away with literal murder—the CND was most likely where he lay buried. It had become common knowledge within the spy community that Frost was pursuing this possibility with ironclad diligence.

"Frost was right about Grimes," Natale said, after thinking about the situation. "He's probably right about a second mole too."

"Langley agreed, for a while. They were even backing Teddy in his search."

"I didn't know."

"Yes. Well, they kept it pretty quiet, especially from people linked to CND. But they did give Frost the green light to go ahead with his second search. And to answer your original question, that's really why Frost is in Rome. Right after I left Moscow, his backers pulled the plug."

"You're kidding me."

"I wish I were. He told me when I spoke to him right after arriving in Nice. They shut him down. I almost turned around and went back to Moscow then, but he told me he was leaving for Rome."

Natale felt a gust of cold wind. "What's Langley's excuse?"

"The black budget, as usual. They actually sent him a ledger showing how much money they'd spent looking for what they're now calling 'Frost's Spook.' They advised him to spend his future time in more productive ways."

Natale was appalled. "What is he going to do?"

"I'm not sure. He's furious, of course."

"I don't blame him."

"It took them sixteen years to nail Grimes, and even then Frost had to step in and hand them the missing pieces," Judith said bitterly.

Natale narrowed his eyes in thought. "So—why aren't they trusting his judgment on this one?"

She shrugged. "Who knows?"

"I can venture an educated guess," Peter said dryly. It always boiled down to politics. The new president had recently appointed a new CIA Director, who was no doubt trying to make his bones by tampering with the long-term employees' ongoing investigations. It happened all the time.

"Anyway, Teddy is fed up with politics."

Natale nodded. "I can see why. The picture presents some dismal possibilities."

They both fell silent, drifting into their respective thoughts.

Natale thought about corruption. There was a lot of money to be made by destroying one's fellow man—or woman. At least one full third of all the money circulating around the planet now was earned through criminal enterprise, mostly through the sale and distribution of illegal drugs.

He thought about Carlo's uncle, *don* Cesare Ricaso, an old man whose eyes glowed with the fires of hell. The man had a satanic hatred for the entire human race, yet he and people like him were ending up with the money that bought the power that dictated the terms of legitimate society. So much power that Peter himself had just turned to them for help rather than to his own colleagues. He thought of the incident with irony.

It had been happening for decades, as Mafia crime lords determined who sat in which office, which police officer ran which district, and even who ruled the armies of the world. Favors were done, favors were called in. But the corruption had never before happened on such a scale or at such a fertile time as this. Entire countries were now succumbing to the influence of organized crime, and the Americans were the only people left on the face of the earth with both the ability and the will to stop them.

If there was a mole, he would be doing some serious damage. It was more vital than ever before that the intelligence community be above corruption.

Judith had been watching him and apparently guessed what was on his mind. She said, "Life doesn't get any easier, does it?"

"Never."

"What, exactly, were you thinking about?"

"Moles, money, a little of everything. Look, Judith. We're in the middle of something pretty strange here. On the one hand, we have Frost interrupting our vacation to send us to Monte Carlo for a couple of days to spy on Prince Veresi. On the other hand, Langley has decided to abort his mole hunt. What's up, anyway?"

"Are you suggesting there might be a connection?"

"What do you think?"

She shrugged. "Who knows?"

"I don't, that's for sure. I don't know much of anything at the moment. But I need to, Judith." He leaned forward, imploring her. "I really need to understand what happened in the hotel this morning. I have to know what that kid wanted, and if that bullet was intended for me."

Judith's facial expression became guarded and disquieting. After a moment, she said, "Let's say that the bullet was for him, Peter. For your intruder. I don't think you need to worry about that."

"Why are you so certain?"

She studied him, the way a child examines a strange insect.

"I have a right to know." He unintentionally raised his voice, as a defensive reaction to her scrutiny. "Tell me, Judith. What is going on here?"

The waitress picked that moment to serve their small snack, bailing Judith out with a frown that accused Peter of mistreatment. He held his tongue, forced a tight smile, waited until she had moved on, then let the smile drop and in a quietly persuasive tone of voice asked, "Why can't you tell me?"

She picked up a croissant, dabbed on some strawberry jam, then took a dainty bite. She kept her eyes lowered, so Natale could not read them, but he saw that her hand was trembling.

He decided that if any woman had the ability to drive him stark crazy, Judith did. He scrutinized her now, as he tried to decide what to say next.

She took a slow sip of hot black coffee.

"Judith—"

Abruptly she looked him dead in the eye, and he saw that an impenetrable resolve had lodged in her.

"I can't—and won't—talk about it, Peter. I have to figure out some things first."

He stifled a rude reply, got himself under control, and said, "You're treating me like you think I might be the mole."

Her eyes were suddenly naked and sad. But her mouth was pursed into silence.

Natale looked down at his coffee in order to mask a new flash of angry frustration.

Other than Judith's minimal explanations for why she had checked them out of Hotel de Mer and her current more open discussion of Teddy Frost and the mole hunt, she'd been like this since she picked him up in front of the Monte Carlo jail. Guarded, cautious about everything. She would start to say something, then stop in mid word.

This lack of communication left Peter feeling awkward and coldly furious. He tugged at his shirt collar, then dragged a heavy hand across his trim beard. He had asked her several times during the short drive and in several different ways if she knew anyone named "Gia." He explained that the man's dying words had been "Tell Gia . . ." and he tried to engage Judith in speculation as to just what this might mean.

She'd grown steely-jawed, then sullen. Natale tried to deflect the anger by putting their relationship on a purely analytical basis, hoping the professional distance would make her relax so he could get at the truth. He needed to know the identity of the man and if there was any connection to Kaleidoscope before he could even think about going after the killer or otherwise resolving the situation.

But that hadn't worked either.

Now he looked up from his coffee to see her gazing at him with a new and impenetrable expression on her face.

He said, "What?"

"I didn't say anything."

"No, but you were sure thinking hard."

"Yes. I guess I was." She paused. "Peter, I've decided not to go to Rome."

He could feel the pain flood his eyes. He quickly looked down again and said, "Frost hasn't cut you loose yet."

"It doesn't matter," she said defiantly.

There was just enough of the old Judith in her words to ring an alarm. His emotional pain was instantly replaced by professional objectivity. He narrowed his eyes, looked at her again, and contemplated what she'd just said.

Judith had been undisciplined and capricious when they'd worked together in Italy/Sicily two years ago. Always unpredictable. And she had become a serious complication in his life. She'd been burning out fast, drinking too much, doing reckless things. He recognized the growing despair in her. He had gone through the same thing himself, when he'd first begun his journey through this corrupted, decayed underbelly of the beast called Power.

As a result of Frost's reshuffling, the IA position came up at Moscow station, and Peter encouraged Judith to take the job. He wanted to get her out of harm's way. He also wanted to distance himself emotionally. He wasn't ready to accept the intensity of his feelings for her.

There had been no other woman after she left Naples. No other woman ever, actually—not compared to her. Finally, after a two-year separation, circumstances took him to Moscow, where he'd confronted the scars of their relationship and tried to regain what he'd lost.

But Judith had changed. She seemed to have found peace and a sense of purpose and approached their relationship with new and disconcerting honesty.

She told him that Moscow was the best thing that had ever happened to her. That she hadn't really loved him because she'd been incapable of love. He could remember exactly what she said to him that day in a safe house outside Moscow. Every word.

"We were huddling together in the darkness, Peter, using each other for courage, for sustenance. We didn't have love, Peter, we had sex. Narcotic sex, to black out our fears. We used each other for anesthesia. Oh, we had friendship too, and I did love you as much as I was able. Unfortunately that wasn't much, because I was using every grain of my emotions to survive the mental strain of the atrocities that were happening around us. I can see now that

I felt a lot of things for you, but real abiding love wasn't one of them. I just didn't have it in me."

She'd been trying to use him to fill the place in her heart and soul that was reserved exclusively for God, she said. Then she explained that she could never have loved him until she'd tapped into the source of love. She said she'd found peace and joy and love—unconditional love—through a relationship with the eternal Savior, Jesus Christ.

But she also agreed to give their own relationship another chance, if Peter was willing to start fresh with just friendship. Natale had eagerly agreed. He had been undergoing some spiritual crises of his own and was ready for something new. They planned a much-needed vacation. Then Kaleidoscope came along, and he'd been tied up completely. She got tied up too, with Frost and his mole hunt apparently. But then, a few weeks ago, Frost finally cut her loose to take a vacation, even offered to pay for the use of a small, secluded villa in the hills above Nice as a bonus for her diligence.

Natale wrapped up his end of Kaleidoscope, and he and Judith flew here to the Mediterranean coast. They spent five glorious days, relaxing, swimming, hiking, and getting reacquainted, finally laughing easily and often, reestablishing friendship, holding hands like teenagers. They soon were talking for hours at a time about spirituality and life and all the things that really mattered. They even touched lightly on the subject of marriage.

But on the sixth day, Teddy Frost arrived in Rome and sent an emissary to summon them back to work.

"You and Judith are only a stone's throw from Monte Carlo, and Clyde Tyler tells me Prince Dante di Veresi has just arrived at Hotel de Mer and needs looking after," Frost said, when Natale reluctantly checked in by phone.

"I've heard the name. What's his angle?"

"He's the Prince of Veresi, the Duke of Orleans, Duc d'Conde, and a distant descendant of both Charles the Fifth and Ferdinand, eighteenth-century King of Naples and Sicily."

"Right," Natale said sarcastically.

If Sicily and Naples had anything, it was an abundance of deposed nobility. The island province was scattered with crumbling castles and palazzos and villas that had once housed these aristocrats.

Most of the European royals who had at one time or another ruled Sicily had left behind their legacy in the form of descendants sprawled across the island, spread out into its sister region Naples, and seeded well into Rome and beyond. Peter knew that the kingdom to which Prince Dante di Veresi's title belonged had vanished when Sicily and Naples became integrated into the Italian kingdom in the late 1800s.

"Don't think that Veresi is just another royal windbag," Frost said. "He's managed to hang onto a few family vineyards, a Sicilian palazzo, and a Neapolitan estate, among other holdings. He's worth a few million American bucks."

"Is he a heavy gambler?" Natale asked, after a moment's reflection.

"Not really. He's careful. We can't figure him out. Keep an eye on him for us, Peter. He's manipulating money—probably laundering it for the Mafia. We want to know exactly what he's doing."

"I'm a little busy at the moment."

Frost chuckled. "I understand. But if anyone can put the pieces together and see exactly what Veresi's up to, you and Judith can."

"Ted, pardon me for seeming selfish, but it took me a while to get Judith here, and I'm not quite ready to leave."

Frost remained cheerfully unperturbed. "This little job really shouldn't be too rough on you. We just need a handle on what he's doing."

"Judith hates Monte Carlo," Natale grumbled. "Matter of fact, so do I."

But Frost was determined. "I don't suppose the prince will stay in Monte Carlo for more than a few days, and then you can get back to the business of relaxing. In fact, why don't you both take an extra week when you're done?"

The lure of an extra week's vacation had been the right bait. Besides, neither Peter Natale nor Judith Davies could ultimately refuse Frost anything, not even an unwelcome stay amid the tarnished grandeur of Monte Carlo with its procession of pimps, frauds, thieves, sun worshipers, deposed royalty, dice addicts, billionaire tax refugees, money launderers, and garden variety criminals.

The surveillance had proved to be simple if tedious. Prince Veresi and his mistress spent both night and day in the casino, gambling away large chunks of money and drinking away what was left of their health.

But going to Monte Carlo had been a definite mistake. He learned nothing whatsoever about the prince, and the second day there Judith grew colder than he would have believed possible.

It had started the afternoon she slipped away to be by herself. Then she grew angry that evening when he tried to learn where she'd been. The iciness manifested itself again late that night, when they were walking along Monte Carlo's waterfront and he proposed marriage. She abruptly changed the subject, then withdrew into herself and refused to come back out.

And then there was the matter of the dead man who'd taken a bullet that was possibly meant for Peter Natale. This wasn't exactly something that Peter was going to let go away.

Natale became suddenly aware that Judith was staring at him with a confrontational look on her face. He realized he'd been coolly appraising her during his reflection on the circuitous path that had brought them to this small airport cafe.

He shifted his position and his approach. "Look, Judith. I thought we'd agreed to help Frost out. It's not like you to jump ship."

She tilted her smooth neck arrogantly, unintentionally showcasing a small gold cross on a chain. "Teddy shouldn't try to involve me in any problems he may be taking on at Rome station. I have plenty to do in Moscow." The waiflike face that was usually far too innocent for her thirty-three years was set in cement again.

Natale was suddenly disgusted with the world. "Why don't you leave the rest of the mop-up at Moscow station to Langley? They're the ones who dropped the ball."

"It's not just that, Peter. It's become a lot more."

"What?"

Her eyes grew luminous with distress. "You were right that I don't trust you."

Natale had already known that, but it hurt to hear the words. "Why on earth not?"

"It's not really you, Peter. It's everyone these days. I guess it's the mole hunt, and all the changes at Langley, personal problems, the chaos in Moscow, just everything. Do you ever have times when you'd like to trust someone but you can't?"

"All the time. It goes with the territory."

She swiftly shook her head. "That's not what I mean. I mean, have you ever been unable to trust others because you really can't trust your own judgment about them?"

His interest quickened. Her face was open and innocent for the first time all day. He said, "Afraid I didn't quite follow that."

"The problem is, I can't trust myself right now, Peter." She almost whispered the words, and she was looking down at her hands, which were twisting her paper napkin into shreds. "I've made a very serious mistake that may have gotten that young man killed."

He felt his throat go dry. His heart seemed to stop beating. He watched her carefully—she seemed to be on the verge of flying apart, like a stone bracing for the impact of a sculptor's chisel.

He said, "Can I help?"

The question seemed to alarm her. She stared at him and shook her head no. "I'm not going to make any more mistakes about this, Peter. Before I do anything, I have to know—"

"Know what?"

"Peter. You mentioned that the man talked about warning someone named Gia about something. Did he mention anything about reptiles? About gold?"

Natale froze in place. He hadn't told her that part of the young man's message. He had focused on learning the identity of the mysterious "Gia." Now he quickly masked his suspicion with a nonchalant air. "As a matter of fact he did. I more or less put it down to confusion."

"Tell me again. What exactly did he say?"

Natale repeated the words, watching her reaction closely.

She shook her head, and Peter saw the anguish in her eyes grow deeper.

"Judith, you're driving me nuts. Tell me!"

But she began to withdraw.

He tried to bring her back to him. "Judith, whatever happened, his death can't be your fault. Everyone makes mistakes sometimes. Tell me what happened. I can help—"

But she had already moved past him and was fully composed, cool as a marble statue. "It doesn't matter. I have to get back to work and figure it out. That's the only way."

"Stay here another day. Just one. I'll phone Frost and tell him we've been delayed."

"No." The alarm turned to panic. "Not now. I have responsibilities, Peter. I can't hang people out to dry, even if I am ready to bail out."

He was genuinely surprised. "You're thinking of quitting the Agency too?"

"Things are changing." An uncharacteristically bitter look tightened her face, and she gazed off into the invisible distance.

"Maybe I could get a temporary reassignment. Come to Moscow with you, after we check things out in Rome. Help you get things squared away."

Her smoky-blue eyes hooded over dangerously. "No."

He was deciding on which avenue of argument to use to break through her thickening armor when they were interrupted by the boarding call for the flight to Rome.

Judith immediately stood, apparently relieved to be done with the conversation.

Peter stepped around the table, took her firmly by the shoulders, and forced her to look up at him.

"There will never be a time when we can be together unless we make one. You know that. We're going to have to deal with the world as it is, Judith. Find our happiness where we can. We need to work this out."

But he saw another bolt of panic come into her eyes, and she stiffened. He felt as if she was going to wrench free, then cut and run.

The loudspeaker interrupted again, a hollow mechanical voice giving the final boarding call in French, Italian, and English.

"You should come to Rome and at least see what's up," Natale said. He stepped back, trying to hide the pain of rejection beneath a casual pose and a hopefully friendly smile. He knew he had made a mistake by trying to press her.

But Judith refused to be persuaded. She had already made a reservation on the 6:30 EuroAir flight to Moscow, she said. She'd be boarding in half an hour, traveling via Milano. She needed to go back.

She did, however, walk with him to the concourse and said a tense good-bye. When Peter tried to take her hand in his, she gently pulled hers back.

But as she turned away, he caught a glimpse of something in her eyes—deep pain seared through with intense loneliness and fear, and the weight of deep responsibility.

Something was seriously wrong.

But even as he had the thought, he was caught in a swirl of passengers and swept forward toward the boarding gate. As he stepped through the entrance, he turned and caught a glimpse of Judith standing at a nearby bank of telephones, holding a receiver and dialing, a worried expression on her face.

He wanted to run to her, hold her. The world would inexorably roll on into a destruction that neither of them was powerful enough to stop anyway. They might as well go away together, live like normal people, and let the world take care of itself.

But he knew he couldn't do that. He couldn't quit fighting the evil that was trying to strangle the world, especially now.

And it wouldn't have mattered anyway. Once Judith made up her mind about something, no one could stop her. He couldn't help her unless she allowed him to.

And she was definitely determined to leave here. And to leave him. He was just going to have to bow out—at least for now.

He strode down the entry ramp and into the Alitalia 727, where he quickly found his aisle seat. The angular, balding man strapped into the window seat was reading the *Riviera Reporter*. He glanced up with a thin smile, and Peter nodded politely, then sat down and strapped himself in.

He leaned back and shut his eyes, ending any threat of conversation. He felt an almost supernatural depression, a tangible weight trying to press him down. But Peter had learned to be resilient. And by the time the plane was taking off he had already worked through the dark mood by offering himself renewed hope.

He would have to give Judith some space. That would help. Give her a week, a little distance, in order to get her mind and feelings untangled. Then he'd contact her, somehow convince her again to go away someplace where they could be alone together and try to start anew.

Rome

To hold a contract for Sicily's taxation offices had long been a sure avenue to power and wealth, for the *esattorie*—the families who collected the regional taxes—had been allowed to keep 10 percent of the revenue as payment for their efforts until as late as 1982. They had also been surreptitiously allowed to use the countless billions of lire they collected until such time as they had to turn it over to the central government. Thus had many Sicilian fortunes been made, among them that of the Chicarelli family.

Access to such enormous amounts of capital had inflamed the interest of all the Sicilian Mafiosi. But the capo-Mafia to whom Volante Chicarelli had long ago pledged his loyalty was a wizened little man from the village of Valletta, *don* Cesare Ricaso.

Chicarelli had chosen well. *Don* Cesare's power had grown until he was now head of the Cupola, the Sicilian Mafia's ruling commission. Indeed, it was his relationship with *don* Cesare that guaranteed Chicarelli's continued wealth and high government position. The tentacles of the octopus that *don* Cesare had created coiled deep into every aspect of Italian life, but most of all into the inferno of politics.

Chicarelli was a young man when he first landed his contract to handle the government's tax money. Soon he was privileged to finance many of the Ricaso crime family's burgeoning heroin deals.

By the time the tax gravy train came to a halt, he was a wealthy man. He owned small shares in the Ricasos' interests in Palermo's most lucrative blocks of real estate. He owned land and buildings throughout mainland Italy and into Switzerland, Germany, and beyond. He held small blocks of stock in the Ricaso family's fleet of fishing trawlers, their two sulfur mines, and their international chain of banks.

This wealth—even his small share of it—brought with it privilege, so that now this small, balding man with his deceptively friendly face was sitting in the Italian Parliament. The next step would be to the European Union, the governing body that loomed like a voracious shadow over the powers of the member nations and that would soon make the economic rules and the social laws that determined the fate of Western Europe.

The presidency rotated among the EU member nations. Next month Italy's turn would begin. To Chicarelli's secret delight, various key members of the EU government had already been well corrupted by the wily old Mafioso who was his padrone. But that was a moot point, because the ability to choose who Italy appointed to sit in the president's seat was all that mattered. And *don* Cesare could certainly accomplish that, in spite of the rising groundswell of support for the appointment of Chicarelli's only rival, Count Benito Jacovetti, a one-time NATO general.

The count was Roman born and bred. He was a long-standing member of the Palazzo, that body of power brokers who determined the rules of Roman politics so long as those rules didn't run afoul of the higher tribunal of the Mafia. Count Jacovetti had served in the EU Council of Ministers ever since the EU became knit together. But the House of Jacovetti was bankrupt; Count Jacovetti had no wealth to splash around. Until now.

Now, suddenly, a flood of secretive money was being spent to tout Jacovetti for president.

Chicarelli frowned as he thought about that. Then he smiled. No matter how much was spent to cultivate those who would make the appointment, Count Jacovetti did not have the secret ingredient that would usher Chicarelli into the position—the Mafia's power and blessing.

The main point of contention seemed to be that the Romans —many of whom would make the final decision—thought a fellow Roman would best serve in the president's office. In addition, many of the growing phalanx of Fascist voters were also monarchists who thought that not only a Roman but a Roman noble should sit on the quasi-throne.

Chicarelli shook off his fears about the count and thought about the future. He would step into the president's role at just the perfect time. *Don* Cesare would see to it. And during the year-long tenure the vote would occur that would make the position of president a permanent office. *Don* Cesare had assured him that, since he would be the incumbent, it would be simple to see that enough votes were thrown his way to quite literally make him—Volante Chicarelli, an Italian peasant's son—the first full president of Europe.

A surge of emotion almost overwhelmed him as he thought about his only son. Luciano would be proud of him. All his life he had worked to give his son a better life than he'd had, to make him proud. Now he was reaching the ultimate goal.

Volante Chicarelli knew he would pay for his prize. Nothing was ever free. His incumbency would give the Mafia enough secretive political clout within the EU to put them in the driver's seat of all the power-making machinery of this revived Roman Empire.

The Mafia had permeated every institution. To get ahead in Italy/Sicily, one had to become one of the *intoccabili*, the untouchables, a man under the Mafia's protective umbrella. But with that power as a foundation, there was no end to the political heights that one could scale. Chicarelli was on the threshold of proving that once and for all.

Still, though the thought of *don* Cesare's blessing on his career brought comfort, a storm cloud of concern arrived swiftly on its heels. Dark undercurrents had been known to snatch the legs out from under politicians, even those with Mafia sponsorship, for the Mafia could be a fickle bedfellow indeed.

Chicarelli thought about his fellow Sicilian Salva Lima, the mayor of Palermo. Lima had also been under Mafia protection. Just like Volante Chicarelli, Lima had served the Mafia long and well. And still he was brutally gunned down in the street as a warning to other politicians and judges who were refusing to throw out a recent series of Mafia murder convictions.

Lima's violent death was a constant reminder to those in positions of political and judicial power that the Mafia could give but they could also swiftly and arbitrarily take away.

Yet Chicarelli had managed to minimize the possibilities of running afoul of *don* Cesare. He had insulated himself well and had mastered a careful balancing act. And thus far, the old Mafioso had delivered enormous blocks of votes from southern Italy, Sicily, Milano, even Rome itself. He would certainly fulfill his promise to give Chicarelli the presidency.

And so Volante Chicarelli sat in his drafty, walnut-paneled office in the Roman parliament building, working late into the night, his mind consumed with this promise. He wanted to do everything possible to make certain that the wily and capricious old capo wouldn't change his mind and give his blessing to Count Jacovetti instead.

When his telephone rang, Volante Chicarelli was still absorbed by these thoughts, so that he absently lifted the receiver on the second ring. *"Buona sera. Signore* Chicarelli speaking."* He tap-tap-tapped the eraser of a pencil on his teak desk.

But suddenly his knuckles went white on the receiver. The healthy color drained from his small, round face. His hazel eyes grew wide, he caught his breath, and his rotund body visibly deflated. At last, in a whispery voice, he said, "But that is impossible. I dropped him off on the Via Italico only a short time ago . . ."

He waited, then said, "Yes. Of course. Whatever you say. Just please don't hurt him. Yes. I see. I'll wait for your call."

He replaced the receiver, then folded his trembling hands and placed them on the desk in front of him as if they were made from fragile china and might break.

He forced himself to breathe slowly, in and out, in and out, till at last he'd calmed himself enough to talk. Then he again picked up the receiver. *Don* Cesare would know precisely, in the most primitive and eternally effective way, just what to do.

But as he was about to dial *don* Cesare's private number, fear hit him with such an impact that he thought he would be sick. He put down the phone. It had crossed his mind that perhaps the Ricasos themselves had taken Luciano, to make some point, to repay him for some unrealized error.

He forced back that fear and said a silent prayer, something he had not done for many years. Again he lifted the receiver.

Woodenly, he dialed the number of the dark empire on Sicily where the contract for his feudalistic bondage had been made, irrevocably, in blood. If *don* Cesare had taken his son, Volante Chicarelli was helpless. What else could he do but find out how he had violated the old man's honor, and plead for Luciano's life?

In a sudden fit of self-pity he felt his eyes fill with tears. And even as they spilled over and two fat teardrops ran down his cheeks, he realized that they were tears not of rage but of fear and shame.

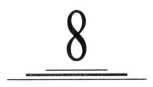

8

Valletta

The Ricaso estate was almost due south of Palermo, north and east of Corleone. The house was massive, dark stone with a gray slate roof, trellises and alcoves, and many extensions and outbuildings, all showcased upon a velvet green lawn framed by orchards and elaborate gardens. The compound was nestled within a sleepy fold of Sicily's volcanic mountains, which rose steeply to cut off the valley from the rest of the island. The entire complex was guarded by invisible sensors and patrolled by armed men and killer guard dogs that managed to blend invisibly into the otherwise pastoral scene.

Two miles due east of *don* Cesare's sprawling estate was the gateway to his empire—the village of Valletta. This was a tiny, carved cameo of picturesque, stacked-stone cottages with tiled roofs, and two-story, terraced shops with weathered faces, all of it set around a wide piazza graced by a small, ancient cathedral.

Though the town might have otherwise been lifted from a bucolic oil painting done during feudal times, there were salient differences. New luxury sedans and sports cars were parked in makeshift driveways. Satellite dishes and electric generators sat in most backyards.

The little old ladies in this village, with their hand-crafted black shawls and hair in gray buns, traveled when they wished to all the European capitals and the United States as well, hand carrying small parcels filled with white powder worth hundreds of thousands of dollars a kilo.

Though they were only a small, peripheral part of the vast army of mules who trafficked *don* Cesare's white powder around the globe, he took especially good care of them. Their sons protected him—sometimes died for him—and because of that he would bail these women out of jail when they were infrequently arrested. Or he would take care of their families—mostly making sure they had enough work—until such time as the mules were free again.

Don Cesare had been born in Valletta. Here his peasant parents labored in the fields and orchards and hog pens until both literally died from overwork. And here, alone in all the world, he visited upon his fellow man the small amount of largesse that he would call charity.

Directly east of the village, rocky crags jutted out of a gray-blue sea, forming the small cove made infamous by Mafia smugglers' ships during the days when the Ricasos were just getting started and still handled the actual heroin themselves. To the west, Valletta was blessed with a wealth of endless orchards, extensive wheat fields, and pastures where goats, cattle, and sheep grazed. These spread all the way to *don* Cesare's remote estate.

Altogether, in spite of the modern conveniences, this was a region so different from Rome that it might have been set back a thousand years in time. Here, feudalistic bondage and vicious brutality reigned. Here, vast corrupted wealth was gained and kept through deep and dangerous conspiracies. Here, *don* Cesare's vineyards grew fat with gold and purple grapes, and here certain of *don* Cesare's meadows were still made fertile by red rivers of blood.

This was the lair of the Octopus, the serene-seeming eye of a ruthless and evil global storm.

And while Volante Chicarelli sat in his Rome office dialing *don* Cesare Ricaso's telephone number, the wily old *don* sat in a dark wicker rocking chair, on the dimly lighted veranda of a sprawling stone house at the center of his empire, all of it submerged in night.

It had become *don* Cesare's habit to discuss the day's financial matters with his nephew Carlo while taking the night air before retiring, as his doctor had advised him to do after his last checkup. And besides, he enjoyed listening to the cicadas' evening song while he talked of his monetary conquests far and wide.

Carlo sat beside his uncle, watching him warily. The *don* was sipping a fruity wine made from the pears and apples that grew in his extensive orchards. The lawn sprinklers made a soothing, swishing sound. An electronic bug-catcher hung from the rafters. It made a small glow of eerie blue light against the black, feathery foliage that separated the house from a high stone wall, which in turn separated the lawns and gardens from the endless surrounding acres of forests and fruit trees and guardhouses and electrified fences and other cutting-edge security.

Don Cesare blinked coldly from time to time, as an insect flew into the trap and was zapped to death. Other than that, the wily old Mafioso had spent the evening totally focused on his favorite subject and his most disturbing problem.

Money.

The problem was not how to get it. That had become simple. One enterprise alone—heroin—now had more than a million guaranteed customers in just the United States. There were more than a million addicts throughout Western Europe, and countless more in other parts of the globe. Needle parks had sprung up in increasing numbers in all major European cities, and business was getting better by the day.

In addition, there was the cocaine and other drugs, the shylocking and blackmailing and controlled prostitution and slave-trading and kidnapping and contract murder and construction bid-rigging and political corruption and dozens of other forms of criminal enterprise.

In fact, the days when the Ricaso family were mere peasants struggling to grub a subsistence income from this land were long, long gone. Now the problem had become what to do with the flood of money that rolled in like a tidal wave, threatening to inundate the family before they could launder it and turn it into legitimate assets.

There were stacks of it, boxes of it, barrels and crates and bales of it, money of every denomination, most of it already rinsed once, money amassed from the tens and twenties that were siphoned out of the pockets of the world's junkies and prostitutes. One level removed from the carnage, the money was transformed into larger bills and other forms of liquid capital, then moved and transformed yet again, and again.

But even by the time everyone in the food chain had taken his cut, the Ricasos found themselves possessing so much money that certain people in law enforcement had accused them of being the twentieth largest nation in terms of Gross National Product, and certain members of the EU called the Mafia the "silent member state."

But anyone in the business long enough came to realize that money was a medium. Possessions were stage props. The true object of the game was power.

Carlo wasn't on top of his game just then, not for any prize. He was, in fact, heavily focused upon himself, a condition that seemed to occur with increasing frequency these days.

Carlo Ricaso was tall and lean, with the haughty demeanor, the pouting mouth, and the handsome face of an aging Italian playboy, a face aged slightly beyond his forty-two years. He seldom let anyone get close enough to realize that this appearance belied a cold, cynical ruthlessness and a violent, hair-trigger temper.

However, at that moment Carlo glanced at his reflection in the glass of the living-room window and realized that his eyes seemed bored, even tired, tonight. His white silk shirt soaked up a tiny portion of the blue bug light. His bottom lip drooped petulantly, and there was a flaccid quality to his face that told him he'd had too much to drink.

He leaned back, drained the last of his wine, and considered the fact that even though he had the ability to order the death of any man on the planet, to purchase anything that was for sale and to take what wasn't, he was feeling increasingly powerless when in the presence of his ruthless aging uncle.

Don Cesare's power lust had taken on a new and darker twist during the past several years. The old man had developed the ability to inspire a deep and abiding terror in Carlo. It was as if the man had been consumed by a new level of power lust that was both demonic and boundless. The change disturbed Carlo to the depths of his soul.

He set down his fluted wine glass and shook his head no, when *don* Cesare immediately picked up the decanter to refill it.

His uncle's smile was deliberately cruel as he poured it full anyway. Then he stared at Carlo, as if to dare him not to drink.

Carlo picked up the glass idly, turning the stem in his hands, and said nothing, studying the man who increasingly tried to rule his every thought, breath, and motion.

Don Cesare was small and frail appearing, but there was dark strength in him that seemed to generate a virtual electric field. In fact, to Carlo, in spite of himself, the old man had begun to appear eternal, invincible. It was in contrast to this growing invincibility that Carlo's own power was seeming, to him, to fade.

He measured his uncle, idly looking for vulnerability of any kind, but the only possible weakness was that *don* Cesare had suffered a small heart attack three years ago. Other than that small lapse into mortality, the aging capo appeared to be in excellent health for his seventy-eight years. His hair was still sleek and mostly dark, and when he unfolded to his full five feet, his back was ramrod straight. His sharp eyes still had twenty-twenty vision, and most of the time they peered with gleaming intensity into the world around him. Or perhaps the eyes merely seemed to peer because of the beaklike nose, which gave him the appearance of a predatory bird.

The *don*'s only deference to age was his hearing, which required the use of a small hearing aid. Therefore Carlo sat in a chair that had been pulled fairly close, at an angle that allowed him to see inside the adjoining living room, with its cherry furniture, Turkish rugs, worn brown-leather sofas, red-granite end tables, and walls full of priceless, pilfered art.

The *don* had been talking about their recent banking problems, lamenting the fact that it was becoming more and more difficult to launder the money that poured in every day from the drug traffic alone.

"Twenty-five percent I'm paying now," he was saying. "These thieves make as much laundering as I do brokering, and it's gotta stop. On top of that, the wider we get spread, the more people I gotta pay off. Fifty million just this week to judges, bankers, politicians—the lice will eat you alive in this business, Carlo."

Carlo nodded indifferently. Though he was heir to the family fortunes and misfortunes, he was not interested in its immense and growing wealth. In his lifetime, wealth had always been there, would always be there. He had learned long ago that money was no object so long as you didn't care what you did to obtain it.

It was those things the Ricaso family did to obtain money that were beginning to seriously bother Carlo. Increasingly any vestige of civility was being crushed beneath the excuse of expediency. Their lower-echelon soldiers were using street kids to carry out crimes, even assassinations. This had resulted in a trend of so-called baby-faced killers here and in Naples. The kids were too young to be sentenced but not too young to be shot in the back of the head so they couldn't confess and implicate their handlers.

The practice sickened Carlo. He tried to stop it wherever he could, but the flood tide of evil seemed to be getting away from him.

And then there was the heroin traffic, a part of the business that had bothered him from the time he was a child and had first come to understand.

Added to that was the black market in armaments. That had once been a lucrative business, one engaged in by every legitimate government in the world, so why not the secret governing body of Sicily? But now the trafficking lanes had turned into pipelines for potential nuclear chaos, another change Carlo deplored but could not change.

Yet another problem was the prostitution. When he'd first started overseeing the family's brothels, street and cafe prostitution, and call-girl agencies, he managed to convince himself that he was helping otherwise penniless women make a living. But now the hustlers on the streets in the European capitals were, more often than not, men masquerading as women, many of whom had had plastic surgery, even sex changes, and many of whom were riddled with AIDS. These men beat up and ran off the women, though the Ricaso crime family still got its *pizzu*—payoff—which kept *don* Cesare happy. When Carlo attempted to intervene, his uncle threatened to chop him up and scatter pieces of him in fifty different countries.

Increasingly Carlo was being forced to give up the rationalizations that had kept him going these many years. He'd always known that the general image of the Mafia was an illusion. But he had believed he could nevertheless have honor and self-respect and still be a Mafioso. There was room for humanity within his other-wise brutal world, if only a person would look for opportunities. Lately the opportunities for compassion were vanishing.

And lately he coped by deadening his sensibilities with alcohol. He knew he was developing a drinking problem, among all his other problems. Still, he took another sip of the fruity wine his uncle had just poured, rolled it on his tongue, then swallowed. Carlo had always despised weakness. When one of their top traffickers got hooked on the heroin he was peddling, Carlo had personally put a bullet in the back of the man's head. It was expressly forbidden for a Mafioso of any rank to use the poison he peddled, for an addict could not be trusted to keep the family secrets. But now Carlo himself had reached a crisis point. He was riding a man-eating tiger that was certain to devour him the instant he tried to climb off. And yet he desperately wanted off.

Because if he didn't get off—and soon—he was going to lose the small remaining portion of his humanity and become just like his evil old uncle—a thought that made him literally shiver.

Cesare snapped, "Whatsa matter?"

Carlo realized that the *don* had been watching him. He pasted another bored look on his face. "Why?"

"You think after all these years I can't read your face? You had that expression, Carlo. Like something's eating at you."

Carlo managed to look blameless. "I have a little problem with a woman. No big deal."

Don Cesare grunted, indicating that he believed not a word Carlo said but was not ready to come right out and call his nephew a liar. "And this Peter Natale? Maybe you got his problems on your mind?"

Carlo was surprised. "Why would I be thinking about Natale?"

"I tell you, this man is a *scassapaghieri*." A small-time hustler. "You would be wise to stay away from him."

"Natale's OK. He can handle himself."

"He works for the CIA, Carlo. You think you have the situation under control?" He snapped his small, thin, tobacco-stained fingers. "That's when they set you up."

Carlo knew what was bothering *don* Cesare.

Since the Single Market had taken effect in the European Union, the Mafia was doing business in the EU nations in a bigger way than ever before. By virtue of the ineffective international laws, barriers had come down for criminals but had gone up for the police who tried to stop them. Which left the Americans as the only effective force standing between *don* Cesare and full free rein.

Carlo agreed that sometimes the Americans seemed to be everywhere with their plans for upgrading police forces, their model racketeering laws, their aid to various underfunded law enforcement agencies, and now the CIA's Anti-Narcotics Division. This was, of course, why *don* Cesare hated them so ferociously.

Cesare often complained that Carlo lacked the true fire of a Sicilian, simply because he had been reared mostly in Brooklyn, where his father and uncle Dominic had emigrated long ago, when the family had first been expanding their heroin business beyond Sicily's borders. Carlo's father had died nearly ten years ago from a heart attack brought on by an extended FBI investigation that had netted no other result.

Dominic, who at the age of seventy-six still lived in Brooklyn, had never really gotten involved in the heavier parts of the family business. He oversaw the banks and other legitimate investments in the United States, the Bahamas, and various South American countries, from a position of semiretirement, and no man was more frightened of Cesare than he.

Carlo considered all this, then tried to reassure Cesare. "Natale is no problem. Don't worry about it."

Cesare's small, narrow jaw set. "I worry, Carlo. When does this man ever come to show me respect? How does he show his loyalty?"

"He's from a different world, that's all."

"Ah, that explains it," the old man said sarcastically. "Some kind of special person. So—how did you put the hooks into him?"

Don Cesare believed people should always be manipulated into a position where any betrayal of the Ricaso crime family would inevitably result in their own destruction. This principle could be instrumented through outright blackmail, through total financial dependence, or—most often—through the instillation of paralyzing, heart-stopping fear.

"No hooks," Carlo said. "I don't need them. Anyway, what's bothering you? You've known about my deal with Peter Natale ever since he helped us out in Russia last year. Why the sudden concern?"

"Because I suddenly see you jeopardizing our interests for someone who doesn't honor us, doesn't earn for us. This thing of ours is for family, Carlo. Family! So you let this American use the people we pay for cover when he whacks someone out? Use our resources to do the work of the American government?" The old man snorted contemptuously. "*Basta,* Carlo. You are a *fesso.* Getting more stupid every day, if that is possible."

Carlo instantly knew that their point man in Monaco had informed *don* Cesare about Peter Natale's fiasco and Carlo's order to fix the problem. He should have expected this. He said, "Peter didn't shoot the man anyway."

"Yeah? That's what he told you? Then why did the gendarmes pull him in?"

"To mess with him because he's American. The real *siccario* got away."

"Who got hit?"

Carlo shrugged. He didn't want to admit that he hadn't bothered to find out.

Cesare's eyes narrowed. "What if it was one of our people, Carlo? I got a man down there laundering a few million dollars, another one handling some traffic out of Marseilles. What if it was one of our workers?"

Surprise forced a wedge into the drunken mass of Carlo's brain, startling him to near sobriety. "Why would one of our workers be in Natale's room?"

"You figure it out."

Carlo was still astonished. "The man who got hit was one of our soldiers?"

Cesare sneered. He leveled his hand and tilted it one way, then the other, in a dismissive gesture. "Not this time, but it doesn't matter. What matters is you take a favor from a friend of ours and give it to an enemy. And money? Ten thousand dollars it cost to straighten this out! Ten thousand dollars in payoffs for us to clean up a hit made in our hotel by your CIA friend. You tell him he's gonna pay us back, Carlo. With interest."

Carlo suddenly saw the problem. His uncle was pathologically cheap. The thought of doing the favor was annoying, but the thought of spending money to do it was more than *don* Cesare could tolerate.

Contracting his arms in a minimal shrug, Carlo said, "It's no big deal. I'll cover the ten thousand."

His uncle's voice turned harsh and sarcastic, and he made a spiteful little half bow. *"Grazie,* Carlo. But your money is my money, you fool. You have nothing that isn't mine. You pay, I pay."

I still have my soul, Carlo thought, with a flash of desperation. *Maybe at least I still have my own soul.*

Don Cesare tilted his head and shot him a warning look, as if he'd sensed the thought. A dangerous glow kindled in his eyes. "What do you tell this *scassapaghieri,* Carlo? Do you talk about our business?"

Carlo's head snapped around, and he stared in disbelief.

"Well, do you talk about it?" the old man persisted. "Has he ever asked questions?"

"He knows better!" Carlo snarled. He measured the frenzied, brutal look in his uncle's eyes. Was the man finally succumbing to the occupational hazard of pathological paranoia? Why on earth would Cesare think he would talk to Peter Natale about the deeper secrets of the Ricasos' business? All he did was use the man to get rid of mutual enemies—and sometimes they talked about personal things, even spiritual things. But to talk serious business with an American spy?

Don Cesare's eyes followed Carlo's as if he again read his mind. "You know, as a man I gotta tell you, Carlo. This Peter Natale is no fool. You talk to him at all, you're asking for trouble. He's always gonna be a step ahead of you. I saw it when you brought him here so I could check him out, and I'm telling you now. Forget about him. We got other people in better positions to help us out, people I've got a hook into that they won't never be able to dig out. And I'm telling you again, this Peter Natale can't be trusted. I don't care what you think. It's time for you to look at the truth."

Carlo looked steadily and contemptuously into his uncle's eyes, matching his stare.

Cesare blinked first, only because he was furious. He stabbed a forefinger at Carlo, almost jabbing him in the chest. Mottled rage flooded into his rodentlike face, and his voice went tight. "You ever mess us up by saying the wrong thing to this *scassaparaghi*, you're dead—blood or no blood."

Carlo was silent. He was thinking about Johnny—his younger brother who had been completely corrupted by Cesare before he'd even had a chance to know that there were other ways to live. Johnny was murdered at the age of thirty-two, when he'd made an ill-conceived attempt to work an especially nasty arms deal on his own, probably in order to exercise some independence from *don* Cesare's stranglehold.

Peter Natale had helped Carlo discover the truth about Johnny's death. But Carlo had learned one thing that he hadn't shared with Natale: *don* Cesare could have easily stopped the hit. Instead, he put business before his nephew's life. Carlo knew the evil old man would do the same to him. He was increasingly confused about where his loyalties should lie, though every fiber of his being had been trained to honor the family—*La Cosa Nostra*—even if it meant his death. When he spoke there was a new weariness in his voice. "My arrangement with Peter Natale has nothing to do with you."

"Yeah?" A surge of perversity seemed to overtake the *don*. "I got one nephew left, one person to teach how to run this family, and he's already such a genius he has everything figured out?"

Carlo tilted the wine glass to take a drink and was surprised to find it empty. He lifted the decanter and refilled it.

Cesare shook his head in disgust. "I'm gonna tell you, Carlo. You pick your friends outa them *scimunitos*, sooner or later you're gonna do something dishonorable." Monkeys. A true Sicilian insult.

"*Zu* Cesare." Carlo's distressed voice came out with effort. "You're my own flesh and blood. I am not going to betray you. I tell you, when it comes to Peter Natale there is no problem."

But the old Sicilian was nothing if not crafty, and now he suddenly softened. "Look, Carlo, forget about it. These things happen. But tell me, what does this man do for us that you should give him such friendship?"

And Carlo saw the trap. *Don* Cesare wanted Natale to do something for them. That's what this was really about.

The *don* apparently knew he'd been discovered. He smiled thinly and shrugged off his duplicity. "You say this man is your friend, Carlo. I ask you, what are friends for?"

"Why can't you just come right out and tell me what you want? Why does everything have to be a manipulation?"

Cesare's grin was like a death mask. "It is such an insignificant thing. A little information for a friend of mine, that's all."

"For who?"

"A lodge-mate, someone in the government, in Rome."

Carlo felt his shoulders sag.

Don Cesare had joined the Order of Caput Mundi some twenty years ago—the Order of the Head of the World. Ancient Rome had been known as *Caput Mundi* when it headed the Roman Empire. Now the name had been adopted for this covert lodge, where member lists and rituals were completely secret.

An invitation to join was an honor that meant a man had arrived in the world. No women were admitted, of course, to this ritual brotherhood, and only the most important men could attend. Cesare used his membership to his own ends. He had managed to co-opt many of the elite members into his own realm of authority, and his access to Italy/Sicily's highest social strata had been considerably broadened. The lodge especially appealed to royals and wealthy men and had many members, with chapters throughout Europe and even into Russia. Cesare was delighted by his membership.

Carlo, however, saw what Cesare didn't. In his mind the lodge had taken the place of religion, for while Cesare had grown up under the rituals of the Catholic faith, he long ago turned away from the church's rule.

Furthermore, Carlo knew that the lodge also served to excite the *don*'s lust for conspiracy. There were inner sanctums within the society, special labyrinths and ceremonies and honors and ranks.

These secret rituals and bondings seemed to give *don* Cesare a dark delight that Carlo could not share, no matter how hard he tried. He despised the organization.

Nor could he share Cesare's interest in hooking Peter Natale into the family circle in order to use his resources to bestow favor upon a lodge-mate. The crudeness of the request surprised him, even though he'd known that this attempt to hook Natale had to happen sooner or later.

His jaw set defiantly. "Natale won't do it."

Don Cesare's eyes narrowed dangerously. Then he turned to stare fiercely out into the darkness.

Carlo silently cursed his uncle for constantly scheming, endlessly scheming, to bend every living, breathing being on the planet to his own dark will.

And yet something was slightly different about this request. There was a tightness and feral hunger in the old man's face that Carlo hadn't seen since the time of Johnny's death. His uncle's head swiveled around, and now Carlo could see the hollow, frightening look in his eyes.

Don Cesare spoke slowly, and anyone who didn't know him might even have thought a pleasant note had crept into his voice.

"You better get yourself straightened out, Carlo. You got your head twisted around backward. No cop, no government man is ever going to do you any good unless you work them the right way."

"Cesare—"

"Things don't stay the same forever, Carlo. You want the family here when you need something, you gotta do your share."

"*Zu* Cesare"—Carlo fell again into the respectful form of address that had been drilled into him from childhood—"it wouldn't matter what I said or did. Peter Natale just wouldn't cooperate. Never. It's impossible. There are certain things he'll do for me as part of our deal, and that is not one of them."

"*Basta!*" snapped the old man. "That's enough!" His twisted sneer was cold.

"I worked on him when we first met. His word is good, but he doesn't bend."

The old Mafioso smiled then—treacherously, but nevertheless it was a smile. "Well," he said, brushing the air back and forth with his hand as if to brush away the smoke of conversation. "You think about what I have said. Give it some time. We'll talk about it later."

Carlo felt drained, so enormous was his sense of relief at being cut loose from the conversation.

Don Cesare swallowed the rest of his wine, then set down the glass on a table. He shut his eyes as though in deep thought and rocked his dark wicker chair back and forth, back and forth, the very picture of aging complacency.

But Carlo could see those dark, frightening eyes moving behind the eyelids, and he knew that the old man was thinking, thinking . . .

Carlo looked past him and out over the dark fields, then upward at the darkened moon. He glanced sharply into the night as a tiny light sparked in the distance. One of the guards, lighting a cigarette.

His uncle's eyes blinked open, and his gaze now followed Carlo's into the distance, as if he were trying to catch his nephew at some deception. But as the old man saw the flash in the dark, he nodded, and his face softened for a moment, showing that he was pleased that the tough, young Sicilian men who shielded him from the world he viciously plundered were on the job.

Then a sudden frown transformed Cesare's face into that of an emaciated and withered toad. He tilted his wine glass and stared at his nephew, studying him over the rim.

"What's wrong?" Carlo asked, taken aback.

"You. I gotta tell you, there is something about you that is bothering me these days."

"Nothing has changed."

"Don't lie. You were thinking of something." The old man's voice was gnawing, prying.

Carlo shook his head. "I'm just distracted. A little tired."

"Then go rest," the old man snapped. "Maria Leona can call you when dinner is ready—"

Don Cesare's words were interrupted by the appearance of his old servant Zaza, a peasant with a face like the roots of a mahogany tree. *"Scusi. Don* Cesare?"

"Si, si." Cesare was irritated by the intrusion.

"Telephono. It is *Signore* Chicarelli, from *Roma."*

"Yes, yes, bring it to me."

Zaza carried the portable phone across the narrow veranda and gave it to Cesare, who immediately spoke into the mouthpiece. "Ciao."

Carlo watched curiously as the batrachian cast of the old man's face intensified, his lips pursed, and suffused rage darkened his skin. He cursed once, listened, cursed again. Finally, he spoke a few castigating words into the instrument, then slammed it down to break the connection, even as he disgorged a full flood of obscenities.

"What's up?"

Don Cesare ignored the question. He refilled his wine glass. Without meeting Carlo's eyes, he tossed off the drink, then poured another. When he had also swallowed that, he finally had enough control over his rage to be able to talk.

He peered at Carlo, his face drawn tight. Behind the skin there was an absence of light that gave it the texture and hardness of a scarab beetle's carapace, the accumulated result of five decades of murders, betrayals, and greed.

"Luciano Chicarelli has been kidnapped," he said in a voice like an open grave.

Carlo was astounded. "By who?" The words rolled out, and immediately he wanted to put them back in again.

The old man sneered. "If I knew, would they still be alive? *Basta!* You are such a fool, Carlo." The old man shook his fist. "But I vow to the saints that whoever has insulted *La Familia* in this manner is *carnazze succese."* Dead meat for the slaughterhouse.

Carlo looked deep into the nakedness of his uncle's eyes, into the vile, dark secrets that lay buried in a poisoned well of hatred.

Cesare saw his scrutiny and blinked, cutting off the dark window to his soul. A sudden crafty look flitted across his face.

"It is because of your friend Peter Natale that this has happened."

Carlo was astonished.

"It is true. We let our enemies use us, and people believe we are growing weak. And I tell you once again, you will either put the hooks into this Natale or he will be *carnazze succese* too."

Carlo knew the old man meant what he said. He'd shoot Natale and have him fed to the pigs just as quickly as he'd ordered thousands of other deaths throughout the decades. Human life no longer had any value whatsoever to *don* Cesare Ricaso.

And suddenly he was gripped by the powerless, futile feeling that he had known often throughout the years. As always, the feeling instantly turned to liquid hate and deep, gnawing fear. He swallowed the fear and let the hatred harden into resolve. He was going to have to make some choices soon, because he had seen through to the pit of hell just now in his uncle's malignant eyes.

"Remember, Carlo. *Chi gioca solo gioca bene.*" The man who plays alone always wins.

"And remember too—" Cesare's eyes slitted up, and an evil light came into them "'A man knows where he is born, but not always where he dies.'"

Carlo knew the old Sicilian parable translated into a threat for both him and Peter Natale.

In that instant, Carlo wanted with every fiber of his being to be far, far away from his vicious relative, to have his soul restored to any form of innocence that a truly benevolent Creator might be able to bestow.

He also wondered, with a sinking, saddened heart, if it wasn't already far, far too late.

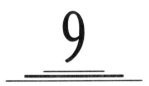

Rome

Peter Natale was unaware that he was the object of a Mafia quarrel. Nor would he have cared had he known. *Don* Cesare's attempts to hook him into subservience would have amused him. And he would have felt empathy for Carlo for having to put up with the brutal old tyrant—though contemptuous of him too for knuckling under. But Natale would have breezed past the situation even at that and filed it away for another time. At that moment he had other, far more pressing, problems.

The Alitalia flight from Nice to Rome had deposited him at Fiumicino Airport just shy of 7:00 P.M. There he was met by a smiling Italian-American junior agent with eager brown eyes and extremely good manners, dressed in dark slacks, a neat white shirt, and wearing a checkered, visored cab-driver's hat perched jauntily on his cropped dark hair.

The young man took Natale's small suitcase and overnighter, then escorted him to one of the many square-cut yellow taxis, where he tossed the light bags into the trunk.

"Grazie," Natale said and yielded to an impulse to hand over a tip.

The driver grinned and pocketed the five American dollars as if it were a private joke between them. He seemed happy to be in the game.

During the tedious, twenty-five minute drive into the city, the young driver offered clipped bits of conversation: the Rome weather (hot tonight, hot all week); the traffic (always impossible). And all the time he eyed Natale in his rearview mirror as if he were observing a rare and endangered species of spy.

Finally Natale slid all the way to one side, turned, and stared out the window.

Eventually they cruised past the antiquated US Embassy at 121 Via Vittorio Veneto and turned onto a side street that led into a leafy, residential area. After another half block the driver yanked the wheel, and they whipped neatly through a heavy iron gate in a high fence masked by dense shrubbery and elegant plane trees. The electric gate had apparently been left open just for them, for some invisible hand caused it to slide shut behind them. Just inside the wall the driver stopped, climbed out, and opened the rear door to usher Natale onto a leaf-sheltered walkway some ten paces from a massive oakwood door.

Peter looked up to see a three-story stone villa with dark, narrow windows. It seemed all but vacant, but he knew that several well-armed guards would be watching him from somewhere.

His attention turned to the door. It was sheltered on both sides by impenetrable shrubbery and flanked by two brass lamps emitting milky light. In the door's upper center was a discrete brass plaque with engraved lettering:

ITALIA IMPORT AND EXPORT:
HOURS 10:00 A.M. to 4:00 P.M.:
WHOLESALE ONLY

Beside the door was an illuminated doorbell.

"We have you checked into the Excelsior," the driver said quietly. "I'll take your bags on ahead."

Natale nodded.

The Excelsior was a luxury hotel in the middle of this muted and elegant quarter that had once been known as Rome's *la dolce vita*. Now the Via Vittorio Veneto was home to airline offices, to small cafes and shops. But the proximity of the American embassy still attracted a number of diplomatic travelers to the Excelsior.

When Natale was in Rome he always stayed there—unless he was working a covert mission—mostly because it was within walking distance of the embassy. The fact that he had been booked into the Excelsior was good news. Maybe he wasn't, after all, being dragged back into a new maelstrom of secret operations.

As the driver prepared to step on the gas, Natale suddenly remembered the finger-printed paper inside his overnight bag. "Hold on," he said. "I'll need my overnighter." He wanted to turn it over to Frost for analysis at the CIA lab.

The driver cheerfully removed the small bag from the trunk, handed it to him, then climbed back inside the car.

Natale was turning toward the door when he remembered something else. "When you've dropped off my other bag at the hotel, would you mind stopping by the Alitalia office? I need a ticket for the morning flight to Naples."

He needed to get home and tie up the paperwork and mop up the aftermath of Kaleidoscope. He acted as paymaster for several Neapolitan members of the network they'd used and otherwise saw to their needs.

And then there was the even more pressing matter of the kid who'd been killed in his room early this morning. He wanted to start that probe from his home base, using his own contacts and resources—people he knew he could trust. Luckily, the other two operations on his agenda were in the hands of two contract agents: an ex-Arafat man who was helping probe the pipeline carrying stolen Russian armaments into Teheran, and an Italian naval intelligence officer who was handling the most recent thefts from the Southern NATO base in Naples.

He needed to catch up on what was happening there too. But most of all he needed to know exactly what had happened in Monte Carlo. Was the kid's death linked into one of his operations, or had it been a random, unconnected act? A lot could ride on the answers, because if the event was connected to something Natale was currently working on, covert agents might be at risk, networks might be blown. At the very least, intelligence had somehow been compromised.

Aside from professional considerations, Natale's interest in the young man's death had also become a personal quest. Understanding would bring a sort of atonement, for the haunting face, the dead-eyed stare kept filtering into his mind like a dark, defiling secret that didn't plan to let him go.

The young driver beamed a smile at Natale, jerking him

back to the present. "The airline office is next door to the hotel," he said. "I'll leave your ticket at the front desk."

"No. Deliver it to me later, please. Bring it to my room." He handed the driver an Agency airline credit card—in an anonymous corporate name, of course—then checked his watch. It was now 7:40. "I should be finished here by midnight at the absolute latest. Just phone before you come up. I want to be absolutely sure that I can get out of here on the first morning flight, and I want my ticket in hand."

The young man nodded agreeably and watched with benign and obvious envy, from his seat within the car, as Natale turned away to press the buzzer.

Peter remembered when he had been like that—innocent, somewhat naive, eager to go out and save the world. And of course to engage in more than a bit of adventure along the way. What else was spy craft all about? That was before he saw all the carnage, the bodies, the deceit and greed and corruption that riddled even the highest and most hallowed places.

Now all Natale felt was tired.

Clyde Tyler, chief of Rome 'station, had apparently been standing just inside the doorway watching, for he answered the buzzer immediately.

Tyler was a square-built, gray-faced, gray-haired man whose forgettable appearance made him the quintessential spy. A station chief did not ordinarily double as a doorman, but this was a very private safe house, used only for high-level strategy meetings. No on-premise servants were allowed.

Clyde Tyler pumped Natale's hand cheerfully, drew him inside with a barrage of greetings, then ushered him down a dimly lighted hallway to a coatrack beside a closed door.

The station chief's air of restrained urgency penetrated Natale's fatigue and began to revive him.

As Peter was hanging up his coat, Tyler said, "You should know that Bob Hammond arrived a couple of hours ago, straight in from Langley."

A stab of dread stopped Natale in mid-motion, but he kept his composure. "That right?"

Hammond was CIA brass of the highest level, the director of operations for the clandestine services sector of the Central Intelligence Agency. Rome station hadn't been graced with such a high-ranking presence for a decade or more, not since Italy had been center stage as one of the true global hot spots. In those days a visit to Italy meant high press for any US politician. Italy invariably grabbed worldwide headlines as the first Western democracy threatening to collapse under the weight of international terrorism.

Nevertheless, the headlines had moved on to other hot spots, and Hammond was a political animal who moved with the headlines. His appearance here now, especially with no notice, meant serious trouble for someone. And suddenly Natale wondered if the trouble was going to land on him.

"Frost tried to phone you on the plane so you'd be prepared," Tyler said.

Peter felt a growing sense of apprehension. "What's up?"

Tyler said he didn't know, but he and Frost were expecting the worst. And anyway, before they stepped into the inner chamber, what exactly had happened in Monte Carlo? Tyler explained that Frost had barely mentioned it to Hammond and him, but it sounded as though Natale had bitten off quite a chunk this time. And where was Judith? Wasn't she supposed to come along? And when was Natale going to give up his exile at Naples station and step into the real action here in Rome?

Natale politely, tersely, and noncommittally answered each question, but Tyler's queries were nervous conversation, and he obviously wasn't focusing on the replies anyway. He opened the door that admitted them both into a well-appointed sitting room.

Peter followed Tyler into the room, then set his small overnighter down on the carpet just inside the door.

He saw the bigger picture first, as he was trained to do: emerald-green carpeting, walls the same color—though with wide, cream-colored vertical stripes and several gold-framed oil paintings of the eighteenth-century Italian countryside. There was a brass-fitted antique fireplace at the far end (unused) and tastefully positioned Queen Anne furnishings throughout, including several claw-footed chairs with oxblood-leather upholstery.

After this split instant's survey, his attention turned to Hammond, who was sitting in an upholstered armchair, watching him. Hammond nodded. Natale returned the silent greeting.

Teddy Frost's portly body was positioned on the edge of a wooden desk at the far side of the room. His arms were folded, his body was at an angle so that one leg appeared to be shorter than the other. Natale now fixed on him, and Frost offered a thin but genuine smile.

Theodore Frost was one of those unique creatures whose name truly fit him. He was almost imperceptibly plump, had a slightly pug nose, the blandly innocent features of a teddy bear, and eyes that were a snappy button-black. His silver-gray hair had recently been razor-cut (in honor of his impending trip to Langley, Natale assumed). Once again Peter reflected on the paradox of Teddy Frost, for no one would ever have guessed that inside this distinguished, kindly looking gentleman there was a nerve network of meshed steel and a mind that dwarfed Machiavelli himself for duplicity.

As usual, Frost was meticulously dressed. Today he wore an iron-blue tailored suit with discrete hand stitching, a blue-white silk shirt, and expensive gold tie tack and cuff links. His silk tie and pocket handkerchief were a tartan in various shades of blue and white; his short arms were folded in front of him. Even as he smiled, his dark eyes measured Natale carefully, as if they were looking for signs of wear.

Peter nodded curtly. "Evening, Ted."

"Good evening, Peter. Glad you could make it." He flicked one manicured hand toward Hammond. "You've met our DO?"

"Once, when he was still station chief in Berlin." Natale directed his full attention to Hammond again and nodded for a second time. "How do you do, sir?"

Hammond nodded back. His pale brows arched into a frown above sun-bleached blue eyes that gazed intently at Natale as if he were trying to remember him. After a moment the gaze broke and moved on to Clyde Tyler, who had seated himself in the chair beside Hammond. Natale also sat down, in a chair a few paces from Frost's desktop perch.

He watched Hammond, leaning back in his chair now, poised and dignified, talking to Tyler about an embassy dinner planned for later that night, which he considered a waste of valuable time. One long leg was crossed over the other to display sharply creased gray trousers running down to a pair of well-shod feet.

Natale reflected that Hammond was still gracefully impressive, as he had been when he ruled Berlin station during the Cold War. But he appeared to have aged a century since he'd left Berlin for the upper ranks, and the pale blue eyes seemed deadened. Peter couldn't quite put his finger on what it was about the man that gave this impression. Perhaps just a gloss of age and exhaustion had settled down over him like fine ash over a spent volcano.

Hammond was stylishly dressed in a lightweight gray linen suit and snow-white shirt instead of the heavy clothing he'd affected the last time Natale had seen him. The hair was still short-clipped and sandy, though the distinguished brush of gray at the temples was substantially thicker. The craggy, oblong face had once been pale from the Berlin winters; now it was sun-tanned leather, the mark of an avid hunter or fisherman—or perhaps of a vain man who made time for the tanning salon.

Hammond was in fact the very picture of what every top-level government administrator should be, a veritable CIA poster boy. And though he was now deeply engaged in a conversation with Tyler, Peter knew that the man was keenly and unpleasantly aware of him.

Hammond was massaging Tyler's ego. "One more week, right? Then you're out to pasture?"

Tyler nodded politely.

"Good time to be leaving government service," Hammond said with forced conviviality. "Bunch of bumbling fools in control, I say. Wish I'd had the sense to get out after I left Berlin, instead of pursuing the piper and landing hip-deep in the middle of the current sewage of Agency politics."

Tyler's reply was noncommittal, socially sympathetic, and the two men talked on, commiserating now about the problems of working at headquarters, a posting that Tyler had also held many years ago, though in a far less exalted position.

Natale waited patiently. He would find out why he was here only when they were ready to tell him. In the meantime, he was a field man among administrators, a fish out of water who was happy to be released from the hook of Hammond's stare. He would be even happier to be released from the man's presence, he decided.

He didn't know much about Hammond, other than the fact that he'd run Berlin station for twenty years during the coldest parts of the Cold War, right up until the day they'd torn down the Wall. Natale burrowed deep, trying to pry open his memory, and managed to dredge up a surprising vignette of a midnight briefing that included information about Hammond's German wife. He had even seen a photograph somewhere of a raven-haired beauty who was said to be a distant relative of the royal House of Brandenburg and who supposedly had several relatives in the West German secret service. He knew that Hammond had moved to Langley, into administration, shortly after leaving Berlin. Then two years ago, former Secretary of State Edgar J. Paxton had been elected president of the United States. Paxton appointed his chief sidekick, Caleb Carey, to the position of Director of the CIA, and the entire Agency had then been reshuffled. A lot of new people landed on top, Hammond among them.

What little else Natale knew about Hammond's professional career was all good, though it wasn't much. There were, of course, the stories about his heyday at Berlin station. His iron-fisted rule there had become legendary.

Natale had heard the stories: refugees trying to escape the terrors of East Germany, coming over the still-standing Wall, the sudden bursts of gunfire, the screams, the abrupt glare of spotlights with one horrified figure skewered in the middle, perhaps a Western spy trying to come back in but betrayed by his fellow man. Another legend had been spun around a high-ranking East German Stasi agent who had burrowed deep into West German intelligence to be single-handedly uncovered by Hammond. The West Germans gave Hammond a military medal for that one—a first for an American spy.

Peter decided that Hammond had apparently earned his stripes and then some. But no matter what he had been in the past, today he was a major cog in the political end of the machine that drove the CIA. Natale, like all true field men, had a healthy and well-earned disdain for the espiocrats who oversaw the field agents' work from positions of absolute safety, so his dislike was not for the man but for the bureaucratic role he inhabited. Desk men were invariably too politicized, too removed from the real world. They had made too many decisions that ruined operations, endangered agents, and even cost agents' lives.

As director of operations, Hammond was the ultimate bureaucrat. His job was to oversee the other bureaucrats in Langley and Washington, who in turn ruled the chiefs of the various CIA stations around the globe, who in turn handled the field men and trainers and case officers who executed the hands-on spy craft that helped protect the global interests of the United States of America.

Hammond shared policy meetings with such luminaries as President Paxton and Paxton's clone, CIA Director Carey. The rumor mill had it that Hammond and the president had become such good friends that they frequently played golf together, to Carey's chagrin. Rumor even had it that Hammond was jockeying for Carey's position as top gun.

And now, for some reason, this very busy political animal had arrived unexpectedly at Rome station—a fact that caused Peter to wonder what political coin Hammond might be seeking here in sunny, sinister Italy.

And Natale was also here, the cat before the king.

He turned to Frost and asked the question again, this time with his eyes: *What's up?*

Frost made a small, almost imperceptible shrug.

Natale leaned closer and said softly, "I guess you know that Judith went on to Moscow?"

Frost shot him a look that said, *Shut up and listen. Don't miss a word.* Aloud he said easily, "She phoned me from the Nice airport as you were taking off. No problem. We can fill her in later."

Natale clamped his mouth shut and tried to look politely interested as Hammond complained to Tyler about this year's black budget and the perpetual problems they were having with the Senate's Intelligence Oversight Committee. Its members were once again demanding that the budget be opened to congressional scrutiny —a plan that would jeopardize whatever secrecy remained within the voluminous agency, Hammond said, for almost any trail worth following could be followed on paper if you had the footprints left by the money.

"Cherchez la cash is about what it adds up to," he said with a scowl. "Follow the money, and I can tell you, certain knee-jerk liberal senators are intending to do just that, even if they give away the farm in the process."

Natale agreed with what Hammond was saying. Nevertheless it was an old complaint, and his foot began a silent, involuntary tapping on the carpet, as his mind traveled on to his own operations and problems.

Frost looked at him and mouthed, *Patience.*

Natale stopped his foot, controlled his agitation, and sat silently. He didn't like the strained look on Frost's face. He didn't like the feeling in the room. It was as if the men were warily skirting around the necessity of announcing a death.

Maybe mine, Natale thought.

Hammond turned to speak to Frost and Natale now, and Peter realized that the DO had been fully aware of the effect he was having on them all along. Hammond had been studying the three of them, taking his time, and apparently whatever criterion he had been applying had produced the right results, for he suddenly became benevolent and affable.

He said, "Well. Yes. I'm running on, aren't I? I always do when I get on the subject of the tomfoolery in the government. And I see that I need to get to the point here." He pasted a sincere, apologetic look on his face. "I know I've made you all nervous by arriving like this—I worked the field myself for many years and believe me I know how unwelcome desk jockeys are when they drop in unexpectedly. But I feel strongly that this is something I need to handle personally. In other words, that this is my problem, so to speak, and therefore mine to straighten out."

He looked around the room, measuring his listeners again, to see how they were responding. He was apparently satisfied, for he continued.

"I'd been on a trip to Asia—coddling the newest Japanese prime minister—or it would never have happened to begin with. I'm talking about your mole hunt, Ted. I'd just returned from Tokyo when I heard that Caleb Carey and his paper-pushing hordes had put the stops to it. And you can imagine how upset I was when I tried to contact you at Moscow station and learned that you'd already stormed Rome, en route to Langley. On your way to voice your disagreement to that decision, am I right? And to tender your resignation? Hmm? I know you that well, Ted. And I wanted to get over here and talk to you before you walked into Langley like a lamb to the slaughter."

"Yes," Frost said. He was studying Hammond with a keen, hard light in his eyes. But his facial expression remained respectful and friendly. "Thank you, I . . . uh . . . appreciate your concern."

"I was out of the Langley loop when the decision was made, or it wouldn't have happened. You can put that in the bank. I wanted to tell you face to face, Ted. I don't like the way they're handling this thing. Not one little bit."

Frost said, "I see . . ."

"I'm completely on your side." Hammond's gaze was fierce and bristling. "I'm going to do my level best to see that the probe is reopened."

Frost blinked hard. It was the first time Natale had seen him speechless.

Hammond offered them a bashful smile. "My wife is a Berliner, you know. She's at the embassy here, visiting with Ambassador Lanza's wife. She demands that I take her to visit her family once or twice a year, so I find myself spending quite a bit of time at Berlin station.

"But frankly, I didn't mind this chance to take a look at what's happening here in Rome. I seem to be getting out of touch lately—they keep whisking me off to Asia. We have a whole new set of problems there now that Korea has nukes and Japan is rebuilding their military. But the EU nations are still the main global arena, and especially Germany, France, and Italy. Mark my words, whatever happens globally in the next few years will find its seed in Europe. Here the future will be made or laid to rest."

He looked around the room, a pleased expression on his face now. He said, "I'm an old warhorse, you all know that. I'm not about to miss out on all the local action. Which is why I decided to personally handle this plate of worms we've been handed with regard to Frost's mole." He nodded briskly, and Peter thought if the nod had been an inch or two deeper it might have passed for a bow.

Teddy Frost's button-black eyes were alive with keen, penetrating interest in what Hammond was saying, but Natale also saw something else there, something masked. He watched Frost curiously, wondering what Machiavellian thoughts were germinating inside the man's brilliant mind.

Hammond unfolded himself, brushed his pants with the palms of both hands, then began to pace lankily, talking as he moved and gazing hard at the floor.

"Thing is, Ted, I don't need to tell you how precarious our situation is right now. There are a lot of power plays going on within the Agency. And we're also under the gun with Congress—you heard me telling Clyde how they're barking about the budget again. And they're still using the Grimes affair to bludgeon us. Nobody wants to worry about another mole in our midst. They want us to purely shut up about it until the budget thing is sorted out and Congress has calmed down.

"Thing is, they're afraid if we keep looking for a mole, we're going to find one." Hammond offered a steely grin. "And I'll tell you up front. If I have my way, we sure as sin will. If there's someone in our ranks doing the devil's work, I will personally have his head."

Frost studied his buffed fingernails. He still sat on the edge of the desk, though he occasionally shifted his weight.

Hammond reached a position across from Natale and close to Frost. He sat down on the edge of a chair, leaned anxiously toward Frost, and peered at him. "I want a private talk with you, Ted, later tonight. Blast that banquet, anyway." He looked at his watch. "What time did you say it started?"

"Eight," Tyler said.

"Well, looks like we're already late. Frankly, I'd skip it if my wife wasn't waiting. And I suppose we might need Ambassador Lanza someday, so better keep the wheels greased. Anyway, Ted, we'll talk some more about your mole later. I need to know exactly what proof you have, what you're basing your opinions on, whether or not you're keeping anything at all from Langley—not that I'd blame you if you did. I'm not sure I'd trust many of my colleagues with my pocket change, much less my life." He chuckled darkly.

Frost was fully composed now. "I'll be happy to talk later."

"I appreciate it. Thing is, Ted, I need something tangible to hang my hat on if I'm going to lay my neck out on this. You understand. I want to do the right thing, but I have to be absolutely certain that it is the right thing. Not that I doubt you. But I have to be able to show the skeptics, you understand, how things work. And I need to know the lay of the land so I won't personally step into any holes."

Frost nodded politely.

Hammond stood again and resumed his pacing. This time, his striding took him around the room to the window, where he pulled aside the heavy drape and peered out. Then he let the drape fall shut, looked at his watch again, and came around to a position across from Natale, where he again sat down, this time on a green high-backed chair facing him. Suddenly he leaned in close and skewered Peter with a penetrating gaze.

"As for you—I hear you had a little trouble in Monte Carlo."

Natale was surprised at the abrupt shift in the subject, but he quickly replied. "Yes, sir. That's certainly true."

"You want to explain what that was all about?"

Natale sat farther back in his chair, uncomfortable with the man's invasion of his personal space. The scent of bay-rum cologne was unpleasantly strong. "Afraid I haven't quite got it figured out yet."

Hammond nodded as if he'd expected as much. "And your friend Carlo Ricaso bailed you out?"

Natale's superiors were aware of his relationship with Carlo. He had to list the Italian as a source in order to explain where he got some of his best intel, though the list was cleared for only a half dozen eyes, Hammond's, Frost's, and Tyler's among them. But this was one of the areas where he tried to feed the Agency only bare bones, for this terrain was a minefield where excessive details had a way of turning into excessive pitfalls, once others got their hands on them.

He tried to dismiss the importance of what had happened with a shrug. "It wasn't much. Carlo pulled some bought-off official's chain. He feels like he still owes me for helping him out in Moscow."

Hammond seemed to chew on the word "Moscow" for a moment. "Well, I personally want to commend you on how you're handling that situation with the Ricaso crime family. Not too much, just a nip here and a tuck there, right? Just stay away from their brothels and hands off their drugs, and you'll see it through." He actually winked, as if he and Peter shared some nasty little secret.

"Thing is," he added—looking at Frost sternly now, all business again—"we can't be too careful these days. The last thing in the world we need is for some reporter to get hold of the fact that one of our star field men is having a little fling with the heir to the Ricaso crime family. We'd have them pawing up bones all over the place, and Congress would be baying at the moon."

The man's words offended Natale, and the use of the word "fling" seemed a deliberate trivialization of what was in fact a very dangerous situation. However, Peter did agree that there was serious need for discretion, especially with regard to the ever-vigilant press corps on both sides of the ocean, who liked nothing better than to unmask a corrupted spy.

Not that the basic parameters of his relationship with Carlo would be a great surprise to the world were they revealed. The CIA had always used criminals as covert sources. The Latin American *Field Operations Manual* actually spelled out the Agency's preference for hiring local crooks to carry out illegal actions within any given country's borders. And in the 1940s the OSS—forerunner of the CIA—used the old Sicilian Mafia as a means of infiltrating the occupied Italian mainland in a brilliant move that helped put an end to the Second World War.

It was only after the OSS rewarded the Mafia by putting them into Sicily's highest political positions that they realized the Mafia's hatred for Mussolini was forged not so much by a longing for democracy as from a desire to wield the dark fascist powers that had once belonged to the Mafia alone and which Mussolini had usurped. By the time the Allies had fully figured this out, the damage had been done.

And then there had been the more recent debacle with Air America during the war in Vietnam. The only way the CIA could get the military information they needed from the mountain warlords was to look the other way with regard to the warlords' opium trafficking. The situation got so bad that for a time the CIA airline, Air America, had actually been used to transport opium to the refineries and then to fly the finished heroin on out to where it could be delivered to the world.

These were dark and well-documented scandals in the history of espionage. But they were also a good lesson. When you made a pact with the devil, it was all too easy for the devil to wrest full control. Natale well knew that—which made Hammond's words a double insult, because they implied that he was vulnerable to the Mafia's many hooks and snares and insinuated that he was the type of man who would spend time in the Mafia's brothels.

The suggestion disgusted him—perhaps all the more so because a Berlin bordello owner and several of his employees had recently become his primary link into the nuclear black market in Germany. After all, if you were going to understand the beast's heartbeat, you sometimes needed to communicate with the people who lived in the belly of the beast. And criminals of every ilk relaxed when they visited brothels.

Though the man who owned the prostitution racket had allowed the Russian Mafia to virtually slave-traffic girls into his establishment, he had drawn the line at helping to facilitate the nuclear black market. He surprised Peter and German intelligence operatives alike by risking his life to provide key information that had helped Natale and his allies make their most recent round of arrests through Operation Kaleidoscope.

For several months, Natale had personally worked that end of the case, living in Berlin and coming to know these people. He learned to understand their bondage—a circumstance he would in no way intensify by patronizing them. Like so many others on the dark side of the world, they coped with their lifestyle by drugging themselves. The idea of exploiting a drugged woman in the pursuit of sexual gratification filled him with such repugnance—not only for the idea of it but also for the man who suggested it—that it was all he could do to keep the revulsion from finding its way to his face.

Natale's disciplined morality was the most powerful weapon he had against being corrupted by the Octopus. The slippery beast lured its prey with greed, with lust, by promising to satiate a thirst for power. He wasn't about to fall into any of those traps, and to imply that he might was a smear on his integrity, the singular quality that had earned Carlo Ricaso's respect and made their relationship possible.

Frost and Tyler were both silent. Tyler seemed embarrassed, and Natale knew from the expression on Frost's face that he was also angry at Hammond for his snide insinuation.

But Hammond appeared impervious to the effect he'd created. He said, "Personally, I'd like to see Cesare and Carlo Ricaso both shot on the spot. Or maybe hung. But I suppose that approach is impractical in these days of high compromise."

He gave Natale a cool, appraising look—almost an accusation—then stood again and returned to the far end of the room, where he hooded his eyes while he lit a cigarette. The smoke billowed. Hammond suddenly looked up to pierce Natale with another stare. "You worked with Frost in Moscow to help us straighten out that synthetic plutonium deal, right?"

"Yes."

"Good job." He smiled tightly. "I wanted to personally thank you. And good work too on helping the Germans wrap up this most recent ring of thieves and drug dealers and nuclear profiteers. I'll personally see to it that you get another intelligence star for handing us this little prize."

"Yes, sir." Natale felt foolish saying it, but he had to say something.

"Yes, well, nothing to sneeze at, this problem with weapons-grade material, and an arrest of this nature certainly helps President Paxton look pretty to the press—even if he has to share some of the glory with the Germans."

There was a sudden, uncomfortable pause in the conversation. Natale disapproved of this misshapen analysis. The politicization of the operation belittled his and Frost's and Tyler's own motivation and efforts. The three men lingered in the tentative silence, and Natale was pleased to sense the silent support of his two friends.

After a moment Hammond stirred as if he were going to speak again, just as a buzzer sounded, causing him to seal his lips and look disgruntled.

Tyler smiled apologetically. He reached in his pocket and pulled out a folded portable phone. He opened it and punched a button. "Yes?"

A scratchy, disembodied voice was audible throughout the room. "The car is still waiting to take you and Mr. Hammond to the embassy, sir. Shall I dismiss the driver?"

Hammond was already in motion. "We're on our way. That's about it for the moment then. Frost, I'll see you later, of course. Sure you won't reconsider and join us for dinner?"

Frost declined.

"Well, later then. Now where did I hang my blasted coat?"

Tyler was ahead of him, opening the door. Frost and Natale said good-bye in a flurry of handshakes, and then Hammond and Tyler were off to play the diplomat's game.

Peter pulled back the heavy green drape and watched the two men from the window as they were ushered into the back of the consulate limo by the liveried chauffeur. Finally, after much ado, the long car backed out of the wrought-iron gate, and the gate automatically slid shut behind them.

10

Rome

Teddy Frost made no secret of the fact that he had learned to value Peter Natale's judgment. Now, ensconced within the well-secured grandeur of the Roman safe house, the two men could finally relax and talk at length.

Peter wanted to know more about the surprise appearance of Bob Hammond. "Isn't our DO slumming a little?"

Frost smiled wearily, but in spite of everything there was a trace of amusement in his button-black eyes. "He's working damage control to try to keep me on as chief of Moscow station, of course. Other than that, your guess is as good as mine."

"Then I'll guess that it has something to do with Washington politics and the president's current low standing in the polls," Natale said dryly.

"I'd call that a good guess, since his next stop is Berlin, heaven help us." Frost pulled a chair around to face Peter, then sat down.

"What's he going to do there?"

"Take credit for the German arrests you and your colleagues just made, I'd expect, and make sure the glory reflects back on President Paxton somehow. A few photo opportunities, a visit to the embassy. Maybe he'll finesse a segment on CNN."

Natale shrugged. "If he can get it past the Germans, it doesn't matter to me. Which brings me to my second question. Why am *I* here?"

A shadow fell across Teddy Frost's face, driving away every trace of good humor. "There's the matter of the young man who died in your hotel room. We need to work on that, of course. But frankly, I decided to invite you here even before that happened. I need to talk to you and Judith about strategy before I go on to Langley and submit my resignation." He frowned and peered into the distance. "I'm not sure I'm making the right decision, but something has to give. My hands are tied more tightly every day, and I've exhausted my patience. I'm starting to feel like I'm no longer up to the job."

"Anything in particular?"

"Everything in particular. On the one hand we have the mushrooming expansion of the crime syndicates—especially the Russians and the Sicilians—"

"A marriage truly made in hell," Natale agreed.

"Amen. And add to that the nuclear black market—as if the drug trafficking and other chaos weren't enough. Then stir in what I'm convinced is one very active mole within the US intelligence community's most hallowed halls, and well—"

"I can see why you might be feeling stressed out. But what exactly can I do for you?"

Frost looked sad. "I don't know, Peter. Frankly, I just don't know. I guess you can begin by telling me what in thunder is going on with Judith. And when you're done explaining that, you can fill me in on exactly what happened at the Hotel de Mer—leaving out absolutely nothing."

Peter leaned back and relaxed. He told Frost everything from beginning to end, although he did leave out his deep feelings for Judith and his suspicions and speculations. Frost would want only the facts anyway. As for Peter and Judith's troubled relationship, Frost probably already knew the truth—at least, as much of it as he was capable of understanding.

When he finished, he unzipped his overnighter, removed the envelope carefully, and handled it by the edges, so as not to smudge the fingerprints on the paper inside. He presented it to Frost. "Wonder if you could check the paper inside here for prints, Ted. I took them off the victim, and it might help us identify him."

"Smart move. Luckily, Tyler and the chief of Rome's Homicide Squad have become close friends, so we've already been given access to his facilities. That will expedite our abilities and substantially broaden our scope."

Natale felt a ray of hope. "Think the chief could find a pretext to contact the Monte Carlo gendarmes and see if they've managed to identify the victim?"

"I thought of that, and it's done."

"No dice?"

"Nothing there. But they had also checked the body for drugs, a common part of any investigation—"

Natale's senses sharpened. "And?"

"Your prowler was a heroin addict. The quantity in his bloodstream indicated that he'd fixed no more than half an hour before climbing into your room. The needle tracks suggest he'd started using only a short time ago—most of his veins were intact, and the scarring was recent. I had about dismissed him as your garden-variety burglar needing money for a quick fix, until you told me he'd used your name."

Natale felt his heart sink. "Anything else?"

"His gun was of Bulgarian manufacture, a knock-off of the Beretta Cougar .23 automatic. That's about it."

Natale nodded. He'd recognized the weapon as a knock-off. He processed the rest of Frost's information, especially the mention of Bulgaria, and wondered what horror he had managed to shake loose now. There was something about Bulgaria . . .

His mind darted this way and that, trying to find any pieces that might fit into this present madness.

Under Communism, the Bulgarian secret police had been the KGB's most apt students of terror, murder, and mayhem. Bulgaria's state-run agency KINTEX ostensibly handled Bulgaria's legitimate trade with the West. In truth, it was responsible for illegally siphoning off hard currency for the Communist bloc. This siphoning took the form of a booming black market in morphine base, heroin, and other addictive drugs, all destined for consumption in Western Europe. This enterprise brought the KGB and their Bulgarian lapdogs into close contact with the Sicilian Mafia.

The KGB colonel who was running the show, Yuri Lepkov, was a wily old fox, and his timing couldn't have been better. Using KINTEX as their central clearinghouse, his network transshipped base from Turkey, Afghanistan, and several Central Asian republics to flood the West anew.

But as Peter Natale considered all this, he also reflected on the surviving spawn of those evil times.

It was common knowledge that some of the KGB's old trafficking networks still lay in place, with or without their former masters. Yuri Lepkov had become a wealthy businessman. His Berlin headquarters acted as an agency for his multitiered and multilayered corporations, which dabbled in just about everything. Other traffickers who had survived the dismantling of Communism had also found niches, often in the criminal world where there was a market for their various skills.

This meant that the man who'd been assassinated in Natale's hotel room might have obtained his gun from a still flourishing market in knock-off weapons. Or perhaps the gun was a relic of former days—which in turn meant that the victim might or might not have some connection to the heroin or armaments traffic . . .

Frost interrupted his thoughts. "I'd like to join Hammond in commending you on the way you smoothed over the incident."

Natale brushed the compliment away. "Actually, Carlo pulled the chain. I just rode along."

"Yes, he definitely has some loyal people on his payroll. If we hadn't requested information as early as we did, the victim would already have been cremated and buried."

"That so?"

Frost nodded. "Even with our request, they couldn't get rid of the body fast enough."

"He's gone?"

"Probably even as we speak. They had him scheduled for the crematorium at eight tonight and assured us there was no way they could wait any longer due to the unpleasant circumstances of the death and their police caseload."

Peter sealed off his feelings with a cold blink to stop the pain before it could set in. "How long will it take to have his fingerprints run?"

Frost had been holding the envelope carefully. Now he leaned over and delicately placed it inside his own briefcase, then zipped the case shut. "We might get results by morning, if I drop it off on my way home."

"It would be nice to have a place to start."

"Yes, I understand. You can't exactly go back there and start turning over rocks."

Frost unconsciously rubbed a hand over his chin. Natale noticed a fine silver stubble beginning to surface. This was the first time he'd ever seen Frost needing a shave.

Teddy pulled his hand away and sat up straight. "Well. In spite of everything else that's happened, I'd still like a report on the antics of Prince Dante di Veresi, if you'd care to indulge my curiosity."

Natale shrugged. "Not much to tell. He and the *contessa* dropped maybe half a mil over a two-night period."

"Did they go to the main casino or stay in the hotel?"

"They played strictly in the Hotel de Mer's gaming rooms. Chemin de fer seems to be their game, and they play only in the private salons with the other high rollers. Nobody really talked to them, nobody came close, though the prince indeed strutted and complained a bit to make sure everyone saw just how much he was losing."

"He bought his chips with paper? Or cash?"

"Cash. Large bills, several currencies."

"And the other players?"

"It was mostly done with signatures and chits, of course, though quite a few people bought their chips with cash. But I didn't see all that much. It's hard to watch the cashier's cage there—you draw the evil eye from the security guards. Mostly the only tangible specie I saw passed anywhere was the chips, between the croupiers and players."

"I actually meant the players at the tables. Was the prince consistently at the table with anyone else?"

Natale thought about that. "There did seem to be one person, a slender nondescript man who looked out of his element but who seemed to be winning heavily." He described the man to Frost.

Frost said, "Beats me. But Tyler tells me they're laundering millions through there. Serious money."

"They may have a croupier who's willing to make some extra money by fixing the game. The dirty money walks into the casino in the prince's pocket, goes across the table and comes out in his partner's pocket as winnings, all neat and ready for taxes and costing the casino absolutely nothing. In fact, they probably leave a percentage as table rent.

"Once the money is in the bank, it can go back out in the form of low-interest loans to various front companies, who can reinvest it in Mafia holdings, which the Mafia can bust out—that is, bankrupt the dummy companies so they never have to pay the money back."

"That's one way to do things," Frost agreed.

"You figure. Veresi dropped two mil in two nights, and the standard percentage for laundering is twenty-five percent. Figure that the prince has a partner who's winning the money. Split that two ways, and both men are earning themselves a tidy quarter of a million apiece for two nights' work, minus the fees to the dealer and maybe the casino manager. Not bad money."

"Maybe it really is time for me to change careers," Frost said wistfully. "The money launderers are making almost as much as the traffickers these days."

"Yes. Well—I'll get a full report to you as soon as I have time to sit down and write it. Maybe then you can figure out what they're doing."

"Whenever you can." Frost made a gesture that said he was in no rush.

Natale frowned. "What's this really all about, anyway? There must be a thousand people around the world laundering Mafia money at this very minute, mostly small fry. You've never bothered me with them before. Why is the prince so hot?"

Frost took a sudden interest in the polished toe of his shoe, turning it this way and that to admire the sheen. When he looked up, he seemed almost embarrassed. "How are you on conspiracy theories?"

Natale was puzzled. "It's not exactly my best subject. I've found that the conspiracy theorists are usually more frightening than the conspiracies they're trying to uncover. Why?"

"Have you ever heard of the Black Nobility?"

Natale scratched at his memory, which rewarded him by conjuring up a jumbled list of so-called conspirator groups that included the Illuminati, the Trilateralists, the Club of Rome, Freemasonry, the US Council on Foreign Relations, the Bilderbergers, and half a dozen other groups that were allegedly out to conquer the world once they'd wiped out their prime enemy, the United States.

Somewhere in there, hanging on at the edges, was the Black Nobility—a group of so-called European royals who, centuries ago, had formed a secret society and had thereby gained formidable, if secretive, political and economic power.

"It rings a very dim bell. Nothing I can really grab onto."

"And that's the way it usually is," Frost agreed. "Once you get past the paranoia, the whole thing goes up in smoke. But not always. Real conspiracies do exist. Therefore, when we get word that something especially heinous is in the works, we look into it even if the trappings have the scent of disinformation or worse."

"Yes . . ." Natale said, even more puzzled.

"Well—we'll leave that for the moment. You have your hands full with other matters. And whether or not a Black Nobility exists is irrelevant to our interest in the prince, because we know, absolutely, that he's one of the key figures in the fascist contingent of the monarchist movement, whatever else he is. A ghostly relic of other times.

"And the real problem is not the money he's laundering, it's his politics. The prince and his pals are serious racists, their party seems to be growing by leaps and bounds, and somebody's pouring in some substantial amounts of money to finance it—including financing their fair-haired child Count Benito Jacovetti.

"Tyler's been keeping an eye on the situation—hence our request that you do likewise. Some unusual movement has recently been taking place within the party that we don't understand."

Natale nodded. He was back on solid ground now. As a full-time resident of Italy, he knew exactly how serious the problem with right-wing fascism had already become.

Fascism had waxed and waned on the Continent since it first found its legs during World War II, but this most recent surge had swept up literally millions of followers in every EU country and in Russia as well.

In Italy, the Fascist party had recently won a landslide in the parliamentary elections. Germany's neo-fascism ran the spectrum from skinhead neo-Nazi street thugs to politically refined politicians who saw a chance to gain new power by manipulating anti-Jewish sentiment. France had her National Front, and Austria had her Freedom Party. Even jolly England was hosting an unprecedented wave of elitist racial hatred.

The fascist mind-set was centered on one central tenet: a totalitarian dictatorship was the preferred way to govern humanity. The only question was, who would be the dictator, and who would be the ruled? Those already pledged to fascism were convinced they'd be on the ruling end of the equation, once the concept came to fruition and the European Union was fully united under one capable man. The royals who were most vociferously throwing themselves behind the cause were those who fiercely believed that they were destined to rule by divine right.

Natale wondered, now, about the link between the resurgence of European fascism and Frost's peculiar question about the Black Nobility. The primary core of Europe's neo-fascism was blended from a strange hodgepodge of deposed royals, street thugs who wanted an excuse to kick others' heads in, power-hungry politicians who knew how to ride a political tide, and—of course—the Sicilian Mafia.

The United States intelligence community had miscalculated the danger the last time fascism gripped Europe's throat. They dismissed Hitler as a nobody whose message of racial hatred would soon wear thin and fade.

This miscalculation kept the United States from intervening in time to stop the Second World War—a possibility then, when the US was the strongest power on earth. The CIA was trying to monitor the European situation more seriously this time.

There was no option this time, Natale thought. The proliferation of nuclear weapons put an entirely different spin on the global balance of power.

"Speaking of fascists," Frost said, interrupting Peter's thoughts, "you should know that I got a call from a friend on Italy's anti-Mafia squad just before you arrived. It seems they put wiretaps on Volante Chicarelli's phone some time ago—"

"No kidding!" Peter grinned. He kept up with the Ricaso crime family's relationships and resources—a necessary part of his survival—which was why he knew that Volante Chicarelli was at the top of the list of Ricaso political henchmen. In fact, he knew a great deal about Volante Chicarelli, and there was nothing he knew that he liked.

The elder Chicarelli was one of *don* Cesare Ricaso's most polished facilitators, a man who had belonged to the Christian Democrat party until the anti-Mafia squads cleaned up that corruption. Then he joined the Fascists. He used tax money to finance early Ricaso heroin deals—which made him every bit as much a murderer as the Ricasos, in Natale's mind.

Don Cesare had helped Chicarelli win political office by killing one rival and blackmailing another, by fixing elections and browbeating voters. In return, Chicarelli helped to enact certain key laws that thwarted the efforts of anti-Mafia law enforcement. He pulled strings with certain judges so that lower court verdicts would be reversed and in this way helped keep the most brutal and bloody Mafiosi free to kill and kill again. As far as Natale was concerned, every evil deed the Sicilian Mafia perpetrated was a deed equally committed by Volante Chicarelli.

Frost said, "The wiretap picked up an interesting piece of information. Seems that Volante's son, Luciano, has been kidnapped."

Natale's eyes snapped wide open. He was astonished. His spectrum of knowledge about Ricaso associates also included Luciano—an innocent, even bewildered, kid who lived, without knowing, in the lair of wolves. He thought for a moment, then said, "I suppose it was just a matter of time before we had another high-profile kidnapping. But Volante Chicarelli's kid?" He emitted a long, low whistle.

"Exactly," said Frost.

"When?"

"Just this afternoon. About the time you were boarding your plane in Nice."

"Any handle on the motive?"

"None. Volante's not even reporting it to the police—he's only asking *don* Cesare to help him."

"Probably the best way. Cesare will certainly be able to hose down the territory and find out who did it. Might have even done it himself."

"That was going to be my next question. Can you imagine any reason why he would want to kidnap Volante's son?"

Natale thought, then said, "From what I know, Volante's been a good boy lately. Spit-shined and polished and ready to step into the EU presidency—with Ricaso's help, of course. Still—there are always the generic reasons."

They both knew what those were: to hook Volante into doing something he wouldn't do otherwise, to extort money, or to punish him.

Natale shook his head. "Frankly, I can't see *don* Cesare kidnapping Volante's son. Things have been moving smoothly in that arena for a while. It just doesn't make sense."

"From what little I know, I have to agree. The wire indicated that Cesare seemed to be as puzzled and angry as Volante. A pretty strange situation."

That led them into a discussion of the possibilities. Some rival might be making a play. One of the remnant terrorist organizations might have gotten hungry. Even some disgruntled person in police work or intelligence might have decided to shoot the moon in an attempt to get rich. Stranger things had happened in Italy.

Finally they exhausted the subject. They moved on to a brighter topic, Natale's most recent success in disrupting the nuclear black market through Operation Kaleidoscope.

After half an hour of filling Frost in on the excellent work the Germans had done on their end, Peter took a break and wandered into the kitchen, where he found a pot of coffee already brewed. He poured two cups and took them back into the sitting room. They each sipped a cup of the foul-tasting brew and talked some more, though now exhaustion was catching up with both of them. Frost confessed he hadn't slept since the day before leaving Moscow.

Shortly after 10:00 P.M. Hammond returned from the banquet. The scent of Scotch was heavy on his breath, and he was wrapped tight, ready to go to work. He immediately turned to Natale. "I need a little time with Ted. Do you mind?"

Natale was actually pleased that he had not been invited to this high-level conference and therefore made privy to yet another aspect of the world's problems. He politely excused himself, then let himself out the front door, conscious of the deadbolt that automatically locked it behind him, conscious again of the invisible eyes that watched his every move from the seemingly empty windows high above.

11

Rome

A fine, cold mist brushed Peter's face as he emerged from the safe house, then paused beneath the sheltering overhang and examined his surroundings.

He was trying to decide whether he wanted to walk the several blocks to the hotel and get soaked or wait for a cab. The flight from Nice and his subsequent talks with Hammond, Tyler, and Frost had left him too tired to walk, but he didn't want to go back in and disturb the two men by using the telephone to call a taxi. Their conference had promised to be a heated one, from the look on Hammond's face.

Still, this section of the city retired early, and a cab might be hard to come by just now. The pedestrian gate buzzed open for him. He stepped forward and held it partially open, gazing past the short driveway to the street as he tried to decide.

Only a handful of pedestrians were within visible distance, only a couple of cars rolling past on the wet pavement. Farther down in the commercial area, the shop windows were shuttered. Their doors would be locked. Even the airline offices that sprinkled the area at the end of the street were firmly bolted against the night, their tasteful neon signs blurred into rainbows by the mist.

As Peter was deciding what to do, two armed *carabinieri* on foot patrol stopped at the corner and turned to look in his direction. The men's blue-black, red-striped uniforms and hats were sheened over by transparent plastic raincoats.

Natale was attracting unnecessary attention. He nodded politely to them, then pushed through the gate and stepped onto the sidewalk, hearing the electronic latch seal the portal behind him with a pneumatic hiss. The two policemen watched curiously as he hunched his shoulders against the rain, tightened his grip on his small overnight bag, and began plodding toward the hotel.

He had made it only one block when a cab drove past, slowly, hunting for a fare. Natale flagged him down, then jumped in, happy to be aboard until the disgruntled, ancient driver, complaining about the lack of business on such a quiet night, perversely dropped him off in the middle of the biggest mud puddle on the street once they reached the hotel. Peter was forced to engage in certain gymnastics in order to get past the filthy water without ruining his shoes.

The hotel, however, was a haven of warmth and light and flowered elegance. The dining room was closed, but the cocktail bar was serving light meals. He sat in a remote corner, away from the smattering of drinkers at the bar, and settled for a bowl of hot minestrone and a small plate of grilled fish with pasta.

The minute he swallowed his last bite, the fatigue in turn swallowed him, so that he almost tripped on the carpet as he left the bar. He felt himself sinking as he rode up the elevator. His last good night of sleep had been the final night he and Judith had spent at the villa above Nice.

Their first night in Monte Carlo had been lost in the glitter of the casino, watching Veresi and his mistress gamble and drink until well after dawn.

The second night was spent mostly in the casino too, and after that he'd stayed awake thinking about his problems with Judith, wide awake in that silent and star-crossed hour before dawn, until the intruder appeared in his balcony doorway to lose his life and blast what was left of Natale's into a tailspin.

More trouble was brewing around that event. He had sensed it in Hammond, in spite of the DO's pleasant words, and he knew the official flak would be just the beginning. But right now he was too tired to worry about it.

He ran a hot bath and soaked for fifteen minutes, falling asleep in the tub. The young driver awakened him by pounding on the door to deliver his airline ticket to Naples. He asked the driver to slip it under the door, then dried himself with a warm fleecy towel, pulled on his pajamas, and slid gratefully into bed, where he fell soundly asleep without bothering to put out the light.

When the telephone rang, he felt as if he were dragging himself up out of coal pitch in order to identify the noise. But finally he picked up the instrument. After fumbling, then dropping it once, he had it in his hands, found his ear, heard himself mumbling, "*Signore* Natale speaking."

"Peter?"

"Yeah. Who's this?"

"Peter, wake up!"

Suddenly Peter recognized Frost's voice. He sat bolt upright. "Yeah. OK. I'm here, what's up?"

"Are you awake now?"

"Regretfully. What do you need?"

"It's Judith."

Natale's chest constricted, and his mouth went dry, so that he had to swallow twice before he could say, "What's wrong?"

"I just got a call from Moscow. She never arrived. Which flight did you say she was on again?"

"The six-thirty P.M. EuroAir, out of Nice, flying via Milano."

"That's what she told me, and what she told our people in Moscow. We checked the flight. She boarded it, but she never arrived."

Natale was struggling to understand. "There must be a mistake. She said she was going to Moscow. Judith may be a lot of things, but I've never known her to lie."

"Did you see her ticket?"

"No."

"If she'd had to change flights, she would have let us know."

"Yes. She'd never worry anyone unnecessarily."

"Anyway, we checked all the other flights that she might have taken. We've covered every angle, Peter. She did get on the plane in Nice. But there are no records of whether or not she got off in Milano, and she certainly didn't arrive in Moscow. She's gone, Peter. Vanished into thin air."

"What about her luggage. Did it arrive?"

"Precisely what the embassy driver wanted to know. What kind of luggage was she carrying?"

"She had two large bags, one carry-on. Louis Vuitton, beige with a tiny flower design. I gave her the set when she worked Naples, so it's a little bit worn."

"I'll relay the message. They hadn't taken the baggage off the plane yet when the driver phoned, but I'll let him know what to look for."

"You're sure she took the plane? Maybe she drove the rental car to Milano instead. Maybe something happened."

"She dropped the car off at the airport return right after you left. Took a shuttle from there back to the terminal."

The sense of dread was growing in Natale. Helplessly he asked, "What do you think might have happened?"

"That's exactly what I was hoping you'd know."

He was standing now, though he didn't remember getting up. He was holding the receiver with one hand, the body of the phone in the other, as he paced back and forth, frowning deeply, occasionally stepping across the cord to keep from tripping.

"Did you two have an argument?"

Natale thought about the scene in the airport cafe, mulled it over. "Like I told you, things have been tense with us since we moved on to Monte Carlo. But she wasn't exactly upset when I left. Just pensive, worried. Something to do with the kid who got killed. Like I said earlier, that last day we were in Monte Carlo, she seemed to change on me."

"Tell me again. In what way?"

"Just what I already said. She became really cold and withdrawn. Like she was worried about something, and I was suddenly in her way. And then when the kid got killed, she really became strange. I'm absolutely certain she recognized him, Ted."

"Think about it again. What did she say?" A razor's edge had come into Frost's voice.

"She as much as admitted she recognized him, though she wouldn't tell me anything else."

"Well . . . there's another thing."

Natale waited.

"You're not going to like this, Peter."

"I don't like a lot of what you tell me."

"The kid who got killed? We identified him for you. And it's just possible that Judith *would* have known him."

"Give me the bad part first."

"I always do. He's a German national who did some odd jobs for Hammond in Berlin for a couple of years, before they tore down the Wall and the CIA station staff got cut back."

Natale felt bewildered, as if he'd just stepped through a looking glass into a dark and distorted world. "You want to hit me with that again?"

"The kid's given name was Rudolph Brandenburg. Nicknamed Rudy, code name Heinz. Hammond recruited him two years before he moved on to Langley. That would make it a little over six years ago. The station was still winding down from the Cold War, and Rudy did contract stuff for them for a while—lightweight of course. He'd never had formal training."

Natale's blood had rushed to his head as he tried to make some sense of this. "You say that kid was one of our agents?"

"That's right. An actual agent, though what we might call a junior one. Now retired, of course—that is, he was retired even before he died. He was recruited by Hammond, but that's not the half of it. You knew that Hammond was married to a German woman?"

Natale's eyes shot wide open. "Brandenburg!"

"That's right. Hammond's wife is a member of the Royal House of Brandenburg, and the kid has the same name because he was the wife's second cousin. He was even in line to inherit some moldering title of one kind or another—I think a baronetcy."

"Incredible! And the wife has relatives in the German secret service?"

"Mostly they were in the old East German Stasi, though a couple of administrators in the Bundesnachrichtenduenst are distantly related. That's a big family, old royalty, on a par with the Hohenzollerns and Hapsburgs. And in fact there was a certain amount of intermarriage—and with all the other old royal houses of Europe as well."

Natale felt as if the world had just shifted beneath him, leaving him suspended in space. He lightly touched the arm of the chair to make contact with something solid. "You want to help me make a little sense of this?"

Frost took a long, exhausted breath. "Very well. I'll just summarize what's in the flash cable I have in front of me. I contacted Moscow station and had them do some clandestine probing on the young man's history.

"Hammond apparently recruited the lad because of the family relationship. My guess is that the kid wanted to be in the heroic middle of things, like most kids do. Hammond was careful never to use him for any rough stuff. In fact, the kid mostly ran supplies and flash information across the Wall to our people in East Germany. A few simple things."

Natale thought about that. The time frame would fit. The man who'd been shot in his hotel room would have been about the right age. And although crossing the border had once been the most dangerous task a spy could undertake, during the last few years of the Wall there had been a softening of hostilities and a lot of traffic between East and West Germany. It wouldn't have been nearly so dangerous as in the old days. But dangerous enough. Covert work was always dangerous enough.

And suddenly Natale again saw the young man's face, twisted in anguished surprise by death. After running supplies and maps and intel back and forth across what had once been the most dangerous border in the world, he had found death on the balcony of one of the world's foremost luxury hotels while trying to talk to a fellow spy.

And that's the way it ends, Natale thought bitterly. Shot in the back, betrayed by either an enemy or a friend.

He forced himself to push past the anger so that once again he was calculating facts instead of feeling emotions. And suddenly the fact that Hammond had arrived in the middle of this incident fully hit him.

"What about Hammond?"

"What about him?"

"Doesn't it strike you as odd that he'd arrive the same day the kid was killed?"

"It does indeed. But then there are a lot of things happening that strike me as odd just now. Take, for instance, the fact that the

House of Brandenburg is also part of the ancient German Order of the Black Nobility—the same order that Prince Dante di Veresi is supposedly reorganizing as a fascist political core."

Natale was silent as he absorbed that, and for an instant he wondered if Frost had indeed been in the thick of battle for too many years.

"But then—any thought of a connection through that mythical order is mere speculation," Frost said. "Pretend you didn't hear that."

"Gladly."

Still, Frost wasn't through speculating. "The Brandenburg family's Berlin estate was also a hotbed of Nazi activity, when such things were fashionable."

Natale processed that information. "What about Hammond's wife?"

"I've met her, and, frankly, I found her to be a gracious and strikingly beautiful woman. But we didn't sit down and have a chat about how her uncles and aunties used to throw parties for Adolph and the boys."

"OK. Then what about Hammond himself? What could he have to do with the kid's death?"

"Nothing, of course. It's just that my devious mind scans every possible connection, sometimes coming to odd conclusions."

Natale was relieved to hear the note of reality that had crept back into Frost's voice. He said, "OK. What else do we know about this?"

"Not much, but I'll give you what we have. Hammond left Berlin for his new job in Langley. As you know, the brass insisted that we cut way back on staff and missions at Berlin station. There was no more work for Rudy-code-name-Heinz, so he floated away into history. Until he turned up on your balcony at the Hotel de Mer, addicted to heroin and using a Bulgarian gun, and whispering dark secrets into your ear."

Frost paused—Natale could almost hear him thinking—then said, "And you'd never seen the lad before?"

"I swear on my life."

"Well, the plot thickens, Peter. Because apparently he got hooked on spy craft when he worked for Hammond. After he left us he freelanced for a year or so, then he went to work for the EIA. They had just decided to open a full intelligence agency in Bonn. Evidently they were scouting around for people with a bit of training, no matter how small. They found several of our leftovers, Rudy included."

Natale thought about that.

The European Intelligence Agency was the EU's answer to the CIA. It had been formed about five years ago by a handful of Western Europe's top intelligence operatives. Already they were giving the CIA a run for its money, not only in Europe but also in other global hot spots. They had the formidable budget of the EU behind them. They also had full access to the world's most awesome computer, which was in a highly secured compound within the EU's government complex in Brussels.

The EU saw the United States as an anachronistic remnant of the five decades following World War II—a benevolent occupying force whose day had ended. They had conveniently forgotten that, without the United States, there would have been a European Union long before now—a Thousand Year Reich, in fact, with Germany at its center and Adolph Hitler as its first emperor.

Natale said, "Does Hammond know the kid's been identified?"

"No. Considering the family connection, I wanted to talk to you first."

"I'm up to my neck."

"I know. I'd make it a point to get back to Naples station as early in the morning as I could, were I you. I think I can run interference, but he's going to want to know what happened."

"Do you trust him?"

"Hammond?"

"Right."

There was a moment's hesitation, then Frost chuckled. "Not for a minute. Do you?"

"No, but then I don't trust anybody who's spent more than a weekend at Langley."

Natale had learned through hard and brutal experience that the farther up the ladder an espiocrat climbed, the more likely that the man had been lured into the old-boy network that placed political camaraderie above common sense—and promotions above the safety of men in the field. Natale was by nature a lone wolf, and what he knew about Langley brass made him more solitary than ever. In fact, the sole reason he stayed aboard the CIA ship was because this was the only vehicle that would propel him anywhere close to where he wanted to be—which was cleaning up the serious problems of the world.

There were still plenty of good men left in the Agency. He knew that. People who put their lives on the line to drive back the growing black tide of evil that was threatening to inundate the planet. But there were always, forever, the traitors, the self-serving, the banal, and the bureaucratic brain dead.

A troubled silence hung between the two men till Natale said, "So where does that leave us?"

"I'd say with Judith missing, one dead ex-agent, and a far-too-coincidental visit from our director of operations."

"A nice summation. So what do you want to do?"

"First we find Judith. I'd like to ask you to handle that, Peter. I know you agree that she's our first priority."

"Absolutely."

"Frankly, my guess is that she disappeared voluntarily. On the other hand, I'm not going to risk her life on my guess."

"Why would she disappear?"

"I haven't a clue. Furthermore, I might be wrong. And just in case I am, I'm going to act accordingly. Because if she intentionally went AWOL, and if Langley gets wind of it, she's going to be disciplined thoroughly, maybe even yanked out of Moscow station or fired, and I'd like to avoid that if possible."

"Maybe that would teach her to have a little more consideration for her loving friends," Natale said, feeling a sudden surge of anger.

"Let's pray things turn out well."

They exchanged a few more clipped comments and a few basic ideas about where Peter should begin his search.

Finally Teddy said, "Look, Peter, I know you're sick about this, just as I am. But she's a survivor. She'll probably be OK."

"Yeah, well . . ."

The conversation dangled, and Peter realized they both had been reduced to empty platitudes. They exchanged good-byes and hung up.

And the minute that connection to sanity was broken, Natale couldn't think, couldn't stop pacing. Every vestige of his predicament with regard to Hammond was shunted to the recesses of his mind, and he had to fight the impulse to bolt, to go looking for Judith. But when he forced himself back into a rational frame of mind he realized that in spite of the few ideas he and Frost had just kicked around, he didn't have so much as a decent hint of a clue as to where to begin.

Then he sat in the semidarkness and thought about her.

Beautiful, haunting Judith of the smoky-blue eyes and the irrational temperament. Judith the martyr, who felt that she was single-handedly obliged to save the world. Judith of the obsessive honesty, of the spiritual seeking, of the complete commitment— once she had decided what she wanted to commit to.

It was indeed likely that she had disappeared voluntarily. Natale remembered the worried expression on her face as she'd made that phone call in Nice. She had said she needed to take care of something important.

But it was also possible that something terrible had happened, perhaps even something to do with her knowledge of the young spy who had been killed.

Natale went over and over everything they'd said to each other, everything they'd done during their brief reunion. At last he went to a window and opened it wide, hoping the fresh air would help him think. He stood with a peculiar stillness, gazing out over the rooftops of Rome, watching and thinking as the first faint glint of morning etched gold into the eastern horizon, then rapidly emptied the darkness from the sky and filled it with fragile blue-gray. The sound of a delivery truck grinding gears was soon joined by a motor scooter puttering along. The Eternal City was awakening around him.

He wished he could also awaken from what was beginning to seem an endless nightmare that somehow kept him blinded to the truth. The truth of Judith, the truth of the spiritual guidelines she professed to apply to her life now. Though he had initially been pleased to see her filled with purpose, genuinely happy, now he thought of the change in her with some bitterness. Her newfound faith seemed to exclude him from the role he wanted to play in her life. He wondered if her professed spiritual awakening was nothing more than an excuse to keep him at a distance, both physically and emotionally.

But these were personal matters, and he needed to focus fully on the professional dimensions of this problem, or Judith might be hurt. Most of all he needed to know the truth of where she was right now, why she had disappeared—or why, for that matter, she had been taken.

Or killed. He didn't want to think about that, but he had to. Death happened in this shadowy world where life was often valued less than secrets. If she was alive, he would find her. And if she was dead, he would avenge her. He made that vow before God, standing before the window and looking out over the Roman morning.

Finally, with daylight fully upon him, Peter showered and packed his bags and phoned a cab. Though the junior agent had delivered his ticket to Naples right on schedule, he was going back to Nice instead.

That was where the trouble had started; it was where his quest would begin. He would personally question the people at the airport, at the car rental agency, to make certain that every possibility had been covered. Only then would he return to Naples and set himself fully to the search.

In Naples he had substantial resources that he could put to work looking for Judith—across Europe and around the globe, if necessary. And among those resources was Carlo Ricaso, whose network of real and potential spies far outnumbered the ranks of the EIA and the CIA combined.

12

Italy, near Naples

In the clear morning light, Gianalisa Lauro Veresi stood beside a whitewashed stone farmhouse on the slopes of Vesuvius. She was immediately south of Naples, looking down over a countryside lush with golden carpets of gorse, with leafy forests, with orchards of gray-leaved olive trees.

She had awakened at first dawn and prepared a small breakfast of fruit and croissants for herself and Luciano, though she had been unable to eat much and Luciano had nibbled only lightly. She fed him and talked to him and tried to make him understand that she was saving his life. He refused to believe her.

She scrubbed the dishes in the small steel sink. She heated a small bit of water in a steel spoon, then dumped in the contents of a glassine bag, dissolving the fine white demon of heroin into invisibility. She poured the contents of the spoon into a bottle cap and had just started to open her kit and take out cotton and a hypodermic needle when the distant noise of an engine surprised her and brought her running outside.

She spotted Rudy's black Volkswagen van, still a quarter of a mile downslope, churning up dust as it traveled the little-used road. But it was indeed Rudy's vehicle. He had come back.

Gianalisa felt a vast wave of relief, for he had planned everything, had shown her how to help Luciano. She was helpless without his direction—and without the heroin he would be bringing, for she had been rationing herself for the past day and had barely enough to keep Luciano sedated and still keep herself from getting sick.

For the entire previous night she had waited for Rudy, ever since Roberto and Marco dropped her and Luciano off here, promising to be back within twelve hours. Rudy had not participated in the kidnapping, but he'd promised to meet her here to help her hide Luciano from the others, and she'd become increasingly worried as the hour of his planned arrival had come and gone—worried more for herself than for him. But whatever had gone wrong was apparently repaired now.

She had pulled out her gun as she left the house. Now she shoved the 10mm Glock automatic back into the reinforced waistband of her denims, then stretched like a cat and waited, as the van made its tortuous way up the serpentine road.

Slightly to her north lay the Bay of Naples and the haze of the city. To her left, gray rivers of frozen lava threaded through the overgrowth that covered the upper slopes of Vesuvius. Though the volcano hadn't erupted since 1944, the Neapolitans still called it the Burning Mountain or the Entrance to Hell.

Last night she had paged through a stack of tattered old *National Geographic*s that had somehow found their way to the farmhouse. In one story, a scientist claimed that the fire in the volcano's belly had been stilled, that the new threat was of earthquake. The last great earthquake had come in November 1980. One hundred thousand people lost their homes, 3,000 lost their lives. The thought of being in such an earthquake sickened and terrified her, even while it kept her from thinking about her present confusion and pain.

Gianalisa was filled with terror by what she was doing, but at the same time she was also smugly pleased with herself. She was playing a cat-and-mouse game with her father, whose property she was using. This farmhouse was at the farthest reaches of one of his vast vineyards.

Since they had kidnapped Luciano yesterday, she also felt as if she were challenging the Mafia and the volcano and the unsteady world around her, all at the same time! It was an exhilarating feeling —or it had been until the heroin had begun to disappear from her system, leaving her with growing unrest and fear—and the threat of unbearable physical pain.

But Rudy was on his way now. She wouldn't have to feel the pain of withdrawal, at least not until they got her to a hospital. Rudy had made a secret promise about that. And as soon as she fixed again, the cobwebs would leave her mind, she would think clearly and would be able to make a decision about her life.

Since Rudy had joined their group two months ago, he had befriended her. He assured her that after they saved Luciano, she could get help for her addiction. He was also going to quit using heroin, he said. He told her privately that he had started using the needle only to make the others think he was like them but had quickly found himself a slave to the drug.

After they had saved Luciano, Roberto and the other evil people would be put in jail—it was her and Rudy's secret—and perhaps she and Luciano could even lead a normal life, far beyond the shadow of the Prince of Darkness. She was increasingly convinced that this was her father's true identity.

She grew sad as she thought about freedom. Luciano had been chained in the small basement cell for more than eighteen hours now. But he was so angry that she knew that if she unchained him he would run away. And then her father and the others would make him tell where he had been and who had taken him, and they'd hurt him, perhaps even kill him so he couldn't tell anyone else, and everything would go back to the way it had been before. Rudy had explained it all.

But the longer Luciano stayed in the basement, the more he seemed to hate her. She thought about that. From love to hatred, overnight. Perhaps he was also secretly serving darkness, for he was really not very dependable after all.

He was furious, of course, that they'd used heroin to keep him under, but what else could they have done to keep him sedated long enough to get him here? It was puzzling. He had been so surprised when he'd looked up and seen her face. She had thought he would know what was happening—they said he had been told. But he didn't know.

She needed Rudy to explain it all to her once again. And now he was on his way up the slope, and things would soon be set right. She would be glad when they had moved Luciano to a better location. The tiny rumblings and minor quakes in the earth beneath the stone house had begun to get on her nerves. She was also worried that one of her father's many workers might accidentally come along, en route to the vineyards, and recognize her and tell her father where she was. He believed she was away in Paris applying for admission to a famous art school—the lies he believed! But of course he did, for he was the Father of Lies that the nuns had warned her about.

She stretched again, gracefully, then breathed in the warming air. She was thin and ethereal, having a frail beauty that might have been a portent of a short and tragic life even had she not become an addict. The luminosity in her eyes might have been madness or genius—a person could read what he wanted to there—although any seasoned doctor or narcotics agent would have immediately read the truth in the dilated pupils and the gaunt cheeks.

She had wanted the heroin. It wasn't something Roberto and the others had to force on her. Once she'd learned what blissful escape lay within the white powder, she eagerly chased the dragon till now it chased her.

Sometimes when she looked at herself in the mirror through the haze of drug-induced delusion, she could still see a true princess, just as in the fairy tales.

At other times, when the drug was wearing off, she looked in the mirror to see a demon locked behind her face, the one that had forced her mother to take her own life and that was tormenting Gianalisa to follow. At those times she would sob, terrified, just as she had when she was a child, and the doctors would come to sedate her or, sometimes, to take her away.

Luciano would hold her in his arms at those times. Gianalisa considered how much she missed that comfort. Perhaps if they moved him they could take off the manacles, and he would get over his anger and hold her once again. Maybe Rudy could make him understand.

The black van crested the hill, and she shielded her eyes against the light and peered to see who was driving, for there were two people in the front seat. One of them raised a hand in salute. She waved back, then turned and went inside the farmhouse.

She took the bottle cap and a book of matches, lifted a wooden trapdoor, then climbed down a steep stone stairway to a concrete pit. Luciano—hair wild, eyes dazed—sat on his haunches, chained to the wall beneath a high, narrow window through which pale sunlight leaked. His clothing was soiled, his unshaven face was haggard, and there was bewildered hatred in his eyes.

"Hello, *cara mia*. Have you been good for me?" Gianalisa reached out and stroked his hair.

Still partly drugged, Luciano stared at the concrete floor.

"Do not hate me so," Gianalisa chided. "This will be your last day here. We will be moving soon." She pulled out the hypodermic and filled it with the fluid from the bottle cap. It was the heroin fix she'd been preparing when she heard the distant drone of the van's engine. She moved closer to Luciano and stroked his head again, then grabbed his arm, worked up the vein, and plunged home the needle. She pressed the syringe till all the fluid had been injected into his bruised arm.

"You'll travel better this way, *cara mia*. Yes, my love, we're going on a journey to keep you safe. Perhaps across the water to your home. I think your father will be waiting for you there, Did you know that? Would you like to go back to Palermo? That's where we'll go, my loved one, to the palace where we will live after I become your wife."

She studied him, watching him get drowsier. She didn't like to use the heroin on him. It was bad enough that she had abandoned herself to it. She knew that she could scarcely think straight most of the time now. All the work with the doctors and nuns at the schools and hospitals had somehow vanished into a growing night.

But Luciano wanted to fight what was happening. She had watched him, had seen the dark fire in his eyes, and she knew that unless he was sedated when Rudy came into the room he would probably fight to the death, straining against the chains until he literally broke his own neck.

She heard the van stop. She climbed back up the stone stairs and exited through the kitchen door, expecting to see Rudy climb out. But as the driver's door opened, she saw the man with the muddy eyes and predatory teeth, the one they called Marco.

"Where's Rudy?" she asked indignantly. "Why are you driving his van?"

The man looked at her with contempt. "Rudy's dead. The plan has changed."

Then Roberto climbed out of the passenger side, and suddenly she knew. Rudy had been a dream. There was no one to save her. And no one to save Luciano now either.

"Wait," she said, trying to grab Roberto's sleeve. "My father will give you gold if you don't hurt Luciano." Her voice turned sly and wheedling, and she pulled at the sleeve. "Really he will. He's a very famous prince, the Prince of Darkness, and he owns all the gold in the world."

Roberto snarled an obscenity. "You fool, don't start that crazy chatter again, or I'll—" He started to bring the rifle butt around to slam into her face.

Marco Guappo was the leader of the neo-terrorist group and also the rebellious son of the Neopolitan Mafia's capo. He stepped between them. "Don't be stupid. I know she's crazy, but we don't have time to deal with it right now."

Roberto stepped back. His eyes were like a snake's.

And Gianalisa understood. The Prince of Darkness, the one who brought all evil to the world, had trapped her once again. He had paid them off, or made them promises, or perhaps he had initiated them into hell itself, as he had Gianalisa's mother so very long ago. For though her father had not wanted her to understand, the nuns in the hospital had read the Bible to her, and she knew about hell, and she knew what her father had been doing.

And suddenly she also knew why her mother had killed herself that anguishing night so very long ago. She had died because there was no other possible way to escape.

13

Naples

Peter spent several hours in Nice, verifying what Frost had already learned about Judith's departure and disappearance. He questioned everyone possible, from the waitress who had served them in the small cafe, to the counter clerk at the car rental agency, to the reservationist who had issued her ticket, then verified that she had boarded the flight. He learned absolutely nothing new, though he felt a bit better for having tried.

As usual, he was unable to sleep during the short flight back across the Tyrrhenian Sea. The gray-haired matron in the seat beside him seemed annoyed by his restlessness. But though he tried to settle down, he kept shifting this way and that as his body reacted to the turmoil in his brain.

He pawed over and over the events of the past few days, looking at everything that had happened from every possible angle, wondering about Frost, analyzing the possibility of another mole at work within the CIA, and lamenting the obvious problems with Langley's administration.

But towering over everything, permeating it all, was his growing concern for Judith—a concern that kept trying to boil up into pure panic, which he arrested only through sheer strength of will.

Peter's flight touched down at Capodichino Airport in Naples late that afternoon. He collected his brown Mercedes sedan from the parking garage, paid an exorbitant parking fee, then drove to his small villa, buff-colored with pale pink trim.

The villa was set amid a shelter of giant ferns and olive trees, high on the hillside above the sweeping bay. It had been a real find in this tough, teeming city of stacked buildings and steep stairways, sprawling slums piled up against extended luxury buildings, crumbling ancient palaces, chaotic shopping stalls, medieval cathedrals, run-down museums, and more.

As he reached the top of the hill, he swung into a driveway off one of the winding alleys, turned into a small garage set into the hillside, and stopped. He retrieved his bags, then climbed a short flight of chipped stone stairs and unlocked his heavy front door with its tiny triangular window.

The first thing he did upon entering was check the answering machine to see if Frost might have phoned with fresh news about Judith. He had used his retrieval code to keep up with messages via long-distance during his travels, and now there was only one message. He played it back and heard Jeremy Ward, the chief of the small Naples station, reminding him to check in as soon as he returned.

Ward was always nagging Natale to conform to regulations, so Peter ignored the testy message and walked over to the seaward side of the house to open the windows and let in fresh air.

His housekeeper, an elderly Neapolitan woman named Sofia Aragona, had a key. Natale was gone a good deal of the time and relied upon her to keep an eye on the house. Now he was pleased to see that she had recently cleaned. The lacquered wooden table and the other shiny surfaces were dust free, the plants were green and well-watered, the mirrors and windows were polished to a sheen, and the small amounts of perishable food he'd forgotten to take out of the refrigerator in his haste to see Judith had vanished without a trace.

He opened the wooden accordion door and stepped out onto his deck to gaze down the steep rocky hillside and out over the great sweep of the bay. The wind was gentle as smoke. In the southern distance, he could see the twin peaks of Vesuvius, tinted pink and vermilion by the dying sun.

The naval base was spread out to the north. A US aircraft carrier had pulled into port during his absence. Its lights twinkled on against the dusk. Perhaps it was conducting exercises with the NATO base, since certain segments of the Sixth Fleet were still home-based here. Since the massive pullout of the US military from Germany, this was one of the few NATO bases to still welcome American forces. There was much political debate about even that.

To his immediate south was the city proper, with its Roman foundations, its graft-riddled government, its poignant beauty and crime-riddled streets and unique Neapolitan fire. Natale had fallen in love with his adopted city, for all her tarnished beauty.

He stretched wearily, pleased to be home, then strode into his small bathroom, flipped on the lights, shed his clothes, stepped into the white-tiled shower stall, and turned on a torrent of steaming hot water.

He stood for a long time, letting the water pound the weariness from his bones. But just as he turned the shower off, he heard the shrill ringing of the telephone.

He wrapped a towel around his waist, stepped into the bedroom, and grabbed up the receiver.

"Natale here."

"Get down here, Peter. Now." It was Jeremy Ward, in a state of high agitation. "You're going to want your hands on this one."

"What's up?"

"Kaleidoscope. And your phone hasn't been swept since you left, so the details can wait till you get here."

Peter felt his jaw tighten. "I'm on my way."

He quickly pulled on a pair of khaki pants and a matching knit shirt, and by the time he was ready to leave a strange calm had descended upon him. This was the way he invariably reacted to crisis. He shut down his emotions and became purely methodical and analytical. This attribute made some call him cold-hearted, while others turned to him as a rational and steadying force.

But Natale never worried about what others thought. His main focus was always on survival, his own as well as the survival of those who depended upon him. And he knew from Ward's tone of voice that this was a life or death problem. He was about to hear some really bad news.

The extreme calm stayed with him as he started the Mercedes and backed out of the garage. But then the anger hit him, and he peeled rubber as he left his driveway, then screeched around the corners as he descended the hill, feeling foolish as he did so but needing to vent his fury. Occasionally he pounded the steering wheel with his fist.

Kaleidoscope was the operation he'd let the Germans wrap up just before his vacation with Judith. He had originated the inquiry, but most of the weapons' grade material that had precipitated the investigation was recovered in Berlin, Munich, and Bonn, and the Germans contested him from the very beginning over jurisdiction. Not that he really wanted any acknowledgment for spearheading the case—his anonymity made that impossible anyway—but he was determined to see that the traffic was stopped and the criminals put away for a long time.

He negotiated long and hard with Karl Dietrich, his liaison with the German secret service, to make certain that the case would be handled exactly right. Finally he decided the Germans were going to do the right thing, and he handed them the evidence he'd put together on the chief trafficker, Harald Rupert, a Berliner who had been top gun of the network.

Rupert and his henchmen had been trafficking not only drugs and conventional armaments but also significant amounts of plutonium-239, uranium-235, and MOX. Natale worked in tandem with the Germans to bust them and stayed on top of the operation until they assured him that they were ready and able to wrap up the case without a hitch. He'd been in and out of Berlin for over six months by then and flew back to be in on the arrests. The Germans entered Rupert's house and arrested him in the middle of the night with no bloodshed. It was a textbook operation. With Rupert behind bars, Peter at last felt free to take his vacation. He met Judith two days later in Nice.

From their remote villa, he kept in touch with Dietrich and followed up on the case. Rupert broke under the weight of German interrogation. More arrests were made, the operation seemed a complete success, and Natale was finally able to focus his attention on Judith.

But life was never easy. Once you stepped into an operation, it had a way of coiling around you like a snake so that you had to play it out to the dead end in order to pry it loose. Natale considered this, then felt his rage gradually dissolve as he resigned himself to the inevitable. After all, certainly the Germans still had Harald Rupert and most of the other gang members in jail. They could not possibly have gotten loose. And with them in jail, how bad could things really be?

By the time he traversed the sweep of the bay to turn toward Naples station, he was fully back on target. And once on target, he had the enviable ability of being able to concentrate fully on whatever he was doing at any given time. His concern over Judith's disappearance had been so intense, his sense of blind futility so complete, that it was almost a relief to get his mind off her—even if temporarily.

He turned again and drove down a broad tree-lined boulevard toward the small, modern building that housed Naples station. He wondered what had gone wrong with Kaleidoscope. And then he wondered why nothing had gone seriously wrong before now. The operation had been tricky from the beginning.

They'd coded the operation Kaleidoscope because the parameters constantly shifted and with such alarming speed that it had been impossible even to keep track of what they were doing, much less manage to unravel all the players and details. The prime objective of the operation had been, as usual, to stop the traffic in black market nuclear materials.

The CIA and its European cohorts had recently managed to push several similar trafficking networks into the ground, only to see others pop up to take their place. A growing sense of futility was beginning to poison all the concerned intelligence agencies, from Russia to Bulgaria to Czechoslovakia to Germany and Italy.

Because of this, Kaleidoscope was especially important, for if it succeeded it would bring a modicum of pride back into the intelligence networks. Natale personally traced the evil web all the way through, outlining every strand and connection.

But even if Kaleidoscope took out one nest of vipers, he knew that the main problem would continue so long as the infrastructure of the former Soviet Union continued to disintegrate. Anarchy and organized crime had become the law of the land. The scientists who manned Russia's nuclear program sometimes went unpaid for months on end. They were not only starving, they were angry, and all it took was one scientist to slip a small package into a briefcase, one guard to look the other way.

Iran, Libya, and Iraq knew fissionable material was out there for the taking. The demise of the USSR had left the ashes of the cold war piled high around Russia and her former satellites: some 140 metric tons of weapons-grade plutonium, another 1,000 metric tons of weapons-grade uranium, and this a conservative estimate. It took only 18 to 55 pounds of these materials to fuel an atomic bomb—assuming one had the necessary expertise and other components.

Everyone in intelligence, everyone in the military knew that this increasing traffic in fissionable materials might well be the worst threat mankind had ever faced: the beginning of the end of the world.

There was big money in weapons-grade materials—millions of dollars and more for one kilogram of fissionable plutonium or uranium or lithium or MOX. Consequently the leaks out of the nuclear facilities were becoming a global flood. Barring some miracle, Natale believed it was just a matter of time until nuclear weapons would fall into the hands of an irrational madman.

It was his job to keep that from happening, though on days like this the job seemed impossible.

He was approaching the building's iron gate. A black and white sign was set in lights over the entrance: INTERTECH DEFENSE INDUSTRIES, NAPLES BRANCH. The widened tarmac that formed the driveway glistened with recent rain.

The technology reference in the false title was designed to mask the reason for the electronics equipment and satellite dish that all but covered the roof.

Natale's thoughts honed in again on Kaleidoscope as he slowed down so that the electronic gate-eye could sense and record his left palm print, which he raised in an Indian salute to the cold-eyed machine. As he waited for the small flash of blue light that would tell him he was cleared for entry, he flashed a smile at the token human gatekeeper, Charley Calveresi.

Charley nodded smartly. His gray hat sat jauntily on his thinning hair. He held up his work-gnarled hand to indicate that he needed to speak with Peter.

Peter pushed a button, and the Mercedes's power window glided down.

Charley said, "Thought you'd like to know, Pietro. The Germans have arrived."

Natale looked past him to where a shiny black Mercedes sedan with diplomatic plates was sheltered, almost invisibly, by the thick grove of trees by the small building's secured side entrance. "Which Germans?"

"Dietrich. His chauffeur drove him in a few minutes ago, like they were fleeing from the devil himself."

Natale thanked Charley, then tooled his own small sedan down the short driveway and parked it between the German limo and the shrubbery. He nodded a greeting to the inconspicuous guard at the glass entryway, again held up his palm for electronic identification, entered a hall as soon as the door slid open, then ignored the security camera that followed his motion as he walked toward Ward's small office, where he knocked smartly on the heavy door. Then, without waiting for a response, he opened it and stepped inside.

The office was much like his own, though larger. There were beige filing cabinets, beige carpet, beige drapes across the double-width window and its special glass that protected against laser-based listening devices.

Two men were in the room: Karl Dietrich, the German secret service's top gun in Naples, and his CIA counterpart, Jeremy Ward.

Dietrich's overt title was German Trade Ambassador, a position that gained him topnotch living quarters at the German Embassy and full diplomatic immunity in the event his true work of spying was unmasked. His assistants did the actual trade negotiations—what little were required.

Italy and Germany were both key members of the European Union. Trade barriers between the two countries had long since fallen and within the year even the simple travel-visa restriction would be lifted.

But there was friction among all the various member nations, as each jockeyed for its share of the EU resources. Thus far Germany, the richest country and therefore the dominant one, was jockeying for a stronger position, which would reflect the amount of money it poured into the Union. France, the next strongest member nation, shared Germany's sentiment and also wanted a stronger proportional vote in EU affairs.

Italy, on the other hand, was a poor country by comparison. Still, Italy had been a founding member of the EU. On this basis and on the basis of its underground power machinations—which were considerable—Italy shared the core of power with Germany and France, even though it did not pay a proportionally large share of the budget. Nevertheless, Italy often felt left out of the decision-making process, even though the rotating presidency itself would be handed to Italy within the month.

In short, there was still enough friction between the various member nations of the EU that it made sense to continue their old pre-union policies of sending diplomatic representatives to one another in order to keep the wheels of commerce and government greased.

Finally, the European Intelligence Agency was beginning to usurp the powers of the various intelligence services of the respective member nations, and this was especially what bothered Peter Natale as he entered Jeremy Ward's office and saw the look of despair on Karl Dietrich's face.

Natale knew that anything he told Dietrich would quickly find its way to the EIA's mammoth computer banks in Brussels. The computer there was capable of processing and regurgitating unfathomable amounts of information. Europol, the European Police Organization, and the EIA were beginning to link the police computers and communications of the EU nations in an attempt to create one massive phalanx against international crime.

Natale understood the need to provide a cohesive front. At the same time, the computers also filled him with a quiet fear. There were raw, formidable powers locked inside such a system. In the wrong hands, those computers could easily become a key tool toward a totalitarian dictatorship unlike any the world had ever known.

All this background came to mind in a single flash of assessment, as Natale stepped into the room to face Karl Dietrich and

Jeremy Ward. And as he remembered, he once again felt the dark mantle of dread drop like a heavy cloak on his shoulders.

Because of the contest for global power between the United States of America and what some were calling the United Nations of Europe, Natale could no longer work in Europe and work alone. He was simply shut off from too much information. That was one reason he had linked up with Carlo Ricaso, who traveled the underworld labyrinths of power. But he also had to hold his own with people such as Dietrich.

Not that Dietrich was in any way contemptible. He had won Natale's respect by demonstrating a firm commitment to stop the traffic in nuclear armaments. Without him, Peter might still be floundering around trying to figure out how to penetrate the German end of Rupert's network.

In fact, Kaleidoscope was a perfect example of the way things worked now. The original information had been a gift from Carlo Ricaso. He contacted Natale almost a year ago and told him about two Mafia-connected brothel owners, Fritz and Eva Breugher, whose Berlin establishment had become an oasis to many international arms and narcotics traffickers.

One patron, a middle-aged German real estate agent named Harald Rupert, had bragged to one of the prostitutes that he was trafficking nuclear materials for the Russian Mafia. Since Carlo drew the line at trafficking fissionable materials, he was enraged that someone was moving in on Ricaso territory to deal in a commodity he'd personally banned. He'd turned the information over to Natale, so that Peter could once again rid him of an enemy.

Natale worked the case himself for several months, until he began to come across the footprints of the German secret service. Then he connected up with Dietrich. Peter offered to share intelligence and to give the Germans all credit in return for their promise to stop Rupert and his people cold.

Dietrich conducted his end of the mission with an iron fist and a well-sealed mouth, and Natale was insulated from any direct interaction with the EIA.

Now the German sat sprawled in one of the dark-brown leather armchairs. He wore black slacks, a gray knit shirt, and a well-cut black-and-gray tweed sports coat. His head was bald, except for a carefully combed gray band around the back and sides that still showed traces of its original dirty blond. His eyes were faded blue, behind gold wire-framed glasses. His eyebrows formed two graying arches upon a putty-colored face. Although Dietrich was an avid sailor who usually sported a Neapolitan suntan, tonight he looked like a captain waiting for his ship to sink and no lifeboat in sight.

Jeremy Ward sat opposite Dietrich and made an exercise in contrast. Ward was short, thin, middle-aged, with kind green eyes that had a stricken look in them at the moment. But his thick, unruly thatch of brown hair and brisk, full mustache made him seem to be sprouting hair everywhere, when compared to Dietrich's near baldness. Hair even sprouted from the back of Ward's hands, which were folded before him as he sat primly behind his desk.

Natale felt the negative charge of trouble crackling in the air even before Dietrich stood up, stepped forward, and shook his hand. But instead of letting go, Dietrich gripped it hard in both of his own, startling Peter with the sudden fierceness of his emotion.

And then Peter saw the fullness of the bruised and sickened look in Dietrich's eyes.

"Peter. I don't know how to tell you. They killed Fritz and Eva this morning, and two of their prostitutes."

Natale felt the impact like a physical blow. His knees tried to buckle, and a wave of nausea hit him.

"Better sit down," Ward said.

Like a wooden marionette, Natale dangled on Ward's command and sagged into a chair.

"We don't know what happened," Dietrich said. He sat back down on the edge of his own chair and leaned forward. "We thought we'd closed off all the seams." His eyes were filled with naked shame.

But Peter had emptied his heart of feeling. He was thinking again about Frost's mole, about what happened when someone deep within the heart of an intelligence agency betrayed his fellow man. Both the United States and Germany were victims of a bureaucratic rot that had set in as a result of lowered standards and moral decay in the political arena. The fault carried over to the intelligence agencies, and from there it sometimes bled into the covert networks.

Now Natale wondered if the leak had come from his side or from Dietrich's. Because the leak had come from inside—there was no other way this could have happened. They had been running a rotten network, perhaps all along.

He felt a deep surge of revulsion at the idea of Fritz and his wife lying dead. He swallowed hard. "What happened?"

Dietrich's attempt to explain kept collapsing into an apology, so Ward took over the report. They had found the bodies this morning, when other employees arrived at the brothel in the Friedrichstrasse section of Berlin where the four people both lived and worked. All four had been strangled, probably with electrical wire, all four in night clothes in their private apartments, perhaps surprised in their sleep.

"The Friedrichstrasse police contacted the central Berlin station, which was flagged to contact us in case of any emergency with our potential witnesses," Dietrich said.

Natale nodded. "Had the news media already picked up on the fact that they were going to be witnesses against Rupert at the trial?"

"Actually, no. That was held private."

Natale nodded again. His theory that the leak came from inside one or the other intelligence agency grew stronger.

"And we've also managed to squelch the story of the murders until tomorrow morning. Then it will hit the Berlin papers and television and probably the international news as well."

"What will you use for an official spin?"

"The usual," Ward said. "People in brothels are fair game in most peoples' eyes. There's a sort of a 'deserve what they get' mentality that will help us keep this under wraps. We'll admit they were involved in a black market in stolen goods and blame their deaths on the Russian Mafia."

"Which is probably true," Ward commented.

"Actually," Dietrich said grimly, "we've had a few new developments since the last time we talked. We confiscated another shipment of MOX at the train station the night before the murders —that would be night before last. Immediately we realized the shipment was part of Rupert's network. His gang's footprints were all over it, and it was being shipped along the same route too, from Moscow to Warsaw, final destination Berlin, where it was to go onto a private airliner for delivery to the buyer—probably Libya or Syria.

"Eva Breugher told us the shipment was coming through, and, sure enough, Harald Rupert's eldest son, Hans, took delivery at the old train station just after midnight. The container held two pounds of weapons-grade plutonium-239 and a dozen grams of uranium-235. A couple of million dollars in nuclear contraband."

"So we hadn't shut down the network after all."

"No. But they'd been living pretty high, and we think we caught them broke. We think they were going for one last shipment, to build up a nest egg before the remaining people disappeared. Though it was pretty stupid of them to keep the same pipeline running after we'd busted Harald."

"If these people were intelligent, they wouldn't be trying to destroy the world. You have Harald's son in jail now?"

Dietrich nodded. "We just got lucky, that's all. Hans Rupert had a favorite prostitute, a Russian girl named Katrina. He was just like his father—he liked to get drunk and brag. He told her what he was doing, promised her jewelry and a new car once the money came in. Katrina told Eva—who told us. I believed then that we'd finally gotten the last shreds of the network—but apparently we missed whoever came back to kill Fritz and Eva." Dietrich's eyes were tormented.

Natale thought about Katrina. He'd met her when he was picking up information from Fritz. She had been pretty once, though now she was broken and her eyes as dead as two tarnished rubles. She had been brought in as a virtual slave by the Russian Mafia, a common practice. She quickly become addicted to heroin, as most of the girls did.

He had to ask. "Was the Russian girl one of the victims?"

"She was."

Natale swallowed the quick stab of sorrow, then stroked his chin and thought more logically about the other victims. The second prostitute had probably just been in the wrong place at the wrong time. But Fritz and Eva had trusted him to keep them safe.

Fritz had been an oily little man with a graying handlebar mustache, whose wife was a surprisingly pretty dumpling of a woman. She had worked in the brothel when she was young.

Though Natale fiercely disapproved of their lifestyle, it was a simple fact that the best way to measure the Octopus's heartbeat was to reach the people who had been swallowed whole by the voracious beast. And no matter how Natale felt about the degradation and sexual bondage, he had been grateful for the quality of information Fritz and Eva provided. Indeed, Fritz, Eva, and their two employees had exhibited much bravery, in spite of whatever else they had been and done. He was deeply saddened by their deaths.

Dietrich talked then, till he'd finally managed to tell Natale everything he knew. Finally the German spy bade the two CIA men farewell.

Natale walked him to the limo, then went back inside.

Ward was already busy on the coded transmitter, passing on the bad news to Wilbur von Wolverton, chief of Berlin station, who probably already knew about it but whom protocol demanded be informed. Von Wolverton had been peripherally involved in Kaleidoscope, simply because he controlled Berlin station and Natale had occasionally needed his resources.

Peter thought about that and realized that Berlin station was yet one more place where the operation might have sprung a leak, yet one more place that might be vulnerable to a mole.

And in spite of himself, he remembered the DO, Bob Hammond, who had shown up on the eve of all this confusion, on his way to the very city where Natale's informants had just been strangled during the night.

He felt uneasy as he put the two thoughts together, as if he detected a slight rush of paranoia, the covert agent's deadly enemy. Once you started imagining things, you got lost in the wilderness of mirrors and could never find your way out again.

But what if it wasn't paranoia? What if he was actually detecting—even unconsciously—certain evidence that needed to be strung together to explain certain aspects of the chaos that was unraveling around him? He shook his head, concerned at the direction his thoughts were taking him, and in that moment he thought about Judith.

He suddenly understood something she had said to him when he last saw her day before yesterday at the Nice airport. She said she couldn't trust anyone anymore, and then she proved it by jumping ship—unless, of course, something worse had happened to her. She didn't even trust him anymore, she said.

Natale was annoyed by the thought. Judith had nothing to do with Kaleidoscope. She'd been talking in the larger context, about Langley's problems, about the mole hunt, examining things from the perspective of an intelligence analyst in anarchic Moscow. She couldn't even trust her own judgment anymore, she said.

And then he had a fleeting memory of her saying she had made a very serious mistake that might have gotten the young man in his hotel room killed. He felt his throat go dry as he abruptly and fully understood just how she'd felt.

It was just possible that he too had made mistakes with Kaleidoscope. He had been too eager to hand things over to the Germans so that he could fly to Nice and be with her. And because he was thinking about his own needs instead of the safety of his informants, he had dropped the investigation before all the possible leaks and venues were sealed off.

I have responsibilities, Peter. I can't hang people out to dry.

He felt a floodtide of shame so deep that it almost made him physically sick. *He* had hung people out to dry. The four people in Berlin were his responsibility, and he stepped away from them at the most crucial time. If he'd been there, to shepherd them through the aftermath of the arrests and to make sure they weren't betrayed, the four of them would still be alive. And no matter what he did to right the situation now, he could never make it right for them.

14

Naples Station

Natale nodded to Jeremy Ward, who was busy on the encryption machine. He went into his own office, picked up the phone, and booked the next direct flight to Berlin. He didn't know if he could do much good there, but he had to find out, because he certainly couldn't sit here and wait to see what happened. As soon as his reservation was made, he hung up and turned on his computer, then fed in the secured access code to the master files.

The background for Kaleidoscope was all there, encrypted, and he wanted another look at it. The people, the purchases, the combinations and connections and contacts. He couldn't quit thinking about Eva and Fritz Breugher.

He'd traced all the threads of the spider's web. He thought he'd covered all the possibilities. But he'd missed something, had overlooked some vital piece of information. Fritz and Eva had been left exposed to an enemy who had brutally murdered them, and it was indeed his fault and his alone. If he'd been thinking clearly, he would have realized then what he now knew with certainty—some deep and destructive layer of Kaleidoscope was still in place.

Natale worked long into the night, pulling up file after file, waiting for the computer to translate the documents from the cipher into English. When that was done, he read each one methodically, every word. He was icy now, determined, looking for something—anything—that he might have missed, some vital secret that might lie embedded somewhere inside the billions of bytes of information that had been locked inside the CIA's electronic memory.

By 3:00 A.M. his eyes were blearing so badly that he could no longer see. He stood and stretched, then realized he was slightly nauseated from the full pot of coffee he'd brewed fresh and finished off during the night. His head was throbbing. He opened a cabinet, took out a bottle of aspirin, and swallowed two tablets with a dredge of cold coffee left in the bottom of his cup. He'd stopped thinking clearly at least an hour ago, and now fatigue had his thoughts scattered all over the place, probing into seemingly unconnected places in a stream of consciousness that had been filled to the banks with the reams of material he'd devoured.

The files had refreshed his memory about the others involved with Operation Kaleidoscope. There were still people out there, other informants—even agents—whose networks could be compromised if Kaleidoscope fell apart. These were real people, on the edge at this very moment, people whose lives were quite literally on the line as they also tried to puzzle out the answers to what was going on, who they could turn to, who they could trust.

And suddenly a surge of dread flooded through him as he remembered how long it had been since anyone had seen or heard from Judith. He reached for the secured telephone and dialed Rome station.

The night cipher clerk picked up the phone.

Natale fed him a code word, then the cipher clerk said, "I'm sorry, *Signore* Natale, but *Signore* Frost and *Signore* Tyler are gone for the night."

Peter felt his shoulders slump. "Anything new on Ms. Davies?"

"Actually, I was just preparing to contact *Signore* Frost. I got some signals traffic about five minutes ago from Moscow station."

Natale stopped breathing. "Did they find her?"

"I'm sorry, sir. I know you are very concerned. But the authorities at Sheremetyevo Airport just informed Moscow station that some unclaimed luggage was discovered in the baggage claim area after all. The tags indicated that the two suitcases and overnight bag were checked through from Nice."

"Judith's luggage!"

"Yes, they were checked to a ticket issued to Judith Davies of the US embassy. They wanted to know if this was the woman who had boarded the EuroAir flight but had not arrived in Moscow."

Natale felt a sudden, murderous impulse. "It's been almost two days! What took them so long?"

"They apologized profusely for overlooking the bags, of course, considering Moscow station's all-out search for them," the young man said sarcastically. "Moscow station is picking up the bags even as we speak, and I'll let you know what they find out."

Natale stifled a curse. He knew Moscow Customs had been holding the bags, perhaps deciding if they could pilfer them with impunity since their owner had vanished. Or perhaps Moscow station's wire traffic had flagged the interest of the detectives at Moscow police. Or the interest of the new KGB, who still listened in on Moscow station every chance they got and who would have then examined the contents of Judith's luggage carefully before turning it over to the embassy.

Natale thanked the cipher clerk, then slammed the phone back into its cradle. In spite of his fatigue, he was wide awake again, and he began to wearily pace the floor.

If Judith's bags were found but Judith was still missing, it seemed more certain than ever that she had either been kidnapped or killed. His chest tightened with unbearable pain at the very thought of losing her, and he had to literally shut off his mind as it began to tabulate the many dangerous things that happened to covert agents operating in enemy territory. And all of Europe, all of Russia, was now enemy territory.

He needed to do something, but what? How could he help when he didn't understand what was happening? There were so many problems, a whole world of problems, each seemingly disconnected from the others. And yet there had to be answers. There had always been answers before.

He wanted to drop everything and bolt, flee into the night, searching randomly for anything at all that might lead him to her. But that was a fool's way to operate, a way to get himself killed, whether or not Judith was still alive. No, he had to plod ahead, think, examine all the possibilities, and find a true and genuine lead into the labyrinth into which she had vanished. Only then could he act.

He forced himself to settle down by repeating Frost's words in his mind, over and over. Judith was indeed sharp, she could take care of herself, she would be OK. *Please, God, let her be OK.* He prayed for a time, fighting back the anxiety.

Then, with a mammoth effort, he managed to tap into his protective tunnel vision and return his attention to the night's other problems.

He'd been scanning any files that might possibly be related to Kaleidoscope, looking randomly for anything that might give him a new slant on things. He finally started pulling up personal files: Carlo Ricaso; *don* Cesare Ricaso; Carlo's deceased brother, Johnny. He rescanned the personnel files on Karl Dietrich, on other German secret service agents who had been involved with Kaleidoscope, even on Wilbur von Wolverton.

Finally he again read the data he had personally coded in on Fritz and Eva. Nothing there. Absolutely nothing. He pulled up files on Frost and Tyler, simply because they had a slight administrative connection with the case, then closed them again in disgust.

There was nothing in any of the files that would help him, no matter where he looked. Whatever he'd missed before was missing still.

He started to turn off the computer. He was ready to give up for the day, perhaps forever. He leaned back and rubbed his eyes, stretched his arms up and yawned.

Ward had two children, and when they first opened the file on Operation Kaleidoscope, it had been just before Peter's birthday. Ward went to a toy shop and purchased a kaleidoscope for him, a children's toy that he kept on his desk as a paperweight. Now he idly picked up the toy as he thought. He turned it this way and that, inspecting the harlequin-patterned outside of the cylinder as he wondered about all that had happened to him these past few days.

He put the toy to his eye like a spyglass and looked through it. He thought about how much the toy was like the operation. Shifting patterns, optical illusions, reflections of shattered, multicolored glass with the brilliance of fine gems.

He put it down, stretched his arms over his head, then looked at the toy with renewed interest and picked it up again. This time he turned toward his desk lamp and looked through it, rotating the cylinder so that the exquisite, multicolored glass snow-flakes shifted into another equally beautiful pattern.

Illusions. All he was seeing were illusions. Loose bits of colored glass and mirrors, not snowflakes. He was looking at the illusion of symmetry, created by reflection.

He turned the cylinder. The world was once more reduced to colors and crystals, no two snowflakes, no two patterns alike. He turned the kaleidoscope again and again, trying to visually separate the real glass fragments from their mirror images, trying to find the near-imperceptible seams where the mirrors converged.

He smiled for the first time all day. This was indeed a remarkable toy, delightful to the senses, opening up the magical wonders of childhood.

The pattern shifted again, then stopped in place as his hand froze. The pattern dissolved, and the brilliantly colored snowflakes in front of his eyes were forgotten as he saw past them into a darkness filled with blood-red shards and sin-black slivers. The patterns, shifting—why hadn't he seen it? He'd been trying to sort out the pattern of Operation Kaleidoscope, he thought he'd found it, had left the operation behind him, and now at least four people were dead. That was the key. The pattern. But what if there was more than one pattern, one superimposed upon another? What if some evil genius had devised a plan so intricate that it had patterns within patterns, layers within layers? A double kaleidoscope, triple, infinite, with separate illusions blending into one another, so that one wasn't clearly visible until the other had been removed! What if some grand pattern connected all the seemingly disjointed events that had been battering at him these past few days? That would explain why he was having so much trouble understanding all the chaos that had entered his life. What if there was a link between the assassination in Monte Carlo and the murders in Berlin?

And what if he'd been looking in the wrong direction with regard to Judith's disappearance? What if that also had something to do with Kaleidoscope? After all, Kaleidoscope linked into Russia, and it was Russian nuclear materials that were being fed into the pipeline. A Russian girl had been murdered in the Berlin brothel. Russia was Judith's domain, and as chief intelligence analyst she was supposed to be more or less on top of anything that was happening there. What if Kaleidoscope had spawned some new horror that had grown to include Judith?

He rolled his eyes toward the ceiling as he had this last thought, and his shoulders slumped. He was grasping at straws indeed. Still, the idea kept nudging him. It nudged him especially hard when he leaned forward again to turn off his computer, so that he stopped short, then folded his fingers to make a cradle for his head as he leaned back to think.

What if?

He began to sum things up in his mind. First, Frost had arrived at Rome station, obsessed with a mole hunt. Next, Frost and Tyler's interest in Prince Dante di Veresi took Judith and him to Monte Carlo. Third, the young German Rudy was killed while entering Peter's hotel room, for no reason he could yet detect. Fourth—and here was the really new slant on things—Rudy had once worked at Berlin station. And so had the CIA's new director of operations, Bob Hammond, who had in fact trained Rudy and who dropped in on Rome station and Natale the very evening following Rudy's death.

Natale didn't believe much in coincidence, especially not when such unusual events happened almost simultaneously and in such dramatic ways.

On the other hand, he had to admit that coincidences did occasionally happen. And Hammond couldn't have known about Rudy's death before he left Langley. Still, he could have certainly known that something dangerous was in the works. He arrived in Rome immediately upon the tail of Frost's arrival and the young man's death, then traveled on to Berlin on a so-called good-will tour at just about the time the Berlin end of Kaleidoscope was blowing up in Natale's face.

Peter realized with irritation that Hammond was probably at Berlin station this very minute, in the CIA's bloc of the elaborate new US embassy on the Pariser Platz, being regaled by Willie von Wolverton with every detail of the Breughers' deaths and Peter Natale's failure to see a vital operation through to its proper conclusion.

At that thought, an anchor of guilt dragged Natale's mind back into disarray, where it began darting here and there, sorting and assessing random pieces of information. With a growing sense of desperation, he tried to force odd segments to match, as if he were working a jigsaw puzzle and the pieces wouldn't quite fit together.

He finally gave up in disgust. He was on the wrong track yet again. Judith's disappearance, Rudy's death, and the blowup of Kaleidoscope were separate problems. He saw no way they could possibly overlap. His sense of helpless frustration returned.

But the chain of reasoning had taken him far afield of Berlin to sail above the bigger picture and examine all the parts. That left him thinking once more of Judith and the events at Monte Carlo. He wondered yet again where she was. As a gnawing fear shot through him, he stopped and prayed that Frost was right about her disappearance being voluntary.

He played back the events of the past week. He thought about being with Judith at the villa above Nice, then about Frost's asking them to go to Monte Carlo for a couple of days to spy on Prince Veresi. He had become curious about the prince during that time. But that had been a busy two days, and he'd had no opportunity to scratch his curiosity.

Now, on impulse, he put his fingers to the keyboard of the still running computer and entered a code word, then checked to see if the CIA computers held any information on the Royal House of Veresi. It was a good bet that they did. They usually had at least some background on the movers and shakers in Italian/Sicilian politics, and according to Frost the prince certainly was that.

He found a small file. He selected the subcategory marked PERSONAL, then watched as Prince Dante di Veresi's full name came up on the amber screen along with his many useless titles, his physical description, and a thin sketch of his sordid background. Natale quickly scanned the information, then scrolled to the second page. Fatigue was setting in again, and he had to blink, then rub his eyes, before he could decipher the words:

PRINCE DANTE DI VERESI: MARRIED ONCE, JULY 8,
1975, TO THE CONTESSA MARIALISA LAURO BRANDENBURG,

DISTANT HEIRESS TO THE GERMAN HOUSE OF BRANDEN-
BURG, DIRECT HEIRESS TO THE NEAPOLITAN HOUSE OF LAURO,
DECEASED THIRTEEN YEARS AFTER MARRIAGE: CAUSE OF
DEATH, SUICIDE. ONE CHILD WAS THE ISSUE OF THAT UNION,
THE PRINCESS GIANALISA LAURO VERESI . . .

Peter snapped wide awake. Gianalisa. Gia.

Suddenly he saw the dying Rudy, his mouth moving sound-
lessly as he tried to wrench his last words out of death itself. "They
lied about everything," he'd said. "Warn her. Tell Gia—"

Rudy died before he could finish his message. Now Natale
knew that he might at last have a chance to reconstruct that message. If he could just find and question the prince's only daughter,
he might be able to make some sense out of Rudy's bewildering
and violent death. That would at least give closure to one of the
many problems that plagued him.

He focused completely on the file now, rereading every word.
But as he reached the third page, a new sense of defeat stormed
into his world. Gianalisa Lauro Veresi was not only the sole issue of
the prince, she was also the issue of madness. Not only had her
mother killed herself, but her grandmother had also put a gun to
her own head and pulled the trigger. And the girl's last known
address was an expensive rehabilitation ward and mental hospital
on the outskirts of Brussels—a long way from Monte Carlo and the
fresh urn of ashes that had once been Rudy Brandenburg.

An addendum to the file came up on the screen. Diagnosed
as a victim of narcotic psychosis, the file said. Treatment: full de-
toxification from narcotic addiction, minimal medication indicated,
long-term institutionalization advised for patient's and others' safety
and for patient's full recovery. Prior institutionalization has resulted
in temporary recovery, but when patient returns to the larger envi-
ronment she invariably returns to the addictive process.

Natale grabbed a medical dictionary from his bookshelf. He
looked up narcotic psychosis and learned that certain people react
to the chemical changes in either narcotics or amphetamines by
manifesting a personality change so dramatic that it is an actual
psychosis. He shut the book and returned to the computer screen.

The attending doctor's diagnosis had been scanned into the
computer:

Believed etiology of narcotics addiction, personality disorders founded in youthful trauma. Subject exhibits a lack of positive identity with females, possibly due to her mother's suicide when she was only ten years of age; also exhibits a tendency to projection and neurotic anxiety. Manifests exaggerated rigidity, varies between controlled behavior and flights of fantasy, prone to delusional thinking. A hyperalert observer, which gives subject a strong ability to sense the unconscious processes of others. This increases the efficacy of subject's exceedingly convincing and manipulative behavior. Suicidal. Possibly homicidal. Exhibits a harsh image of her father, to the point of identifying him as the literal Prince of Darkness. Blames father for mother's suicide, with no rational basis; mother was possibly also psychotic, though no medical records exist.

Peter felt fatigue settle down on him like a leaden cloak. He shut off the computer. This couldn't possibly be the mysterious Gia. He was back to square one, with no clue as to why his informant had been murdered, no clue as to why the woman he loved had vanished into thin air.

He struggled with that for a moment. His exhaustion and discouragement weighed on him so heavily that he felt as though the world had shifted and deposited its full weight on him. And in that moment he decided his priorities. With regard to Judith he had to do something, and there seemed to be only one avenue left open.

He reached again for the phone and dialed the private and secured telephone number of Carlo Ricaso. Carlo had more people at his disposal than the CIA and the EIA combined, most of them very well positioned when it came to knowing what was happening in the international pipelines and the streets.

When someone picked up the phone at the other end, Natale started to speak. But before he could get the polite words out of his mouth, a coarse, irritated voice informed him that "the Signore" wasn't in and wasn't expected back until the following night. Peter asked if he could leave a message and was rudely advised that he could.

He used his cover name, left a fictitious number—Carlo already had his home number—and asked for Signore Ricaso to phone him immediately on a matter of the utmost urgency.

Then he shut off his office lights, locked the door, dragged himself past the guards and to his Mercedes. As he drove home, he reflected on the past few days' events and the chaos that had swirled into his life.

The next flight to Berlin didn't leave until 2:00 P.M. He would at least have time to sleep for a few hours in his own bed for a change. And then he could step back into that other firefight, as he took a firsthand look at the damage to Kaleidoscope, talked to the Germans, and tried to decide what to do next.

As that door shut in his mind, the one that held the specter of Judith immediately popped open, and an uncharacteristically selfish thought struck him. He knew that whatever else was happening with Judith, she at least had some answers about Rudy Brandenburg. On that basis alone, he had to find her, just in case Rudy's death was somehow connected to Kaleidoscope.

He had to find the answers. If he didn't get some answers soon, he was going to join the prince's disturbed daughter Gianalisa in her very pricey Belgian mental ward.

He phoned Jeremy Ward and asked him to send a flash query to Rome station, requesting additional information on Gianalisa Lauro Veresi and asking verification of her location. Then he walked wearily into his bedroom, kicked off his shoes, lay down on the bed still fully dressed, and was instantly asleep.

15

Naples

One additional incident occurred that day in capricious Naples to lengthen the imponderable chain of events that was wrapping like a set of powerful black tentacles around the frustrated and exhausted Peter Natale.

At 7:00 P.M. the Ricaso Mafia Family's black-and-silver Gulfstream jet touched down at Capodichino Airport, whined down the runway, then slowed to a smooth stop. *Don* Cesare and Carlo had just arrived from Palermo.

A discreet black Rolls Royce limo slid up to within a breath of the plane's unfolded steps. Cesare and Carlo stepped into the passenger compartment and were swept away from the airport, sped into the city and along the waterfront, then deposited beside the private elevator in the parking garage of the Hotel Sempreverde. This was the classiest hotel in Naples and another of the crown jewels in the Ricasos' chain of luxury establishments, second only to the grand old Hotel de Mer itself.

The Ricasos dined in their penthouse suite in a room with walls of polished glass that framed the tarnished shimmer of city lights. The music of Naples's favorite son, Enrico Caruso, played softly in the background. The long, white-clothed table was set with immaculate crystal, weighty silver utensils, and gold-trimmed thirteenth-century dinner plates that had once graced the king's table at Castel Nuovo.

Several Ricaso henchmen, doubling as waiters, drifted in and out like well-mannered, well-armed ghosts, serving the food prepared specially by the hotel's master chef.

Don Cesare kept badgering Carlo and their solitary guest, Vincente Guappo, to eat.

"Have a little taste of this *gatto*. It contains real mozzarella, made from the milk from Battipaglia's most generous buffalo. Ah, *bellissimo!* And there, there, try another slice of the *braciola alla napoletana*. Another dish the chef makes special for me. You'll never find better anywhere."

Carlo ate sparingly. He was used to his uncle's enthusiasm for food—and in fact, this was the only enthusiasm the wily old man ever showed for anything but money. And his lodge. There was always his obsession with the lodge.

However, Vincente Guappo apparently needed no encouragement to shovel vast quantities of the excellent food into his mouth. He was the corpulent and brutal head of the Camorra, Naples's home-grown Mafia, and Carlo knew that he considered his girth a manifestation of his value as a man. He was dressed in an expensive black cashmere suit and white silk shirt, but the rumpled, ill-fitting clothing only emphasized the expanse of his body.

In the early seventies, the Sicilian Mafia had started doing large volumes of business with the Camorra, and in order to keep control they swore in key Camorra members as "made men." Immediately the Sicilians started tilting things to their own advantage, and the *Camorristi* rebelled. Now, after a recent war that left nearly a hundred *Camorristi* dead, the Camorra had effectively been swallowed whole by the Sicilians, as had the smaller Italian Mafia, the 'Ndrangheta in Calabria province. Both organizations were allowed to operate as separate cells beneath the Sicilian umbrella only so long as they understood who was boss.

The three Mafiosi murmured polite questions and took turns making pithy replies until the last swallow of *gnocchetti al salmon* was savored and the dessert of *sfogliatella*—a puff pastry filled with cheese, candied nuts, and cinnamon—had been consumed and complimented.

Then *don* Cesare offered the men Cuban cigars—Carlo declined—while one of the servants poured after-dinner whiskeys, which Carlo avidly accepted.

After Cesare had clipped, dampened, and lighted his evil-smelling smoke, he tilted his head in a haughty manner and put on his death's-head grin.

He said to Guappo, "Any message of hope for my dear friend Volante?"

Vincente Guappo blanched, then belched, then smiled weakly. "I am sorry, *Padrone*. My men have combed every inch of Neapolitan soil—I have even forced them into the pits of the volcano itself. The young man is not being kept here—assuming he is still alive."

"He's alive." The old capo said it with absolute certainty.

"You have heard something?"

"No. The kidnappers are still silent. But I know he isn't worth anything dead, and why kidnap him except for money? Keep looking. My respect for *Signore* Volante Chicarelli far exceeds my respect for you, *amico*. I don't need to repeat what will happen if it turns out his son was kept somewhere in your territory and was not found."

Guappo paled further and stared helplessly at the floor.

There was a long silence before *don* Cesare spoke in a less threatening tone of voice. "But enough of business, Vincente. The kid will turn up. And if he doesn't? *Faugh.*" He made a twisted face. "He was a weakling anyway. So be it."

For some reason that Carlo could not fathom, that caused both men to break into scabrous, riotous laughter that reminded him of grave robbers or trolls.

Then Cesare turned serious. "Anyway, tonight we should celebrate. We have the honor of admitting Marco to the Third Order of the Caput Mundi."

Guappo made a little bow and lifted his glass in salute. "I am grateful for your sponsorship."

Don Cesare's eyes glittered with a dark pleasure that Carlo fully understood. *Don* Cesare knew that Guappo wasn't grateful, and in fact neither Guappo nor his son Marco even wanted to belong to the lodge. But *don* Cesare delighted in making people bend to his will. Everything was a life or death contest with him, and he had a pathological need to control everyone around him, right down to their thoughts. Even Carlo. Especially Carlo, who looked at his uncle and suddenly felt steel bands tightening on his chest.

"I commend you for turning Marco from a trouble-making young thief into a true man of respect," Cesare said, still looking at Vincente Guappo. Then he twisted the knife. "He now serves us well."

Guappo offered a forced smile that showed a gold-capped front tooth. "Marco is a good boy. A good, good boy. He has assured me he will always be there to help you."

Don Cesare nodded knowingly and puffed on his cigar.

Carlo knew what kind of help they could expect from Marco. The twisted young man was a skilled assassin, whose primary training had come during his teens when he'd gone to a Bulgarian terrorist training camp during a flight of rebellion against his family. Several years later he changed his mind and, in order to redeem himself, betrayed a fellow assassin who was trafficking KGB drugs in Camorra territory. After that, Marco had been further tutored by Vincente Guappo himself and had become one of the Camorra's busiest men, feared by even other Mafiosi.

Marco Guappo had been known to kill with the *lupara*, with other types of shotgun, with hand grenades, by the garrotte, with poison, baseball bats, piano wire, and tire irons. He was responsible for many of the murder victims who were known in Sicily and Naples as "Distinguished Cadavers," that is, men in high places who refused to knuckle under to Mafia demands and paid with their lives. There were thousands of such men, fallen victims in the anti-Mafia wars. Marco alone was responsible for the deaths of judges, policemen, journalists, educators, priests, members of any political opposition, and countless active Mafia members whose own time—for one reason or another—had come.

Carlo felt a grim repugnance for both Vincente Guappo and his death-addicted son. In fact, Marco and other sanctioned serial killers like him were yet another reason that Carlo was beginning to seriously question his position within the Mafia and his will to continue the family legacy.

As *don* Cesare and Vincente Guappo continued their conversation, circling one another like vultures looking for exposed flesh, Carlo thought about the bigger picture. He still did not understand why Cesare had sponsored Marco as a lodge member—unless it gave the *don* an added vestige of control over a man who was essentially a mad dog.

Nor did he understand why *don* Cesare found such evil delight in stringing along his subordinates—as he was doing now with Guappo—only to inevitably pull the rug out from under them at the worst possible time, in order to "teach them a lesson." In a world filled with so much hatred, why deliberately create more?

In fact, there was much about the pathological psychology of his crafty old uncle that Carlo did not understand—and much that he hoped he would never understand. But one thing he did know. Vincente Guappo's deference was a mask that did a poor job of hiding the man's deep and abiding hatred. *Don* Cesare had best never turn his back on this man.

A servant approached with the whiskey decanter, and Carlo held up his glass for a refill.

As he sipped the amber liquid, he idly surveyed the man, noting with contempt that Guappo had stained his diamond-studded cravat with a dollop of cheese from the rich dessert. His small and pointed nose seemed arbitrarily attached to his flabby cheeks and receding chin, and his tiny, rosebud mouth was still moist from his last sip of whiskey. His black, gray-flecked hair was pomaded like a thick layer of axle grease across his bulbous head.

In fact, Vincente Guappo's appearance was almost comical, so wide was the margin by which it failed to capture the essence of style. But if Guappo was a clown, he was an evil clown. When he and *don* Cesare began discussing the aspects of Mafia business that gave Guappo pleasure—murder, violence, pornography—the Neapolitan's eyes rolled back for a split instant to show the whites. When they returned, the pupils had turned to piercing black gimlets that revolted Carlo with the hellish excitement he saw there.

"A shame Marco could not join us for dinner," Cesare said politely, after they had talked for a time about corrupting a new Neapolitan police officer.

A shame he wasn't invited, Carlo thought cynically.

He knew that Marco would already be at the lodge, undergoing the special purification ceremony that preceded the actual ritual of advancement. But Carlo's mood was surly. He hated this manipulation, hated these rituals as much as his evil old uncle loved them. In fact, he accompanied *don* Cesare to Naples and attended these Machiavellian dinners and the subsequent lodge meetings solely to keep a vestige of peace in the family.

Once a month, always on schedule, the Order of the Caput Mundi met at the ancient temple in Naples to engage in the stodgy, tedious ceremonies that kept the members of this secret society convinced that they were somehow superior to the rest of the world.

And once a month, if he was foolish enough to be in Sicily, Carlo was obliged to join them. He had long ago been admitted to the Third Order of the Outer Circle as an Adeptus Minor. He'd also made clear to *don* Cesare that he considered the entire brotherhood to be an exercise in adolescent fraternity and that the Third Order was three orders higher than he cared to climb.

Carlo looked back with longing to the time when Mafiosi had been prohibited from joining other secret societies.

But within the past two decades, most high-ranking Mafiosi had seen the advantages of hidden access to the men who seemed to gravitate to such secret lodges as the Knights Templar, the Rosicrucians, the Capati, and the Freemasons. The men who belonged to these organizations were generally movers and shakers who also joined lodges in order to form relationships that might give them an edge. Any thinking Mafioso would never miss such an opportunity to rub shoulders with men he so zealously longed to corrupt. Certain lodge members also wanted to have a Mafia lodge-mate to hold up to competitors as a tacit threat.

In order to facilitate these mutually beneficial couplings, many lodges had incorporated a standing tenet whereby the Mafiosi could learn the secrets of the lodge but the lodge would never be able to learn the secrets of the Mafia. In addition, the blood oaths required for membership in the lodges would be automatically overridden by any similar blood oaths made to the Mafia.

Because of these concessions, it was now common for Mafiosi to link up with one fraternal lodge or another, though most seemed to prefer the Freemasons. *Don* Cesare himself had belonged to the Trapanese and Neapolitan affiliates for a time, for these were also covered societies, whose member lists were more carefully guarded than the most dangerous state secrets. Above all things, *don* Cesare valued secrecy when plotting his conspiracies.

But the Caput Mundi was a far more secretive and exclusive brotherhood than even the Freemasons or Knights Templar. It brought together the highest ranking nobles, politicians, and businessmen, not only from Sicily but from the entire European continent, and bound these men together in an oath unto death. For *don* Cesare, who craved power and lusted for conspiracy, the combination was absolutely perfect.

Carlo didn't know the identities of the Inner Circle members. They met secretly and wore black pointed hoods reminiscent of the Spanish Inquisition, except when in their private chamber. But he did know that Prince Dante di Veresi was the master of their particular lodge—*don* Cesare hadn't been able to resist imparting that gem of information. And though the lodge had a branch in Sicily, the prince officiated here at the Naples lodge—therefore, *don* Cesare insisted that they fly to Naples every month to attend.

This interested Carlo. The Veresi family had a long-standing bond with the Ricasos, and for once he understood his wily uncle's motives.

Prince Veresi's family had come to Sicily when Alphonso of Aragon united the crowns of Sicily and Naples in 1442. The Veresis were eventually granted title to vast regions of Sicilian land, which included the small village of Valletta and all the surrounding valleys. When the island was united with Italy in 1860, the feudalistic grip of the Veresi family was loosened only slightly. Until the end of World War II, they still sucked the blood from the land and all the peasants who toiled upon it, to forge that blood and toil into golden ballrooms, plush-lined carriages, hundreds of servants, opulent gems, luxurious travel, and every other extravagance imaginable.

Two of the peasants exploited for the Veresi family's gain were *don* Cesare Ricaso's parents.

Carlo could remember the stories well, told by both his uncle and his now-dead father. As children, the Ricaso brothers had seen the Veresis when the royal family came to their vacation estate south of Valletta for the high days of summer. The contrast between the Veresis' wealth and the Ricasos' poverty had gnawed on *don* Cesare all his life.

But things changed. Now Cesare held title to the land around Valletta and a good slice of the rest of Sicily besides. The prince's parents had both died, and the prince's vast fortune had dwindled substantially. But Carlo knew that the famous Sicilian saying "Revenge is a dish the Sicilian eats cold" summed up the situation completely. *Don* Cesare still felt the gnawing wounds of childhood poverty. He still loathed the nobles and their *gabelloti*—managers. They had enforced a social order that created misery at best, overt slavery at worst. And Cesare blamed the current prince for the misery of his parents, the misery of his grandparents, and for all the family's early deaths from sickness and malnutrition.

Carlo knew all this. And he realized that by joining this particular lodge, *don* Cesare was not only indulging himself in his fascination for ritualistic secrecy. He was also getting even.

Crafty, evil, Cesare had immediately embarked upon a carefully designed campaign to bring the prince fully under his heel. He studied the prince's vices, which included licentiousness as well as greed, a harrowing amount of pride, and a severe case of alcohol dependency. The cunning old Mafioso took much pleasure in constantly and cleverly trying to manipulate the prince into situations that would debauch him completely.

Cesare had also coerced the prince into promoting him directly into the most secretive cabal within this already secretive order. Now *don* Cesare Ricaso was one of the few non-titled members of the Royal Invisible Order of the Caput Mundi, known less formally as the Black Nobility.

When the *don* had revealed this to his nephew, Carlo had barely hidden his sneer. Since childhood, Carlo had heard rumors that an ancient cabal of highly powerful royals existed. But such rumors came from conspiracy theorists whose logic was so muddled that he could not possibly give them credence. In these paranoid analyses of reality, the Black Nobility existed as a fiendish ancient cult intent upon instrumenting a One World Order with themselves at the helm, having already subverted such diverse organizations as the CIA, the United Nations, most global governments, the Mafia itself, and all Christian religions.

Carlo frankly could not believe that his uncle would fall for such foolishness. To be sure, he could indeed see the world moving toward a certain uniformity. But to him it seemed obvious that the changes were built into the very nature of global economics and the nature of modern communications, rather than being instrumented by some dark and sinister hand.

Carlo finally decided that this order was capitalizing upon the legend of a vastly powerful and evil Black Nobility in order to tap into the aura of sinister mystery. For these Black Nobility certainly thrived on mystery. Everyone now knew that there was a Mafia. But in spite of Carlo's access to the most secretive sides of Italian society, he had not known that the Black Nobility actually existed until Cesare joined the lodge, then bragged to him about his conquest.

Well—whatever other purposes the sect might serve, at least for once the old Mafioso's lust for conspiracy and secrecy had been sated. After his initiation, he had walked around with a smug look for days.

These memories drifted back as Carlo listened to the two Mafia *dons* talk of the business of running the darker side of the city of Naples. There was a discussion of a recent murder Marco had carried out, a hit on a banker who was refusing to honor a Mafia loan—which would not have been paid back, of course. The two crime families' mutual rackets and vices were discussed, though briefly, for Cesare had sub-capos who handled most of the lower echelon business.

Finally, at 9:30 P.M. it was time for the three men to descend again to the parking garage. There they climbed into the limo and glided the several blocks to the lodge.

The building itself was a mysterious, three-story, black stone structure with a small iron carving of a winged sphinx set on the gable above the front door. The few narrow windows appeared like slits in a medieval prison, and the edifice was set well back within a disguise of thick shrubbery and several acres of lawn and sheltering trees. A heavy, spiked iron wall surrounded the entire compound.

This was the Naples temple of the Order of Caput Mundi. The gate was guarded by an electronic beam and by two guards who wore black, gold-trimmed dress uniforms as smart as those of Benito Mussolini's most elegantly decorated officers.

Don Cesare spoke a password, shared a secret handshake, and the three men were admitted through the massive front door by a hooded gatekeeper who wore a flowing black robe and pointed, anonymous black hood. They passed beneath a Gothic arch with a carved capstone, then walked down a dark and intricate passage adorned with somber armorial trophies and carvings of dragons, stars, and zodiacal and mythological creatures.

Cesare spoke a second password to another robed, hooded gatekeeper, who stepped aside so they could walk beneath a second capstone. This one was adorned with a pyramid enclosing the great, all-seeing eye of Osiris. Feeble gleams of encrimsoned light filtered through a partially opened doorway at the far end of the hall. The building was so silent Carlo could hear the faraway drone of voices.

As always, he felt the air of sorrow and irredeemable gloom that seemed to pervade this building. He wished he'd had the presence of mind to bring a flask of whiskey with him to further deaden his senses to the oppressive surroundings.

The anteroom they entered had red velvet tapestries draped here and there, and the walls were adorned with various swords and knives and certain royal crests. Varnished human skulls were set upon dark sideboards, and flags showing death's-heads hung from brass poles stuck into the walls at an angle, like medieval tapers. Behind a wide doorway was a closet, and within this, in a wide bank of private lockers, hung ceremonial robes of all sizes and colors.

Each man selected and donned the robe that exemplified his respective rank. Carlo's was a rich, royal blue satin with gold pentagrams and winged sphinxes embroidered into the lapel; Vincente Guappo, who had been promoted to the Tenth Order of the Outer Circle because of Cesare's constant badgering, wore an emerald green satin robe appropriately embroidered with gold skulls and crossbones, hybrid beasts and scimitars.

Don Cesare's was, of course, the most impressive. It was made of the richest black velvet, and a wide band at the hem of the otherwise austere garment was adorned with a gossamer of golden thread and precious gemstones in designs that included stars, sun, moon, angels, clouds, pillars, pyramids, various medieval instruments, ancient cabalistic letters, and countless other designs, all of which symbolized the deepest universal mysteries.

Next, they donned their matching ceremonial headdresses, the inquisitors' masks, which served to keep them hidden from their lodge-mates until such time as they were ordered to reveal themselves. Carlo felt foolish, as always.

The three of them walked down the hall and into the sanctuary. As they entered the wide room and sat down, he reflected once again on the similarities between this lodge and a church sanctuary —though no church had ever filled him with this feeling of dread.

The large, dimly lit room smelled of varnish and floor wax. The walls were of highly polished wood, the ceiling was lofty and slightly domed, the rows of seats looked remarkably like pews, and an ornate golden altar had been placed at the front of the otherwise Spartan room. About five feet behind it was a platform, and in the center of this stood a high-backed wooden throne, fronted by a simple pulpit made of the same expensive and polished wood as the walls. The throne-chair was backed by milky tiles tinted with naked pastel figures of mythological gods and goddesses and bordered by black signs from the ancient Jewish cabala. To both sides of the simple throne sat heavy, carved chairs, filled at the moment with figures in red satin robes and hoods.

Apparently the Ricaso party was the last to arrive. As soon as they sat down, a gatekeeper pulled the heavy door shut with a sharp, grating sound, locked it, then turned, stiffened to attention, and said in a mournful voice, "Men faithful and true, men who value honor over life. Stand and be counted!"

The thirty or so men in attendance all stood and put right hands across their hearts in a silent pledge of allegiance.

A bailiff in a black robe stepped to a position in front of the pulpit. He said, "Sun-crossed men, men of courage. Men of sterling worth. Who among you dares to approach the celestial mysteries?"

The men made a ritualized response of three words in Latin.

At that moment, the prince entered with a theatrical flourish through the door behind the podium. He wore a black robe with gold trim, much like Cesare's, and for the initiation ceremonies he wore no hood.

He was a small man with an aged face and thinning black hair, which he probably dyed and which he combed crossways to hide his balding spots. His well-trimmed black goatee and mustache—also surely dyed and appearing odd against the pallor of his skin—made him resemble most depictions of Mephistopheles, an affectation Carlo believed was deliberate and which was exaggerated by the man's flowing black velvet robe.

The prince strode to the podium, posed in a style reminiscent of a thousand tyrants, and arched his dark eyebrows. "I bid you welcome, men of the sun." He made hand motions that were vaguely reminiscent of the sign of the cross. Then he raised his hand, as if to bless the small group, and repeated the intonation: "Sun-crossed men, men of courage. Men of sterling worth. Who among you dares to approach the celestial mysteries?"

The answer was a unified murmur. "We are not worthy, Your Excellency."

Veresi nodded once, abruptly, then moved back and sat down on the throne with dramatic flair.

As soon as he was seated, a tall, thin man in a billowing red satin robe and a hood entered through the door behind the podium.

This man was known as the Grand Masterful Priest, the man who officiated at these initiations. Behind him came Marco, looking awkward in his yellow satin initiate's robe. His headpiece was carried awkwardly beneath his arm, his muddy eyes were suspicious and ticking across the room. Carlo had the feeling that Marco was trying to make eye contact with someone, anyone, so as to dare him to comment unfavorably on his unusual appearance.

But there was nothing amusing about Marco. Or about this sinister room. As usual, Carlo was aware of unpleasant sensations that had nothing to do with the five drinks he had consumed after dinner in an attempt to prepare himself for this unpleasant attempt at fraternity.

The Grand Masterful Priest positioned himself behind the podium, while Marco—obviously rehearsed—stepped to the altar and turned to face the priest.

The priest said, "Who dares to seek admission to the mysterious celestial kingdom? Who dares approach the men of sun-crossed worth?"

Marco spoke his name, and Carlo actually thought he heard a muted curse mixed therein. He looked closer and saw that Marco was thoroughly disgusted. He seemingly was here under extreme duress. *Don* Cesare was getting his money's worth today.

The priest said, "Who comes here?"

Marco recited the answer. "I am a blind man, seeking light."

"And who holds this light?"

"The keeper of the celestial mysteries."

The ritual continued. The same words in different variations were spoken over and over again, and soon the men in the audience stood and also began to respond with prescribed ritualistic intonations. Carlo stood among them, fighting a growing sense of oppression and apathy that threatened to collapse him into a stupor.

And finally Marco had waded through all the ritual and reached the point of actual initiation.

The two red-robed figures spread a white sheet on the floor in front of him. It was symbolic of graveclothes and an open grave. The priest intoned, "Repeat after me: If I betray the celestial mysteries of this excellent order, may I die and be placed in this grave."

Marco held up his right hand over the symbolic sheet and repeated the oath.

Next, one of the red satin figures stepped forward and handed Marco the picture of a saint and a lighted red candle.

Again repeating the words and directions of the priest, Marco set fire to the picture and watched the paper curl in the flame. He said, "May I burn in hell like this sacred image if I betray any of my brethren in the Order of Caput Mundi."

Carlo felt a growing pressure in his head. Unwanted memories drifted into his mind, memories of his own initiation into this peculiar and boring cult. And at the same time, he felt the wan, emaciated fingers of another memory grip his heart and squeeze it dry of blood.

This fraternal oath was so much like the Mafia's blood oath that the difference scarcely mattered. As Marco was now vowing to die rather than dishonor his lodge-mates, so Carlo had sworn on his eternal soul to die before dishonoring the *Cosa Nostra*—"Our Thing."

Carlo had been informed at that time that he would indeed die for the Mafia, for he was going in alive and he would go out only when he was dead. He had sworn a blood oath to that too. What else could he do? He had been born to the Mafia, he had grown up within the Mafia, and once in, never out. He was obliged unto death to blindly obey every order his capo—in this case his uncle—dispensed. To even think of treason was punishable by death, if the capo got wind of the potential defection.

Back then, Carlo had meant every word he'd said. Now, he was more and more certain that he had made a mistake. He thought of his many years of brutality and bloodshed and immeasurable greed. He thought again about his own initiation into the dark brotherhood, while still in his teens.

In the Ricaso form of the Mafia initiation ceremony, the picture of Saint Rosalia—Sicily's patron saint—was burned. And after that, Carlo's finger had been sliced—he looked down at the small scar, still visible after all these years. The blood had dripped to the floor, to the white, symbolic sheet, as ever more sinister vows were made—upon the saints, upon the cross, upon his life.

And finally, when the ritual seemed complete and the half-dozen withered old Mafiosi in attendance were stirring in anticipation of the following food and drinks, *don* Cesare handed Carlo a Beretta small-frame automatic.

A large portrait of Jesus Christ hung in the front of the small stuccoed and whitewashed room. It was a serene print showing the Christ with shining, long brown hair and a beatific expression of love for all mankind. The portrait had surprised and disturbed Carlo when he had first entered the remote peasant's cottage, and it had made him uncomfortable throughout the ritual. By making these vows, he was literally turning his back on God's laws and therefore on God Himself. The picture represented something that should not have been in evidence that day, in that room where such sinister vows were being made.

Cesare then satisfied his curiosity about the reason for the picture of Jesus. "Today," he said, "you become a man of honor.

You give *La Familia*"—The Family—"your body and soul. You have sworn this day to die for *La Cosa Nostra* rather than betray any one of us. To these men of respect, you have sworn *omerta* and love. You have mingled your blood with ours and sworn to obey. Now, Carlo, you must show us that you will indeed obey, even if your father calls you from his deathbed. Even if your mother calls you from beyond the grave. First of all and above all, you must forever obey *La Cosa Nostra*."

He handed the gun to Carlo then. "If you cannot shoot the Christ, then you will not shoot your mother, you will not shoot your father. You will not give your first love and loyalty to *La Familia*. And so, Carlo, you must shoot this picture as if you were shooting the true Son of God."

Carlo had ignored the dark shiver that threatened to envelop him, catapult him into a dark eternity. He wanted to be admitted to this society, he wanted to be thought of as a true man of honor. So he raised the pistol, took aim, and fired.

He knew that what they said was true. If he would shoot the Christ—even a holy picture—he would have truly turned his back on his childhood, on the church. He would belong only to the Mafia, forever.

Carlo had grown up in a Mafia family. He killed his first man at the age of sixteen. There was little that turned his stomach, little that bothered him, nothing that he feared. But shooting the picture of Jesus full of holes left him shaken, as if the Christ were staring straight at him with sad and loving eyes, forgiving him even as he pulled the trigger and fired and fired again until the gun was empty, leaving the picture in shreds, the figure of Christ destroyed as the real Christ had been destroyed on the cross in order to give Carlo eternal life.

Now, these twenty long years later, Carlo was once again thinking about that night, as the occultic ritual initiating Marco Guappo to a higher level in the lodge droned on.

He had sworn, that long-ago day, to burn in hell if he broke a Mafia rule or disobeyed an order. But now he saw the truth—it was the keeping of the Mafia oaths that would sooner or later catapult him into hell. In fact, *La Familia* had already turned his life into a hell, just as they had stolen his eternal soul.

The lesson had been long in coming, but he knew now that everything in the Mafia was a hideous lie. The money turned to ashes, the loyalty to betrayal, the love to burning, hellish hatred. His fellow Mafiosi had turned everything upside down and backward, just as these people in the Caput Mundi were now doing.

Suddenly he felt suffocated by the sensation of evil, as if a weight were pressing on his heart. He stood, ignoring the startled and angry look that *don* Cesare shot at him. He pushed past his uncle, pushed past Guappo, and made for the door, which the surprised gatekeeper opened for him.

He ripped off his robe the instant he reached the hallway and threw it on a bench padded with crimson silk. Then he glared at the gatekeeper at the front door as he approached, so that by the time he reached the door it was already open for him and the man had stepped well to one side.

The limo driver had the car waiting in front. Carlo mumbled something about being sick. He ordered the startled man to take him back to the hotel, then to return for *don* Cesare and the Guappos. His uncle was going to be murderously furious at him for leaving like that, but at that moment Carlo simply did not care.

He stood alone in the suite, gazing through the polished glass walls that spread out the night glitter of Naples before him like a glistening magic carpet of vices. This was his domain, the world he and his uncle ruled through life and death. But the lights were garish, like carnival neon. The world had turned to ashes on his tongue, to gunmetal at the back of his throat. He felt as if the forces of the universe were swirling around him, demons were howling at him.

He threw open the door to his bedroom and made straight for the sideboard, where the whiskey bottle and glasses had been set. He uncapped the bourbon and drank it straight, letting the fire of the alcohol burn down his throat to quench the other fires that were boiling up in his soul.

After a moment the horror was somewhat dampened. Carlo shook his head to clear it, wondering at the madness of his sudden mood. He glanced over to the phone at the side of his bed. The red message light was blinking. Something was up.

164

He had settled down enough now to pour his next shot of whiskey into a water glass. He drained it, poured another, then picked up the telephone and dialed the front desk. He waited while the operator put him through to Sicily, then he listened to the terse, clipped words of the man who handled his messages.

Peter Natale had tried to contact him and had asked him to call back right away. "On a matter of utmost urgency," the messenger said.

At that moment Carlo could think of no one he'd rather talk to than Pietro Natale. He quickly dialed Peter's home phone number in Naples and let the phone ring ten times. Then he hung up and tried the private number Peter had given him at Naples station. This time the phone was answered.

"Prego. Pizzerie di Cefalu."

Carlo said the appropriate words, then hung up. He had drained another half glass of whiskey and was just beginning to truly regret leaving the lodge—though the regret was actually because of what he was going to have to put up with from his uncle—when the phone rang.

"Ciao."

Peter Natale said, "Your phone clear?"

"Always," said Carlo. He was surprised at how pleased he was to hear Natale's voice and by how quickly his message had been relayed to wherever Pietro had been.

Peter immediately got to the point. Judith was missing. He gave a brief summary of as much of the rest of the situation as he could offer without breaching security. Then he asked Carlo for help.

Carlo remembered Judith from when she'd worked out of Naples station. He'd also met her again in Moscow last year. He liked her, he was willing to help, but most of all he was relieved to have something to take his mind off the lingering scent of sulfur that had followed him from the lodge.

He asked a few clipped questions, got a bit more information from Peter, then he said, "I'll get my people on this right away."

"Thanks, Carlo. I owe you big time on this one."

"Forget about it. What are friends for?" Carlo could hear his own voice getting fuzzy from the whiskey. "I mean it, *paisano*. Don't worry about it. If she's anywhere at all, we'll find her."

But after Natale hung up, Carlo thought about *don* Cesare's hatred of the CIA man and how he would react if he knew the family resources were once again being used—with no recompense—by the CIA.

He could help Peter. His connections spanned Europe and the rest of the world. And when the Mafia wanted to find a person, no one could hide—a fact attested to by thousands of graves around the globe. But he was going to have to handle this slowly and carefully. Otherwise he would invite even more wrath from his ever-contentious uncle. And he already had all the pressure he could handle from that direction.

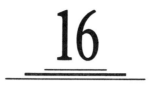

16

Innsbruck

Many of Europe's most beautiful cities originated as Roman forts during the Empire's conquest of what is now Western Europe. Among these was the quaint Austrian city of Innsbruck, a rough-cut jewel cupped in the sheltering hands of the jagged die Zweitausender Alps. Here Judith Davies stood on a wrought-iron balcony as the violet, velvet promise of first dawn wrapped around her like a cloak, and she watched the city begin to stir against the coming day.

Judith had indeed disembarked from her Moscow flight during its short layover in Milano. She spent the first night in a small hotel near the airport, worrying for hours about whether or not she was doing the right thing.

Half a dozen times she picked up the telephone, wanting to contact either Teddy Frost or Peter. But each time a gentle, invisible hand seemed to stop her—just as, in midflight, a silent, near-imperceptible voice told her to get off the plane in Milano, something was wrong, desperately wrong, and there was something she needed to do.

She tried to ignore the impulse, but almost involuntarily she found herself departing the plane during the fifteen-minute layover, leaving her luggage and even her overnight bag aboard and questioning her sanity with every step she took.

Fortunately she had adequate cash in her handbag to rent a cheap hotel room. The next morning she arrived at the Milanese branch of Eurobank as soon as it opened. She took the ecu equivalent of US $5,000 out of her savings account so she wouldn't have to use the easily tracked and computerized smart cards everyone carried these days.

Then she went to a beauty shop and had her honey-blonde hair cropped off stylishly short and lightened to a Scandinavian white-blonde hue. The hairdo made her Mediterranean tan seem more golden, her smoky-blue eyes even wider and more pronounced. But that couldn't be helped. She had no time to obtain colored contact lenses.

The disguise was superficial at best. She still carried her own identification. She would have to do better if she was going to escape the CIA's wide net, for it would be just a matter of time before Frost and Peter attempted to track her down. And she knew—irrationally—that she couldn't let that happen.

Judith was still uncertain about what she was doing. Whatever was happening to her had its seed in the tragic assassination that had occurred in Peter Natale's room at the Hotel de Mer. She had at least figured out that much. Though now that she thought about it again in the clear, cold violet light of the coming day, she realized that the incident had actually begun earlier that afternoon.

Rudy Brandenburg. Yes, she had known the young man, at least for a few hours. She had met him that same afternoon, and she regretted with every fiber of her being that she had not trusted him enough to at least listen carefully to what he said. She knew now that he had been fighting for his life. He had come to her as perhaps a last source of help. And she almost laughed out loud at him. She bit her lip, hard, and felt a flood of shame.

Like Peter, she had been annoyed when Frost interrupted their well-deserved vacation and asked them to go to Monte Carlo. But she had agreed with him that Frost wouldn't have asked unless he felt that it was vitally important. Plus, the extra week's vacation was a good trade-off, and so they'd gone.

She was aware of Frost's growing fascination with the ancient order called the Black Nobility, and she would have considered that fascination odd except that he placed it within the context of the dark growing fascism that was sweeping Europe. Any manifestation of fascism was a legitimate—even a primary—concern for any CIA operative, and if it took the form of some obscure, even occultic, order, so be it.

As Frost's chief intelligence analyst, she'd been asked to comb through musty documents, to trace certain allegations and legends about the Black Nobility through the various royal houses and even through the lineage of the tsars of Russia.

It was no surprise that so many nobles were drawn to fascism. Fascism was born from elitism, and most nobles were nothing if not elitists. At the same time, Judith was relieved to learn that many members of the old noble houses of Europe had adjusted quite well to their present common lives and leaned no more toward fascism than did any other group.

Still, her charts and trees and computer models were beginning to provide evidence that Frost's theory of a Black Nobility fomenting some kind of power grab was accurate. It seemed to Judith that the current Black Nobility was buried within a lodge, and this lodge had ancient roots: some obscure writings placed a Black Nobility within an ancient Roman order known as Caput Mundi.

She reported this to Frost, but suddenly his attention shifted back to his old nemesis—the mole within the CIA.

Judith was used to these sudden shifts. Frost grew obsessed with everything he did. He was a pure perfectionist. He advised her to start poring over the old files and documents that had been left over from Cold War days, when the mole Grimes had penetrated Moscow station. He locked himself away for a week or so with other files, refusing to see anyone. When he came out he was furious and had already been packing his bags for his confrontation with Langley's espiocrats.

Judith didn't understand it all. She had learned to stay out of Frost's way when he got like this. Anyway, she was burned out, for a lot of reasons, and when Frost suggested that now might be a good time for her to go to Nice and take that vacation she'd been planning with Peter, she truly thought it was a gesture of kindness. He even found and paid for their villa, telling her it was a bonus for work well done. He told her that when he came back from Langley —*if* he came back—they were going to be very busy. If she wanted to get away, she'd better go now.

She hadn't suspected a setup until Frost sent a messenger to them on their fifth day at the villa and asked them to go to Monte Carlo. When she learned that the surveillance target was Prince Dante di Veresi, a man whose paper trail she'd been chasing for several weeks, she was certain that Frost had sent her to the Côte d' Azur for his own purposes, and she in turn was furious.

Nevertheless she was mildly interested the first time she actually saw the prince and also found his mistress interesting, if dissipated. But the novelty wore off quickly. After several hours of pretending to gamble, chat, and otherwise circulate inside the private casino's rooms, Judith decided that the prince and *contessa* were impossible, the surveillance monotonous and almost unbearable. She could manage to stick with it only because of the promise that she and Peter could soon return to their lovely little villa on the perfect hillside above Nice.

The trouble started on the second day. She awakened to a swift surge of anxiety followed by a dark mist of oppression that stayed with her and made her alternately snap at Peter, then treat him to a frozen silence.

She attributed the irritation to her anger at Frost, coupled with Peter's profound courtesy and constant attentiveness. After two years on her own she was no longer comfortable with so much attention, and she was also having a lot of trouble with her feelings for Peter, a problem that reduced to a growing confusion.

She felt as if a spiritual war was being fought within her. The old war between good and evil. On the one hand she appreciated Peter, appreciated his efforts, his constant concern—his love, for he did love her. There was no other word for it.

On the other hand, she was determined not to return to the old destructive relationship they had once had, and, by being with him so much, she felt as if she were slipping away from the only true joy and peace she had ever known, a blessing she had found as part of her commitment to Jesus Christ.

She felt sure that there was no way she could have both Peter and this wonderful spiritual purity, especially since their former physical relationship had been forged as much in anger and despair as in love. And yet she wanted the intimacy they'd once had. The passionate times, yes, but mostly the quiet times, the sense of belonging fully to someone, the possibility of marriage and a family, of a normal life someday.

Finally, about two o'clock, her mood turned fully black, and she told Peter that she needed to get away from the cold, glitzy patina of the guests at the Hotel de Mer—a truth but not all of the truth. She mostly wanted a break from him—or so she thought. She felt as if she were suffocating.

She went for a solitary walk in the Romanesque garden, a morass of tangled greenery and white marble statuary with broken torsos, busts with chipped noses and missing arms and hands, all relics of classical Rome and all nestled like wonderful surprises within the shrubbery and leaves and trees. The gardens at Hotel de Mer were seldom used. The guests were either in the casino or on the beach below. So she found herself alone. The trees enveloped her, the birdsong soothed her, and the perfume of the pastel roses enchanted her and relaxed her mood so that she sat on a bench for a long time and soaked up the warm afternoon and prayed for patience and for guidance.

Feeling rejuvenated, she started up the leafy pathway back toward the hotel. She paused to appreciate an ivy-draped statue of a faun and was starting to walk toward a broken depiction of the mythological Roman twins, Romulus and Remus, when a young man stepped from behind a tree, startling her to an abrupt halt.

He dipped his head in apology. "I'm sorry, *Fraulein*. I didn't mean to frighten you."

He spoke English, with a hint of German accent. She would have known he was Germanic at any rate, just from his thin, poetic face and coloring. She thought he looked very young, no more than twenty-five. He was about a foot taller than she and dressed casually in black denims and a black short-sleeved T-shirt. His eyes were a pleasant deep blue, his hair was thick, rich corn silk, but there was such an expression of intensity on his face, even though he was trying to be charming, that she instantly knew he had been waiting for her.

The signals she picked up were mixed. On the one hand, he seemed young and innocent as he stood there flashing an embarrassed and cordial grin. However, she also sensed a gloss of danger that seemed to hang over him like an invisible cloak, so that her initial alarm grew more intense.

"I'm in a hurry," she said and started to step around him.

He moved forward to fully block the narrow path.

"I've been following you and watching you." His eyes still watched her. "Since you left the lobby of the hotel."

She frowned and wondered if he was going to try to pick her up. Still, curiosity prevailed over caution. "Why?"

"I have something you want." He glanced around, as if making sure they were still alone.

She felt the blood rush to her face, and she became more suspicious. "Really. And what is that?"

"Gold," he said, and as he gazed fully into her eyes, she saw a flat, cold deadness that made her think of a circling shark.

She wondered for an instant if he thought she was a prostitute. But surely not. This was not a place for that sort of assignation. And then she wondered if he was a rapist or perhaps was otherwise disturbed and capable of violence. She glanced around, looking for a means of escape, but the foliage was thick here, and once she left the path she'd be far more vulnerable than she was now. She decided confrontation would be the best strategy after all. "Why would I be in this garden looking for gold?" she said with a forced smile. "People looking for gold stay in the casino."

His eyes narrowed with annoyance. He studied her for a moment as if making up his mind about something, then he said, "You'd best be careful in gardens. I've heard certain reptiles like to hide in them."

She was struck speechless by the oddness of the comment.

"But I'm forgetting my manners. Let me introduce myself. My name is Rudy Brandenburg." He bowed with a little flourish.

"As in the Royal House of Brandenburg?" She managed to keep the amusement out of her voice, nevertheless she was instantly certain that she finally had him pegged. She'd been targeted as a potential victim by one of the numerous frauds and gigolos who worked the fringes of the casinos.

"As a matter of fact, I *am* a member of the Royal House," the young man said with irritation.

Something in his eyes kept Judith from pursuing the point. She said, "And?"

"You and I have mutual friends."

"Who?" Judith didn't like this at all.

His smile was bitter. "Secret friends in very high places," he said. "People who apparently like gold a great deal better than you do." His voice seethed with contempt.

She hid a shiver as a sudden thought struck her. Was this going to be an attempt to recruit her to work as a double agent for some as-yet-undisclosed intelligence service? Since the end of the Cold War, such recruitment activity had dwindled to a mere trickle. The Russians were no longer spending millions to co-opt spies. But there were still enemy services who tried to penetrate the CIA, and even offers to work for services that professed to be friends.

She started to tell him she didn't understand what he was talking about, but something in his eyes told her it would do no good. He really did know something about her work.

"Gold buys reptiles," he said. He was watching her closely, as if he didn't want to miss so much as a flick of an eyelash.

"I—I really don't understand."

"I'm sure you don't. If you did, you wouldn't be wandering around gardens alone."

"This place is perfectly safe," she said defensively.

"You're wrong. This is a very dangerous place." He paused and reflected, "I believe a recent director of the organization you serve said that your country had slain the dragon, only to find that the world is now filled with a bewildering variety of poisonous snakes."

Judith recognized the paraphrased words of one-time CIA Director James Woolsey. She felt a chill. This young man indeed knew who she was and what she did.

His eyes grew flatter, colder. "I have some information for you. That's why I've been following you. I want to tell you that the dragon has come back to life, and he's busily buying up the reptiles and training them to his ends."

"What exactly do you mean by 'reptiles'?" The British secret service informally referred to moles and other enemy agents as 'reptiles.'

"There are reptiles everyplace, even in your own cloistered garden. In fact, especially in your own garden—and very close to you."

She was beginning to feel spooked.

He appeared to be getting edgy too. He glanced around again, and a look of anxiety crept into his face. "I have to get back."

Judith felt relieved.

"People are waiting for me. But promise me, don't tell anyone—no one at all—that I talked to you." And suddenly his eyes were naked with apprehension.

The abrupt vulnerability was so unexpected that she involuntarily lifted her arms, as if to catch someone who was about to fall off a cliff.

He stepped back. "Promise me."

She dropped her arms helplessly and nodded.

He glanced over his shoulder, then turned back to face her. He seemed to have made a decision about something. "I used to do some contract work for the CIA in Berlin, before they cut back their staff."

"You shouldn't be telling me this. I'm an analyst now. That's classified for Berlin only."

He ignored her. "I'm no longer affiliated with Berlin. You can check on me with the EIA's Bonn station. Dennis Kreidler. Call him, ask if you can trust Rudy Brandenburg."

"I don't know him personally. How do I know if I can trust *him?*"

He just stared at her.

"Anyway, why don't you go to him with your information? Why are you approaching me?"

"Because you're here, and he isn't."

"Then tell me what you want! You don't have to talk so cryptically."

He stared into her eyes, as if looking for something. "You are a Christian, right?"

She was taken aback. How would he know that? Then she remembered the small gold cross around her neck. She touched it and nodded.

"Then promise me in the name of God that you will never tell anyone what I have said to you here today."

She felt a stubborn frown come to her face. "You haven't said anything I could understand anyway."

"You will understand," he said. "I'm risking my life at this very moment by being here, and I'm telling you as much as you need to know."

"Then I'm going to leave here knowing no more than I did when I came in. Why don't you just get to the point?"

He nodded, as though to himself. "First, promise before the God you believe in."

She found herself promising. The man was so persistent and determined that she felt a need to placate him.

"I don't think you'll believe me until you have more evidence," he said.

"Try me."

He studied her, then shook his head as if expecting the worst. "Very well, I will tell you. I know what happened to the Red Gold."

Judith had all she could do to stifle a snort of disbelief. She couldn't count how many scams had been built around the "Red Gold" that had vanished out of the Moscow Central Bank vaults during the transition from Soviet to Russian rule. Every criminal and con man on the face of the planet knew the story, every intelligence operative on earth had searched diligently for the gold for the better part of three years, but it was missing still, probably melted down and lost in the multitrillion-dollar global economy. She was once again convinced that she'd run into a con man, though a first-class one, she had to admit.

"I saw you and your partner in the casino. I know who he is."

A surge of alarm washed away the amusement.

"You're watching the prince," he said. "You're looking in the right place."

"Look—I don't care about any Red Gold. I'm here on vacation, and I have to go."

"I know it sounds incredible, but I swear on my life that it's true. Come back tonight, and I can prove it."

"I'm afraid I have plans." She and Peter were going to be watching Veresi and his mistress as they compulsively gambled the night and their lives away.

As she tried again to step around him, a stricken, even frightened look came into his eyes, so that she wondered for an instant if she was missing something here, something immensely important.

At that awkward moment a pair of young lovers—honeymooners by the look of them—strolled into view. Rudy Brandenburg wrapped even tighter, his fists actually knotted. He looked at them almost confrontationally, then before Judith could say another word he leveled one long, scrutinizing look at her, mouthed the words *Be here, seven o'clock*, then spun on his heels and strode down a path that let him avoid the approaching lovers.

She thought about following him and demanding to know just how stupid he thought she really was—and how much money he'd thought he could extort from her in order to feed her yet another fanciful story about the US $256 billion in pirated Red Gold.

As Judith walked slowly back to the hotel, the encounter began to seem more and more surreal. She finally decided to write it off as a bad experience but nothing to really worry about. It happened sometimes that you were recognized, and perhaps the young man had really been an agent. Or maybe he'd been at the embassy in Moscow at one time or another.

Still, the more she thought about it, the more curious she became. By 5:00 P.M. she'd actually decided to return to the garden at 7:00 in order to quiz the young man further. But at about 6:30 the prince and his mistress became especially busy at the gaming tables. They lost perhaps a quarter of a million dollars in one fell swoop. By the time she was able to break away, it was well after 8:00—too late to meet the troubled young man.

She and Peter watched Veresi and his mistress gambling until well after midnight. But throughout the evening, the encounter with Rudy Brandenburg haunted her. Later, when she and Peter were walking on the waterfront, she started to tell him about the incident. But he chose just that moment to propose marriage!

She returned to her room to fret and toss and turn, till she finally got up, put on her robe, brushed her hair, and sat reading her Bible.

The gunshots exploded her meditation. She rushed to Peter's room—and there on his floor was the body of the young man who had identified himself as Rudy Brandenburg.

In that scalding moment she knew that she'd made a serious mistake in judgment. If only she'd read the situation correctly, she might have saved the young man's life.

Now, standing on the balcony in Innsbruck, watching the first faint etchings of gold melt into the violet sky, Judith shivered and wrapped her arms around herself. She had thought of little other than Rudy's words ever since he'd died, and now she was beginning to realize that it might be true that he had actually discovered something about the Red Gold.

But if that was true, she didn't know what to do. She'd wanted to talk to Peter, but something immovable had stopped her tongue each time she started to speak. She'd wanted to tell Teddy Frost when she talked to him on the telephone, but the same strange thing had happened.

And then, when she'd been flying back to Moscow, the small silent voice had instructed her, and she'd found herself in Milano, disguising herself as much as was possible and trying to understand whether or not she was going mad.

After getting her hair cut and dyed, she rented a car, using her credit card. A plane ticket was easy to trace, though even use of a card would soon be tracked down by Frost's people. But something told her that she needed to fly solo for a while. Frost, Peter, nobody could help her just now. Only God Himself.

She left Milano in the heavy flow of traffic that streamed northward at yesterday's end. She drove across the Brenner pass late last night, past the fortifications and monuments, through the towering mountains, and finally across the long Europa Bridge that ushered her into Austria and to Innsbruck.

Now she was here, inside this narrow red-brick hotel with its Gothic facade, on the Maria Theresien Strasse in the center of town.

She watched the sun painting gold into the morning and looked once again at her watch. At nine o'clock the shops would open. Then she could contact Seigfried Shaver, the old freelance forger who had once created perfect identification kits for agents of all nationalities and political bents during the heaviest days of the Cold War. She knew he was still in Innsbruck, still in business at his small jewelry engraving shop.

She gazed out over the awakening city. She thought about the miles and endless miles she had traveled to get here, the years of despair in Naples station, the growing problems in her relationship with Peter, her new posting in Moscow and the wonderful spiritual renewal she'd found there as she'd learned to trust God.

She knew now that, even though she didn't understand what was happening, her encounter with Rudy Brandenburg had been more than an act of serendipity. In fact, on the basis of the steady, guiding hand she seemed to feel pressing her forward, ever forward, she was beginning to think the encounter might have even been an act of providence.

17

Berlin

Berlin's present chief of station, Wilhelm von Wolverton—Willie —stood up, surprised, as Peter Natale entered his office.

"Peter, good to see you again." Though Wolverton was of American-German descent, his eighteen years in West Germany had left him with the hint of a German accent. He smiled and extended his hand for a shake.

"My pleasure." Natale returned the courtesy. "Sorry to drop in on you like this."

"No, really, it is good to see you."

Natale grinned and sat down on a gray-leather chair. "Nice office." The new embassy complex had been finished within the last year and had cost the American taxpayers a small fortune. Wolverton's office was all dark polished wood with a wine-colored Persian carpet and expensive new furniture.

"Yes, they're treating us well these days."

"The DO still in town?"

"Hammond? He's off having lunch with one of his relatives, I'm afraid. Did you need to see him?"

"Needed not to, if I have a choice."

Wolverton nodded judiciously. "He's not really angry, you know. He understands that Rudy's death wasn't your fault. But he's going to be furious if someone doesn't soon figure out who killed the young man, and why."

"Yes, well, I'm working on it, but without much luck."

"Still, you might have let us know you were coming."

"You knew."

Wolverton smiled dryly. "Yes, I suppose I did know you'd

be here to try to clean up the aftermath of Kaleidoscope. I'm sorry about your informants, Peter. That's always hard. But great scot, what do you expect? These Mafia arms and drug runners are spreading out across Europe like a storm of biblical locusts! Look at it, man! Do you actually think you and a few German cops are going to stop them?"

"We have to try."

"Yes, I respect that about you. No matter how bad the odds, you never quit trying."

Peter was mildly surprised by the left-handed compliment. He always felt that Wolverton was a threat to him, and that feeling was very much with him right now.

Not that the man's appearance was in any way menacing. Wolverton's blue eyes were bleary behind his bifocals, his colorless hair was thinning, his face was long and sorrowful, and his brown suit rumpled and ill-fitting. But Natale knew from both personal experience and rumor that Wolverton was merciless and unscrupulous when it came to getting what he wanted. Because of this he had managed, at one time or another, to alienate every potential ally within the German and Russian intelligence communities.

And that was one reason Natale had kept Operation Kaleidoscope at arms' length from this CIA station. Wolverton hadn't known much of what was actually happening until well after the arrests were made. It was also why he was going to make this a quick, obligatory courtesy visit. Then he'd cut out and contact the German intelligence operatives who'd put their lives on the line in order to help him crack open Kaleidoscope.

"I ran into Paul Kurtz yesterday," Wolverton said with a contemptuous sneer. Kurtz was the key German case agent on Kaleidoscope, and Wolverton had disliked him since Cold War days. "They've made a proper mess of things. Apparently Harald Rupert has stopped talking and is changing his story about the others he's already implicated."

"I wouldn't be surprised. With Fritz and Eva dead, Rupert stands a far better chance of beating the charges. We don't have much left to bargain with."

"Maybe the Germans will barter with his son's charges. They wrapped him up pretty good."

"Maybe. But as far as I'm concerned, the whole operation is pretty much blown. The Germans should have had Fritz and Eva in protective custody, but I guess they refused to go."

"It's the money," Wolverton said smugly. "Those kinds of people would rather die than miss a red cent."

Natale ignored the comment. "I'll get all the gruesome details soon enough. I'm meeting Kurtz in half an hour. In the meantime"—he offered a cordial smile—"I'd appreciate a little more information on Hammond's cousin."

Wolverton blinked. "I thought the files had all been sent to Naples station."

"They hadn't arrived by the time I left. Anyway, I want the information that isn't in the files. The speculation, innuendo, and dirt. After all, if I don't get this thing straightened out, I'm out of a job." He didn't add that the information might also help him understand what was happening with Kaleidoscope.

Wolverton checked his watch. "I have a conference in about five minutes. But we're having a dinner for Hammond tonight. He goes back to Langley tomorrow. Why don't you drop by the ambassador's residence, and we can talk then."

"I really need to work things out with Kurtz."

"Yes, well, if you don't want to smooth things out with Hammond, if you really want him going back to Langley to arrange for your head to arrive shortly thereafter . . . on a block . . ."

"I'm not much in a mood to kowtow," Natale said with a flash of temper.

"I'll pass that along." Wolverton was suddenly haughty.

"Look, I didn't mean to imply that you do. Kowtow, that is. It's just that I'm catching an evening plane back to Naples." Peter forced himself to calm down. "I just dropped by to say hello to you, and I don't want to deal with Hammond right now."

Wolverton appeared to be placated. He stood and walked Natale across the rich carpet to the door, shook his hand again, and said, "Well, if you miss your plane or change your mind, dinner starts at seven, cocktails and conversation around nine. Wear a jacket."

"Thanks. But I do need to get back."

18

Berlin

Yuri Lepkov set his glass of slivovitz on the pink marble mantle-piece in his bedroom, then peered once again into the full-length gilt-edged mirror. He admired the granite directness of his gaze, the clean-shaven Slavic contours of his face, the way his hair was graying in a distinguished manner in spite of the fact that it continued to recede. Perhaps someday he would indulge in a hair transplant, when he had a bit more time. At the moment, he was fully absorbed by the intoxicating power game he was orchestrating. He had no time to indulge his conceit.

He stepped back and admired the cut of his new black suit, then nodded with satisfaction. In his role as Russian/German businessman, he had of course been invited to the US ambassador's informal dinner. He made it a point to always be the picture of affluence and success. A wunderkind, the German financiers called him. Especially the ones who reaped the largesse of his money-laundering schemes for the Russian, Sicilian, and Colombian Mafias.

He glanced at his watch. He had almost an hour, just enough time to catch the antics of his most important tamed politician. His wife was dressing in her own suite. He stepped out of the new suit and hung it on a padded hanger, then hastily pulled on a royal-blue silk robe over his sleeveless undershirt and boxer shorts. He picked up his vodka and sank onto the gold-and-white satin divan, then clicked on the television remote, which was tuned to the EuroNews Network, ENN.

As the screen faded from black, a wide shot of the newly built EU Ministers' building in Brussels appeared. It was a ten-story, crescent-shaped, white marble structure fronted by classic

Roman pillars and tall flagpoles. The building, driveways, and walkways were already ablaze with light, though dusk was just settling over the city. The EU flag, displaying a circle of golden stars against a royal blue background, flew in the central place of honor, flanked by the banners of the EU member nations, which rippled in a light evening breeze.

Classical music played in the TV background—Lepkov recognized it as Brahms. A cultivated female voice-over was explaining that the European Union's Council of Ministers was now in session, and the key evening speaker would be Count Benito Jacovetti, the Italian minister of finance, who would be addressing the Council momentarily.

Lepkov smiled cruelly. He had his hands on the invisible strings that moved this Roman puppet, even from a thousand miles away. He thought about how incredibly easy it had been to deceive, then corrupt, the man. How easy it was to corrupt anyone when you had unlimited connections and resources.

His smile deepened. He recalled the reputed words of some earlier political figure: "What we want is a man of sufficient stature to hold the allegiance of all people and to lift us out of the economic morass into which we are sinking. Send us such a man and be he god or devil, we will receive him."

During his years in the KGB, he had been more and more amazed by the Western mind-set; by the Americans' foolish belief that their puny two-hundred-year-old republic had always existed and would always exist; by the total ignorance most of them and the Europeans displayed with regard to the rest of the world.

The CIA mole Grimes was a perfect example of Western ignorance, indifference, and ineptitude. Though Lepkov had never controlled Grimes, he had benefited more than once from information Grimes had delivered to the KGB. For years everything the Americans did was relayed back to the KGB, and it had taken Langley sixteen long years to catch the man. They still hadn't caught Grimes's twin viper, who was coiled tightly in the middle of the American spies' nest at this very moment, serving the enemy still.

Lepkov chuckled. He, of course, was still the enemy. How could he help himself? With such people, dominance was inevitable. It was only a matter of time. And so it was too with the European Union. The massive, still-growing bureaucracy had become so ingrown and convoluted that the power structure was fair game for all.

His eyes grazed over the picture on the television screen. He had no god on hand to deliver up to the world, but he would happily send them a devil. And a fool and buffoon, for Count Benito Jacovetti had sold his soul in order to dangle forever on someone else's hook.

The purchase of the count had set Lepkov's reptile fund back almost $100 million, by the time he'd added in all the peripheral expenses, including a couple of murders that had taken key political rivals out of the way. There had also been the sky-rocketing cost of laundering the pilfered gold into usable cash.

Still, for that price Lepkov had bought the central seat of power in the Europe Union—assuming Jacovetti indeed won the presidential appointment. But with Volante Chicarelli out of the way, that appointment was an ironclad certainty.

And Chicarelli was weakening by the day. Marco said the old man was pleading with them now when they called to taunt him about his kidnapped son. Lepkov had decided to hang onto the boy until the presidential appointment next week, and by then Volante Chicarelli would be a quivering, incapable mass of fear who would easily yield the appointment to Jacovetti.

It was a nuisance, though, overseeing Marco in this matter and keeping track of what was going on. He initially wanted to just kill Volante and have done with the problem, but there was always public sentiment to be considered. A murder might have backfired.

Besides, Chicarelli would stay in the Italian parliament and might be useful someday in other ways. He had followed Lepkov's orders not to divulge the kidnapping to anyone—except *don* Cesare, of course. That had been inevitable. Still, with no news of the kidnapping hitting the news media, it would be simple to claim that Chicarelli had simply bowed out of contention for health reasons. Jacovetti would be the only possible replacement. Perfect, so far.

There could still be problems with *don* Cesare Ricaso if he found out he had been played for a fool. That was the only potential flaw in the plan. But for once the wily old capo seemed incapable of finding the boy. In fact, Cesare had actually contacted Lepkov—covertly, of course—and asked him to keep an eye out in Germany for the lad. Incredible, how easy it was becoming to deceive these men. If Lepkov believed in such things, he'd almost say that some supernatural power was clearing the way and giving him wings.

The TV caught his eye as the scene cut to the interior of the Ministry. The great auditorium reminded him of the Kremlin's Hall of Congresses, right down to the thousands of padded seats in a tiered, semicircular pattern. Every seat was filled tonight with men in black suits and women in tasteful dresses.

The vast backdrop behind the podium displayed a giant mural of Europa, the beautiful, mythical Grecian goddess who was the namesake of the continent and the Union. She was draped in white, riding sideways on a beautiful scarlet beast, a bull with curly ringlets, who represented the god Zeus. The entire montage was set within the circle of golden stars that represented the EU member nations, against the same royal-blue background as the EU flag.

Lepkov was familiar with the Europa symbol only because of the parliamentary debate when the emblem had been chosen to adorn the EU's currency. Soon all currency would be obsolete anyway, as ID microchip implants replaced both bankcards and hard assets.

Unfortunately, cash was still the blood that pumped through the criminal milieu's veins to keep the Octopus and all its affiliate tentacles healthy and viable. The looming threat of a global cashless society made it all the more essential that the EU's laws remain loose, the central banks permeable, if the various Mafias and facilitators such as Lepkov were to stay in business. The only certain way to make this occur was to control whoever ran the government.

Lepkov leaned back and sipped his vodka. One man could make the difference. History had proved that time and time again. All great dictators had ruled single-handedly, though of course they'd used many others to achieve their aims. Lepkov felt certain that, under his keen eye and steady hand, the man who would be the next president of Europe would deliver an equal amount of power, once he sat firmly upon the quasi-throne.

Lepkov needed to steer certain edicts through the newly emergent EU. He took a vast gulp of vodka as he thought about that, and a rare current of uncertainty surged through him.

The EU central government's grip on the money supply was tightening. There was even talk of making private possession of gold illegal. If that law were enacted, the value of Lepkov's trove of Red Gold would take a nosedive. That was yet another reason that he needed to pull the strings within the central government.

He had easily helped friends in the KGB and Politburo plunder tons of Red Gold from the Soviet vaults during the collapse of Communism. The trouble had started only after he had the gold in hand, for what could you do with such a vast amount of precious metal, all of it minted with a special chemical signature that made it impossible to pass it off as anything but Red Gold?

Every policeman, every intelligence operative had been after the gold as soon as it was declared missing. He'd quickly buried his share, fortunately. He'd kept most of it on ice, had scarcely touched it, due to the difficulties of laundering such a vast amount. He was almost discovered just last year when he tried to move a few thousand bars past the Central Bullion Clearinghouse at the EU Central Bank, the only way to get it out of Europe. He considered using the Colombian Mafia's South American banks to launder it—but they would take a vast amount as a laundering fee, and they would also know then that he had it.

He cursed. It was humiliating. Though he was the most skillful money launderer in all of Europe, his own financial reserves still sat in half a dozen potentially leaky bank vaults, from Berlin to Brussels to Luxembourg to Zurich to Monte Carlo to Milano, while he was forced to resort to the archaic tactic of having the Red Gold laundered here and there, a few scant bars at a time.

There was other income, of course, but expenses were phenomenal. He had just invested half a billion in a new shopping center in central Berlin, and the hotel in Baden Baden had cost $100 million. It hadn't been that easy to come up with another

$100 million to finance Jacovetti, even considering the substantial proceeds from the traffic in heroin, cocaine, and nuclear materials.

There were many other expenses, many things going wrong. The recent disruption of the end of the pipeline handled by Harald Rupert had cost Lepkov more than $10 million just this month. And then yesterday Rupert's peculiar son had brought one more shipment through—and he'd been busted as well!

Lepkov was insulated from the actual trafficking, of course, but he'd had to have Marco come in to eliminate the informants anyway, once his CIA source told him who they were. He was also going to have to take care of Harald Rupert and his eccentric son as soon as they were accessible. They were the only ones who could link that network to him, and yesterday's incident proved they were too stupid to be allowed to live.

Fortunately the Ricaso crime family had bought the Hotel de Mer in order to use the casino as a laundry, and they encouraged Lepkov to rinse their end of the Russian heroin and cocaine money by simply sending couriers to the hotel to lose it at the gaming tables. He was moving ten or twenty bars of gold with each delivery, along with a few pounds of gold coins. He paid off the manager who oversaw the laundering, and the man now traded small amounts of the Red Gold for gambling chips, which were then turned into cash at the end of a gaming day.

Lepkov smiled as he thought about what he was doing. The seeds of his financial skills had come from *don* Cesare himself, back when the greedy mobster had contracted with KINTEX to supply morphine base to Sicilian labs. Lepkov had learned a great deal about the administration of iron-backed power from the KGB, but he had learned everything he knew about gold-backed power from the Mafia. *Don* Cesare had taught him precisely what he needed to know in order to usurp any amount of power from the shrewd old Mafioso.

Prince Veresi and his fascist minions also used the Hotel de Mer's casino to pass the laundered assets on to the various reptiles who were working furiously underground to help bring Jacovetti to power. That was even more risky, and Lepkov disliked that end of the situation. Besides, the prince was a snob. He wanted Jacovetti in power because Jacovetti was a count. But the prince thought he was using Lepkov, rather than the other way around, and Lepkov resented the insult.

He thought of the two CIA operatives watching the prince at Hotel de Mer, and he felt a chill, then cursed. That woman . . . Judith Davies . . . all the way from Moscow.

Lepkov's attention snapped back to the television screen as Count Jacovetti stepped up to the podium in the Hall of Ministers. He knew the pulpit-shaped dais had been raised to accommodate the man's five-foot-six-inch frame, but the hard-faced old Italian cut a compelling presence in spite of his size.

He was strongly built and kept himself fit, though he looked pale and out of humor as he riffled the notes in his hand, a fact that made Lepkov frown. The man was nervous and high-strung at times, in keeping with his fanatical commitment to the fascist cause. He required careful tending, and Lepkov was constantly scanning for any signs of serious trouble.

Jacovetti looked up, and his satin-black eyes gleamed in the bright light. There was a heavy round of applause. He stood staring out at the audience, displaying the familiar forward thrust of his obstinate jaw. When the applause died down, he spoke.

"My fellow citizens of Europe and fellow architects of the New World Order. Since the Treaty of Rome was signed in 1957, the European Union has slowly been emerging as the key force in global power. We have been building a great *Pax* Romana that dwarfs the thousand-year Roman empire that once held Western Europe in its iron grip."

There was sudden, angry silence from the audience, then an occasional audible grumble and a buzzing, as people whispered their outrage to one another.

The shadow of Rome's former colonization of most of the EU member nations had been a point of contention among people who wanted to halt Italy's turn at the presidential seat. This president would be in a position to easily win the permanent elected position, and there was a strong lobby to put a German in office instead. That was why Lepkov's speech writer had suggested that Jacovetti address the issue up front, depriving his enemies of their ammunition.

Lepkov was pleased with the results so far. The use of the term *Pax Romana* was brilliant. The old Roman Empire had established their Peace of Rome over a vast empire that included most portions of the EU nations. Its unified government and singular set of laws had endured for centuries. Lepkov smiled. This new *Pax Romana* might just as easily be called a *Pax* Mafiosa, if one were to factor in Lepkov's link to the Octopus and the way its tentacles held so many of the EU power brokers by the throat.

"The ancient Roman Empire fell almost two millenniums ago," Jacovetti said. "As it should have. It was a brutal system, and we are fortunate that it is crushed beneath the ashes of the centuries, for no sane man would wish for such a world today."

Lepkov carefully watched the audience's response. Good. They thawed at that, almost visibly, and many of them were listening intently now.

Jacovetti spoke further about the New World Order and the flaws in the former Roman Empire and how fortunate they were to be able to build anew. Then he deftly changed the subject and began the voluminous acknowledgments required by protocol. There were brief smatterings of applause as he mentioned each minister who had accomplished anything of note within the past month.

Lepkov paid little attention to the words. He was studying Jacovetti's speaking ability. The man had a rounded, resounding voice, strong and clear, the kind of voice people listened to. And as he stood at the podium, a presence seemed to fill him. Lepkov thought that the lessons in oratory had paid off.

Next, the count went into a lengthy rhapsody about how great Europe was becoming. He especially complimented the newly appointed EU defense minister from Germany, who was singularly vociferous when it came to getting the Americans out of NATO so that the EuroCorp, centered on German troops, would be the only viable regional military power.

Good, thought Lepkov. *Pull someone else into the battle with us, plant some ideas, appeal to their European chauvinism.*

"We at last have the opportunity to establish a just and comprehensive order of peace in Europe—after these many centuries of bloody division," Jacovetti said. "We must do everything possible to make sure that order is not disrupted for the economic gain of any other alliance, whether they be enemy or friend. For though we are stronger by the day, the economic future of the European Union remains fragile and must be tended with care."

The United States had been trying to cut some trade deals favorable to themselves. Jacovetti had just skillfully suggested that the United States of America might be deliberately standing in the way of a fully integrated, prosperous, and peaceful Europe, and therefore their presence must be quashed.

He started talking about the trade issues facing Europe. But Lepkov tuned out and thought about his last private conversation with Jacovetti, a week ago. The man was a skilled actor, no doubt about it. Nobody who watched him tonight would have ever believed the fanatical commitment he had to fascism or his true ideas about mankind.

"The masses are herds of sheep," he'd told Lepkov.

The two men were walking along a leafy avenue near the EU headquarters. Lepkov had just hand-delivered a very large check in order to take Jacovetti's measure firsthand before tonight's speech.

"I do not so much dislike the masses as distrust them," Jacovetti continued. "They are completely incapable of ruling themselves."

Lepkov agreed.

"Any man who believes he can rule with kindness instead of an iron fist is in grave danger," Jacovetti went on. "A ruler must control the masses like a master artist, knowing every nuance, every breath of the political wind."

Lepkov wondered then if the man hadn't developed too much of a taste for power. He started to say something, but then decided he would give Jacovetti his head until after the election. Then he'd yank on the hook he'd put into the count's jaw.

Jacovetti said something to the audience that Lepkov missed, and suddenly the crowd was on its feet, cheering. Lepkov frowned and peered intently at the man. A close-up showed that his eyes had taken on a red, glassy light.

And then Jacovetti broke into a pyrogenic speech that Lepkov could scarcely believe. It was filled with the fascist rhetoric of every dictator who had ever bloodied the continent, and the audience was on its feet still, cheering, stomping, mad with delight, as

Jacovetti held up his arm, openly, in the stiff-armed salute made famous by Mussolini and by Hitler's brown-shirted throngs.

Lepkov froze in alarm. He'd never seen the man so animated, had never dreamed he could actually so control the masses he held in such contempt.

But just as quickly the diatribe was over, and Jacovetti became himself again, dignified, modest, telling the audience that he did not deserve such acclaim and thanking them for their attention. Then, with a bow, he left the podium, and the audience was still cheering.

Lepkov was confused. This had not been the scripted speech at all. He had the distinct feeling that something had slipped through his hands and that something was very, very wrong.

Before he could think the matter through, his private telephone rang. He lifted the receiver, still watching the television screen, his eyes slitted dangerously. "Yes?"

It was Wolverton from the CIA station, breathless with worry. "Yuri, you know Peter Natale? The Naples man I told you about, who originated the operation that brought down Harald Rupert's network?"

"Yes." Lepkov knew his phones were swept for bugs on a regular basis, but he was still uncomfortable talking on them.

"He's here," Wolverton said. "To check into Fritz and Eva Breugher's deaths."

"Why didn't you tell me he was coming?"

"I—I didn't know."

"Send him back to Naples," Lepkov demanded.

"I can't. You—you just don't do those things to Natale. And I don't know what else to do with him," Wolverton whined. "He's getting close. What if he finds out—"

"Shut up," said Lepkov. "I can't stand to listen to you anymore. I'll handle everything. Just shut your mouth and say no more."

He slammed down the phone. He wished Marco were still in town. He could always depend upon Marco. But things were never perfect. He thought for a moment, lifted the receiver again, spoke into it, then dropped it gently into the cradle, and shifted his eyes back to the television screen.

Jacovetti was gone, the Hall of Ministers was gone. The exterior shot of the EU building was back on the screen, though it was dark now and people were coming down the steps, leaving the meeting.

He looked at his watch, cursed, stood up, and grabbed his suit. He was going to be late for the US ambassador's dinner on top of everything else. Suddenly what had started off as a very good day indeed was not going well at all.

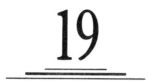

19

Berlin

"The operation sprang a leak," Kurtz said. "Nothing else makes sense." He wore an ominous frown as he paced back and forth in his small, simple office.

Natale stood beside the window listening intently, also too keyed up to sit down.

Joseph Kurtz was broad and easily five inches taller than Peter, which made him a huge man. His red-rimmed eyes were a perfect match for a craggy, florid face, and his unruly copper hair had the consistency of steel wool. He had been with the German intelligence networks for two perilous decades, and he was fond of telling Natale that intelligence work was more dangerous now than it had been during even the most evil depths of the Cold War.

"It's impossible to trust anyone now," he said, when Peter first offered to link up on Kaleidoscope. "But I'm going to make one exception and trust you."

Now Natale had brought the proud old spy into a corrupted operation. The two key informants had been murdered, the key trafficker had changed his mind about testifying, and half a dozen other nuclear black marketeers were soon going to walk if the situation didn't change.

"Where do you think the leak began?"

"It didn't come from our end." Kurtz barely managed to meet Natale's gaze before looking away in disgust.

Natale's first instinct was to defend himself and the CIA, but then he thought about Frost's mole. He knew that, in spite of his careful shepherding of the case, Wolverton, Hammond, and a few others in Langley had seen the portions of his reports that he had to submit to his superiors. Kutz's accusation could all too easily be true.

He asked, "Do you have a handle yet on who actually killed Eva and Fritz?"

"We do," Kurtz said bitterly. "But we aren't going to be able to go after them."

Natale knew he was referring to the Datenschutz law. Instrumented in the wake of the totalitarian rule of Adolph Hitler, Germany's basic privacy law was as strongly protective as any law in the world. Unfortunately, the same law that protected an honest citizen's privacy also protected the criminals. Germany's liberal laws were the key reason that the Sicilian Mafia had targeted Germany as a colony, and why they had been buying up and corrupting the country's infrastructure with ease for three profitable decades.

Some seventy thousand legitimate Italian workers lived in Germany, and the Italian/Sicilian criminals—whether heroin traffickers or hit squads—hid among them. Chains of Sicilian pizza parlors and restaurants had sprung up throughout the country like dragons' teeth. These were often fronts for Mafia business, usually extortion and heroin. In fact, in Germany they no longer called it the Sicilian Mafia—they called it the EuroMafia. Its tentacles had indeed grown long, and in Berlin they were especially entwined with those of a smaller yet equally deadly Octopus, the Russian Mafia.

"Maybe I can help," Natale offered. It was easier for him to work illegally than for the locals to break laws.

"It won't be easy."

Natale shrugged. "I'm still listening."

Kurtz studied him, as though trying to make up his mind about something, while Peter patiently waited. He understood the problem.

The German laws made it impossible for the German police —or spies—to use phone taps or any other form of covert surveillance against any citizen, even a suspected murderer. Extradition was equally difficult. Because of the diverse laws and remaining jealousies, it was impossible for law enforcers to cross the EU national borders to catch criminals. In most EU nations, money laundering was still legal. A known trafficker with a million dirty ecus or deutsche marks in his pocket could walk through customs with impunity.

Kurtz indeed had his hands tied.

"Look, Joseph. I know how you must feel right now. But I really might be able to help, if you'll let me."

The thorny German rubbed his eyes wearily with the heel of his hands. "I'm sorry, Peter. Dietrich tells me I can trust you, and there's no man in the world I respect more than him. But I must tell you, I've considered every possibility, and there's no place else a leak could have begun except within your organization."

"I'm willing to consider that possibility. We can talk off the record."

Kurtz nodded cynically. "Considering the way my own hands are tied, I don't have much choice. Very well. The assassin's name is Marco. That's all I know. He's apparently one of the Sicilian's *kanonenfutter*."

Natale recognized the term. It meant one of the throw-away workers the Sicilians sent north in order to do dirty jobs such as hits, arsons, and other criminal enterprise. The people had no intrinsic value to the Mafia, and therefore they could be terminated if they brought any heat home with them.

"We've learned that this Marco flew in from Naples and met with two local men who have not yet been identified. Apparently they committed the murders under Marco's direction, then Marco flew back to Naples."

"How do you know this?"

Kurtz looked uncomfortable. "I'd rather not share my sources at the moment."

Peter was offended, but at the same time he understood. "I know a hit man named Marco who works out of Naples," he explained. "And he's anything but cannon fodder. In fact, he's a blood-thirsty serial killer whose work is sanctioned by his father, Vincente Guappo, who just happens to be the head of the Neapolitan Camorra. Marco runs hit squads all over the Continent."

Kurtz raised his eyebrows. "So this links directly into Sicily."

"Exactly. *Don* Cesare Ricaso and Vincente Guappo are thick as thieves. Guappo is actually Cesare's lieutenant in charge of the Neapolitan territory these days."

He wasn't going to add that *don* Cesare's nephew and heir apparent had given him a great deal of the information that had helped them penetrate Kaleidoscope's pipelines. Such a bizarre statement would certainly destroy any shred of trust remaining.

Kurtz was frowning, thinking hard.

Peter said, "I'd like to hear what's on your mind."

"OK, look at it." Kurtz began to count the points off on his thick fingers. "We have the Russian traffickers connected to certain corrupted nuclear physicists the Russians have rounded up."

"The tip of the iceberg," Natale commented, "but at least the Russian police should still be able to put away a few of the people on their end."

"Here in Germany, we have Harald Rupert and his son, Hans. The main traffickers for this portion of the pipeline. We still have them in custody, along with a few of their subordinates."

"Right."

"That should have been the network. All the way to the top."

"Or so we thought."

"We stopped too soon."

"Exactly. We thought Rupert was the top dog, but someone was pulling his chain."

"And that person hired Marco to kill our informants."

"Exactly."

Kurtz paused, and the room was silent except for the sound of someone typing at a computer in an adjoining office. Finally, he said, "We stopped a shipment of a half kilo of uranium-235 yesterday in Baden-Wurttemberg. We've kept it out of the news. The shipment had the same footprints we found all the way through Kaleidoscope. Our analysts say it originated from the same Russian stockpiles, and it came through the same pipelines, though by way of a slightly different trafficking route."

Natale's felt as if something had clutched him by the throat. "Then that's it. Something a lot bigger is still out there."

Kurtz agreed.

Natale's shoulders sagged. "So—what now?"

"We'll have to start over. We can still try to convict Rupert and his people, but that's not going to happen. I think we just have to cut our losses and start all over again."

The sense of defeat in Kurtz's voice stayed with Natale as he left the building and climbed into his rented car. Now, driving toward Tegel Airport to catch his flight to Naples, he was still thinking about everything he and Kurtz had discussed, and his own sense of failure was enveloping him.

He veered out of the heavy traffic that plagued central Berlin and headed for the narrow side street that would get him past the worst of the logjam. He was driving fast. He'd spent far too long talking to Kurtz, trying to lift his spirits and put some hope back into the situation. He was going to miss his flight if he didn't hurry. He checked his watch and let his foot grow a little heavier on the gas pedal.

A brown Audi cut into the lane in front of him. He swerved into the next lane to avoid hitting the car, glanced at his speedometer, realized how fast he was driving, and grudgingly lifted his foot from the gas.

The Audi also slowed down, so that he came alongside and started to pass it. The car's windows were tinted a smoky gray; he couldn't see inside. That was fine. He and the driver had narrowly avoided what would have been a very nasty collision, and the driver was surely glaring.

Peter deliberately stared straight ahead and stepped on the gas again to move away, but the Audi speeded up to pace him. His shoulders heaved in resignation. What a time to bump into a driver who held a grudge.

He started to make a sharp left, planning to go around the block to break up the potential quarrel before it could escalate. But as he turned, the Audi accelerated and followed. Its tires screeched as it made the sudden turn with him.

Natale didn't realize what was happening until the dark-tinted window slid halfway down and a gun muzzle jutted out. Fear jolted him then, and he yanked the wheel to swerve out of the line of fire.

A barrage of machine-gun fire exploded. Suddenly the world was moving at the speed of light as shattered glass pierced his face and blood streamed into his eyes, almost blinding him. The rented Mercedes fishtailed, he was losing control, he saw the blur of the

Audi falling back. But before he could process what that meant, a building suddenly loomed directly ahead, and he realized the street was dead-ending in a T-intersection.

He had to lift his foot from the gas in order to make the sharp turn into the cross street, and the Audi caught up. It pulled alongside again, and the fenders of the two cars scraped in a scream of ripping metal.

Natale wiped his brow with the back of his hand so he could see what was happening. The blood was a thick sheet now, and he looked out just as the gun barrel came up again, an evil, black cylinder that seemed thick as his arm. His head jerked back and forth as he tried to find an escape, but the road was narrow, and there were no exits—only stacked red-brick apartment buildings on both sides.

The gun barrel was swinging back and forth too, as the trigger-german tried to fix him in his sights.

Natale prayed, eyes wide open, as the blood salted and stung his eyes and terror so gripped him by the throat that he could hardly breathe.

At that perfect instant, a green tour bus slowly rounded a corner, filling the narrow street. Peter was speeding straight at it, with the Audi right behind. The machine gun fired again, but the Audi's driver hit the brakes in order to avoid a collision with the bus, and the shots went wide, breaking a strip of red brick dust out of a building.

Peter stomped on his brakes, yanked the steering wheel, and managed to slide to a stop a fraction of an inch away from the bus. The Audi skidded to a stop and left tread on the sidewalk, barely missing a collision with Natale's car. The driver threw the Audi into reverse, and it began to back up, faster and faster, until it backed the full length of the short street. Then it rounded the corner into the larger street, tires smoking, gears grinding, vanished behind a building, and was gone.

Peter looked through streaming blood at the green metal side of the bus. He still couldn't believe he'd avoided an accident. His heart was racing, his breath was ragged, and he was hanging onto the wheel with an iron grip.

The bus driver—a thin, gray-haired German *Fraulein* in an equally gray uniform—jumped out of the bus.

Dazed, he watched her approach. The other passengers stayed glued inside, their frightened faces pressed against the windows. *"Mein Gott in Himmel,"* the driver said, as she stared through the shattered glass at his bleeding face and white-knuckled hands. "What have those devils been doing to you?"

My God in heaven, thought Natale. He put his arms carefully on the steering wheel, then lowered his head. *Thank You, Father, for letting me get away. Thank You for letting me live.*

20

Berlin

The elderly bus driver helped him stop the bleeding, using her first-aid kit to clean up his facial cuts.

Natale was able to drive after half an hour or so. He stopped at a gas station and washed himself, left the shot-up Mercedes in the parking lot beside the station, phoned the rental car company and told them where to find it. Then he took a cab back to the embassy complex. He knocked on the rear door of the ambassador's glittering residence and asked the maid to find Wolverton.

Now he stood in semidarkness, staring at the elegantly attired station chief, who was blearing in and out of his vision with a startled look on his face.

"You're surprised to see me," Natale said to Wolverton.

"Your appearance is a little—well—disruptive," Wolverton said. "Your face is cut up."

"Sorry." He knew that he had half a dozen small cuts crosshatching his face, and a growing black-and-blue knot on his head. In addition, his white knit shirt was stained red across the front.

"We have guests," Wolverton said, his eyes slitted. "And not exactly the kind of people who want covert operatives appearing at the ambassador's door looking like they've just cleaned a slaughterhouse. Let's get out of here and go to my office."

"Fine by me." Natale felt a surge of weakness. He gritted his teeth and forced himself back to full consciousness. The cuts were better, the heaviest part of the sting had gone away. But he'd hit his head against the windshield sometime during the confusion, and his head throbbed.

"Wait here," Wolverton snapped.

Natale nodded and wondered why he hadn't gone to a hotel or why he hadn't gone to Kurtz for help instead. And then he thought about what that would have looked like. It would have been an open admission that he didn't trust his own people. Then he wondered how much longer he could stand up.

A moment later Wolverton reappeared, and Hammond stormed out right behind him. The two men all but frog-marched Peter across the wide green lawn, into the office complex, then up an elevator and into Wolverton's plush new office.

Only then did Hammond speak. "Now what happened?"

The irritation in his voice stung Natale. He regretted even more deeply that he'd come here, but he'd had to go somewhere.

He'd missed his flight to Naples, though he knew that there was another flight going out in about two hours. But he had planned to fly in and fly back out, an eighteen-hour trip. He hadn't brought a change of clothes, and he didn't want to walk into a department store and shop for a new shirt—he wasn't sure he could manage without folding up. And he couldn't travel like this. He'd be stopped by one airport guard or another, under suspicion of being involved in some bloody crime. He also had an obligation to report this incident to Berlin station, just in case it had more to do with their operations than with him. So here he was, just like the rule book said, welcome or not.

Wolverton picked something invisible from between his front teeth with his little fingernail, then said, "OK, let's have it."

"Two men in a gray Audi tried to kill me."

Hammond and Wolverton stared at each other in alarm. Then Hammond said, "How?"

Natale explained.

"Did you get their license number?"

"I did." He rattled it off. "But these were professionals. The car had to be stolen. Except for the literal grace of God, I'd be on a slab right now."

He suddenly became aware of the heavy tension both men were generating, like massive turbines under intense steam pressure pumping out negative energy full blast. For the first time he realized that he might have interrupted something, that the double-dose of hostility wasn't all because of him.

Wolverton eyed Natale. "There are bandages in the bathroom."

"Thanks." Peter didn't move. "Do you have any coffee?" He didn't know whether there was a chill in the room or he was going into a mild state of shock.

Wolverton disappeared into the small adjoining kitchen, then returned almost immediately with a cup of thick black liquid. "It's been sitting for a while. I could make some fresh."

Natale was grateful for the warmth of the cup. "This will be fine." He took a sip, and the warm, bitter fluid felt good going down.

Wolverton looked at Hammond, and their eyes locked. Then Wolverton turned to Natale. "Look, do you need a doctor? Maybe we should call an ambulance . . ."

Natale felt his head clearing, and he felt his confidence coming back. "I'll be fine."

Hammond suddenly glared. "How do you get yourself into these things, Peter? I have a hundred agents working all throughout Europe, and you cause more trouble than all the rest of them combined. Which reminds me, what's happening with the last fiasco you were involved in—Rudy Brandenburg's murder? My wife is furious with me for not getting to the bottom of that."

Natale realized that Hammond's surly mood was partly the result of too much alcohol, but also the man was on edge as he'd never seen him before. Peter glared back. Then he turned to Wolverton. "If you could fix me up with a clean shirt and reserve a seat on the next flight to Naples, I'll be happy to get out of your hair."

Both Wolverton and Hammond were silent for a long time. Finally Wolverton said, "What about the men who tried to kill you?"

"I'll have to deal with them another time."

Hammond shot Wolverton another alarmed look.

"We can talk to the authorities," Wolverton said. "See what we can find out."

"I'd be more likely to understand it by going in from the other direction." He was still thinking about Marco, about all that Kurtz had told him, but he wasn't about to share that information with either of these two.

"Carlo Ricaso," Hammond said contemptuously. "You think he can turn over some rocks with his networks here and find out what happened? Fine, unless he happens to be the one who ordered the attack."

Natale couldn't stop the astonished look that he knew leaped to his face. "Why would he want to do that?"

"We've been hearing rumors, Peter. Things aren't going all that well in the Ricaso camp."

"There's no problem between Carlo and me."

"But perhaps the old man—"

Wolverton shot Hammond a furious look. "I think I have a shirt around here somewhere. I'll have to find it. We'll get you cleaned up a little. An embassy driver can take you to the airport."

Natale was becoming increasingly certain that he'd stepped into the middle of something and landed in a place where he most definitely wasn't wanted. His eyes focused again on Hammond.

He saw the DO's eyes catch and lock again with Wolverton's, and in that instant a message was telegraphed between the two men that Peter inadvertently intercepted.

Something heavy was going on at Berlin station. And if he stumbled further into whatever it was, these two men might easily turn into the worst enemies he'd ever had. He hid his thoughts and went through the motions, only to find his suspicions reinforced some five minutes later when Hammond left.

Wolverton was still looking for a clean shirt, and Natale stood at the window. Through a crack in the drape he watched Hammond stroll across the lighted lawn toward the ambassador's residence.

When the DO was about halfway across, a man came out of the dark trees, a man dressed in a black dress suit and white shirt similar to Hammond's, so that Natale assumed he was also attending the dinner. The man walked up to meet Hammond, who stopped just outside the brightest oval of light.

They talked with animation, both gesticulating widely, then Hammond made an offhand gesture toward the window where Peter stood concealed by the heavy drape.

The stranger looked up, and in spite of the distance Natale could see his full face, illumined by the yard light. The man's face was clean-shaven. He had a chiseled face and a smooth, wide fore-head that emphasized his receding hairline. His hair was cropped short, and though Peter couldn't see his eyes, the body language told him that they were alive with anger.

He felt a rush of alarm that further cleared his head, and upon the crest of that wave came a sudden fleeting memory. He thought he had seen this man briefly as he entered the lobby of the Hotel de Mer, when he and Judith were checking into the prince's money laundering.

He wondered momentarily if he was hallucinating from the blow to his head. Both men were now looking toward the window, and Hammond was making agitated gestures, apparently explaining something to the other man, who continued to gaze upward, scowling.

At that moment Wolverton walked back into the room. Natale quickly dropped the drape and turned around.

Wolverton smiled tightly. "Are you sure you're up to traveling?"

"I'll be fine."

"Well, your ticket is waiting at the airport check-in, and here's a shirt. The driver will be here any minute. You can wait downstairs for him. I have to get back to the dinner. My wife is going to be furious with me."

Wolverton walked him to the foyer that led into the office building and informed the guard that *Herr* Natale would be waiting for the embassy driver. But as he started to walk through the door, he turned and smiled sadly. "Peter. I know you didn't get a very warm reception here. But some things are happening just now, some manipulations to get the Americans out of the country, us included. It was a bad time for any sort of incident. We appreciate your willingness to step past it. We won't let it rest, though, I can assure you. As soon as we get this little political hassle straightened out, we really will check into what happened to you."

Natale felt foolish for thanking him, but he didn't know what else to say.

The ride to the airport was uneventful, the driver supplied him with a mineral water and some aspirin that helped take the edge off his headache. He actually arrived for his flight half an hour early, and as he made for the concourse he passed a bank of pay phones.

On an impulse, he stopped, put his Agency smart card into the slot, and dialed Carlo's private number in Palermo.

After several rings, the line was answered by the gruffly mysterious voice that always answered Carlo's private phone.

Natale asked to speak with Carlo, got the obligatory pause, then the voice surprised him by growling, "Mr. Natale? Mr. Ricaso is out for the evening, but he left a message for you. I am to tell you that the person you are looking for has been spotted in Milano, two days ago. She rented a car there."

Judith! Suddenly everything else was forgotten.

"What else?" His voice was trembling.

"I'm sorry, *Signore*, that is all."

"I have to get in touch with Carlo right now! I don't care where he is, phone him, send for him. I have to talk to him. I'm at"—he read off the phone number—"in Berlin. I'm going to stand here at this pay phone and wait for *Signore* Ricaso's call, so I'd suggest you contact him right away."

In only ten minutes, the phone rang.

Natale jumped up from where he'd been sprawled on a nearby seat and grabbed the receiver. He didn't even bother with the preliminary identifications. "Where is she, Carlo? Has anybody actually seen her?"

"She rented a car in Milano day before yesterday. My police contacts there checked the car rental companies. They've had the company report the car as stolen, and the plate number has been fed into the EuroPol computer network. That should flush her out."

Natale felt a surge of protective anger. It could also get Judith arrested and cause a nasty incident if she was picked up in the wrong place. On the other hand, the Ricasos had connections into nearly every police department in Italy and well into all surrounding countries. If they'd put out the word that they were looking for Judith and she was then arrested, Carlo would be notified almost before she was locked in a cell.

"Tell your contacts to just hold her, not to arrest her."

Carlo chuckled. "That's already done, *amico*. Don't worry about it. We'll take good care of your lady. Now, you interrupted some business. Anything else?"

Natale had initially phoned Carlo to ask some generic questions about Berlin's assassination networks. He could probably have asked outright about Marco and even told Carlo about the two men who'd tried to kill him. But there were still certain boundaries in their relationship, and he was careful not to step across them. The more he expected of Carlo, the more Carlo would expect from him.

Besides, he'd be back in Naples tomorrow, and they could talk then. The flight home would give him a chance to think things over, and he'd know exactly where he needed to begin.

He made one more quick call. To Kurtz. He told him about the two men in the Audi and warned him to watch himself. Kurtz assured him he would do everything possible to find out who the men were.

But as Natale walked down the passageway and across the concourse to the boarding gate, he felt little assurance that the two assassins would ever be found. There were so many for hire in Europe these days, of every nationality, every background.

Still, he was certain of one thing. Whoever hired them had just decreased his own lifespan as a free man. Natale was absolutely certain that the attempt had something to do with Operation Kaleidoscope, and he was going to clean up that network even if it did literally cost him his life.

21

Valletta

On that troubled evening, as velvet shadows hung long over the laurel hedges and peach trees, Carlo and *don* Cesare once again sat on the elevated veranda on the west side of the secluded villa they used as their primary fortress against the world they ruled.

The polished lava stone was again cool beneath their feet, though the lawn sprinklers were silent. The rainy season was beginning, Cesare's estate was more than ever lushly green. There was a new chill in the air, so that the *don* had draped a seedy woolen sweater around his frail shoulders. The rooks swirled low in the evening light, while the cicadas lamented summer's approaching end.

The torrential rains of winter would soon drive out the last of summer's hot sirocco winds. But this was not the only impending change. Both men were tense these days, silent and brooding. They sensed a darker wind that was ushering in a growing, evil shadow, and the wind grew stronger, the shadow grew darker, with every new problem and every passing day.

Don Cesare had been talking, as always, about the widespread and complicated family business. "We must take stock, Carlo. Sicily, Naples, Berlin—all the key centers of operation along our pipelines are being glutted with worthless *ncarugnutu* who use our networks and resources but who do not feel loyalty. We must weed them out to keep our family strong."

"With every solution comes a problem," Carlo said wearily. He took a sip of the golden Marsala he'd taken out of the wine cellar an hour before. The bottle was already half gone.

Cesare nodded. "You will understand even better when you are capo-Mafia. The problems never end."

As the old man stared into the dark surrounding shrubbery, an intense sinister genius made his eyes shine like those of a jungle animal. He turned to Carlo and said quietly, "I am an old man, and the old ways are disappearing like water into sand. We must not be fools. Together we must handle whatever comes next."

Carlo remained silent and waited for his uncle to say what was on his mind. An unusual sadness was emanating from the capo, and Carlo respected the rare sense of camaraderie they shared at that moment.

Don Cesare took a sip of wine. "I have been talking today with Volante."

Carlo nodded. He had suspected as much.

"There are problems I haven't told you about with regard to the kidnapping of Luciano."

Carlo remained silent. He knew that an effort had been made to find the young man, but the effort had failed.

"Volante must be the next president of the European Union. There is no other possibility for us."

Carlo considered this. With Volante in office, the already porous EU laws could be tailor-made to suit Ricaso needs.

"But there is a problem with this as well, Carlo."

Carlo waited wearily to hear yet again about his uncle's most devious and obsessive plot. He took a long swallow of wine.

"It is the Americans. I need to remind you again, Carlo. They are no longer our friends. There was a time when we needed them to keep the Communists from taking over Italy. Now there is no power greater than our own. But the Americans are still here, still bumbling around in our business. The NATO base in Naples, Carlo. If the Americans would only leave there, we could soon get rid of the rest of the interfering fools who still think they can stop the tides of the future."

"The Americans will leave soon without any effort on our part."

"Yes. But perhaps not soon enough. I will be frank with you. This Counternarcotics Division of theirs is beginning to concern me. They are giving our people trouble in Munich, in Rome, in Monaco. Is this where your friend Peter Natale now sows his seeds of discord? Is that why he was at Hotel de Mer?"

Carlo shrugged. "I don't know. It really doesn't matter. He helps me, I help him. Other than that, we both do what we have to do."

He had expected a flash of anger from his uncle, but instead the old man gazed again into the dark foliage, frowning. "This is not a light matter, Carlo. I don't need to tell you that whoever rules the EU presidency and parliament will rule Europe, and if it is not us it will be our enemies."

Carlo had heard this argument often enough. It was the family's justification for everything they did. If it were not for *La Familia*, even more malevolent crime consortiums would grip the world by the throat and reduce it to ashes. In this version of things, the Mafiosi were the guardians of the poor, the providers of jobs for those who were cruelly cast off by conventional society. The Mafia enterprises provided money to buy political protection for those who were powerless.

There were dozens of other exonerations for what the Ricasos did—Carlo had heard them all throughout the years. And he had known, even as a child, that there were certain truths in the argument. The world was indeed full of butchers and madmen who would stop at nothing to pick up the reins of power. The Colombians, the Russians, the new and smaller Mafias around the globe were proving this every day.

But Carlo also knew that even within the Ricaso crime family there was an insidious decay that helped foment such travesties. And now he could see the family reacting to the pressure from ever more sinister forces, so that they were no longer a counterforce—if ever they had been—but were now one of the forces that were ushering in what Carlo sometimes thought was the end of the world.

He looked at his uncle with an objective eye and realized just how much raw power this frail old man actually wielded—and how much he himself would one day wield when he inherited the leadership.

So long as *don* Cesare was alive, Carlo would be only a secondary force, dominated like everyone else by this predatory little dictator whose genius was helping enslave the world. But one day this malignant wedge of the world would be his to further corrupt, his to control. He felt certain, though, that by the time that happened the world would certainly be reduced to ashes.

He said, "Maybe it's time for us to get out of the heroin business and tighten up on the armaments."

Don Cesare turned to stare coldly at him.

Carlo persisted. "I'm serious. Think about it. Look at what's happening. We lose one of our Berlin pipelines because some swine are using it to traffic nuclear materials. It costs us ten million dollars in lost heroin profits in just under a month, not counting the aggravation. It's not good business anymore, *Zu* Cesare. We don't need the problems. We can get where we want to be with the legitimate assets we already have."

Cesare looked at him with sudden loathing. "*You* think about it. You don't know what you're talking about. Money is only as valuable as the power behind it, otherwise it's just metal and green paper. Without the heroin pipelines and the human assets we buy with our profits, we would be nothing. Mark my words. The minute the Ricasos step out of the heroin business, a thousand madmen will step in, and people will be on their knees praying to go back to the days when we kept the business organized and cleaned off the scum."

Carlo knew there was some truth in the old man's statement. Heroin was still the most valuable commodity on earth, worth fifty times its weight in gold or more, depending on the market. It also had the added advantage of being addictive, which meant the market would always be there.

He decided to change the subject before the discussion collapsed into an argument. "What's happening with Volante?"

"I worry about him." Cesare's eyes shifted deviously. "I no longer trust him."

Carlo was surprised. "Why? He hasn't even reported the kidnapping to the police, and it's been over a week now. He's trusting you all the way."

"No, you are wrong. He no longer trusts me, in spite of my reassurances. He thinks I am behind the kidnapping."

"You!"

"*Si*. It is crazy but true. He is crumbling apart from the pressure. I sense it, I see it. And I am not sure yet what to do about it."

"Why don't we just find Luciano?"

Don Cesare's smile was withering. "We will find him. It is just a matter of time."

Carlo was silent.

Cesare shifted positions and locked eyes with Carlo. "Volante heard again from the kidnappers today."

"Did they finally stop playing games and say how much they want?" Carlo felt the same hot fury as his uncle now, as if it had been shot into him by the eye contact.

The old man's teeth bared in a predatory snarl. "They are not after money, Carlo. They are trying to disrupt Volante's appointment as EU president."

Carlo was doubly astounded. "That's all they want?"

Don Cesare's face was suddenly something terrible to see. "That's *all?* Let me tell you, Carlo, that is everything. Whoever is holding Luciano is not after Volante—they are after me! Us! They are dead men already. They have no idea who they are betraying."

Carlo nodded, agreeing for once. "But first we have to find them. What's the plan?"

It was the old man's turn to shrug the small, almost imperceptible shrug that spoke volumes of Sicilian conspiracy. "They say they will hold Luciano until after the Italian president of the EU is selected by the parliament next month."

Carlo felt renewed rage. "I'll handle these *pesecanos*. You can pull your soldiers back. Long before the time comes for the parliament to make their decision, we'll have Luciano back." Carlo thought, then said, "The question is, will Volante hold together in the meantime?"

Cesare blinked once, hard, like a bird of prey startled in its savage speculations. "*Si avi corpa di cortella*, Carlo. A man who is really a man reveals nothing, not even with a dagger through his heart. But Volante is not a man. He is a puppet, dancing on my chain. I have made him, I hold his hand through every little problem, and now perhaps I will have to kill him. I do not know."

Carlo's anger vanished as he looked into Cesare's flat, dead eyes and saw his own future reflected there. He suppressed a shudder. He couldn't imagine a life where he was consumed by such a terrible desire to annihilate and destroy everything that opposed his will.

Even as a child, Carlo had seen death in his uncle *don* Cesare's hard face and lusterless eyes. Now he suddenly thought about how odd it was that death merchants inevitably murdered, first of all, the most vital parts of themselves.

His father too had shown the gradual erosion. He'd lost the capacity for joy, became obsessed with a need to strangle others' freedom and control them. Carlo had wanted to be a doctor, before he'd known his heritage. His father murdered that dream when he manipulated him into the Mafia, for Carlo was, after all, the first son. The only son, now that Johnny was dead.

Through the years, Carlo had watched his father wither as he became almost psychotic, suppressing life in all its aspects, courting death and administering it until finally his own death had swallowed him.

Carlo tried to come to terms with the fact that he had also become a death merchant. During his twenty years as the family scion, he'd done evil things. But he believed that he still had a gentler side to his nature, that he had managed to nurture the spark of life that welcomed joy. He was still certain that he lacked the cold, lifeless edge that *don* Cesare possessed.

Cesare was so astute at picking up people's facial nuances and body language that he was almost telepathic. Now he glared at Carlo. "Do think I should coddle the fool?"

"You've been friends for almost thirty years. I just wonder that you can abruptly cut someone off like that." In truth, he was wondering if Cesare would be able to suddenly cut him off too.

Contempt flooded the old man's face. "You got a problem, Carlo. You're going soft."

"At least I'm still human!" He immediately regretted the defiant words.

"You think you're better than me?" The fury that always lay just beneath the surface of Cesare's withered skin now erupted, so that the man spoke in a tone of voice like seething molten lava.

"You're a *fesso*, Carlo. A fool, and getting worse! I watch you these days. Don't you think I see? You're a do-gooder. You think I do certain things because I want to. You don't see yet that certain things have to be done. This world is not easy, like you've had it. And what do you do? I'm telling you, if you don't watch yourself, you're gonna spend the rest of your life trying to pick all the maggots off the face of the earth, and every time you peel one off, three more's gonna grow back."

Carlo stared at the transformation in his old uncle and knew that he was looking at something primitive and evil.

"You're gonna spend your life feeding pigs, Carlo. Because you ain't gonna change the world, no matter how hard you try. It don't want to be changed, and you're too stupid to know that it's not our fault."

"I don't want to change the world. I just want to change myself," Carlo said in defense.

Resentment thickened Cesare's features. "You don't understand nothing. Not the business anymore, not the way the world works. I'm telling you again, you're trusting the wrong people. I told you, you were gonna find yourself in a position where you'd have to do something to hurt us. I'm telling you, you get rid of that Peter Natale, or it's just a matter of time."

Carlo recognized the thinly veiled threat. *Don* Cesare was seriously thinking about putting a contract out on Pietro.

Cesare tilted his head, studying him now with a new and gentler expression on his face. "We have responsibilities, Carlo, so many *picciotti d'honore*, the young men of honor who look up to you, who are born to the *Onorata Societa*." The Honored Society, the Mafia. "And there are the older men, of my generation, who have seen the blood, who know how hard we have fought. The trouble comes because you are not of our generation, Carlo. You do not understand yet that we Mafiosi must know what others will not look at. Sometimes it is a dark wisdom, but it is wisdom nonetheless."

Carlo responded to his uncle's more persuasive tone of voice. "You've made more money than you could spend in a thousand years. You could live however you wanted to."

"Sicily is my home, and violence is Sicily's most lucrative business. Surely you know that by now. I must stay strong, or the *scassapaghieri* will take what I have, no matter how much it is. That is a law of life."

"But surely there are other ways—"

"Ah, Carlo. Someday you will see it. Perhaps before it is too late. People do not let you stop. I am capo-Mafia, more powerful than the pope, more powerful than the president of any country, more powerful than any other capo in Sicily or beyond. I have become a myth to people. But if a myth is shattered, the people tear you limb from limb. I have seen it in my life. You will see it too, one day, if you are not careful."

"But you created the myth."

"No, Carlo. Nor did your father. The people themselves created it, because they needed to believe. You do not understand. I remember when I killed my first man, so many, many years ago . . . ah so very much blood since then. There was a capo of sorts in Valletta then, though he was not thought of as Mafia. He was a *gabellotti*, the manager for the Veresi estates that owned your grandparents' small bit of land and the stone shanty that we lived in. Even the pigs and goats and chickens that slept inside with us when it rained were theirs. I was a handsome young man then, and I had caught the eye of a girl the manager wanted for his own—for immoral purposes, you understand. He would never have honored a peasant girl by marrying her."

Carlo almost smiled at that. It never failed to amaze him how his uncle, who could rake money off the most atrocious forms of pornography and prostitution, always spoke of intimate matters with the careful delicacy of the most devout Catholic peasant woman —a trait he was sure had been inherited from his peasant grandmother.

"The man attacked me and your father one night, when we were walking back to the village from this very valley, after herding the estate's goats all day. He beat your father, beat me—he was a grown man, stronger by far. We went home and got the one important thing our father owned—a *lupara*. Even the poorest Sicilians kept such shotguns back then. We loaded it, went back to the road, and waited until the *gabellotti* started home from the village later that evening.

"I had been beaten the worst, so I pulled the trigger. I blew his head off, and we threw him down a ravine, and the Veresi family never did find out who did it, for when they asked the villagers who the killers were, the peasants would only say, 'Why, is somebody dead?'

"But Sicilians always know. And we were suddenly the *Padrinos* of the village. Robin Hoods. We were suddenly called upon to protect the people, to settle disputes, even sometimes to provide for them. The Veresi family sent a new manager, someone less inclined to get himself killed. And then the war came. You know the rest."

"When my father went to the United States just before the war to open up the territory over there, you stayed here and became capo-Mafia."

"I did. And I learned that if I did not defend myself, nobody would. I learned that there would be many who would rely on me to also defend them, people who wanted me to be their patron saint." His face suddenly turned dark. "But I also learned that these people, like my enemies, gave back nothing unless they were forced to. You have to see it, Carlo. On the one hand, there is a mob of violent fools who would destroy the very world for gain. On the other there are swarms of *pidocchii*—lice—who want it all done for them. They have no honor, they whine and take, and then, when you call upon them to do something to help you keep the power that feeds and clothes and defends them, they call you a criminal and a thug and try to put you in jail."

"But Volante! You're not even certain that he'll betray you."

"He will."

"Maybe not. After all, you've made him rich, you've put him into the parliament, and he's human, after all . . ."

"Ah, *bueno*, Carlo. You are beginning to see. Yes, he is human. Which is why I must stop him before he betrays me."

Carlo shook his head. "You really have so much contempt for every man?"

Don Cesare smiled darkly. "I trust only money, Carlo. Money never lies. You never find it in bed with your wife. When you are old and sick, your friends leave you, but the money stays. People are for sale anyway, Carlo. I can buy any one of them with money. Money is the only truth. One day you will learn that, and then you will at last have earned the right to be capo-Mafia."

"Volante has helped you. He's never betrayed you before."

"He is a stepping-stone I used to get to the top. Don't be so simpleminded, Carlo. In the beginning he was my enemy. He wanted to stand in my way, but I bought him off. You will learn one day that people stand in your way on purpose—to stop you from accomplishing anything. They are nothing, they do nothing, they resent others who manage to achieve power or wealth. They stand in the way deliberately and refuse to move, so you have to step over them or on them if you are to do anything."

Carlo was listening intently. He was fascinated by the insight into the dark and withered old soul, but he also wondered why this was happening. Cesare did nothing without a reason, so he kept waiting for the other shoe to drop.

"I wanted only a decent life," Cesare said. "I planned to work the land and marry, like other young men in Valletta did in those times. My wife, Maria, was a village girl, dead before your birth." He looked down and made the sign of the cross. "I wanted to give her children. I did not want to hold her in my arms while she died from typhus because we had no money for decent food or for medicine. But she died, and that loss hurt me so deeply that I never had the will to marry again. I had no desire to be capo-Mafia of Valletta or capo-di-tutti-capi of all of Sicily, for that matter. But life thrusts things upon us, and we do what we must.

"You do not know about the early years. When I first started making money with the *cinniri*, I helped people in Sicily, I gave money away. I gave money to the church for an orphanage in Palermo. But the people resented me, they laughed behind my back, they called me *Il Papa*, the pope, and they did not mean it respectfully back then as they do now when they speak of me." A poisonous look swept into the old man's eyes.

"Carlo. You must learn this, you must know, for one day I will be gone, and you must survive alone. People are filled with malice. They let you steal for them, kill for them; they take your money and your honor and use you in every way. And then they try to destroy you, simply because you are what they cannot be. So you see, Carlo? Now, if a man tries to run out on a debt or a responsibility to me, I fracture his kneecaps so he can run no more. I put a bullet in his head. And make no mistake about it, I will kill Volante if I get even an inkling that he is betraying me."

Cesare had fixed Carlo with a coldly devastating stare, and suddenly Carlo saw the true point that was being delivered in a wrapping of memories.

"*Zu* Cesare. I tell you again. All people are not like that."

But the old man was growing tired of conversation and was drawing back inside the carapace that covered him most of the time like a scarab beetle's shell. There was an accusing and betrayed look in his eyes, both at the same time. "You will not understand until you have lived long enough to see," he said cryptically. "I am soiling myself at this very moment by trying to explain it to you."

Carlo was wise enough to stay silent.

After a moment, Cesare said, "I will say this, Carlo. Let other men be honorable, and I will honor them. When my truths are no longer trampled by pigs, I'll end my deceptions. But in the meantime, if any man gets in my way, even if he is my own flesh and blood, I will either move him out of my way or kill him."

The statement was accompanied by a chilling gaze that left no question about exactly what the old man meant.

Carlo felt a soul-deep sadness. Still, he felt no reciprocal hostility. "*Zu* Cesare, I must tell you respectfully. If your dark perceptions are the true measure of life, it is not worth the price you have paid to live it."

But the rare moment was past, and *don* Cesare suddenly stood, preparing to go in for dinner. He gave Carlo a cold, dismissive blink. "*Faugh,* Carlo. You are such a fool. I am telling you again. Stop spending time with Peter Natale. The man is headed toward no good end, and I would hate to see you end up at the bottom of one of the shafts in our sulfur mines along with him."

Carlo had lost his appetite. He sat alone and gazed out at the darkening pastures and wondered what had happened to the small light of hope he had seen as a child, when he'd first realized the dark legacy to which he had been born. All his life he had wanted to be free from the pervasive sorrow that was an inevitable counterpoint to his family's evil power. But he had never been able to break away.

Now the responsibility was growing heavier, and he was feeling smothered by the death and power lust and greed and pain. And in that moment he could see only the grim inevitability of his future, as he at last succumbed fully to his cruelly powerful heritage.

22

Bonn

Judith awakened, suddenly, to the mournful sound of a ship's horn. The cabin was cold. She shivered as she dragged herself out of the small berth, then pulled back the curtain that covered the brass-rimmed porthole. The predawn sky was gray, and a cold, fine rain needled the river. Feeble yellow lights defined the looming prehensile skeletons of giant loading cranes, one with jaws poised hungrily above a barge heaped high with cargo containers.

Other lights winked through the downpour, outlining narrow cobbled alleys and rain-misted, gabled warehouses beside the docks. She heard the melancholy sound again and craned her neck. A tugboat was moving alongside her cabin liner, easing it into a mooring at the end of a crowded pier. She checked her watch. Five-thirty. This part of the journey was over.

Someone tapped on the door.

"Yes?"

"Ms. Livman. We have reached Bonn. Breakfast will be served in one-half hour, after which we will spend the day touring Drachenfels castle and the city."

"Thank you."

She would not be taking the tour. She was here only to check out Rudy's story about working for the CIA in Berlin and the EIA in Bonn.

"Call Dennis Kreidler at the EIA," he had said. "Ask if you can trust Rudy Brandenburg."

She thought about how she might contact Kreidler. She had risked phoning from Zurich to see if he was in residence at the Bonn EIA complex. The EU embassy clerk pressed her for an identification and a reason for calling, but she hung up without answering.

She took a quick shower and dressed in a white cotton blouse and khaki slacks with matching safari jacket, then packed her few possessions into a large canvas tote bag.

In the grim gray light of morning, the idea of approaching an EIA man—any EIA man—seemed senseless, even dangerous. But checking in now with the Bonn CIA station was impossible. By now they must be looking for her. She had bought a ticket all the way to Amsterdam to throw them off her trail if they picked it up in Basel. But sooner or later she was going to have to surface somewhere, if she were to learn what she needed to know. It might as well be in Bonn.

Judith did a last-minute check of the cabin. Suddenly she wanted to stop right there, drop her bag, drop her career, stay in the secure little cabin and float down the Rhine to Rotterdam, then on out to sea. She was tired of the CIA's internal corruption and equally tired of her dirty, dangerous profession. But on the heels of that thought, a new surge of energy lifted her. She had to continue on her strange path, no matter where it took her. She had to know the truth.

She lifted the canvas bag and placed it across her shoulder. Then she took one last look about the tiny cabin—her womb of security in a very dark world—and bowed her head in prayer. She went out the door, shut it quietly behind her, and climbed the metal stairs.

As she hit the deck, a gust of wind raged up and slanted rain into her eyes, blinding her. She raised her hand to shield her eyes, and suddenly someone was close behind her, blocking the wind. The smell of tobacco smoke and stale breath was strong. She felt a man's hand fumbling at her arm, then seizing it in a viselike grip. A massive body slammed into her, taking her breath, spinning her into reaction.

She jerked away, shoving the attacker backward as she wheeled around, poised for flight.

She was face to face with *Herr* Muller. His fleshy face was twisted, his heavy brows furrowed in a scowl as he tottered backward, then forward, then seemed to right himself. He was a Berlin banker—newly widowed, he said—traveling down the Rhine to forget. She had refused his clumsy advances two nights in a row in the cruiser's dining room, and now she was uncertain as to whether this encounter was deliberate or accidental.

"You must forgive me, *Fraulein*. I had intended only to bid you good morning, but I lost my footing. See, the deck is slick—" he slid his leather-soled shoe across it to demonstrate "—and I almost fell. I am sorry to alarm you."

Judith mumbled a response, then darted toward the boarding ramp. She descended it, then stepped onto the quay, where she turned to look back at the small, warm cabin steamer. She was still reluctant to leave it.

Finally she turned away toward the small city. A supply truck was unloading linens and fresh produce for the steamer. Three blue taxis sat beneath a dimming streetlight near the ticket offices, and she hurried toward one of these, tapped on the window to awaken the bleary-eyed driver, then climbed inside the rear compartment.

Her watch now said 6:30. It was far too early to contact anyone. She asked the driver to take her to the nearest clean hotel.

By midmorning, she had done a lot of nervous pacing and thinking. At 9:00 she phoned the EIA station, told the nosy clerk that she had a private message for *Herr* Kreidler from the Brandenburg family, and was instantly put through.

She didn't care now if the EIA's satellites tracked her call. She was getting closer, she could sense it, and she had to go forward. It was a good bet the computers would ignore the call anyway, unless they'd been specifically programmed to download messages coming into EIA offices—unlikely, since the EIA offices had their own recording systems.

Kreidler's voice was young, even timid. He identified himself, then said, *"Frau* Brandenburg?"

Judith smiled. "I'm afraid not. Actually, I'm a friend of Rudy's."

Kreidler audibly sucked in air through his teeth, then said quickly, "What do you have for me?"

"I'll have to see you personally."

"Yes, yes, of course. Right away." Kreidler said he'd prefer they meet in his office.

Judith decided it really didn't matter. She had already dived in, and he would either betray her or not, no matter where they met.

Bonn had been the western capital during the division of Germany. Now that the country was reunified, the complex of government buildings beside the river housed only the remnants of bureaucracy that had not yet been transferred to the spanking new quarters in Berlin. Within this complex, nested deep in the monotony of concrete and steel, the EIA's Bonn station was a nondescript office suite with the typical furnishings and personnel of any low-level bureaucracy.

However, when a clerk led Judith past the facade and toward Kreidler's office, she caught a glimpse of a vast white room where banks of floor-to-ceiling computers hummed softly. One giant empty screen gleamed like a newly blinded giant's eye. The room seemed to be poised, waiting for something ominous. She quickly stepped past and was ushered into Kreidler's office.

The clerk left her there, and Kreidler stood as she entered. He was about thirty-five and rail thin. His light-brown hair was cut with military precision; he had a thin mustache and ash-blue, opaque eyes that were impenetrable. He stepped from behind a walnut desk and introduced himself, then motioned for her to sit, sat back down himself, and said, "What do you have for me?" He watched her carefully.

She decided not to waste time. "I met Rudy only briefly, but he asked me to give you a message. I am to tell you that he 'found it.' It seemed very important that you know."

Kreidler's face went cold. "Found what?"

Judith shrugged and put on her most innocent face. "Whatever he was looking for, I assume."

"He told you he was working for us?"

"Yes."

Kreidler leaned forward. His eyes narrowed, and he seemed to peer into the far distance. What he saw there appeared to anger him. "I know what he told you," he said. "Anyway I know some of what he told you, though I didn't know he'd broken his security and confessed his role as spy."

"But how—"

"Rudy contacted me and told me of your encounter."

Judith had wondered about this. She'd gotten into his office too easily. She said, "I see." She really didn't.

Kreidler rubbed his forehead. "His funeral was only yesterday."

That surprised her. "They brought the body back to Bonn?"

"The ashes. They wasted no time cremating him. They brought the urn to the aunt who raised him after his parents died. The Archduchess Marlena Brandenburg. But then you know that. The Monte Carlo police were notified of his identity by certain authorities in Rome, I am told. We assume your people had something to do with that."

"My people?"

He smiled. "I know that you are a CIA intelligence analyst in Moscow, *Fraulein*. What I do not know is why you are here."

"Fast work."

"Not so fast. We take the death of an agent seriously, of course. And our agent did die in Peter Natale's hotel room. I ran your face print through our computer scan while you were in the waiting room, just to confirm your identity. You are not Una Livman, vacationing schoolteacher from Copenhagen. You are Judith Davies of the CIA's Moscow station, ex-partner of Peter Natale and his recent companion in Monte Carlo."

Judith hid the surge of alarm that raced through her.

Kreidler smiled tightly. "You are AWOL, as you Americans say. Away from Moscow station without leave."

"I'm on vacation," she said defensively.

"Then you have failed to inform your employer," he said with a cold smile. "We have learned from EIA-Moscow that your people are concerned you might have been abducted or murdered."

Judith was silent. She was suddenly ashamed that she hadn't contacted Frost or Natale. She said, "I suppose I should check in with them."

"I am not trying to interfere," Kreidler said politely. "I only wish to know why you are here instead of there."

Judith decided to be honest. "I frankly don't know. It has something to do with Rudy's death. I let him down, and it keeps gnawing at me. I suppose I'm making a detour on my way home—to learn what I can."

Kreidler leaned back, relaxing a bit. "Well. I suppose there's no harm in admitting that Rudy was one of ours. It can't matter now. You have that in your records anyway, since he belonged to you first."

Judith hadn't seen the records. She was puzzled.

"Come now, don't be coy. Rudy had nothing to be ashamed of. He had a good record in the CIA, in spite of the fact that his distant cousin got him the job.

"Cousin?"

"There really is no reason for all this guile. Bob Hammond, your ex-chief of Berlin station. We know that Rudy was his distant cousin. It's not unusual for the jaded descendants of Europe's old royal families to look for some adventure in their lives. Some drive race cars, some climb mountains. Some become criminals—or spies. In spite of the nepotism, Rudy did quite well. We were happy to hire him when he came to us."

"Hammond was Rudy's distant cousin?"

"His wife was related to Rudy by marriage. Didn't you know?"

Judith was stunned speechless. She had been locked away in Moscow, involved in other things. Still, she should have known.

Kreidler grinned, enjoying the surprise he'd elicited. "I expect you've wondered why Rudy picked you out of the crowd."

She nodded dumbly.

"Rudy knew you and Peter Natale would be in Monte Carlo because I told him to watch for you," Kreidler said, adding another layer of intrigue to the mystery. "Our satellite trawl intercepted communications between Natale and *Herr* Frost at Rome station. The key word was Prince Dante di Veresi. We were watching the prince too."

Judith silently chastised Peter for using a public phone to check in with Frost. She said, "Why?"

"I admit that fascism seems to be the fashion of the moment, but there are still a few of us who'd like to stop the rising tides of tyranny. Prince Veresi and his clique of well-heeled royals are backing Count Benito Jacovetti's upcoming bid for the permanent

EU presidency. Certain very serious EU factions want to keep Jacovetti out of the race."

"This whole thing reduces to politics?"

His smile was dark and devastating. "Politics is the art of administering social and economic power. Everything reduces to power."

Judith said, "And the German candidate for the permanent presidency? Doesn't he have a fascist bent too?"

Kreidler's face went stiff. "Nothing so dramatic as the second incarnation of Mussolini the Italians want to foist upon us."

Judith decided to change the subject before she alienated him completely. "Rudy mentioned something about the missing Soviet gold and a reptile fund. What was that all about?"

Kreidler leaned forward and stared. "He said *what?*"

Judith felt a rush of adrenaline. She was at last getting close to what she needed to know. But if she was going to learn more, she would have to give something up first, because she had Kreidler alarmed now. She decided to make the trade. "Rudy told me he had secret friends in high places, people who like gold. He said the dragon was loose again and was using the gold to buy up the reptiles. I assumed that he'd uncovered some sort of reptile fund."

Judith saw something hot and deadly come into Kreidler's eyes. It was quickly followed by the same flash of fear and determination that she'd seen in Rudy Brandenburg's eyes not long before he died.

"He told me he was in danger," she persisted. "I didn't believe him. He was high. Did you know that? Using heroin, I think."

Kreidler cursed. "I should have pulled him out of there. In fact I tried, but he wouldn't listen."

"He said there were reptiles everyplace, even in my own cloistered garden. That's exactly what he said. I believe he was trying to tell me that he'd uncovered a mole."

Kreidler glanced around, startled, then reached under his desk, brought out a tape recorder, hit the STOP button, and rewound it. "I hadn't realized where this conversation would go," he said by way of apology.

"I had hoped this would be confidential."

"Yes. I agree now. This is a most unexpected turn of events."

"How good was Rudy?"

Kreidler stroked his narrow chin. "He was getting very good, though far too reckless. He had that in common with your Peter Natale."

Judith raised her eyebrows in question.

"We of course checked Peter Natale out thoroughly when we learned the circumstances of Rudy's death. We suspected he was involved for a while."

"Involved in Rudy's death?"

Kreidler pursed his lips as if to seal them, then nodded in spite of it. "We are aware of Mr. Natale's relationship with the Ricaso family. That sort of link makes people suspicious."

Judith nodded. It did indeed. "Why did Rudy go to Peter's room?" It was a question that had been eating her like acid. "Was it because I let him down?"

"Not at all. Something new came up that afternoon. He told me he had found the method of conversion. I had told him Peter could be trusted. He was going to elicit Peter's help in breaking into the casino."

"*What?*"

"Exactly my reaction. When he told me he was going to break into the casino, I said he was crazy. I demanded he take some time off."

"He didn't listen, and now he's dead."

"Yes."

"But why?" She knew he was touching only the surface of what he actually knew. "What method of conversion? And what were they converting? Drug money? The Red Gold?"

Kreidler pursed his mouth shut, then changed his mind and said, "Rudy had indeed discovered a mole. Though I'm not sure if the mole had penetrated your agency or ours—or both. He told me not long ago that he had in fact worked with this mole for a time, though on matters unrelated to intelligence."

"What matters?"

"I'm not at liberty to answer that."

"You trusted Rudy's version of events, even though he was on heroin?"

Kreidler got angry. "All spies can't sit behind desks and issue memorandums, *Fraulein*. Some have to go where it gets dirty. Rudy volunteered to penetrate a very violent paramilitary force of ex-terrorists. They traffic in armaments, heroin, and many of them are addicts. Rudy dabbled with drugs during his interim between the CIA and us. He was willing to fix heroin so they would think he was one of them, but he overestimated his ability to control the drug."

"These people killed him?"

"Most likely."

"Why do you think it was them? Why not the prince's people? You said he was watching Veresi, and the stakes for the EU presidency are high."

Kreidler stiffened. "My dear, they *were* the prince's people, at least, after a fashion."

"What do they have to do with the prince?"

"They handle odd jobs for him, for the Sicilians, for anyone else who can pay them."

"So the prince might have ordered the hit? Because Rudy knew what he was doing? I'm sorry. I still don't understand."

He studied her, then sighed. "You are familiar with Ernst Adler?"

"I know who he was."

Adler had been Germany's favorite to win the permanent presidency of the EU, the only man strong enough to go up against an incumbent. Adler had so much support throughout the European Union that he would have easily won the post. But Adler had been brutally gunned down in a Berlin street a year ago—by thieves, the story went. Shortly thereafter, the only other non-Italian challenger was found dead at his home of an apparent heart attack. Most intelligence operatives believed this also was murder.

"You're saying that Jacovetti is murdering his way into office, and the prince in involved."

"It looks that way, yes. We hadn't suspected at first. We were looking at the Ricaso crime family. Volante Chicarelli was expected to win the seat, Jacovetti and Chicarelli are long-time rivals, so what would Jacovetti have to gain? But now we have learned that something is seriously wrong in Chicarelli's camp. He has implied that he may not accept the seat even if he's appointed. Jacovetti would win the position by default. There's no one strong enough left to stand against him."

"Rudy was involved in all that?"

"Peripherally." Kreidler's mouth clamped shut.

Judith could see he was beginning to regret talking so freely. It happened that way sometimes. People tended to confide in her, then blamed her for learning so much.

"Let me speculate. All this had something to do with the Red Gold and the reptile fund. And Rudy found the link?"

Kreidler shot her a look of pure hatred, then looked abruptly away, as if he could no longer stand to look at her.

She was momentarily stunned by the sudden change. It was time to back off, to give something up. She said, "I'm sorry if I've offended you. I just don't understand what I've stumbled into here. Rudy also made me promise that if anything happened to him, I should tell you to take care of Gia, because she believed in him."

Kreidler's face took on a strangled look, and his eyes showed surprise.

"Who's Gia?"

Kreidler shook his head, as if giving up. "Look, she's just another junkie, another confused and destructive child of Europe's jaded royalty. Sometimes I think half of this generation is crazy and the other half is drugged."

"Whose child exactly?"

"Fraulein, you surprise me. You really don't know?"

Judith shook her head no.

"She's Prince Dante di Veresi's daughter, of course. Weren't you briefed at all?"

Judith thought about the vague references to the prince's daughter in the research on the Black Nobility she'd done for Frost, but no specific name had been mentioned. She realized now that the papers had been faulted and dated.

Kreidler seemed to read her mind. "The girl is a basket case. She's been in and out of mental hospitals and private schools since she was ten, when her mother killed herself. Last year she was cut loose from a school, and she went wild again. She began buying drugs from certain members of the Black Brigade, then got involved with them—we think perhaps they targeted her.

"Rudy was an idealist of the first order, in spite of his own problems. When he realized what was going on, he actually thought that if he could get her away from them and off the heroin, he could slay the dragon, save the beautiful princess, and everyone would live happily ever after."

"The dragon. The same dragon Rudy was talking about. You did send him after the Red Gold," Judith said. "We suspected you were still looking—halfheartedly, like the rest of us."

He shot her a sudden look of suspicion.

"Rudy told me quite a bit."

"Really." He measured her fully, then smiled a cold, frightening smile. "Did he tell you that he helped steal the Red Gold to begin with, when he was working Berlin station?"

Judith's throat went dry.

"Oh, yes, we weren't supposed to know that, but we were watching him. We figured it out. Why do you think we were so eager to have him on board, drugs and all? Did he tell you that your own CIA helped the KGB move half the gold bars out of Russia?"

She felt the blood leave her face. She hadn't wanted to hear that. She'd kept the possibility shifted to the edge of her mind. But the clues had been there, peppered throughout everything she'd learned about the pilfered gold. Now that the words had been said, she knew they were true, and she knew that she had the better part of what she had come to find out.

"Rudy knew where to find the Red Gold, all right." Kreidler watched her carefully. "He helped move part of it out of Russia and through East Berlin. It wasn't the mother lode, but one small vein, which he mined quite well for several years.

"But he had his own problems with drugs off and on. He helped his aunt, who had fallen on hard times, and he gambled. He fell for the wrong women. He spent his own share, then we suspect he began to tap the others for more than he'd contracted for. They wouldn't give it to him.

"He came to me and told me he'd had a part in the robbery when he'd been stationed at the CIA's Berlin station. He said he was sorry now that he'd gotten involved, he was beginning to realize the depraved nature of the people he'd helped. He was going to redeem himself by unraveling the theft. He was going to save the world and end up wealthy besides. In truth, he was just going to get even."

"That was why you were watching the prince? He was laundering this gold at Hotel de Mer?"

Kreidler's eyes glittered coldly.

"Rudy said if we were watching the prince, we were looking in the right direction."

Kreidler abruptly stood. His face turned to stone. "I've told you as much as I can and enough to lose my job and perhaps my life if you decide to betray my trust."

"I won't. I swear I won't. I'm genuinely grateful for your confidence." She stood up too. She wanted to ask more questions about the Red Gold, about the CIA's part in the heist. But she knew it would do no good. She could see he was still wondering if he'd made the right decision by talking to her.

He said, "If you'll excuse me, I have a meeting in just a few minutes."

Judith put her hands on his desk and leaned across, face to face with him. "Look," she said. "I don't really care about the Red Gold. That's a side issue. I came to see you because I want to know whether or not I could have done anything to stop Rudy's death. I really need to know that. You never told me who actually killed him."

Kreidler's face stayed cold, but his voice softened. "The Black Brigade."

"Not the old Black Brigade trained by the KGB in Bulgaria during the terrorist era?"

"A remnant. The spawn of the old Black Brigade but grown up now. They're working for the key KGB man who helped steal the gold—Yuri Lepkov—currently in Berlin. I am surprised you haven't heard of them."

Judith recognized the name. Lepkov had been a legendary KGB man, a serious enemy who would stop at nothing to destroy the Western world. And she had also read confidential memos stating that certain fascist groups were offering their services to various criminals again.

"They killed Rudy because of what he learned?"

"Most likely because of what *they* learned. They discovered he was a spy, that's all. He shouldn't have come to you. He was watched, he told me, and they also made you as a CIA agent. But you must not blame yourself, *Fraulein*. Rudy was too young, too idealistic to be in that line of work anyway. He always trusted the wrong people, and on top of that he had the problem with drugs. He befriended the girl Gia. I believe he told her too much, and she passed it on to the others—whether on purpose or because she wasn't thinking straight. And now Rudy's dead." He shrugged matter-of-factly. "Death will come to us all someday."

"Why did he come to me? What did he want me to do?"

"He was already in trouble. If anything, he was looking for a way out, and he wanted to enlist you in his attempted revenge. In fact, it's far more likely that he jeopardized you than you him. I had supposed that might be the reason for your disappearance."

Judith thought about that. She wondered if she might have actually been a target. Perhaps that was why she'd been silently but certainly urged to get off the plane in Milano and go into hiding for a couple of days. "Tell me what you can about this new Black Brigade."

Kreidler's blue eyes turned cold again. "They're basically a band of paramilitary thugs and hit men. The leader is a Neapolitan named Marco Guappo. You must know of him."

Judith did indeed. "He's Neapolitan Mafia."

"That is correct. But at one time he was also a terrorist. He was trained in Bulgaria."

"Bulgaria. That country keeps coming up."

"A lot of connections were made back when the KGB used that country as their spawning ground and nexus of crime. The sewage spills over to the present." Kreidler looked at his watch, then at the door. "I have a meeting, *Fraulein*."

"I'd like to speak with Rudy's aunt."

"That's a bad idea. Rudy's aunt is old, half senile. Rudy was the only family member she was still close to, and she had to bury him yesterday. I wouldn't feel good about bothering her."

"Maybe she'd like to talk to someone who saw him recently."

"No." But his face was twisted with indecision.

Kreidler moved in her direction and tried to usher her out of the room ahead of him, but Judith's stubborn streak emerged, and she stood firm, looking at him expectantly.

Finally he sighed heavily, turned back to his desk, and scribbled something on a note pad, then handed it to her. It was the Archduchess Marlena Brandenburg's phone number and address.

"Have your little visit. Then go back to Moscow, Judith Davies. This problem is way beyond you. I've heard about you. You're a misfit, like Rudy. Only instead of being an avenger, you're a crusader, a champion of the poor and oppressed. But your high goals aren't going to help you in this. You're going to end up like Rudy if you don't leave this alone."

"Are you threatening me?"

He laughed mirthlessly. "Hardly. If anything, the threat comes to me. There are a few of us in the EIA who genuinely want to build a better world, *Fraulein*. I am not talking to you with the sanction of my superiors."

"I can't leave this alone. I honestly wish I could."

"Go speak with Rudy's aunt. Watch out for her nasty little circle of fascist nobles. But watch out most of all for your own people. You must understand that. They are being pressed to the wall in many ways—they have the most to lose. And the men who helped Rudy steal the gold are going to stop at nothing now to hide their bloodied tracks."

"Who are they?"

His eye ticked across her face, and she knew he saw the anxiety there. "I've already said too much."

"Yes," Judith said. "I appreciate the risk you've taken. Thank you. And you'll be relieved to know that I will be leaving Bonn just as soon as I speak with Rudy's aunt."

But as she left the building and hailed a cab, she wondered if she knew what she was doing after all. There had only been two men controlling American interests in Berlin station at the time the Red Gold was stolen from the Soviet central reserve—Bob Hammond, who had shot up the CIA ladder like a skyrocket after leaving Berlin, and Willie von Wolverton, the present chief of Berlin station, whom Hammond still controlled with an iron hand.

Both were powerful men. And if they were indeed implicated in the theft of the Red Gold, chances were good that they were also involved in other crimes against the United States and Russia.

She thought about the mole, about the Grimes case and the betrayed networks in Moscow, all the dead agents over the years, and she shuddered. It wasn't over yet. These people were as evil as anyone in the Mafia, as evil as anyone in the European Union's power structure. They would kill just as quickly, just as ruthlessly. And they would lie just as effectively too. And they probably already knew she was on their trail.

It was still raining as she walked to the car rental center. She knew now why the strong, silent hand had steered her away from informing anybody in the CIA of her suspicions. She knew why she'd had to come alone to find out what had happened to Rudy Brandenburg. She thought about his peculiar statements to her that day in the hotel's garden, and a new surge of anxiety hit her. She knew that it was almost time to come in from the cold, and when she did she was going to start a fire that would burn all the way to Langley, all the way to the EU president's chair and well beyond.

She thought about Rudy Brandenburg, about his cold, horrified face, frozen in death, looking back at an assassin he'd never seen. And she knew that if things went wrong, she might well become nothing more than an anonymous star on the marble wall at CIA HQ at Langley. The wall was reserved as a memorial for covert agents who had died in the field, betrayed by their enemies or their confederates. Even in death, they remained anonymous, their deeds left unsung. Nobody would ever know the terrible secret she had uncovered.

She shivered, then shook off the dread. She needed to contact Frost and tell him, enlist his help in bringing Hammond down. But first of all, she needed to be absolutely certain she wasn't wrapped up in some Gordian spy-knot, being twisted to someone else's ends.

That was why she needed to talk to the Archduchess Marlena von Brandenburg and why she needed to fully understand the pipeline that had transferred the stolen Red Gold.

23

Naples

Peter Natale was wrapped tight and wired, alternately depressed and astounded at the enormity of what he had stumbled into. He drove toward the NATO base, where yet another set of problems awaited him. While he drove, he fought off a sense of unreality as he considered the size of the storm that now swirled up around him.

His probe into Judith's Milano rental car had hit a dead end. The car had been found at a train station in Zurich, and Carlo's people lost her trail after that. Peter wanted to call out the troops, get every available CIA man in the country looking for her—she was, after all, a missing agent, presumed kidnapped or dead according to protocol and deserving of the CIA's full resources in finding out what had happened.

On the other hand, if she had voluntarily vanished, such a move might be the end of her career.

No, he couldn't report her yet. There was too much going on in Langley, too much corruption to deal with throughout Europe and Russia. He'd give it another day, maybe two.

Frost was due back from Langley soon. He'd notified Naples station that he would be stopping here to brief them on certain matters pertinent to the NATO base. Natale could just imagine what that would be. There were forces at work in the US government that wanted to eliminate the American presence in Europe just as badly as most of the European intelligence networks wanted the Americans out. With the US military gone, the rationale for keeping the CIA in Naples was also gone. Maybe they would even be closing Naples station. At any rate, whatever was going on, he would wait till he talked to Frost before he called out the CIA hounds on Judith.

Every time he thought about her, he felt as if someone had hit him in the chest with a hammer, so after a while he made himself stop thinking about her. He focused on the rest of the problem, which was equally confusing. Still, he was getting close to figuring it out. He knew he was in the home stretch now.

He had been lucky to spot Lepkov arguing with Hammond at the Berlin embassy. The circumstances of the argument were alarming. After all, less than an hour before that, two men in a gray Audi had tried to kill him. And then there was Hammond, arguing with a vaguely familiar man, probably arguing about him—at least, Peter thought the argument had been about him. Why else would they be gesturing toward Wolverton's office, where he stood watching from behind a partly drawn drape?

It had taken him twelve hours to match the man's face to an KGB file. Yuri Lepkov. He then searched for connections, for possibilities. Now he had a dozen or more. For the first time, things were beginning to make some sense.

The key was KINTEX, the old Bulgarian trade empire. Lepkov had run the show there. As soon as Peter saw the file, he remembered the name. He in fact saw Lepkov's face in other contexts with regard to the trafficking networks across Europe and Russia, but the pictures were dated. Lepkov had then worn a shock of brown hair and a trim beard and mustache. Now he was clean-shaven and balding. But he was still one of the KGB renegades who had translated the collapse of Communism into a vast personal fortune.

Natale decided that Lepkov might still be running the show —the one he'd stumbled into. Maybe he had even written the script. There was Red Gold in the puzzle, and everyone agreed that the Red Gold could not have left Russia without the help of the intelligence networks. The sum was too vast, the disappearance too complete.

He knew there were also remnants of the old Bulgarian pipelines in place. He had stumbled across that information while looking through lists of Lepkov's dark accomplishments. The list of known terrorists trained by the KGB in Bulgaria included Marco Guappo, son of Cammora thug Vincente Guappo.

Marco had apparently gone through the crisis of identity that seems to hit most teenagers at one time or another. He tried to leave the Mafia and become a terrorist—Lepkov trained him in the terrorist camps in Bulgaria—only to learn that the two ideologies were one and the same.

Lepkov had also delivered countless tons of morphine base to the Ricaso family's heroin labs. *Don* Cesare now ruled Vincente Guappo's Neapolitan crime network, probably including Marco. The connections were getting so thick that Natale felt as if he'd stumbled into a thick, giant spider's web. He was just waiting to discover the spider.

He had been interrupted in his research by a phone call from one of his junior agents, a man who'd been probing into some arms thefts from the NATO base. Natale felt ashamed that he'd left his two juniors on their own for so long. Officially, he'd told them to act as if he were still on vacation.

Now the agent had run into a problem with Military Intelligence. He needed someone to cut through some red tape. It was nothing much, just a minor turf war, but Natale decided he needed to do his job and get it straightened out.

He hung a left on the Viale Augusto. As he turned toward the coastal highway, he saw a woman standing beside a green Fiat Uno parked at the side of the road. A tire was obviously flat. She waved, and for a moment he started to go on past. The crime rate was so high in Naples, the scams so various and plentiful, that his first thought was of robbers.

He in fact drove past her. But as he glanced back he saw such a look of disappointment on her face that his compassion kicked in and he decided he could spend a moment after all. He pulled to the shoulder and looked around. No place a partner could be waiting. He backed up on the shoulder, swung out into the road when he reached the Fiat, then reversed into a position behind the stalled auto. He rolled his window down, feeling like a Good Samaritan. His gun was in the door pouch if anything went wrong, inches away from his left hand.

The woman was young and plain, with brown straggly hair. Her eyes were hidden behind sunglasses. She wore a white T-shirt and denim slacks, and there was something faintly suggestive about the way she bent over so close she almost filled the car window. She brushed a strand of hair off her forehead.

"Mi scusi," she said, smiling at him. "Would you help me?" She spoke Italian with a Neapolitan dialect, which meant she was a native.

Natale didn't like her closeness, and he drew back. There was a scent of stale cigarette smoke and something oppressive about her. He said, "Let me take a look," and started to open the car door.

She continued to lean against it, and Peter realized she was blocking his view of the road.

She said, "Maybe it would be better to leave my car here and just have it towed."

Natale frowned. "I'm not going back toward the city just now. I'd better have a look." He wanted to push her away, but she was, after all, a woman. He pushed gently on the door and waited for her to get the message. He pushed harder then and finally pressed her back in order to climb out.

Abruptly she caught him off guard and shoved him forward with surprising strength, knocking him off balance. It took an instant to catch himself. And in that instant there was a screech of brakes, and a black Volkswagen van skidded to a stop feet away.

Natale couldn't believe it was happening. He was being kidnapped?

The man who leaped from the passenger side of the van was wearing black from head to toe, including a black mountaineer's mask. He also held a Skorpion submachine gun, aimed dead at Peter. Any thoughts Natale had of going for his gun instantly vanished.

Traffic was getting thicker. He hoped for an instant that one of the many drivers flowing past would stop to help him. But this was, after all, Naples. People knew the Camorra. They knew the Mafia rules. Nobody ever wanted to get involved, because as long as you could look the other way you would be safe.

He watched for any chance at all.

The van driver shouted, *"Pronto! Dai!"*

The man with the Skorpion barely turned his head and shouted back a reply.

Peter dove into him. His shoulder slammed into the man's side. The Skorpion went flying.

And then Natale was being dragged to his feet. He swiveled his head to see Marco Guappo, muddy eyes gloating, the woman beside him, Guappo smiling as he heaved Peter up by his belt. Then Guappo wheeled him around and slammed a gun butt into his face.

Natale could feel his forehead bleeding. He held his arms out at his sides, indicating submission. "What do you want?"

Marco brought the gun up again. Natale raised his hands without thinking to shield himself from the death he saw in the man's eyes. The other man had his Skorpion aimed at him again. There was no point in fighting back and dying a hero.

The driver shouted again, *"Pronto! Dai!"*

Marco's expression changed. He glanced backward at the highway. Several cars were approaching, among them a brown military truck. He jabbed the gun muzzle into Natale's side. He and the woman pressed Peter forward, forward, and suddenly the side door of the van slid open. Peter had a glimpse of tangled bedding, a small stack of guns, a wooden case of bullets, and the remnants of take-out meals.

He was willing to get into the van—he knew when he was outgunned. Besides, Guappo was subordinate to Carlo Ricaso. There was some mistake here. He said, "Call Carlo. He'll straighten this out—"

But the words were cut off before he finished. Something hit him in the back of the head, a wave of nauseous darkness shot into fireworks. And then he felt himself sag forward, felt hands drag him inside. He heard the door slide shut, heard someone talking though he couldn't make out what was said. He felt a surge of shame at his stupidity, a sense of anger that his desire to help had been betrayed.

Then the world went mercifully black.

24

The Rhine River Valley, near Bonn

Judith left Bonn at 4:00 P.M. and drove back up the Rhine River Valley. She hunched in the driver's seat of her rental car and glanced frequently into the rearview mirror. After five tedious miles, she was finally satisfied that no one was following her.

The gloomy morning had turned into a rainy afternoon, but she was scarcely aware of the weather. She traveled past vineyards and through several small villages with golden-spired churches and gabled wooden houses. The valley was rich with castles that seemed to materialize out of the mists of time. Some were crumbled ruins, others had been renovated by Europe's noveau riche. As she spotted the castle known as Drachenfels, perched high on a hilltop, she remembered that this was where Richard Wagner's *Neiblung* hero Siegfried had supposedly slain the dragon.

That thought reminded her of Rudy Brandenburg's cryptic words: "Your country had slain the dragon, only to find that the world is now filled with a bewildering variety of poisonous snakes."

Dragons. Rhinegold. Maybe even Red Gold. This ancient valley held legends of lustful, destructive wealth; it held political realities that slept fitfully beneath the picturesque surface, fermenting into poison. Here the Nazi party was growing strong again.

As she passed beneath Drachenfels castle, the dark, heavy clouds sank lower to cloak the gloomy valley. The river had been a placid blue during her journey down from the Alps. Now it was deep gray and turbulent. Barges struggled against the heavy current and chop.

The depressing mood of the countryside exactly matched her own. Her sense of mission had vanished, she felt foolish and alone

—and a bit afraid of what she was doing. She considered what would happen when she returned to Moscow station, and then she thought about Frost and about Peter Natale.

She hated the fact that she'd worried them, yet she'd been afraid to tell them the truth. Frost especially. He would have ordered her back to Moscow immediately and demanded she stay there till he had his end of the problem straightened out.

Maybe that's what she should have done. She was definitely in over her head now. Depression settled over her like black fog.

When she reached the small hamlet of Bad Honef, she turned inland through the rain-streaked vineyards. The road wound upward toward a mountain valley, and after a twenty-minute drive she made a hard right turn, then slid to a stop in front of an iron-barred gate that had been hidden by a sudden heavy cover of trees.

A sign was wired to the gate: Verboten. Just in case the reader didn't speak German, the sign also said Forbidden to Enter, Closed to Visitors, in English and Italian and French.

Judith climbed out and checked the gate, which was the only way through a high stone wall. Three massive padlocks sealed it tight.

She shielded her eyes against the rain and peered through the trees. She saw a large unkempt lawn, a wide serpentine driveway, crumbling French gardens off to the left. There were also outbuildings, and in the center of the dense trees and shrubs she could make out the castle itself—or rather, what was left of a castle complex, for the moat, walls, ramparts, and bulwarks had long ago been torn down to leave only the castle keep.

It was a square, four-story edifice of gray stone, with turrets rising on all four corners. It was small by the standards of most Rhineland castles, and there was an air of crumbling disrepair about it. But the dwelling was immense indeed when compared to the homes of the common folk.

Pale light poured through French windows in the right lower corner. Judith went back to the car, pulled it off the road, locked it, then scaled the gate and began walking down the driveway in the rain.

She was just catching the antiquated mood of the place when

a sudden bedlam of guard dogs came snarling and barking, whirling toward her like a devil wind hidden in the trees.

She spun around and ran back to the gate. As she scrambled over, a male voice yelled at the dogs in German, and the bedlam died to a mild, disgruntled yipping as a man appeared out of the forest.

He was apparently the caretaker. He was wearing greasy coveralls and a weathered raincap. His face was weather-beaten yet guileless. His eyes were bleared by age. Three tan-and-black German shepherds trotted obediently behind him.

"*Jah?*" he said loudly. Too loudly. Judith realized he was hard of hearing. He walked toward the gate. Two of the dogs' tails were actually wagging now. "What is it you want?"

"I am a friend of Rudy's." She raised her voice. "I phoned ahead."

The man looked her over. "Ms. Livman, *jah?*"

Judith nodded, acknowledging her assumed name. She felt uncomfortable under his scrutiny. She was tired, disheveled from travel, feeling older by the moment as she stood there being pelted by the driving rain.

"You are early. No matter. Come."

The man opened the padlocks with a set of keys. She went back to the car, drove through, waited while he locked it again. Then she invited him inside, and they drove down the serpentine driveway. She parked in front of the stone castle. It seemed larger and older up close. Stones were crumbling, the roof was in disrepair. Debris was stacked in several places near small outbuildings.

The front door was massive carved oak. The man opened it for her and ushered her into the front hall, where he left her for a moment, then reappeared with a clean though frayed kitchen towel. He invited her to dry off, waited while she dabbed water from her face, then silently gestured for her to follow him.

It was the sort of house where it always seems to be night. The hallway was narrow, the walls were dark, polished wood. Most of the windows appeared to be permanently shut.

The caretaker escorted her into a large library, and Judith stared at endless volumes of leather-bound books that filled three walls from the floor to the high, vaulted ceiling. There was an overabundance of furniture and whatnots in the room, a worn green Persian rug. Belgian lace throws covered the backs of claw-footed dark brown sofas. There was also a walk-in stone fireplace in a far corner, where a small fire had been lit. Beside the fireplace were the French windows through which she'd seen the light.

The Archduchess Marlena Brandenburg sat beside the fire, tucked into a wheelchair, a tan afghan thrown across her lap. She was at the edge of the yellow lamplight, and the darkness spread out around her. The table at her side was littered with papers. The floor was stacked high with leather-bound photograph albums.

"Thank you for coming," the old woman said, wheeling her chair slightly so that she faced Judith. She nodded regally.

Judith thanked her in turn. She had an eerie feeling that she'd stepped back in time, for everything in the room seemed to come from the past, and the woman herself was well over ninety years old. The gleaming brass fireplace fittings were turn of the century, the aging furniture was a mixture of eras, stopping sometime in the forties. The walnut picture frames on the mantelpiece and wall displayed brown photographs of men in Nazi uniform.

The archduchess was small and slender, and she held her age well. She had a frail, perfect jawline and parchment-thin skin with just a hint of crepe at her throat. Her carriage was erect, even while sitting. There was a queenly tilt to her head.

Her long silver hair was wrapped neatly into a chignon, and she wore a fortune in large, flawless diamonds against a black crepe dress.

Her left shoulder displayed a huge brooch in the shape of a rose. Huge rings adorned every finger. A necklace that sparkled like fire hung from her neck, nearly covering it, and thick bracelets banded each wrist. Judith could see that the woman had once been a great beauty. She was beautiful still.

But there was something disquieting about her, a thin trace of contempt permanently stenciled into her pursed lips, a discontented frown etched permanently in the small wrinkles between her eyes, a haughtiness in the inclination of her head.

The archduchess patted a small brown sofa next to her, and Judith sat down. A light dust rose up from the upholstery as her weight pressed into it. It made her sad, somehow, that it had been so long since anyone had used or cleaned this sofa.

The archduchess smiled thinly, as Judith noticed a collection of silver-framed photographs arranged on a small table beside her. The clothing and hairstyles were reminiscent of the 1930s. One photograph especially caught her eye. It captured a glittering crowd standing in front of an opera house, the men in formal attire and military uniform, the women in gowns and tiaras and furs. Judith realized that the woman next to the end was the youthful arch-duchess: she had been indeed exquisite, with white-blonde hair and wide innocent eyes, holding a bejeweled cigarette holder co-quettishly between her fingers.

Judith thought she was so beautiful she was almost ethereal. And then the sensation was drawn inside out and became a claw of dread, for Judith recognized the man standing beside her, his hand possessively gripping her arm. It was Adolph Hitler, young, prob-ably in the beginning of his rule, with the spark of evil madness already traced into his eyes.

Judith felt a chill creep into the room. Mentally she dis-tanced herself from the old woman beside her.

"You have come about Rudy," the archduchess said.

Judith heard a tremor of grief in her voice. "I wanted to pay my respects. I understand the funeral was yesterday."

"If funeral is what you want to call it. I was the only one there." The elderly woman shot her an accusing look.

"I'm sorry," Judith said. "I didn't know."

"Yes, well—the family in Berlin chose not to come. My niece and her husband are in Washington. What could I do on such short notice anyway?"

"I really wish I could have been here."

"Rudy was your friend?" The Archduchess Marlena said it hungrily, as if she needed to talk about her lost nephew.

"I was with him shortly before he died."

"Before he was murdered," the archduchess said, anger flash-ing in her rheumy eyes.

"I had wondered about that," Judith said innocently.

The archduchess flicked her hand dismissively. The blue di-amonds gleamed as firelight caught the bracelets. "Please don't patronize me, young woman. I was dabbling in political intrigue long before you were born. You are American, are you not?"

Judith nodded, a bit embarrassed.

"Then you no doubt know my American nephew by marriage, Robert Hammond?"

Judith felt a chill of trepidation. "I do."

"He is an American spy. A disgrace to the family. Are you a spy too?"

The question startled Judith. "I—not at the moment."

"Then how do you know Rudy?"

"I met him in Monte Carlo."

"Just before he died?" The question was sharp.

"I . . . uh . . . yes."

"Then what do you want from me?" The woman was suddenly imperious, her nostrils flaring, her head tilted at a dangerous angle.

Judith decided that a direct approach was probably the only one that was going to work, even though it was risky. She told the truth.

"I don't know what happened to him," she concluded, "but I do know that he came to me for help, and I let him down."

The archduchess thought for a moment, then nodded. "I believe your story."

"I wish it *weren't* true."

"You're not the only one who let him down," the old woman said bitterly. There were tears in her eyes. "Everyone let him down. Everyone used him."

"Who used him?"

The old woman looked suspiciously at her and fell silent. The fog and darkness seemed to fill the French windows, and the caretaker—apparently the only servant on the premises—came in and pulled the drapes against the growing night, then turned on two lamps. The extra light was immediately swallowed by shadows.

Judith became uncomfortable. "I'm sorry. I really don't know why I've come."

The woman ignored her. Her jaw grew taut as she seemed to think of other things. "Was Rudy using drugs again?"

Judith thought before she answered and decided to again be honest. "Yes. I think so."

The old woman winced as if someone had slapped her. "It is hard for the children of the nobility today. They are born to rule, and the world refuses them."

Judith again felt the vast distance between herself and this domineering old lady.

But the archduchess was in her own thoughts and didn't notice. "And Rudy said he had gold?"

"Well—he said he had found it."

She surprised Judith then by letting her face relax into a faint smile. "Rudy was a good boy."

"I wish I'd known him better."

"Yes, you would have liked him." She stopped and looked speculatively at Judith, then added, "If he only would have married, things might have been different."

Judith smiled. "He'd have needed someone closer to his own age."

The archduchess smiled weakly, though sadly. "Yes. There was a young girl in Naples, a princess, someone he cared about. He spoke of her the last time he was here. A pity. He would have made a good husband for someone. He was so attentive, so thoughtful. He gave me these, you know." She fingered the diamonds at her throat, touched the brooch, then displayed her diamond-studded fingers and wrists.

Judith wondered where Rudy had gotten the diamonds. There was a fortune there.

A shrewd look came over the old woman's face, as if she guessed Judith's thoughts. "Rudy took care of me. You must not think badly of him. After the war, when the Americans came, we had nothing left, you see—at least those of us who refused to renounce our beliefs had nothing. It was all given to the *Jews* again." She virtually spat out the word.

Judith had to look down to avoid reacting. Her grandmother had been Jewish. Judith's Christianity made her deeply respect God's Chosen People, and she deplored what the Nazis had done.

The archduchess shot her a peculiar look, part defensive, part curious, as if defying her to contradict the statement. When

Judith remained silent, her eyes masked, the old woman said, "Rudy was coming next week to take me to Bayreuth." She tipped her head and peered at Judith. "Do you go to Bayreuth, my dear?"

"I—I'm afraid you have me at a disadvantage."

"The opera." The woman said. *"The Ring.* Surely you've been to see *The Ring* at least once?" The question was anxious, as if she were desperately seeking common ground.

Judith surprised herself by suddenly remembering the whole theme. Bayreuth was the home of the Festpielhaus, the opera house Richard Wagner had founded over a century ago to show-case his series of operas *Der Ring des Nibelungen.* The operas were about Nordic and Teutonic pre-Christian gods. They centered on the tale of the Rhinegold, which lay at the bottom of the River Rhine, guarded by the ethereal Rhine Maidens.

She thought some of the most wonderful music ever written came from that opera. But with it also came some of the most racist propaganda ever devised.

Wagner had been and was the darling of the Nazi party. His combination of subtle German elitism and brilliant music had drawn them by the droves. Wotan, the god of war, had been a hero of Hitler's. Some said the demented tyrant actually believed himself possessed by this evil god made famous by Wagner.

Judith suppressed a shiver. "I've never gone to Bayreuth, but I've seen the opera. I love Wagner's music." It was true. It was hauntingly beautiful. It was his racism she despised.

The archduchess offered up a charming if withered smile. "I see. A pity you can't go. If Rudy was here, I'm sure he'd want you to come with us." She paused, suddenly worried, then said, "Did Rudy give you anything to bring to me?"

Judith frowned, puzzled. "I—I'm sorry, no."

"Nothing?"

"I'm sorry."

"But he said he would send it—ah, of course he will. He has always taken care of me."

Judith noticed the change of tense as the old lady thought about her deceased nephew. She remembered Kreidler's saying the woman was slightly senile.

"My Rudy was a remarkable person," the archduchess said, again placing him in the past. "A hero, like Seigfried. You know, my Rudy actually discovered the Rhinegold. Many years ago, when he worked in Berlin. Without it, I would have lost this castle and all the vineyards. Without him, I would have no hope." She shot Judith a probing look. "And you say he sent nothing?"

"No. What were you expecting?"

The archduchess's lashes swept her eyes, coyly. She raised a shoulder and tilted her head, in a posture both regal and coquettish. "Perhaps I misunderstood. I must speak with him again."

"Excuse me?"

The archduchess smiled such a superior smile that Judith felt as if she'd been slapped. "You must stay for dinner, then the seance," she said. "We will have several guests tonight."

Judith felt the room turn cold. There was a sudden sense of decay around her. "I'm afraid I must get back."

"Please stay. Rudy will speak to us. He will tell me when to expect the . . . the . . ." Her voice tapered off.

Judith suddenly understood. The old woman had been hoping that she was bringing money from Rudy. He had still been supporting her. She wondered about the Berlin side of the family. She'd heard they were still wealthy. Why weren't they helping? Then she wondered again about the rest of the missing Red Gold.

A stricken, almost frightened look came into the old woman's eyes as Judith started to stand up. The surface of her face seemed to crumble. "Perhaps he left something with the girl he was seeing."

"I can check if you wish."

The archduchess looked relieved. She reached up and pulled a cord.

The caretaker came into the room, a cook's apron wrapped around his thin waist.

"Wolfe, please get my brocaded box from my dresser," she said.

The old man nodded, and Judith saw a gentle respect in his eyes as he looked at the archduchess.

"Would you like to see my photographs while we wait?"

Judith nodded and accepted the top album from the stack beside the wheelchair. She opened it, turned so the woman could see the pictures too, then looked at the page to see a young Rudy Brandenburg smiling up at her. The following pages showed more of him, with his parents, then alone, then with the archduchess and her late husband, a man with a stance and face like a Prussian general. The archduchess had been sitting here alone, looking at the albums, lost in memories and grief.

But then the archduchess picked up another album, and now they were farther in the past. These photographs were of still more men in Nazi uniform, of women with adoring smiles on their faces as they looked up at them. Finally, with the third album, the photographs became sepia-tinted with age, and then there was an album of actual tintypes. There were castles, portraits of elaborate balls, of Germanic people at the turn of the century, Teutonic, Bavarian, regal and haughty. And there were symbols in the background of some of the tintypes, symbols of the Baravian Black Nobility and the branch that held the House of Brandenburg.

Judith waited until one unusual symbol caught her eye. It was a reverse swastika imprinted in a brooch worn by a woman who had obviously lived and died long before Hitler's time. Beside it, in the same brooch, was the *sig rune*—the double lightning bolt—which was supposed to be highly magical.

She pointed. "These symbols preceded the Nazi symbols? What do they mean?"

"These are concealed matters." The archduchess's eyes slitted dangerously. "To understand, you must commit yourself fully and study for years."

Judith nodded and decided to ask no more questions, in spite of her consuming curiosity. She could guess the truth anyway. Both were mystical symbols found heavily throughout all the occultic traditions of the Black Nobility. Both indicated that the family had been steeped in occultic tradition for at least a century.

She felt a sudden chill as she thought about the old woman's short time left on earth and the depths of the deception within which she lived. She prayed fervently that God would give her the right words to say to help the archduchess, knowing that anything she said on her own would be met with anger and rejection.

She couldn't just leave it alone. Finally, in spite of some reservations, she blurted out, "Do you believe in God?"

The old woman looked at her haughtily. "Which god?"

"The Creator. God."

"Why on earth do you ask such a question?"

Judith forged ahead. "I wonder if you believe in life after death?"

"Of course. I have studied with the Thule society and also under the Vrilists. I am Aryan, my dear. We are a race of giants, superior people, surely you know. But I do not believe in a Christian God. That being is for fools. Rudy's spirit is still with me, right here, and he will join me in the Fourth Reich."

Judith felt her heart sink. "Have you ever known Jesus?" she asked, not knowing how else to say it except directly.

"What foolish talk. And I thought you seemed such a bright young girl." There was livid, scathing hatred hidden behind the woman's demeaning words.

Judith hesitated, unsure of what to say or do next.

At that moment the old man returned and handed a brocaded box to the archduchess. She opened it, rummaged among some papers, then pulled out a small, thin scrap. "Ah, here it is."

She handed it over with reluctance, as if she were giving up a treasure map.

Judith took it respectfully, turned it right side up, and froze as she read the words: "Gianalisa Lauro. Contact through Serena Porcellana." The name was followed by a Palermo address, in the ancient palazzo district beside the street known as the Viale della Libertà.

Judith remembered from her Moscow research that one of the prince's two palaces was in Palermo, the other outside Naples.

She said, "I'll copy this down. I have a friend in Palermo. Perhaps he can find her for you." She rummaged in her handbag, pulled out a pencil and a small notepad, then wrote down the name and address.

The archduchess became childish when Judith said she had to leave. She began to devise reasons to hang onto her longer, as if Judith were a last hope. So Judith looked at more albums, listened to inconsequential talk about long-dead relatives and the opera in

Bayreuth. She wanted to talk to the old woman about her eternal soul, about the Savior who could lift her out of the tradition of darkness. She kept looking for a way to talk, kept praying that God would lead her.

She had stayed long enough to realize that there were no guests coming. Any seance would be a solitary affair with the archduchess sitting, talking to the ghosts of the dead past.

Finally the old woman fell asleep in her chair beside the fire, and the caretaker came in and suggested Judith come back another day.

She left reluctantly. She felt a vast, pitying sadness.

Judith prayed on the way back to Bonn, first for the tired old woman who would soon step into an eternity she was unprepared to meet, then about everything that had happened to bring her to that woman's doorstep. Finally, as she reached the Bonn city limits, bypassed downtown, and drove toward the airport, the sense of oppression lifted, and she suddenly felt refreshed.

She would write to the archduchess, send her cards, and try to help her. That was as much as she could do. As far as finances were concerned, perhaps the old lady would have to sell her castle and her diamonds. She'd probably live well for the rest of her life on the proceeds from that alone.

Her encounter with the archduchess had diverted Judith's attention from her own problems for a time. Now she was back in her own world, and she was at last beginning to fully understand the circuitous path she had taken from the time she'd jumped ship in Milano until now.

She needed to find Gianalisa and talk to her about Rudy. That might put one more small piece into the puzzle. But whether or not she had a chance to talk to the young princess, Judith was finished with her secret quest. She knew that much.

She needed to fly back to Naples and start the firestorm that would inevitably erupt. It was time to enlist Peter to help her, to bring Frost into the game. Together they could bring this whole crazy fiasco to an end—with God's continued help.

25

Valletta

The Sicilian sky was overcast, the humidity was oppressive. Hot dry winds had gathered their breath in the scorching sands of the Sahara, then screamed across the Mediterranean, soaking up moisture from the sea as they came. They whined now with near-gale force through the valley where lay *don* Cesare Ricaso's estate.

The Ricaso family had been busy during the past week. Carlo's nerves were on edge, his skin was itchy. *Don* Cesare, on the other hand, seemed to be lost in a brooding melancholy as he watched his nephew's efforts to find the kidnapped young Luciano Chicarelli.

Don Cesare was deeply worried about losing his one solid shot at controlling the European Union's presidency, which would soon usurp the dictates of the governments he already controlled in Palermo and Rome. The worry ate at him like water eroding a stone.

Cesare and Carlo had watched Benito Jacovetti's pyrogenic speech on the ENN network, and *don* Cesare didn't sleep at all that night. Carlo could hear him pacing, back and forth, back and forth, stopping, then pacing once again.

The following morning, the wily old *don* informed Carlo that he himself would take over the campaign to find Luciano, that now he would stop at nothing. Carlo noted the hellish light burning in his uncle's eyes and stepped out of his way.

The sirocco winds made tangible the dark, evil storm-currents surging through *don* Cesare's heart and the hearts of his men. They came and went, speaking in clipped sentences, communicating with dark looks and near-imperceptible glances.

Carlo watched and waited while his evil uncle called up the full power of his dark empire. But Luciano Chicarelli had disappeared days ago, and he still could not be found.

The date of selection of the EU president was fast approaching, and Volante Chicarelli continued to fall apart. He called the Ricaso estate every day now, pleading for his son's life, apparently further convincing himself that *don* Cesare had spirited the lad away.

Carlo was sickened by what was happening. He was showing his blood now, issuing orders in a rage, then reacting eagerly each time the telephone rang or a car raced into the well-guarded driveway, believing the boy would soon be located. At the same time, *don* Cesare's men ruthlessly combed Sicily, the Italian mainland, any possible place the kidnappers might hold Luciano.

From Palermo to Trapani to Reggio dei Calabria and Naples, from Rome to Milano to Brussels, suspected collaborators were gunned down in broad daylight. Cars were blown up, businesses bombed. Corpses were found in parks, at the airport, in bars, alleys, dumpsters. Throughout this, *don* Cesare showed the bitter concentration of a general staging his most vital campaign. And as each assault, each death, was reported to him, he discussed his strategy with Carlo, asked Carlo's opinion, solicited Carlo's advice, and craved his praise.

And still they had not found Luciano.

"We'll get the *pesecano* who did this." Cesare's choleric face was dark as a rat's skin. "Wherever he is, whoever he is, the *'ncarugnutu* is *carnazze succese.*"

Carlo could see, now, why *don* Cesare was the most powerful of Sicily's capos. He would destroy the very world to achieve his ends. Still, in this instance Carlo mostly approved of his uncle's campaign. The last few weeks had changed him, and he felt as if his soul were dusted with a soot made from the ground glass of bitterness. This kidnapping had whetted his natural bent toward revenge and had solidified the logic that were it not for the Ricasos' power, truly evil men would spring up like dragons' teeth to completely devour the planet.

Carlo knew he was being sucked further into this violent

world, and for the first time he fully understood what drove men like *don* Cesare and his late father.

One part of that understanding was a new knowledge of the contempt that Dominic and Cesare had always shown for most people in positions of governmental authority. The public officials and police who paid obeisance to *don* Cesare were despicable, spineless men. Even though Cesare had quietly engaged them in the search for Luciano, they were as good as useless when doing anything besides selling out their fellow men. *Don* Cesare was right about them. They closed their eyes to bloodstains and atrocities in return for a feathered nest, and the price of their feathers was cheap at that.

Carlo was also beginning to understand why Cesare placed such low value on these men's lives. They surrounded him, fawned on him until they were sickening. They could be used but never trusted. Nor would they stand up under pressure, for they were apt as not to change sides with the changing wind—or, at very least, to turn tail and run when they were most needed. As now.

The entire situation set Carlo to thinking. Perhaps for this time and place, *La Familia* was the only way. In the world that was Sicily a person survived only by bloodletting and/or cunning—or one was inundated by the pervasive moral rot that had overspread and eaten through the very culture like the fine, tangled webwork of decay that sometimes ate into the stones beneath Sicily's lush hanging gardens.

The kidnapping also polished to darkness Carlo's lust for revenge, the seeds of which had found fertile soil the previous year in his younger brother Johnny's brutal murder. Or perhaps the seeds had been planted all the way back, before Carlo had been born, in the lives of a family of Sicilian peasants who had learned deception, violence, and *omerta* in order to simply survive.

In a word, he was beginning to see with the vision of those who were Mafia—a people alienated from others, a people aware that others fed on their pain and amused themselves with their bloodshed. They'd been forced to breed dark strengths, thereby developing a frightening contempt for those who lived in safer and simpler worlds.

Now Carlo felt contempt for the man he had been. In a situation like this, it was apparent that a man of honor had few options for survival.

Still, even a Mafioso could have friends.

When Carlo Ricaso tried to contact Peter Natale and was told that Natale had disappeared the day before, his car found abandoned on the road to the NATO base, Carlo suddenly understood Volante Chicarelli's misgivings about his uncle.

He wondered if *don* Cesare knew Carlo had been using Mafia resources to help Pietro search for Judith. He remembered the old man's threats after he helped bail Natale out of the scrape at Hotel de Mer. And he wondered if Cesare had finally decided to destroy his relationship with Peter Natale in a permanent way.

Carlo reactivated the small group of men he could personally trust—not many, for most would sell him out in a heartbeat in order to gain points with *don* Cesare. Natale had disappeared as mysteriously as Luciano Chicarelli, and Carlo thought there might be a connection of sorts. But by the second day of searching, he and his men had learned nothing about Peter, nothing more about Luciano, and *don* Cesare continued his own brutal search.

Carlo decided that his uncle was not to blame after all for Natale's disappearance. Both Luciano and Pietro were more likely pawns in a greater game. Some master hand was tempting the Ricaso family, some master hand was trifling with death. Carlo or *don* Cesare would find them. Soon. And then these enemies of *La Familia* were going to be dead, no matter how much blood had to be shed toward that end.

26

Naples

Peter Natale heard a distant buzzing. His eyelids were heavy, his body felt like lead, though he was at least conscious again. His wrists were chained to the wall, he was on the stone floor, curled up in a fetal position. He was also deathly nauseous. He knew he had been drugged.

The faraway buzz of voices grew louder, and he realized the noise had awakened him. He tried to make out the words but could only tell that they were spoken in angry Italian. And then he heard a fragment, a man's voice saying, "A last resort . . . go with the Sixth Fleet . . . lose some people, doesn't matter . . . Lepkov is right."

He wanted to hear more, but his stomach betrayed him. He gagged, then rolled his head to one side and vomited up the only thing left in his stomach—coffee and bile. He heard people in the room with him now, behind him, and for a second he felt strangely embarrassed that he'd thrown up on their concrete floor. Heroin. They had given him heroin. It often made the nonaddicted user sick. A boot kicked him in the rib cage from behind, and the shame turned to instant agony.

Just as they rolled him over, he opened his eyes to stare at a single light bulb dangling from the high ceiling. Then he was looking up into a Mephistophelian face, a small rat's mouth. The man had an aged countenance and thinning black hair, which Natale knew was dyed. It was combed crossways to hide the bald spots. His well-trimmed black goatee and mustache—also dyed jet black —were what gave him the Mephistophelian air. It seemed even blacker against the pallor of his skin.

Natale knew him, of course. He had watched this man and his alcoholic mistress for two tedious nights as they'd gambled and postured and thrown away chips to the croupiers in the casino at Hotel de Mer.

The prince's mouth was frozen in cruelty. His thin hair was mussed, as if he'd been running his fingers through it, worrying. Strangely, he wore brown French-striped pajamas and a brown wool robe. Natale wondered if they were in the prince's home.

Veresi arched his dark eyebrows. Peter could see the hatred in his eyes, could see that the man wanted to reach down and grab him by the throat and strangle him. But the prince controlled his primitive blood lust, stepped back, turned his head, and said, "Call someone. Have this mess cleaned up."

Marco Guappo stepped into Natale's line of vision. He said to the prince, "What do you want me to do?"

"Find out what he knows. Everything. And if he won't talk, kill him."

Marco's smile was manifested evil, enough to make Natale wonder if demons could take human form.

He could see the prince turn and walk away, then look back once at him with no expression on his face. And then Marco was over him, smiling, talking. "You Americans are going to pay for every dollar you've cost us."

Marco yanked him into a sitting position, so that the manacles scraped his wrists. Then he kicked Peter in the ribs again, and Natale felt the nausea well up.

"Do you know where you are?" Marco asked.

Natale shook his head no.

"You are standing in the doorway to hell. And I'm going to shove you in and watch you burn. Now. Tell me. Why are you and your friends so interested in Prince Dante di Veresi?"

Natale tried to remember. His mind was clouded by pain. His head lolled back against the cold stone wall.

"Don't lie. You were seen, watching him at the casino in Hotel de Mer. What do you want with him?"

He tried to remember. It seemed so very long ago. So much had happened since then. He rolled his head back and forth, indicating a negative reply. His mind felt as if it were filled with mud. His body seemed to have been flushed through with prussic acid.

"Where is your nosy girlfriend?"

Peter became alert but managed to hide it. Judith. They were talking about Judith. Were they after her too? If they were, at least they didn't have her. Otherwise they wouldn't be asking about her. Maybe she was still OK.

Marco kicked him again, harder. "Where? What is she doing?" He spat out the words.

Natale wanted to answer. The drugs were still in his system, and they made him strangely passive and compliant. But he really didn't know.

The inquisition continued only a moment longer, then something seemed to snap in Marco, and the questions stopped. He began to beat Peter methodically, sadistically, in the face, the kidneys, the stomach, until Natale, trying his best to defend himself in spite of his chains, felt himself gagging on his own blood, realized he was lightheaded and far too weak to win—and with despair realized he was going to pass out again. He prayed silently as he felt his body sag.

The blows finally stopped. Marco Guappo was still cursing as he called for the guards, and Peter heard new footsteps approaching.

"Call me when he wakes up," Guappo said.

And then he was gone, and Natale sagged all the way into black oblivion.

27

Palermo

After Marco and Roberto had taken her from the farmhouse above Naples, the Princess Gianalisa Lauro Veresi had been locked in one of her father's dungeon apartments, where she was kept by two fat, evil trolls.

Twice a day the trolls pretended to be her father's servants and brought her trays of food. At other times they appeared with white coats on, masquerading as doctors bringing shiny clean hypodermic needles on white enamel trays.

Gia recognized the dissolved white powder, and she gratefully put out her arm for the injections. This was better than suicide. Sometimes she would cry as the needle penetrated her skin, but sometimes she would smile peacefully as the fluid found its way into her royal blood.

She would be OK for a time after that. She would feel her head sag to her chest, and she'd be in and out of oblivion for a while. Then she'd awaken to float aloft with the translucent, silken-winged angels and cherubs who drifted across the ceiling—though when the trolls returned, the angelic beings quickly embedded themselves back into the luminous, milky tiles that made up a huge Olympian fresco on the room's wide-domed ceiling.

Sometimes, even when the trolls were here, Gia could see the angels secretly laughing at her.

The trolls had come with her medicine more than two hours ago. They would be back with food later, when the sun went down, though Gia only knew when the sun set because the room grew dark and she had to put on the lights. Now it was still filled with golden afternoon sunlight that filtered through the high, barred windows. She lay on her back on a silk-covered couch and looked up at the painted languid Venus and thought about her mother.

This lavish dungeon, with its dappled mirrors, gilded silk furniture, and enameled floor was her mother's tomb. She was sure of it, though she'd been unable to find any trace of her mother's body or blood. Perhaps her mother had disappeared into the milky depths of the fresco, or perhaps she had escaped through one of the secret passages that made up a labyrinth within the lower regions of the palace.

Or perhaps she hadn't escaped at all. Perhaps she was still locked in the secret apartment beneath this one, crying and crying, her sobs making the passageways reverberate with an echo that turned into the thunder that shook the hills. Perhaps it was her mother's screams she had heard last night, then again this morning. Perhaps her mother wasn't dead yet after all.

Gianalisa shuddered and forced herself to sit up and stare at the wall instead of the ceiling. If she ignored the ceiling, the painted beings would leave her alone for a while. She thought about her mother escaping, and she knew that she too would escape. Tonight.

She had thought of nothing else since being imprisoned here. She'd been planning all the time, drawing maps with her thumbnail in the silken upholstery as she remembered from childhood the honeycomb of secret passages that ran through the palace, then out into the gardens and courtyards. She discovered that she could remember secret doors and apartments and suites that had been forgotten years ago.

She dared a small glance upward, and saw the Venus smiling again. Gia took that as a sign that she could break free from the Prince of Darkness and his frightening trolls.

Ginanalisa had grown up in this enormous palazzo, built by Prince Giordino di Veresi in the seventeenth century as a combination citadel and residence. It had been renovated and added to throughout the years so that now it was a forty-room complex of salons, galleries, kitchens, passageways, opulent stairways, marble-encrusted ballrooms, towers, terraces, courtyards, sculpted cornices, elaborate balustrades, secret balconies, and forgotten attics filled with cobwebs and ghosts and the clutter of the centuries.

Gianalisa had been a lonely child. She had entertained and frightened herself by taking her doll to explore every part of the Palazzo di Veresi, from the oldest section that had suffered earthquake damage—where one could still step through a doorway and into a room collapsed to rubble—to the newer part built during the baroque era when Sicily's nobles had celebrated their golden age with palaces and castles second to none in the world.

She knew this palace. She knew its secrets. And she knew that something new had happened last night. Someone new had been brought to the basements, where the rooms with bars and whips and chains were hidden, the rooms where they had put Luciano, the only part of the palace she had never dared explore.

She had tried to find Luciano though. She had quashed her fear and climbed down the stone steps, only to find the passage blocked by a guard. That was why they had locked her in here. But she knew how to get out now, and so she would.

At 7:00 P.M. the trolls brought her a tray with aranice—tiny fried rice balls filled with meat and peas. On the tray was a silver pitcher of fresh cold water and a small helping of pasta and a slice of fish. She threw the food on the floor, then made evil faces at the trolls to get them to go away.

When they cleaned up the food, then left, grumbling and warning her that the prince would punish her severely when he was told, she smiled sweetly to confuse them, and they finally shut the door, cursing, and locked her in for the night.

And then she had started looking again.

She remembered this room from childhood, the Venus especially, and she knew that she had once come into this room through a secret panel. Now, with each lucid moment, she'd been busily looking for that doorway to her freedom.

At 10:00 P.M., when the few full-time servants in the palazzo were sleeping soundly, Gianalisa pulled aside a polished yellowwood cabinet with black enamel inlay. The massive ancient cupboard featured hollows, recesses, shelves, and drawers, and it took her half an hour to inch it out from the wall. But the moment she saw the panel behind it, she knew she'd at last succeeded in finding her way out.

She pressed here and there upon the partition. Finally, as she applied the full pressure of her body to one side, it slowly creaked open.

A musty, oppressive passageway opened before her. It promised to rob her very breath as soon as she shut the wooden section behind her. But she had to leave just as her mother had left, and if death waited for her in the depths as it had for her mother, so be it. Either way she would be free.

Still, she left the panel slightly open, so that some light streamed into the passage. Then she descended the crumbling slate stairway and moved into a narrow catacomb that was dimly illuminated from a high window. She had vague memories of traveling through odorous rooms and stuffy passages to an abandoned apartment that had been uninhabited for centuries, and now she tried to retrace the memory.

Most of all, she was afraid that she would get lost and find herself in the secret rooms where her mother had cried herself to death. She had seen into them once, the simple wooden decor and the plain, almost puritanical furniture. She had wondered then what could happen in such a common place to make her mother so sad, but she had also vowed to never find out.

She prayed as she went, as much as she was able. The nuns had taught her certain prayers in school, and now she tried to use them, though the words often became jumbled. She waded through rat-infested water and swatted at cobwebs, but in truth she remembered the labyrinths to be far worse than they were.

After fifteen minutes of wandering through murky light, then darkness, then murky light again, Gianalisa suddenly stopped as she spied a small barred window set into the stone wall, just high enough so that she would have to stand on tiptoe to look into it.

But she did, and when she tilted her head at an angle, she could look down into the semidarkness, and she saw a stone cell, with something crumpled on the floor, perhaps old rags. The room made her faintly ill for some reason. It reminded her of pain. But it fascinated her too.

She stepped down, then up again, and looked down into the room. And this time she saw that the rags on the floor had turned into a man, a bearded man, crumpled up. His eyes were open, and he seemed to be staring up at her in astonishment.

She stepped back, frightened, and heard him say, "Wait! Who are you?" The words were faint, as if the man were sick.

She didn't want to answer him. What if it was a trick of her father's to catch her before she could get away? What if he was also a troll? What if he had murdered her mother?

The man said, "Wait!" again. Then he said, "Please help me."

She was sure that was what she heard. She stood on tiptoe again and peered down at him.

He said it again. "Who are you?"

This time, she thought it was an impertinent question. "I am the Princess Gia, and this is my palace. My father is the Prince of Darkness."

"Where are we?" the man said.

"In a palace, I told you."

"But where is this palace?"

"In Sicily, of course. The one in Naples is being used by devils."

"Help me," the strange man said again. "Find Carlo Ricaso. Tell him where I am."

She had a crafty thought. "Have you seen Luciano?"

"Who?"

She was suddenly suspicious again and decided not to repeat the question.

He turned his head slightly, and she looked at him closer and saw that his face was puffy and crusted with blood and his hair was matted. His wrists were chained to the wall.

Suddenly she was terrified. She ran down the stone passage, then through an arched doorway and upward, upward, until she came to another narrow stone stair and saw the courtyard of the Three Mysteries down a short cobbled hallway before her. It was connected to an informal garden beside the high stone wall that separated it from the street, and she suddenly forgot all about the strange bloodied man, and she realized what the exit meant. She was free.

Gia walked carefully through the garden, hiding behind bushes and trees but pausing to appreciate the silvery moonlight and the spray of orange blossoms it illuminated. She could hear the sounds of the city outside the wall now and could see the streetlights.

Palermo was a jumbled mass of periods and styles, a staggered mixture of poverty and plenty. The palazzi in this district were separated from the bustle of the streets only by huge stone walls and vast gardens. The street beside the Palazzo di Veresi was a busy one. There would be life there, and many kinds of people amid whom she could hide herself.

When Gia reached the gate it was locked, and she panicked for a moment. The stone wall was far too high to climb over, and besides it had iron spikes all along the top. Then she remembered the key and found it where it had been kept for years, within a niche in the wall.

The gate creaked as she opened it. She stopped, listening. She heard the shriek of sirens coming from the waterfront, and the bark of a dog nearby. But mostly she heard the steady grinding of the traffic, the background noises of the city night. She stepped out onto the wide sidewalk, and the headlights of passing cars swept her down the Viale della Libertà toward the dilapidated red-light district known as the *Vucciria*—the "Meat Market."

She walked past a dark yard with a burned-out villa—it was common for tottering nobility to hire Mafia arsonists who could transform their crumbling old palaces and villas to cash. Some penurious nobles even lived in the top floors of stately old palazzi and rented the bottom floors to art galleries and boutiques and coffeehouses, all closed now.

She shivered as she walked past the main entrance of the black hulk of burned stone, for two chipped gargoyles with gaping mouths glared down at her from their perch atop the crumbling gates.

Nearby was the region where children begged for their bread. She had been there. She had taken them things from the palace for a while, until the trolls stopped her. Beyond that was a tangle of dark alleys where the prostitutes tarnished themselves by selling their bodies. And she had been there too, for this was where the people lived who had sold her medicine, before she had met Marco and Roberto and Rudy. She would need medicine. She would either have to find a doctor right away or go back to the dungeon.

She walked past the concert hall and admired its dwarf palms, its yuccas, its palms and bamboo. It was good to be out again. The cool air was tainted by exhaust and the scent of rotting garbage, but at least it wasn't stale with centuries of torment and pain. Perhaps she would stay away from the palace forever this time, if her father did not find her.

The wind rushed through a bank of nearby palms, rustling like torn silk. For a moment she was afraid that Roberto and Marco had come after her like ghosts, but the fear passed, and she walked on toward the Mafia-encrusted slums that lay nearby.

As she passed the dark cathedral on the corner, she tried to pray again. Perhaps this was all her fault. And she decided that she would have to do penance, perhaps for the rest of her life, because she knew now that she should never have trusted Rudy, should never have helped him and Marco and Roberto spirit Luciano away.

28

Palermo

"She says she's a princess." The barman sneered, then fell back into a servility that Carlo found disgusting.

He was a thick-set, graying man whose Sicilian heritage was apparent in his broad nose and high cheekbones. He had thick wrinkles in his face from drink and toil and dissipation. He wrung the towel he was using as if it were someone's neck. Carlo knew he was showing off.

Carlo looked the girl over. She sat on a stool at the smoky, seedy, crumbling waterfront bar, and she could not have been more out of place. She was perhaps nineteen or twenty. She wore no makeup and was dressed in faded denims and an expensive pink cotton blouse, unlike the bedraggled slum prostitutes who favored skimpy silks and satin. This young woman had dark luminous eyes that made her quietly beautiful in spite of her unkempt hair. Carlo thought she seemed both innocent and strangely jaded.

He could see from her posture and jaundiced coloring that she was in the first stages of heroin withdrawal. Not surprising, in this part of town. He leaned forward like a proprietor, starting to pull back her sleeve to check for track marks, but she drew herself up and shot fire with her eyes. "You may not touch me."

Carlo frowned and stopped in mid-motion. This young woman was strange indeed. There was more in her eyes by far than the normal pain of the streets. Profound horror and madness were there but also pride and a terrible fear.

He sensed a sudden affinity with this strange young woman. He knew intuitively that they had shared the same darkness, and suddenly he wanted to help her.

He turned to the bartender. "She mentioned Luciano Chicarelli?"

The barman nodded. "Not the last name, just the first." He shrugged. "A lot of Lucianos in Italy. It may or may not be your man. But I phoned Rocco. Just in case."

Carlo nodded. Rocco was an enforcer for *don* Cesare, who had rewarded him by naming him sub-copo for this red-light district. The barman was his cousin by marriage. The Ricasos had put out a $50,000 reward for anyone who could help them find Luciano. Carlo had been getting all sorts of strange tips and had followed this one up only because he was truly desperate.

"What did the girl say?"

"Not much. She came in here and asked for a doctor. I had the feeling she used to buy here, you know. Maybe when Carmine DiCallo ran things. I told her I didn't have anything for her, and she asked me then if I could help her talk to Luciano. She said her father would pay me. I dunno what she meant. Maybe she's just nuts. But I knew you were looking for the Chicarelli kid, so I thought it was worth a shot. I told her I hadn't seen him and asked if she knew where he was. She said yes."

"Good that you asked."

It had been years since a Ricaso had actually handled the heroin the family brokered and trafficked. The low-level managers and street soldiers took care of that end of the business. Now Carlo considered getting a bag of heroin from the barman—it was everywhere down here, though they were careful not to sell to strangers.

But he also knew that the quality would be poor. It had certainly been cut a dozen times or more by the time it hit these streets, and who knew with what. Though he and his uncle insisted on a certain level of quality control even in the streets, people got greedy. You couldn't watch them all.

He said, "I'll take care of her. Call Dr. Basconi. He's in the phone book. Tell him to come to my place right away and to bring morphine."

The girl's eyes widened when he mentioned a doctor. She followed him obediently, like a stray dog who's found a new master, he thought. She was silent during the drive back to his apartment, and he sensed that this was not the time to question her.

She remained silent during the trip up the elevator, past the hard-faced *picciotti* who always guarded his penthouse home. But when he ushered her into the smoky-white and rose interior of his sunken living room and gestured her toward a white leather couch, she got a sudden haunted look on her face. She walked to the window instead, where she stood with a sad expression on her face and looked out over the tarnished city lights.

Carlo saw that she was shivering now. She wrapped herself in her arms, and he wondered how long it would be before the doctor arrived with morphine, how long it would be before the girl got really sick.

He said, "You say you are a princess?" He thought he was humoring her.

In spite of her pain, she turned and tilted her head regally. "I am the Princess Gianalisa Lauro Veresi, and my father owns Palermo."

Carlo felt a shock wave like a physical blow. "The prince is your *father?*"

"The Prince of Darkness."

Carlo's mind was racing now. He knew the prince had a daughter. He had even known the young woman was seeing Luciano. Volante had said they were to meet for dinner the night Luciano was kidnapped. But the prince and *don* Cesare were lodgemates—they had talked together several times since Luciano's disappearance. *Don* Cesare told Carlo that he'd asked about the daughter, if she had seen or heard from Luciano. The prince had assured him that the girl was back in the hospital—that Luciano's disappearance had triggered a relapse in her fragile mental condition, and she had been sent away.

Now the girl stood before him, shivering from heroin withdrawal, and he felt like someone had stabbed him in the heart.

Had his uncle lied to him? Or had Veresi lied to his uncle? Or perhaps it was true that the girl had been in the hospital at that time. Perhaps she was newly released, though Carlo knew from looking at her that a mental condition was hardly her worst problem.

He said, "Do you know Luciano Chicarelli?"

"We are to be married," she said simply. Then she shivered again and gripped her stomach.

Carlo knew she was cramping. Soon she would be too sick to talk, and when the doctor came and injected her with morphine she'd be on the nod for a while. He had to find out now. He said, "Where is Luciano?"

She turned to look at him, and her eyes were flooded with suspicion. "Why?"

"I want to help him."

She made a piteous noise. "I do not even know who you are."

"I am Carlo Ricaso."

She looked at him in amazement, the name making such an impression that she actually dropped her arms and stopped shivering for a moment. She lifted her head and stared. "I know about you."

He smiled. "I'm not quite as bad as they say."

"Who is 'they'?"

"Everybody."

He examined her with his eyes. Her logic was confusing. She lived in a different world. He didn't know exactly how to question her.

She said sweetly, "Do you know my father? People say he is bad too."

Carlo started to admit he knew the prince, but a sudden guarded fear in her eyes stopped him. He was about to lose her. On an impulse he said, "No. I don't know your father. Is he really bad?"

"He is evil." She shrugged as if she could blanket that fact with indifference. She looked back out the window to the city, and the shivering began again. "My mother killed herself to get away from him. But I heard her screaming last night."

Carlo frowned. He had heard the rumors, the tales of occultic practices and even torture within the Order of Caput Mundi's innermost cabal, the Black Nobility.

Don Cesare said the rumors were nonsense, and Carlo knew the old *don* would never engage in violence unless it furthered his business. But his uncle had been a member of the Black Nobility only a short time; there was no guarantee he'd know everything that happened.

Carlo also knew that there were rooms in Italy's and Sicily's crumbling old palaces that held ancient manacles and chains and torture devices. Many of the palaces had been built when such things were necessary if men were to keep their wealth and power, though most had been gutted or sealed off.

He considered Gianalisa's words. Perhaps the prince engaged in the sick practice of sadomasochism and made use of his ancient torture chambers as titillation. This would be nothing new among the jaded European royals—or among other degenerated people for that matter. This would account for the wife's suicide.

But if not that, what was this girl talking about? Was it something to do with the lodge? He knew the prince was obsessed with secret societies. He dabbled in many things. But a medieval torture chamber? People screaming in the night? Dead people? He suddenly looked at Gianalisa with a new eye. She was indeed mad.

She looked back at him. "There is a man in the dungeon who asked for you."

"What?"

"In the dungeon," she said, "the dark dungeon, not the light one where I live."

He walked over and faced her, and he could see that she was even more sallow and sickly looking than before. He cursed the doctor for taking so long, cursed himself for getting involved in this mess.

"He had blood on his face," she said. "I saw him through the window when I was coming out. He said to tell you—"

Suddenly Carlo realized she was telling the truth. He grabbed her by both arms and almost shook her. "Was it Luciano?"

She whimpered. "You're hurting me."

He stepped back and let go of her. "I'm sorry. Please tell me. Is there really someone in your father's dungeon?"

"At the palace," she said. "A man with a beard—"

But she was talking to air.

Carlo sprinted into the kitchen, snatched up the phone, and called his second-in-command, Tomasso Pico. Then he grabbed his holstered gun off the wall peg in the closet, raced to the elevator, and collared one of the guards. He told him to go up and take care of Gia. "The doctor should be here shortly. She's going through withdrawal. Have him take care of her."

The guard nodded and was gone, and Carlo was also gone, into his car, out the garage, speeding through Palermo's dark, ancient streets toward the Palazzo di Veresi. He would meet Tomasso a block from the palace, and then he would find out firsthand if Gianalisa was telling the truth or if he had believed a tale of madness.

A grating, metallic noise clanged through Peter's slumber. He tried to roll over, then shot awake as he was brought up short by chains. As his eyes flew open, he realized that the left one was nearly swollen shut. He could taste blood.

His arms and legs were cramping. He tried to extend an arm and was again jerked up short. A wave of claustrophobic panic shot through him as he realized how tightly he was manacled. Then the panic crested in a flash of rage as he remembered Marco Guappo, standing over him, beating him senselessly, hitting him again and again and again.

The echo of someone cursing touched his ears, so faintly that he believed he was hearing his own mind. The fear began to grow in him, but that too was brought up short by a sudden grating as a rusted door opened somewhere.

Guappo was coming back, to beat him. He shut his eyes and gritted his teeth and prayed. He had been praying over and over again. Praying was all he could do.

Suddenly gunshots echoed, so loud they nearly broke his eardrums. Natale recoiled at the sound. Close by, down the hallway, someone was screaming in rage, and someone else was crying, crying, and then the sound of gunfire came again, several calibers of guns, followed by screams of pain. Then silence.

Peter lay terrified. Were they murdering the inmates of this hideous prison? Were they coming for him? He heard the jangle of keys and shut his eyes tight. He didn't want to see. He prayed fervently that God would bring him safely home. The blackness of eternity seemed to swallow him already.

He felt someone moving his legs, and he braced for the inevitable blow. But instead he heard a voice, a familiar voice, then a comforting hand touched his forehead. His eyes shot wide open in astonishment, and he was staring up into the worried and sickened face of Carlo Ricaso.

"Don't worry, *paisano*. We've got you now. Those *pesecanos* who were guarding you are dead." Carlo had the keys to the wrist manacles, and he took them off.

"Marco." Natale barely managed to mutter the word. He flexed his hands. They were numb.

Carlo sat back, surprised. "Marco Guappo? He was *here?*"

Natale nodded. And then, again, the world went mercifully black.

He awakened as they were lifting him into the elegant cabin of a private jet.

Carlo was beside him. He said, "We're taking you to Naples. Get some rest. We're keeping Luciano here—taking him to the hospital. You're gonna be all right, *amico*. Your people know you're coming. You're in good hands."

Natale fell asleep on a wide padded seat, buckled in for the flight. He didn't know why Carlo was talking about Luciano. He was still unsure of what had happened, but he knew that whatever it was, it had definitely been an answer to his prayers.

29

Berlin

Yuri Lepkov's fist slammed into the plate-glass balcony door, shattering it into a million pieces. Sheets slid down like small guillotines, and a half dozen cuts spurted blood..

He turned and stomped back into his office and slammed his bloodied fist into the wall. He was so filled with rage that he didn't even feel the pain, though later he would learn that he'd broken several small bones in addition to the cuts. He yanked a handkerchief from his pocket and awkwardly arranged it to absorb the blood.

His left hand held a portable, encrypted telephone, held to his ear. He was talking to Marco Guappo, and he wished fervently that the fool were here, this moment, so he could put his hands around the thick Neapolitan throat and squeeze and squeeze until he felt the last drop of life leave the man.

But the idiot was in Naples, hiding out, and Luciano had been discovered, Peter Natale had been discovered, the entire scheme was disintegrating around him, turning to ashes, and it was all Guappo's fault.

"I told you to kill Natale," he said. "Why did you keep him for questioning? The fool doesn't know a thing."

"The prince said to question him," Guappo whined.

"You are to listen to me, not that molding, satanic aristocrat. He's my puppet, do you understand?"

Marco was silent.

"Anyway, *do* something," Lepkov said.

"What?"

"How do I know? Do something about the Americans. They're the ones who are always messing things up."

"The Americans?"

"You idiot, didn't you learn anything from me? I don't care what you do. Blow up their bases, set their houses on fire, bomb their airplanes. Get them out of Italy. Get rid of them. Nothing is going to work right until they're gone."

Marco was silent for a time, and then he said, "Fright Decade Four?"

"What are you muttering about?" Lepkov dropped the handkerchief and picked up a brass paperweight, thinking of throwing it into the original Van Gogh on his wall.

"The training camp in Bulgaria—remember the plan? That's what we called it. Fright Decade Four."

Lepkov set down the paperweight. He did remember. His anger began to drain away. Back then, Italy had been the weakest link in the Western democracies. That was the primary reason the KGB had targeted them for such a heavy dose of terrorism. The Communist party was strong then, and the KGB commanded a serious following within the country.

There were still Communists in Italy, but they were different now, independent, not so manipulable. But there were the growing numbers of Fascists, who hated the Americans more than the Communists ever had.

Lepkov said, "Can you do it?"

"Maybe. I could use the Blacks instead of the Reds."

Lepkov thought. It had worked before. Why not now? Earlier, the Red and Black terrorism had almost brought Italy to her knees. "How long will it take to set it up?" he asked.

A new note of confidence crept into Marco's voice. "There's an international air show at the NATO base this Saturday. A family affair, people come with picnic lunches, everything. I can make it happen then, but it will be expensive. Wire me some money."

"How much?"

"If I can spread around a half million, I promise you the best show Italy will ever see."

"What about the news media? Can you control them?"

"Enough of them. Several papers already lean our way, and we can put anything we want into the papers my father owns. And we can buy one of the news directors at ENN. He agrees with your cause, and he's made it known that he needs money. He can make certain that the events are slanted the right way, though his time is expensive."

Lepkov thought. "We can't use Hotel de Mer for a while. The Ricasos are going to be all over the prince, all over everything."

"The prince is in hiding in Naples."

"I don't care. Kill him. Who needs him anyway?"

"What about Count Jacovetti?"

"He's mine. I don't need Veresi."

Marco said, "OK. Ciao. I know what to do. Just wire the money directly to my father's bank account in Naples. By the time anyone could check it, the whole thing will be done."

"It will be, or you will," Lepkov said ominously. "This is the last chance you have."

30

Naples

"Peter."

Peter Natale opened his eyes, then shut them again. He was dreaming, and he didn't want to wake up. Besides, the hair was wrong. It was short and white-blonde, not the shoulder-length, honey-blonde hair he knew.

"Peter. Are you awake?"

It was Judith's voice. It wasn't a dream. He opened his eyes again, and she was indeed standing there, looking down at him, her smoky-blue eyes wide with concern. But she had cut and dyed her hair, and she was wearing an oversized buff-colored shirt and jeans. She looked like a Swedish college student.

He said, "What did you do to your hair?"

She laughed. "What did you do to your face?"

He reached up and touched it, and suddenly he remembered the horror and went stiff.

He felt a hand stroke his cheek, and the horror vanished.

"Don't," Judith said. "You're all right now."

He looked around. He was in a blue bedroom with satin brocade drapes and Charles III furnishings. Opulent, but somehow comfortable. "Where am I?"

"Naples. The safe house in Vomero. After Carlo's Gulfstream delivered you to the base, we had you checked out by one of the best military doctors. You're bruised and beaten, but you're tough as nails, Peter Natale. You're going to be just fine."

"How long have I been here?"

"Two days."

He felt a sudden surge of fury as he remembered. He said, "And Marco Guappo?"

"He's in the wind, but we'll find him."

"Carlo?"

"He's OK. He's been phoning to check on you. They've got Luciano in the hospital. He says Marco and Rudy Brandenburg were behind the kidnapping. They had Luciano stashed in the basement of the prince's palazzo."

"Rudy helped them kidnap Luciano?"

"We have a lot to catch up on, Peter. Frost is flying in later tonight. He's finished with Langley."

"What happened there?"

"He couldn't talk about it long-distance. Just said he was on his way here. But frankly, you're pumped full of pain-killers— you'll be drifting off again soon. Let's wait till Teddy arrives. Then we'll try to patch this all together."

Peter felt a vast sense of relief that he didn't have to pick up the ball yet. He was feeling his eyes grow heavy. But a sudden thought startled him back awake. "Where were you? Why didn't you call?"

"I couldn't risk a satellite pickup, but there's more, of course. Some of it I really don't understand. Shhh, now. Go back to sleep. We'll talk about it later."

She smiled at him, and the smile made him feel like a million bucks. He smiled back, but the smile seemed to crack his skin. It was stiff and sore.

He didn't understand what she meant about satellite pick-ups, but then it really didn't matter anyway. He was drifting back into that safe black place where he'd been hiding, and she was back. And with luck this time she would stay with him for good.

31

Valletta

In the picturesque region above the Ricaso estate, a crumbling stone temple clung giddily to a hillside. It was a remnant of the Carthaginian occupation in the fifth century.

On the lush mountainside above the ancient ruins, *don* Cesare Ricaso had built a small lava-stone chapel and a white marble sarcophagus. He had moved his parents here from the peasant cemetery in Valletta, after he'd made enough money to buy the land. They had been dead more than twenty years by that time, almost half a century by now.

The chapel had been built to please Cesare's sister, Maria. She wanted a place where she could light candles and pray for her parents' souls. Now Maria too was dead, buried with her ne'er-do-well husband south of the city. After her death Cesare padlocked the chapel, so long ago that the lock had rusted shut. He despised nothing more than prayer, hated nothing more than the thought of eternity.

Don Cesare had been driven up the tangled, rutted road by one of the young Sicilian men who swarmed to him, willing to do anything for a taste of his dark power. He sent the driver away, and now he sat alone upon a stone bench in the leafy grove that held the chapel and sarcophagus.

He had come here to make the final decision about what to do about Carlo. It was, after all, a decision that would determine the crime family's future, and he wanted to sift through his memories as he made up his mind.

Directly in front of him was a white marble statue of the archangel Michael slaying a dragon, an object selected by Maria to adorn the gravesite. The old man found himself gazing at it and thinking of the day it had been erected, and of his childhood and his brutal, difficult life.

He had grown up Catholic, as had most Sicilians of his era. His peasant parents revered the pope and the archbishops. Cesare felt the stick when he refused to go to Communion in the small village church, though the Latin liturgy had been remote and cold to him. But the church was the only safe harbor in the harsh Sicilian world, and he had nevertheless spent long, agonizing hours in the confessional trying to make sense of his boyish sins.

Ah, that had been so many years ago. Now *don* Cesare had concluded that any God who would create such a world as this one could not possibly be a God worthy of worship. To him, any church was a fraud. The concept of religion had turned to ashes in his mouth.

But then, nothing and no one else could be trusted either. Not even his own nephew, the man he had treated like a son, had groomed to inherit his crime empire and carry on his hard-won legacy. Carlo had betrayed him too.

Cesare had brought a microcasette player with him, and now he pulled it out of the pocket of his seedy wool sweater and hit the PLAY button.

Peter Natale's voice came on. "Where is she, Carlo? Has anybody actually seen her?"

Carlo's voice replied. "She rented a car in Milano day before yesterday. My police contacts there checked the car rental companies. They've had the company report the car as stolen . . ."

"Tell your contacts to just hold her, not to arrest her."

"That's already done, *amico*. Don't worry about it. We'll take good care of your lady. Now, you interrupted some business. Anything else?"

Cesare felt a knife turn in his heart every time he listened to the words, and he had listened to them over and over again, often enough to be absolutely certain that Carlo was still using *don* Cesare's hard-won resources to facilitate the activities of the crime family's worst enemies! The old man uttered a curse. Carlo was never going to learn.

That wasn't the only tape. *Don* Cesare had his own espionage network, as befitted a man who controlled a shadow government. The collection of surveillance tapes gathered from Carlo's private telephone had been growing, and each one added yet more weight to the burden of decision that the *don* would have to make today.

There were conversations with Volante Chicarelli, wherein the parliamentarian contacted Carlo directly and pleaded with him to intervene in his son's kidnapping. Volante came right out and told Carlo that he now trusted him much more than the *don*. Carlo had never mentioned a word of any of those conversations to his uncle, thus compounding the betrayal.

The problem was that Carlo had been raised in Brooklyn instead of Sicily. He was not a man of honor, not a Sicilian in his heart. The old man was certain of that now. Sometimes he was actually a fool.

Cesare shook his head in disgust, turned off the tape player, and listened to the sighing wind. A fool could never control this dark empire he had built. It required genius and courage and a complete absence of compassion, and that was where Carlo failed most of all.

Several years ago, Cesare realized Carlo was different from his father, different from his younger brother, who had masterminded the heroin empire until his death. Carlo had started harassing him to get out of the criminal enterprises and make do with the hundreds of millions they had already managed to launder into a legitimate empire.

Carlo couldn't understand that the Ricaso empire rested in blood, and that it would crumble into decay once that blood stopped pumping. Carlo refused to believe that the only true power was power backed up with a bullet. Even the United States government knew that. They had their armies, their other military, their agents who carried bombs and guns. Carlo was a fool indeed.

Don Cesare started keeping business secrets from Carlo. Now, because Carlo was in the dark about so many things, he was making serious mistakes.

Take, for instance, the problem with the Berlin network, the one penetrated by the CIA's Operation Kaleidoscope. Carlo hadn't known Cesare was using the pipeline that ran through Berlin and

Munich and Milano, the one managed by Harald Rupert and his dissipated son. Carlo had unfortunately picked up some fringe information about the network and had passed that information on to Peter Natale. He had almost handed *don* Cesare's head to Peter Natale, for that network linked Cesare with his most valuable trading partner, Yuri Lepkov.

Cesare had known from the beginning that Carlo was to blame for that leak. Carlo hated the black market in nuclear materials. He was far too soft for this world, but Cesare wasn't about to bypass such a prosperous enterprise. Cesare and Lepkov tried to fix things by having Marco kill the informants, Fritz and Eva Breugher. That had at least stopped that end of the problem. But still Peter Natale was everywhere—in Naples, in Palermo, in Berlin, and it was just a matter of time before they locked horns again.

It was Carlo's fault. Carlo had befriended a man who had dedicated his life to destroying everything *La Familia* stood for, everything *don* Cesare had worked and killed for. It was like befriending the man who was cutting your heart out with a knife. The old man shook his head in disgust. Carlo had chosen the wrong side.

And now he had taken the Gulfstream, had flown it into the American section of the NATO base with Peter Natale aboard. Another breach of Mafia ethics, for hadn't Carlo sworn on his life to always honor the orders of his capo-Mafia? Hadn't he sworn in blood that he would die rather than betray him? Cesare was tired of telling Carlo time and again to sever his friendship with Natale. Carlo wouldn't listen.

To be sure, Carlo had freed Luciano. *Don* Cesare was pleased, Volante was pitifully grateful. But Carlo had also stepped fully out from under Cesare's dominion for the first time in his forty-two years, and the *don* was seriously disturbed by this.

He was also disturbed by where Carlo had found Luciano. In the prince's dungeon. *Don* Cesare was a brilliant if evil man. His genius for deception told him immediately what this meant. The prince had not been under his thumb after all. He had been manipulating Cesare while the wily old *don* thought *he* was pulling the chains.

It was a humiliation that cut like acid, and he had himself to blame. Like Carlo, he had been trying to belong to a world that was not his, and he had ended up feathering the nest of his enemy.

He had been betrayed. Laughed at and dishonored. Now he would avenge that betrayal. He felt hatred seethe through his soul.

A cloud drifted over the sun, a shadow shifted, illuminating the white statue of Michael slaying the dragon-beast. It caught *don* Cesare's eye, and he scrutinized the simple curves of the sculptor's work, the symmetry of the sword as it struck the dragon's head, the intricate carving in the hilt.

He sneered at the symbolism. If there was a beast loose upon the earth, it was he. He had learned the dark secret of endless power, and now he would implement every grain of what he had learned. He would do what he had to, to straighten this mess out and reclaim his rightful place as the true Prince of Sicily.

He turned away from the statue and gazed down over his valley, over the slate roof of his sprawling house, far away now. The almond trees were in blossom. Their lilac-gray petals tinted the emerald green grass of the pastures, scented the valley with perfume. The olive orchards spread out almost all the way to the village. The stream that ran through the valley was a thin green ribbon.

From here he could not see the sensors that lay beneath his emerald lawns. He could not see the two dozen killer dogs that patrolled his grounds at night or the hard-faced men who protected the compound with their lives. These men would be needed more than ever now. His long and difficult plan would still bear fruit, just as the peach, pear, and orange trees in the valley beneath him poured their sweet, swollen bounty into his hands.

And if those such as Peter Natale would not get out of his way? Well, he no longer believed in the eternal flames that swallowed those who broke God's laws. But he believed in hell. He himself could unleash hell on earth. He had done it many times before and would do it again, with relish.

Another shadow crossed the sun. The wind sighed through the trees, rustling the leaves. He looked again at the statue, then looked again, closer. There was something sickly under the dragon's carved scales, something living that had grown there. He stood up and stepped closer, then closer still.

Michael himself was still smooth, still saintly in his white, furious splendor. But the dragon had been covered over with a fine, near-invisible webwork of decay.

32

Naples

The CIA safe house was a nineteenth-century villa in the Vomero section of Naples. It had been purchased just after the war, when property could be had for a song. The living room was furnished in the blue-and-silver style of Charles III, and the finery remained, though mirrors and plants had been added to soften the effect.

It was 2:30 A.M. but the house guests were still wide awake, though Natale wore his pajamas. He sat on a blue silk sofa. Judith sat across from him on a brocaded settee.

Teddy Frost had arrived from Langley, flying commercial, and had been picked up at the airport by Jeremy Ward. Ward dropped him off at the safe house, and Frost had just entered the room. He seated himself in a black walnut chair beside a matching antique desk, leaned forward with a worried frown, and said, "Judith. Glad you found your way home. Peter? I want to warn you, Hammond's furious with you. He's flying in this morning. Let's get this sorted out before he gets here."

Natale was still bruised, sore, and confused from his abduction and the subsequent beatings, though Judith's presence was working miracles. "Where do I begin?"

Frost's button-black eyes blazed impatiently. "With Kaleidoscope. That's where you came into the picture."

"Kaleidoscope?"

Judith had been stroking her chin lightly with her forefinger, thinking. Now she said, "Kaleidoscope was your end of the problem. Teddy set us up, you know." She turned to Frost and gave him an icy stare. "Didn't you?"

Frost's smile was sheepish. "Yes and no. I sent you to Monte Carlo because I needed to know what the prince was doing. I admit I paid for the villa so you'd be close by in case I needed you."

"You knew you'd need us," Judith said, "and you knew we'd be there for you. So why didn't you just brief us on the operation instead of sending us in blind?"

"Because I was blind myself. I was still turning over rocks, trying to see what might crawl out. I decided it was wiser to let you feel your own way than to confuse you with my unsubstantiated speculations."

Judith smiled thinly, unconvinced.

Natale cocked an eyebrow. "This all had to do with your mole hunt?"

"Right." Judith answered for Frost. She eyed Teddy speculatively. "And you've found your mole, haven't you, Ted? You went to Langley to nail him down, and now you have him."

Frost emitted an exhausted sigh. "I learned what I needed to know. But I'm not likely to convince anyone else soon."

"Why do I get the feeling I'm being left out of something?" Peter asked.

"Because you picked up the problem from another end," Judith replied. "You caught the pipeline in Berlin and Naples. We climbed on board in Moscow."

"And then there's the big picture," Frost added. "The corruption in Langley hangs like a shadow over it all."

"Tell you what," Judith said, "let's look at the puzzle one piece at a time. Then maybe we can fit it all together."

Natale and Frost both agreed.

"It starts with Ted's mole hunt," she said. "Ted knew that Al Grimes had worked with a partner, and he knew the partner was still burrowed away." She paused, chewed on her lip for a moment. "We're talking about Bob Hammond, of course."

Natale felt a clawing sensation as he heard his suspicions confirmed. He stood up, agitated, and went to the window. Then he walked back and leaned against the radiator, too tense to sit back down.

Frost said, "Hammond met me in Rome to find out how much I'd learned. Then he tried to convince me that he was on my side. Fortunately I still have friends in high places. They tipped me that Hammond was really the one who had stopped my mole hunt. He was brilliant in shifting the blame, and he almost got away with it. But not quite." He made a sour face.

"All the blown networks, the dead agents, everything was done with Hammond's help." Judith shifted, so that she was staring dead at Natale. "He'd been running dirty networks for the last ten years he worked Berlin station, and he took his corruption with him to Langley."

"Then why didn't Grimes give Hammond away when he was arrested—in order to cut a better deal?" Natale asked.

"That puzzled me too," Frost said, frowning. "But I discovered evidence in Langley that Hammond was going to let Grimes do a couple of years in prison, then he was going to cut him loose, pay him off in return for his silence. The groundwork was laid. Hammond was going to uncover new evidence and have his golfing buddy in the White House hand Grimes a presidential pardon. You know how it goes."

Peter did, and it made him sick.

Judith picked up the story. "Hammond was smart enough to keep his fingerprints off the action. But he was in the thick of things. The heroin traffic, the black markets, the dirty espionage. He'd linked up with the KGB shortly after taking over Berlin station."

"They doubled him?"

Frost shook his head. "Not directly. He met his wife at an embassy ball and married straight into the murky labyrinths of the European Black Nobility."

"Right." Judith had a pen in her hand, and now she fidgeted with it, turning it end over end. "His wife's family were and are neo-Nazis—pro-Fascist, virulently anti-American, typical of that group. Two of his wife's uncles were in banking. They had estates and extensive businesses in the Pankow district as well as in Central Berlin and the Rhineland. After World War II they found their mansions and central banking operations on the Soviet side of the Wall. So they cut a deal with the KGB—they got to keep their wealth in return for helping facilitate the German end of the KGB's black market. When Hammond came along, they wasted no time embracing—then corrupting—him."

"So Hammond and his fellow thugs had the whole system wired from both ends," Natale said. He stepped to the window, pulled back the drape, and glanced out as if he were expecting to find Hammond himself peering in at them. But nothing was there except the faint glimmer of city lights spread out below them, capricious corrupted Naples, then the wide, black sea.

He shook his head in self-disgust at the twitch of paranoia, then walked back to the sofa and sat down again.

Frost nodded. "It was the beginning of a troika. A triple play that's still working. And here's where you and Kaleidoscope begin to fit in. There were three key rats in this rats' nest." He held up his fingers and counted them off. "First, there was Hammond, with access to all the CIA's assets. He brought a very big stick to the game and became an invaluable player.

"Second, there was a KGB colonel named Yuri Lepkov. He was the chief of the Bulgarian networks, and, as you know, Bulgaria was the center of the KGB's terrorist and narcotics campaign against the West. It was also the center of the Soviet black market."

"I stumbled onto Lepkov too," Natale said. "I pulled his file and refreshed my memory after I spotted him with Hammond in Berlin. He was the real force behind Kaleidoscope, wasn't he?"

"Right. And he's still in the thick of things, though he's traded his KGB office at KINTEX for a glass-and-steel high-rise in Berlin." Frost paused, then added, "Hammond still controls Berlin station, of course. Wolverton is dirty too. Hammond bought him off way back when.

"When you busted into their Berlin pipeline with Kaleidoscope, you really stirred things up. Lepkov was top dog; Hammond was his silent partner. Hammond started gumming things up the minute he got wind of your investigation, and he managed to seal off the top levels before you got to them."

Peter thought about the dead informants in the Berlin brothel, people who had trusted him with their lives. He thought about the Bulgarian pistol found in the dead Rudy Brandenburg's hand. He thought about the men who had tried to gun him down on a Berlin street.

286

He leaned forward. "KINTEX supplied all the Ricaso family's morphine base for years in an attempt to help destabilize the West. *Don* Cesare is the third member of the troika, right?"

Frost said, "He is indeed. His heroin empire was already corroding the foundations of Western civilization. The KGB was all too happy to help him."

Natale shook his head, puzzled. "But Carlo gave me information on the Berlin network, especially the nuclear contraband. Why would Carlo blow the whistle on his own family's operations?"

"I can't answer that," Frost said. "But I do know that *don* Cesare, Lepkov, and Hammond are all linked together."

"And now we come to the Red Gold," Judith said.

"Cherchez la cash," Peter said. "Hammond said it. Follow the money, and sooner or later you'll figure things out."

"It's quite a trail," she said. "When the Communist government was falling, the Communist Mafia—the people Lepkov and Hammond were essentially serving—decided to loot the USSR's central gold reserves. But it's not all that easy to move two thousand tons of gold, not even when there's white-hot boiling chaos everywhere. They needed a pipeline that was already in place. Lepkov was already in the loop. He knew how to move large amounts of contraband. He actually helped his buddies in the Politburo cook up the scheme. Then he brought in Hammond, who could blow enough smoke to keep the Western intelligence agencies confused."

Natale whistled. "You're saying that *we*—the CIA—helped loot the Red Gold?"

"Not all of the CIA, please. Just one despicable rat," Judith said. "Anyway, the gold vanished without a trace in 1991, two thousand tons. The central gold vault was left empty. Nobody could find so much as a nugget lying around. Enter our dauntless friend Teddy Frost." Judith shot him a mischievous grin. "Teddy kept looking for the gold—and for the mole—and he finally uncovered one gold seam. That's why he sent us to Hotel de Mer." She turned to Frost. "Right?"

Frost nodded.

Natale said, "We've jumped from Moscow to Monte Carlo. How did Prince Veresi get into this?"

"He's top dog in the secret order of the Black Nobility," she explained, "and they're at the fermenting center of the whole escapade—at least the European end. Hammond and the Black Nobles were shooting their own angles, and every roll of the dice was fixed."

Frost waved a hand. "It's the old relationship between power and servility. Power corrupts. Absolute power corrupts absolutely, and Hammond and Lepkov got a whopping good taste of power when they were serving the KGB. They wanted more and more and more, and all of it for themselves this time. Their end of the gold could buy a lot of potential power."

"Power becomes an addiction," Peter agreed. "Especially when you've sold your soul to get it. So what was Veresi's angle?"

Frost picked up the narrative. "Veresi is a high priest in a secret society known as the Order of Caput Mundi. That's the so-called fraternal lodge that's been built up around the Black Nobility's secret core."

"The Black Nobility shows up everywhere," Peter said.

"Yes, and interestingly enough the society began in ancient Rome, during the pagan era. Its headquarters was moved here to Naples centuries ago after a run-in with the Vatican. The various popes disapproved of the Nobility's secretive, pagan, occultic traditions. With good reason. The membership is powerful enough to threaten the Vatican's power base, the Italian government's power base—even the EU.

"Judith uncovered the member list for the Naples lodge while doing paper research in Moscow: there are parliamentarians, judges, prime ministers, bankers, businessmen, EuroCorp generals —you name it. The members take a blood oath just like the Mafia. Divulging the membership list is punishable by death. Veresi's family has been involved in the Black Nobility since its inception— Judith, why don't you fill Peter in?"

"Gladly. The ancient Caput Mundi worshiped the Roman gods and goddesses, Peter. When the Christian era began in Rome, they went underground and became a subversive power base for corrupted nobles. Over the centuries, the order evolved into a kind of lodge, with the Black Nobility at the invisible center. During the Dark Ages a sort of spiritualism began to creep in—secret meetings, seances, and that sort of thing."

"Creepy." Natale had his legs stretched out in front of him. He shifted, pulling them back, leaning forward.

"Yes. It is. Still, the origins of the Order are purely fascistic. The original *fasces* was a Roman symbol—a bunch of sticks bonded together with leather strapping. It was the emblem of the ancient Roman military, meaning solidarity as equal to strength. The Caput Mundi adopted the symbol as their own long before Mussolini discovered it and decided to call his totalitarian form of government Fascism."

"This is beginning to make sense," Natale said.

"The Black Nobility's occultic power nexus is definitely elitist and anti-Christian. They're also avidly anti-American."

"Sounds like a bunch of misfits trying to convince themselves of their superiority."

"Hardly misfits. There seems to be at least one royal house from every European nation involved, though most of them are long-since deposed. The Brandenburgs ruled parts of Germany and Bavaria during the Dark Ages. They lost power centuries ago. Nevertheless, they've played a role in affairs one way or another ever since. They had a strong hand in helping Adolph Hitler rise to power. That's the German end of the stick. And then there's Prince Dante di Veresi and the Veresi relatives, the Italian end. They intermarried with the Brandenburgs way back when."

Natale nodded. His mouth was drawn into a thin, worried line.

"And then there's the Mafia. Your old buddy Carlo is also a member of Caput Mundi, though of the lower order."

Natale wasn't surprised. He knew that Mafiosi saw the advantages of fraternizing with legitimate businessmen, politicians, and others in seats of power. And such men seemed to gravitate to lodges and secret fraternal societies.

"Vincente Guappo and his vicious son, Marco, also belong to the lower order of the lodge. That one surprised even me. But *don* Cesare Ricaso was the real surprise. He belongs to the Black Nobility itself!"

Natale frowned. "So the center isn't strictly reserved for nobles?"

Judith shrugged. "The nobles have made a few exceptions through the centuries, based on money, power, patronage. The Mafia can be very, very useful to the old guard, and vice versa. Think about it."

Peter did. There really wasn't much difference between today's Mafia and some of the brutal old nobles who'd gained their land and gold by pillaging and shedding blood. He could see how the Black Nobility might find the Ricaso crime family useful. But the Ricasos were far more adept at using others than at letting themselves be used. If *don* Cesare belonged to a secret society in addition to the Mafia, he would have a very good reason indeed.

"The Black Nobility is gathering strength like a threatening storm," Judith said. "They're backing Jacovetti, and in return they'll own him. They already have people sitting in the EU parliament, in the EU central courts and banks. They want the whole banana, and they think Jacovetti can hand it to them."

"It seems incredible." He shook his head in disbelief.

"Yes," Frost said, seeing the look on Peter's face. "Nevertheless, Judith's research uncovered a political spider's web that spans across the borders of all the EU countries. The Fascists are stronger than they've been at any time since Hitler and Mussolini. Part of this is backlash against the socialism that ruined Europe's economies—and against Communism. But whatever the reasons, we've certainly seen a fascist mentality grip Europe and Russia these past few years.

"But there's also some invisible hand stirring the fascist broth, manipulating the people who are blind to what's going on. We believe that hand is the Black Nobility. They're desperate to see a royal at the head of the EU. Jacovetti is of 'noble blood,' even if he is just a lowly count."

"He's distantly related to the Veresis," Judith explained. "He's been inactive in the Black Nobility since he joined the EU parliament, but we believe that's just smoke and mirrors. He usually hides his fascist mentality—but a recent speech in Brussels surprised a few of us. He even gave the audience the old Fascist hand salute. It looks like he's developing the oratory and charisma to carry quite a crowd."

Natale rolled his eyes. "Where does Lepkov come into this? Don't tell me he's an heir to the tsarist throne?"

Judith grinned. "He's an heir to the tsar's gold. That's enough to buy him a ticket. Most of the nobles are a bit down at the heels. Lepkov and his thugs also want a say in what's happening in Europe, and he's bankrolling some of the corruption with his share of the Red Gold in return for a certain say in what happens after the EU elections."

"Incredible."

"It is. But it's still true. And it still boils down to money. Think about it. All three rats in the troika have stockpiles of money all over the globe—maybe billions sitting in warehouses, vaults, anywhere they can put it. Once they get the hard cash into the banks, they don't have to worry about it anymore. It's gone. Kaput. Vanishes into the electronic wire transfer network to appear as whatever currency they need, wherever they need it.

"The big problem is getting it into the banks. Even though they own banks, they still have to worry about transporting the actual cash and about laundering fees. People have to be paid off to handle it, customs guards paid to look the other way. The cost of laundering is running them about twenty-five percent of the haul right now. And they can't find enough people they trust to move it all, so they still have all this money sitting around, waiting to be rinsed so they can use it to buy up the legitimate world."

Natale thought about the problem from that point of view. *Cherchez la* cash. Some of the Mafia's money would be in US currency, sitting in warehouses and bunkers and bank vaults throughout the United States, waiting for a pipeline out. That was a problem; they were losing money through inflation every day it sat there.

But European currency was an even bigger problem. Since the American market in narcotics and cocaine became saturated during the late 1980s, the EuroMafia had turned their main attention toward Europe. Most of their money would therefore be locked into European currencies.

"And it's less than six months until the EU consolidates all

European currency into the ecu," Judith said. "That's partly what this is all about."

Natale understood only too well. When that happened, the crime troika might as well burn their stockpiles of European currency, because they couldn't show up with a half trillion or so pounds or lire or deutsche marks or anything else to trade for ecus unless they could also show where it came from. Laws had already been enacted to weed out all dirty currency at the time of the restructuring.

Judith said, "The EuroMafia needs some very good friends in very high places, people who can slowly feed their money into the system and exchange it for ecus for a couple of years or so after the ecu becomes the common currency. People who can soften or negate laws, build boondoggles, otherwise facilitate the Mafia's pipelines."

"Makes sense to me," Natale said. "What I can't figure out is how *don* Cesare got into this. He's backing Volante Chicarelli for the presidency. He's had the man in his pocket for decades. I can see him wanting to launder his hidden drug money—he probably has a few billion sitting around—but Chicarelli is his best man for the job. Why would he shift his allegiance to Jacovetti?"

Judith smiled wryly. "That's where it gets interesting. The Black Nobility want their own man in the driver's seat. It looks like Lepkov is siding with Hammond and his nasty in-laws and is backing Jacovetti behind *don* Cesare's back. A prime double-cross. It always happens sooner or later when you're dealing with rats. They practice rat-think, and at the moment, Lepkov and Hammond and Veresi are trying to undermine the Ricaso family's power base in order to become king rats."

"Sounds fanciful."

"Does it? Who do you think kidnapped Luciano Chicarelli? Tyler is still in Rome station—he postponed his retirement to help Teddy get this straightened out. He cabled us the transcripts from the latest Chicarelli phone intercepts. The motive was to get Chicarelli out of the race. And it was working—he was caving in until Carlo found Luciano in the prince's dungeon. And you, of course. Now, who knows?"

"Who knows, indeed? I still can't figure out why Guappo kidnapped *me*." He rubbed his wrist, remembering the manacles.

"He's a hired gun, working for anyone in the cabal who'll have him. A hit for *don* Cesare today, an arson for his father tomorrow. Whatever. We believe Lepkov and Hammond hired him to kill you. Fortunately he didn't follow orders, though we aren't sure why. He took you to the prince's palace instead."

"Everyone makes mistakes," Frost said.

Natale cocked an eyebrow defensively.

"From their point of view," Frost explained. "We're hoping that kidnapping you was their big mistake."

"Anyway, let's sum up the big picture. We know for sure that these people plan to bribe and murder their way into the permanent presidency of the EU. At least we have that. And we know that Jacovetti is their man. That's absolute too. I already had a handle on that much before I sent you to Hotel de Mer—though I was hoping you'd stumble into something more definite. Instead, you tripped over a dead EIA spy."

"Rudy Brandenburg." Judith's face saddened. "Another piece of the puzzle."

Natale recalled the moonlit night at Monte Carlo, the body on his hotel room floor. "Where does he fit in?" he asked.

"He was a wild card," she said. "He helped Hammond move the gold when he worked with him in Berlin. Then when Hammond went to Langley, Rudy got left out of the main shuffle. He got mad and decided to get even. He went to work for the EIA and pretended to be helping Hammond. The EIA let him target Marco's gang. But Rudy was working his own angles too. He was close to the edge—he knew it. He was addicted to heroin, and Marco's thugs were onto him. He decided to pull a grandstand act. He was going to tip us off about Hammond, Lepkov, and the gold, then rip off the casino vault as revenge and either disappear or go out in a blaze of glory. At least that's the way it looks to me."

Natale had intended for the question to be speculative. He was surprised that Judith knew the answer. He stared at her.

She smiled with embarrassment. "I guess I've been busy." She explained what she'd learned in Bonn, told them about her visit to the Archduchess Brandenburg's castle. And then she turned to Peter and told him about Rudy's confronting her in the garden at the Hotel de Mer.

"So he was going to break into the vault."

"Apparently. Maybe that's why he went to your room. In his drugged frame of mind, he thought he was going to con you into helping him."

"Who killed him?"

"Marco's toughs, according to Kreidler. But Hammond or Lepkov must have ordered the hit."

"Why wouldn't you tell me what was going on?" His jaw set in anger.

Judith looked at the floor, suddenly seeming uncomfortable. "I was confused, Peter. I promised before God that I wouldn't say anything to anyone, and I felt I should keep that promise. Beyond that, I didn't trust my own judgment. I really thought I'd let Rudy down and got him killed."

"So why the disappearing act? What was the point?"

A cloud crossed her face. Her eyes grew luminous with distress. "I don't really understand it. When I reached Milano, I just knew I had to get off the plane. Something seemed to be gently steering me. And once off, it seemed like momentum took over, and I ended up in Bonn, trying to check out the story Rudy told me."

"Maybe someone was watching you," Natale said. She had told them about her fear that the EIA satellites might intercept any phone messages if she tried to contact him or Frost. "I've had that uneasy feeling at times when I was under physical surveillance."

"No, it wasn't that kind of feeling." Her smoky-blue eyes suddenly hooded over. "That wasn't it at all."

"Then what? You had us crazy with worry, Judith. Why did you bail out like that?"

"I really don't understand. But I know it was something I absolutely had to do." She looked down at the floor as if ashamed.

Natale was silent. Frost was also quiet for a time. Peter noticed that Teddy's shoulders were sagging and his face was gray now with fatigue.

Natale turned to him. "What's on your mind?"

Frost looked up, worried. "We've been monitoring some serious anti-American activism in Naples these past few days. Almost as bad as during the terrorist days."

"And?"

Frost looked almost embarrassed. "This is going to sound preposterous . . ."

"Try me."

"I can see something frightening happening in this country, Peter. It crosses my mind that the only thing that held back the tide of Italy's fascism for the past seventy years was the Communists, and they're all but gone."

Natale looked puzzled. "You're lamenting the death of the USSR and the Italian Communist party?"

"Hardly. I'm lamenting the fact that the fall of Communism left so much empty and fertile ground. Any form of totalitarianism could easily take root here."

"The Mafia already has," Judith commented.

"Not totally," Peter said. "The Octopus's tentacles strangle most of the country but not all of it. There's plenty of room for other types of fascists, so long as they don't go one-on-one with *don* Cesare."

Frost sighed. "I have a very bad feeling about things."

"That's because Hammond is flying in," Judith said.

"That's right, back to Hammond." He turned to look fully at Peter, and there was a sincerity in his face that added impact to the concern in his eyes. "Hammond got in a flash transmission just before I left Langley—that Carlo had freed you and Luciano. One of my friends was watching him and copied the message. Peter, he knows we're getting close to nailing him. He's not going to let that happen, even if he has to kill all three of us."

"He'd be crazy to try that," Judith protested.

"He'd be crazy not to, from his point of view," Peter said. "Look what he's already gotten away with."

Frost leaned forward. "He's starting with you, Peter, because you're the most direct threat. I didn't want to say this till I had a better handle on what was happening, but it all fits together now. While I was in Langley, Hammond asked for a hearing into the way you handled Kaleidoscope. He's setting you up so no one will believe anything you say. He claims the informants were murdered because of you, that your interaction with the German secret police was mangled from the beginning, damaging already fragile relations. He's using your relationship with Carlo to convince people that you've gone dirty and are into the black market and heroin traffic. That's going to be his entry card to taking you down."

Anger sparked in Peter's eyes. He started to say something, but Frost held up his hand.

"Let me finish. Here's the way I see it now. Lepkov and Hammond want you out of the picture. Marco kidnapped you on their orders, but for whatever reason he took you to the prince's palace, and Carlo got you out. Now Hammond is going to arrive in a white-hot rage. He's going to discredit you before you can talk. He's going to yank you back to Langley, probably in chains, and pull you up on charges—unless he finds an easy way to get rid of you before then, of course.

"His back is to the wall, and he doesn't know yet how much I've figured out, or how much Judith has figured out. But he knows you're on the brink of uncovering him, and that makes you the immediate target. He's more dangerous than ever, Peter. Believe me when I say that. I want you to leave here, fly anywhere he can't find you till we get this straightened out."

Peter felt a tangible weight trying to press him down, and suddenly his head began to hurt, the place where his shoulder was bandaged began to throb, even his teeth ached. He said, "That's a really bad idea."

"He'll nail you, then we'll be next." Judith's pale eyebrows dipped into an angry frown.

Natale felt his own face collapse into a scowl. He abruptly got up and went into the kitchen. He needed to move, to get rid of the stiffness that was setting in with the pain. He needed to think. He poured three steaming cups of coffee while he swiftly worked things out, then he took them back into the living room and set one cup on the end table beside Frost, who was staring out the window, and another beside Judith.

The expression on her face was darkly distant. She was lost in her own troubled world.

Frost sipped his coffee politely and looked at Natale, waiting.

Finally Peter said, "You know, friends, we've stumbled into something that is evil incarnate."

"Yes," Judith said softly. "Exactly."

"There's a force underlying it. A spiritual force. Black quicksand, and something serpentine and evil lives there."

Judith inclined her head as if she knew exactly what he meant.

"It wants power. A black, evil power." He stopped, looked at Frost.

Frost said, "I'm listening."

Natale's eyes kindled. "You know what? I don't believe in darkness. I believe in the light." He looked at Judith for approval.

She smiled at him. They were her words, spoken while they were discussing spiritual matters during their short stay at the villa in the hills above Nice.

"We have to take down Hammond and the whole rats' nest," Peter said. "We don't have a choice."

Judith set her jaw stubbornly. "Where do we begin?"

"How about with Marco Guappo? I'd like to personally ask him why he kidnapped me." Natale's face was cold, determined.

Frost studied his fingers, found an invisible speck beneath a manicured nail, worked diligently at removing it. After a moment, he made a gesture of resignation. "I suppose I could keep Hammond diverted for a little while."

"How long?"

Frost glanced at his watch. "It's almost four A.M. That gives us about five hours till he arrives. He's coming by CIA jet to visit General Barkoff and view the air show, which starts at ten this morning. Something for the press. Then he's going to come for you, Peter, probably with a couple of soldiers on each arm. I can keep him busy for a while, even at that. But I can't say for how long. Stay away from Naples station today. That will help. I'll buy you all the time I can, but at some point he's going to go out of control."

"That at least gives us time to start," Judith said.

"To start precisely what?" Frost asked.

Peter could see he was really worried. "To start looking for a way to bring Hammond down. To drive a stake through his shriveled heart."

"And if you can't pull it off?"

Natale looked at Frost's furrowed brow, at Judith's stubborn chin jutting out. He said, "Then we pray."

"It might be a good idea to start praying right now," Judith said. She suddenly smiled, and her face became radiant.

Natale smiled back, though it hurt.

But the pain was only superficial. It would heal. The rest of the world might be rocketing into oblivion, the bad guys might be gunning for him and already digging his grave. But Judith had come back. That was a miracle and an answer to prayer.

With Judith at his side, maybe they could still stop the world from plummeting into the hideous, growing darkness that seemed to spread with paralyzing thickness all around them.

33

Valletta

Carlo had just entered the doorway of *don* Cesare's dark stone house when he felt something hard and cylindrical ram into his back.

"Don't move. Don't do nothing, or you're dead."

The voice was familiar.

"Rocco? What in—"

"I'm sorry, but I got to follow orders. *Don* Cesare said to cuff you when you got inside the house."

Carlo felt his heart turn to ice. His voice was equally cold. "I'm telling you, Rocco, you don't let me go, you'll be on a slab in the morgue or down a mine shaft before the sun comes up."

"You ain't going to be able," Rocco said. "Move." The gun pressed into Carlo's back and shoved him forward to where another *picciotti*, Roberto Antonini, was waiting with a pair of handcuffs.

Roberto yanked Carlo's hands together in front of him, put on the cuffs, and ratcheted them tight.

Carlo didn't struggle. These men were professionals. If he made one wrong move, his back and chest would be instantly blown away. At the same time, he knew what the cuffs meant. Either way, he was about to meet Sicily's White Death. His body would be dropped out at sea or down a shaft, fed to the pigs, or otherwise made to disappear. He hadn't thought it would happen. He really hadn't believed *don* Cesare could murder his own flesh and blood.

But as the two killers pushed him forward and out onto the stone veranda, he thought about every other form of atrocity he'd seen his evil uncle administer over the long and brutal years, and he had to face the truth. His uncle—his family—had made a pact with death long ago, and now it was his turn.

"Carlo." Cesare was seated in his dark wicker rocker. A lamp was lit beside him. His voice was curiously devoid of emotion. He patted Carlo's chair. "Sit down." The old man smiled, then the smile slithered away, leaving the face of a poisonous snake.

Carlo obediently sat, leaning forward at an uncomfortable angle to accommodate the handcuffs. It was well past 2:00 A.M. He had been in Palermo taking care of business. The orchards and fields, the lawns and guardhouses were dark beneath a sharp sliver of moon. Carlo felt death pressing on him, suffocating him. He could smell the freshly turned earth of his own grave.

"I'm gonna explain this. You at least deserve to know," the old capo said. He was cold, tensile. "I gave you every chance in the world, but you ain't ever gonna listen."

"You're crazy. Lepkov and Veresi set you up like you wouldn't believe, and you're pulling the gun on *me?*"

"You shouldn't have gone into the prince's palace, not even to get Luciano. You should of cleared it with me first. There were other ways to handle things. I have my own action going with the prince, things you couldn't understand. I can't have my left hand fighting with my right hand, Carlo. It opens the door to my enemies."

"Your enemies already had you by the throat."

"*Basta,* Carlo. That's enough! I done everything to get you straightened out. But you chose to help Peter Natale. You chose the wrong side. The friend of my enemies becomes my enemy, Carlo. You pushed me as far as I can go. You give me no other choice than to do what I gotta do."

"Why are you so angry about my breaking into the prince's palace? I don't get it."

"Why? Why?" the old man mimicked in a whining tone of voice. "Why do I have to live with a traitor in my own house, that's what I want to know?"

"I'm not a traitor."

"*Basta,* Carlo. If you'd been anyone else, you would of been dead years ago."

"*Zu* Cesare—"

"It's over, Carlo. Maybe things coulda been different if you'd grown up in Sicily. Or maybe your blood was just bad from the start. Who knows? But I'm telling you, things are happening. The Americans are about to get blown out of Italy, and once that happens I can relax and take care of business without worrying about their spy satellites and their narcotics agents and their money-laundering task forces, and most of all about what my own flesh-and-blood relative is telling them behind my back."

Carlo stopped breathing. "What do you mean, 'blown out of Italy'?"

"Lepkov and the others are taking care of the Americans at NATO, Carlo. We're going to get things straightened out. You don't understand anything. I need Lepkov and the prince, Carlo, just for the moment. They're taking care of certain things that need to be done. When they're through—" he flicked his fingers dismissively "—they can be discarded. In the meantime, you don't know how to handle my action, but you ain't got the sense to stay out of it. I'm sorry it's gotta be this way, but I gave you every chance." He made a tiny movement with his wrist, as if to bat an insect away.

Rocco and Roberto had been standing with their guns aimed dead at Carlo. Now Rocco stepped forward and started to pull a hood over Carlo's head.

Carlo held his breath and tensed till Rocco was at just the right angle. Then he spun, kicked out, made contact, and Rocco sprawled to the stone floor. Roberto lunged, and Carlo brought the cuffs around and slammed both arms into him, sending the second man reeling too.

Both men were shouting now, *don* Cesare was lurching to his feet, glaring, yelling. Carlo could see the hellish flames behind the black glass of his uncle's eyes.

Something whacked him on the head. He stumbled forward, then heard *don* Cesare spit out the words: "Don't shoot him here. I don't wanta see it happen."

Carlo glanced up and saw Rocco standing, coming around to hit him again. The gun was angled so that the butt would impact his temple with the force of a hammer.

He waited till the last second and dodged, then wheeled around, snap-kicked Rocco in the side. The man doubled up, gagged, and the gun went spinning across the lava-stone floor.

Carlo scooted after the gun, feeling the wind as Roberto reached him, then rolled onto his back. He brought the gun up just as Roberto dove into him, going for the weapon. Carlo squeezed the trigger, then fired again.

There was a terrible groan. Roberto seemed to hesitate in midair, then slammed into him from above like a side of slaughtered beef. Carlo shoved, rolled Roberto off him just in time to feel Rocco grab his arm.

Then Carlo was rolling up and out of the position, the rage of centuries boiling up in him as he reacted, simply reacted, came around, saw Rocco hurtling at him. He brought the gun up again, and fired, fired. The report was deafening in the silent night. And then the gun was empty, and Rocco and Roberto both lay on the stone floor, their faces frozen in surprise as they glimpsed eternity's horror.

Carlo was standing, panting, his lungs aching from the absence of air. He still held the empty gun. He quickly surveyed the bodies, then whipped around, expecting to see *don* Cesare holding a *lupara* on him, but the old man's hands were empty.

Don Cesare was tense, his head was tilted, he watched Carlo with narrowed, dangerous eyes, but in fact he seemed almost amused. He said, *"Buono,* Carlo. I didn't know you had it in you."

Carlo snarled, "Get the key. Get me out of these cuffs."

"Si, Carlo. I will let you go. We can put this problem off for a while. If you would fight as hard against our enemies as you do against our friends, we might even get it straightened out."

Carlo's adrenaline had been pumping. Now he felt himself begin to wind down. Still, he watched Cesare carefully as the *don* bent stiffly over Rocco's body. He fished in a pocket, then came out with the handcuff key.

Carlo felt anger toward his uncle, along with a sickening sense of betrayal. But most of all he felt as if he were studying some deceptively dangerous species of beast, something rising up out of black poisonous quicksand.

Cesare moved gingerly toward him, and Carlo said, "Get these things off me."

"*Si*, Carlo, *si*. You are always so impatient."

Cesare dipped, seemed to be fiddling with the cuffs, the key, but in the instant that the cuffs came off, he suddenly lunged upward. Something tight ripped into Carlo's throat. He stumbled forward and struggled, but the agile little capo scrambled around and was on his back like a monkey.

Carlo realized the truth—his uncle had whipped a thin wire garrote around his neck, was behind him and pulling with all his strength. He cursed his own stupidity even as he struggled to breathe, then with a massive effort he heaved up his shoulders and threw the old man backward across the room.

He whirled to face him and simultaneously ripped the garrote from his throat. His hands came away bloodied from where the wire had cut deep into the skin.

"You *scimunito*," his uncle spat, lying on his back, breathing harshly. "You are not my blood. I denounce you, everything about you. You are a traitor, you are not Mafia—" The old man struggled to his feet, and a flood of obscenities came from his mouth.

Carlo was amazed at the man's strength. But a sad realization gripped him at the same time—his uncle was either going to kill him, or he was going to have to kill his uncle. There was no other way.

Don Cesare was up and moving toward him. His hands thrust out stiffly like claws longing to grip his throat, and Carlo could see that the *don* was crazed with the scent of death. He wondered yet again what would happen if he allowed himself to kill the old man. Would that same murderous evil that gripped Cesare come into him? Would he forever forfeit any chance to be free from the vileness that continued to swallow up his life?

Cesare lurched another step forward, and Carlo braced himself for a renewed attack. But the man stopped, stiffened, staggered, moving woodenly. He grabbed his throat and made a strange gagging sound.

Carlo stared.

Cesare lurched forward another step.

Carlo hesitated, puzzled.

The capo made a croaking sound, another. It crossed Carlo's mind that the old man had overexcited himself. But even as the thought flitted through his head, Cesare's face twisted into agony, then froze, and Carlo realized that something was terribly wrong.

Don Cesare was lurching again, starting, stopping, gaining only inches with each distorted step. His face was turning darker, sweat was breaking out in beads on the wrinkled forehead. The old man's face remained frozen in a contorted position. A new, deep terror flooded his eyes.

He reeled forward again, then his legs buckled, and he toppled to the floor. His right hand seemed to be frozen into one of the predatory claws that had threatened Carlo just moments ago.

Carlo suddenly thought he understood what was happening. His uncle was suffering a stroke. His rage had activated his old illness and fueled his own destruction. For just an instant Carlo felt a sweeping sense of relief.

But in almost the same instant he felt guilty and knew he couldn't leave it like this. He couldn't let his uncle die. If he did, he would indeed be offering his soul to the same demons that had driven *don* Cesare.

Carlo swept the old man up in his arms, surprised at how small he really was, how frail he seemed. He caught up a throw from the sofa and wrapped the old man in it, then held him tenderly as he hurried to his car.

He was driving the Alfa Romeo today. He placed his uncle in the backseat, seeing the horror still growing in the old man's eyes. He also saw the weakness now, and he knew it had always possessed the man. He tucked the *don* into the seat belt, then leaped into the driver's seat.

He sped down the palm-lined driveway, raised a hand to signal a guard to open the gate, and then he was on the highway, racing to save his uncle's life, while *don* Cesare lay in the backseat making terrible, rasping sounds.

At the hospital in Palermo, time dragged by. Carlo had been given a private room where he waited for word on his uncle's condition, waited to see if the old man would die.

He thought about all that was happening. Even if *don* Cesare lived, Carlo would have to take the reins of power now. No other option was open to him. The lifetime of dread had turned into reality. His most fearsome nightmare had come true.

He had just become the Ricaso family capo, which made him the capo *di tutti capi* of all Sicily—unless he decided to walk away and let the butchers and madmen take over the territories. They would take control of the blind and venal world and administer a totally new layer of madness and violence that would catch him up in it. Inevitably it would destroy him, because he had always known that there were only two kinds of people in Sicily—the Mafia and their victims. He would either be capo-Mafia, or he would become the victim of the new capo-Mafia. There was no other choice.

Carlo stared into the darkness until it melted into the first faint traces of dawn. But the gray light brought only a fresh, harsh look at the Sicilian mountains and even grimmer thoughts of what his future would hold.

At 6:00 A.M., when the skyline was fully visible, the doctor came out of the emergency operating room with a sad look on his face. "He's alive," he said. "But he will never be the same again. I'm sorry, Carlo. I did everything I could."

He heard the surgeon's words in a daze. *Don* Cesare would need round-the-clock care now, someone to feed him, help him use the bathroom, even move him. His full left side, his legs and arms, were paralyzed. He had suffered massive intracranial bleed. He would never talk right again. His mental processes might be damaged. Certain anticoagulant drugs might keep him alive—or there could be faster degeneration, unpleasant side effects.

Carlo nodded to the doctor, but he had stopped listening. A realization had gripped him and turned his throat dry. *Don* Cesare had just suffered something far, far worse than death.

Control. Power. Control had been everything to Cesare. It had filled the emptiness at the old man's center of being, an emptiness that Peter Natale said could be filled only by God. Now, in an instant, Cesare had lost control over not only the world he had pillaged and bloodied but over even his own ravaged body.

Carlo felt the claustrophobic horror, felt the suffocation and the helpless fear.

The doctor left, and a nurse led Carlo down a corridor. He thought of what Peter Natale had said about the emptiness at the core of being that could be filled only by God. He remembered his uncle's cryptic statement about the Americans being blown out of Italy. He thought of Lepkov, the prince—all his family's enemies, men his uncle had thought he controlled, but who had turned the tables on him. In fact, they had been controlling *him*. These men were still out there, still fomenting their madness, still a threat to him and to everyone else.

Carlo asked the nurse to direct him to the closest phone, where he called Naples station and asked for Natale. The cipher clerk said he was not in. Carlo left his private number and his code name. He made two more quick calls, then he walked back down the corridor and into the room where they had wheeled his old uncle.

Cesare was pale, deflated, head swathed in bandages, and sound asleep. His face was still twisted in permanent agony, his hand was still clawlike. He was attached to IV drips and machines and so many monitors that he seemed more machine than human.

Carlo felt a sudden, gripping sense of loss that belied every other emotion he'd ever felt toward this man. All the anger, the outrage, the fear seemed to vanish into the dust that his uncle would soon become.

He stepped back, surprised by his feelings, and chanced to see a scuffed leather Bible on a table in the corner. He moved over, opened it, found himself reading the Twenty-third Psalm, something he had not done since childhood.

He sat down beside his uncle. "The Lord is my Shepherd. I shall not want." He read the first verse out loud. And then, finding a strange comfort in the words, he continued to read, another verse, then another, until he realized he was no longer reading aloud but silently, hungrily, to himself now.

A nurse came in to check the monitors, and Carlo shut the Bible, embarrassed to be caught. At the same time he felt a strange sense of renewed hope. Perhaps for him there was still time to discover a world forged from something besides deception, greed, and blood. Perhaps the secrets indeed lay hidden here in this Book.

He was tired. Too tired to walk down the corridor again. But there was no reason for it anyway. He picked up the bedside phone and tried to call Peter Natale again. The clerk advised him that Natale had not checked in yet with Naples station.

"Get a message to him, right away," Carlo said. "Tell him that something's up with the NATO base. Something urgent. I don't know what, and I don't know when. But I know it's big, and you'd best let Natale know immediately so he can check it out."

He hung up the phone, then looked up to see black, shining hatred gleaming through the drug-misted lenses of *don* Cesare's swollen eyes. The old man had awakened, had heard and understood the words Carlo spoke into the phone.

"Sorry, *Zu* Cesare," Carlo said. "But your way no longer works. I am capo now, and I will take care of you, just as you've always taken care of me. But I will not be like you. Never, no matter what. In this moment, I make a new vow. No matter what happens, no matter what it costs me, I will never let *La Mafia* cause me to forfeit my eternal soul."

Cesare's eyes were stricken with panic now. He was trying to move his hand, and Carlo could see that his uncle was beginning to realize what had happened to him.

Carlo felt the panic too. He didn't know what to say. He didn't know what to do. Automatically he picked up the Bible and opened it.

Again he began to read. "The Lord is my Shepherd. I shall not want. . . ."

Cesare's eyes filled with even deeper hatred.

But Carlo ignored him. This time, deliberately, he continued to read. Out loud.

34

Naples

At 5:30 A.M. Marco Guappo sat at a wrought-iron table on the balcony of an apartment in the Neapolitan suburb of Bagnoli and thought about how a terrorist network had brought Italy to her knees back during the 1970s. But at that time the Red Brigade had made the fatal mistake of kidnapping an American NATO general, and the US military retaliated by spearheading an all-out attack on terrorism that had brought down the terrorists—all the various factions. Now the odds had shifted. The Americans were no longer wanted in Europe. Things would be different this time.

Marco was not an intelligent man, but he was extremely cunning. His craftiness showed in the glitter of his black eyes, in the jut of his heavy jaw. He felt more than analyzed, as he considered the work ahead of him and all it would mean.

He was no longer foolish enough to have political motives. Perhaps he had never been. Looking back, he could see that he'd joined Lepkov's terrorist brigade because he'd wanted action, blood, an excuse to blow up airliners and assassinate strangers and otherwise vent his rage on the world. Now, as a Mafia enforcer, he had all the action and vengeance he could handle.

What he didn't have was his own territory. He wanted money, he wanted full control of Naples's heroin market. The Ricaso family was in his way, and he hated them with an acidic hatred that made him ready for any plan that would harm them. He had been happy to work against them by kidnapping Luciano Chicarelli and Peter Natale. He spat as he thought about how Carlo Ricaso had freed them and made a fool of him.

But he couldn't think about that today. Today he would only think about how much he hated the Americans, especially for their attempts to help beef up Italy's anti-Mafia, anti-drug squads. He agreed with Lepkov that the American presence in Europe had to come to an end, and he was ready to make that happen.

Marco's face twisted in an evil smile. Today would begin that era the terrorists had called Fright Decade Four. Today the Americans would be driven from Italy, the power base would shift, opportunities would open up for those who dared rush in, and Marco would be leading the pack.

NATO's CINCSOUTH was the key. Though NATO had been stripped down throughout the rest of Europe and largely replaced by the militia of the anti-American EuroCorp, its Naples base remained strong and strongly pro-American. Its arsenal still included atomic rockets, nuclear missiles, tanks, jet fighters, and all other necessary infrastructure to fight a global war, including the spy networks and intelligence-gathering satellites.

The centerpiece of operations in southern NATO remained the US Navy's Sixth Fleet. The fleet spent half its time at sea, the other half in the various ports it visited. But several supply ships were permanently docked at Naples, and the fleet's land staff was attached to AFSOUTH, NATO's regional HQ.

AFSOUTH also had a number of American and Italian fighter jets and support planes at its disposal, and today the Italians and Americans would demonstrate their skill and solidarity by working together in NATO's annual air show.

Marco's borrowed apartment was on the hillside. Before him lay the Bay of Naples and the Cape of Misena. From this vantage point, he could see that the US aircraft carrier Thomas Jefferson had come into port during the night, along with its escort ships. The sailors would get leave. They would be at the air show.

He hadn't considered this possibility, and for a minute he was worried. But then he changed his mind. He had used all his connections. He had spread an ample amount of Lepkov's money around the Neapolitan slums. There would be enough people in the anti-American demonstration today to rout any number of patriotic sailors, even if they were drunk on Neapolitan beer and wine and ready to defend their country's honor with their fists.

Marco gazed eagerly at the ships' lights. His eyes measured the sky, trying to foresee the day's weather. If there were heavy showers as yesterday, NATO might cancel the air show. But no, there it was—the dawn had just edged pink light into a cloudless sky. In his mind he could see the NATO and allied flags flapping in the predawn breeze at the entrance to AFSOUTH HQ. Already they would be setting up bleachers and checking the Thunderbolt fighter jets that would be the stars of the show.

He hadn't been able to sleep. The details of the operation kept playing in his mind, and he had been in radio communication all night with the two other Black Brigade members who were assisting with this operation. They assured him they'd paid off the military policeman who was helping them. The anti-aircraft missile was well concealed and in place.

Marco had done many things, killed many people. But never before had he felt as if he were waging a war all by himself. It was an intoxicating feeling. He would make a good commander in chief for the Naples Mafia, far better than his father had ever been. But that was a problem for the future, and to think about his father would make him lose his taste for the moment.

He used his radio to once again contact his men. They informed him that everything was in place. By the time the sun set tonight, the American military in NATO would be a smoking, defeated ruin, and the Americans would be forced to leave the country.

And then—but he couldn't let himself think that far. His hatred for his father had swallowed him so completely that the thought of freedom had shrunk down to a tiny, secret core that he sometimes hid even from himself.

He checked his watch again—5:45. Suddenly he stood and gazed in the direction of Bertinelli Field. The air show would begin at 10:00. He felt a stirring as he thought of the enormous crowds, the chaos, and the pleasure, the inevitable pleasure, of destroying a world that had tried for so long to destroy him.

35

Judith spent some hard, early-morning hours on the telephone, verifying certain link-ups and otherwise adding to the growing bank of knowledge about the madness that was threatening to swallow them all. Peter stayed at the safe house with her, working his own connections, helping her put together a strategy that would help them unmask Hammond before Hammond could activate his substantial resources and get to them first.

They had their own convictions, added to a good deal of general background information that might sooner or later lead to evidence. But they needed immediate, ironclad proof if they were going to accuse the CIA's director of operations of two decades of corruption and make the charge stick.

Both were tense, pale, weighted down by the enormity of the problem. Peter was keenly aware of how close they were to having their hands permanently tied with regard to all that was happening in Europe. He knew that the American presence was crucial in the global war against drugs. Though there were still many honest policemen and honest antidrug agents in Europe, there was no substantial and viable foundation for them if the Americans pulled out.

Furthermore, if European power fell to the EuroMafia, the United States itself would soon be buried under a renewed avalanche of drugs and corruption, and this time they'd have no global nexus from which to fight back.

At 8:30 Frost left for the base. He would meet Hammond's plane, then stay with him during the air show. He would try to buy

Natale some time afterward, but Teddy was tired, worried. Natale could tell he wasn't feeling confident that they could pull this off.

After Frost left, Peter also began to feel defeated. Maybe he should consider jumping ship. The only thing that prevented him was Judith.

She sat, eyes shining with determination, at the computer console. She picked up the telephone and talked to people at various CIA stations, getting a scrap of information here, a morsel there. She was determined to unmask the mole.

He could not leave her alone, especially now that she'd shown her motives to so many people in so many places.

He thought about the simplicity of their lives when they'd stolen those five days at the retreat above Nice. He wanted to be back there, with her—or perhaps in some similarly simple place in Brazil or the South Pacific.

But there was no way she'd jump ship with him, even though she'd taken off on her own not long ago. That had been an aberration, totally unlike her, and now she was back to her old stubborn self. She wouldn't give up. She wouldn't run from anything. He couldn't even mention the possibility to her. He didn't want to see the disappointment in her eyes.

At 9:00 Peter phoned Naples station to see if anything new had come up. He would be unable to contact them later in the day, for Hammond would have the dogs out, and he didn't want to jeopardize Jeremy Ward or the others who manned the station.

Ward hadn't come in yet. Things were quiet—except for a message from Carlo Ricaso. Natale listened, said a few words, waited for a long time, then spoke again and hung up.

"Judith." He turned, woodenly, and looked at her.

She glanced up from the computer console, then did a double-take. "What's wrong? You're white as a sheet."

"A message from Carlo. Something's up with the NATO base. I think this thing is coming to a head."

"What?"

"He didn't know, but he says it's big. He's got a sixth sense about these things."

"You talked to him?"

"I waited while the cipher clerk tried to patch me through. Carlo's not there, and the man who answers his phone doesn't know anything about the message, doesn't know where he is."

Judith thought. "Maybe someone is going to be assassinated today. Big crowds, a lot of turmoil." She narrowed her eyes. "Maybe Hammond." There was no malice in her face or voice, though Peter checked to make sure. And then her face froze. "Or maybe Teddy Frost."

Natale grabbed up a phone and talked to NATO's US Military Police, then turned back to Judith. "The MPs also had an anonymous tip. They say they have the base and the airfield fully secured, but they don't have the manpower to actually cover every contingency." He grinned wryly. "I have a feeling Carlo called them too."

"Probably."

"The MPs say that there are some pretty serious demonstrations outside the gate—more trouble than usual. The MPs are keeping them outside the airfield—"

"What kind of demonstrators?"

"Fascists, a few Communists. Anti-Americans. People calling for the US to get out of Europe."

"Maybe that's it. Maybe they're going to do something more than demonstrate this year."

"Maybe."

"What do we do?"

"Maybe we should go to the base and see what's up."

"With Hammond there?"

"Why not? There are going to be hundreds, maybe thousands, of people at the air show, military families, civilian families having picnics, Italians, Americans. Hammond and Frost will be with the big shots on the viewing stands. We can blend into the crowd, stay away from that area, see what's what."

Judith looked with disgust at the computer terminal, then at the telephone. "I'm not getting anywhere here. Let's do it."

"Let me make one more quick call," Peter said. He dialed Naples's SISMI headquarters—the Italian intelligence network, roughly equivalent to the CIA.

He usually stayed well away from SISMI, simply because of the enormity of their bureaucracy and the plodding way in which they got things done. He had worked with them from time to time, however, when no other option was possible. Other than their bureaucratic sludge, he found them compatible.

Natale asked for a man named Tony Scorzini, who listened to what he said with interest, then replied that they had also been tipped. Something big was in the wind with regard to the air show, something that would make the Americans persona non grata in all of Italy.

Scorzini admitted that anti-American sentiment had been growing recently, with several demonstrations erupting into violence. He and his partner were just leaving SISMI HQ for the NATO base. Would Natale like to link up with them?

Natale cupped a hand over the receiver as they quickly discussed it. He had been kidnapped and out of the picture for a few days, Judith had been in the wind. Both had missed the TV news, the papers.

But he knew that political demonstrations were seldom spontaneous. Almost always there were organizers behind them, people making some kind of power grab. Whoever it was this time had managed to get way ahead of them. Now they had to at least try to find out what was wrong. Because trouble was coming. It was coming as surely as the violent sirocco winds always returned with the deep heat of summer, as surely as the torrential winter rains always arrived to drench Naples and all the rest of southern Italy and Sicily.

"Tell them yes," Judith said. "We're totally blind on this one. We can use all the help we can get."

SISMI headquarters was a few short blocks out of the way. Natale and Judith stopped long enough to pick up the two SISMI men. The portly Antonio "Tony" Scorzini was pleased to see Judith and saluted smartly. His partner, Antonino "Tony" Barco was a tall thin man with a mournful face, whose smile was more a grimace. They were known within the intelligence community as the Two Tonys, and Natale agreed with Judith that they were both honest and hard-working men who were completely aware of the shortcomings of the bureaucracy they served—and who would be an asset in any operation.

The Two Tonys climbed into the backseat of Natale's brown Mercedes, and Peter was stepping on the gas, starting to turn away from the building and into the street, when an aide raced down the steps yelling. "Sir? Sir! Stop!"

Natale stepped on the brakes, and Tony One rolled down the rear window. "What is it? We have—"

"Sir. This is just in and urgent. The commander wanted you to know before you left. The head of the Naples Fascist party—Paolo Tomassini? He has just been shot to death at the demonstration outside the gates at NATO. The assassin was in the uniform of an American soldier. He disappeared into the crowd. The situation is getting ugly, sir. He wanted you to know."

"This is it," Natale said. "They've just lit the flame, and there's no telling how much trouble it's going to ignite." He threw the car in gear and stomped on the gas.

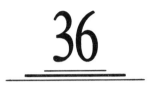

36

Naples, Bertinelli Airfield

Natale leaned forward, his eyes ticking off every car he passed, every street sign. He was speeding toward a possible conflagration. With all the anti-American sentiment currently in the air, the shooting at Bertinelli Airfield could easily erupt into chaos.

Was that the problem Carlo had warned them about? If so, the shooting wasn't an accident. And if it wasn't an accident, chances were good that the assassin wasn't an American but was merely set up to seem American. Natale was suddenly weighted down with possibilities.

His three passengers were silent, stony faced. He glanced in his rearview mirror, saw the Two Tonys checking their sidearms. He felt a rush of panic, saw the sensation reflected in Judith's ashen face.

As he approached the gates, the traffic became more congested, then slowed, then came to a near stop. A mob of protesters was disrupting the flow of cars, trucks, military Jeeps. People on foot and on motorbikes were going around the larger vehicles. The situation was disintegrating.

The protesters had the hungry, angry look of striking workers, except for the huge, black ensigns they carried. Scores of black flags flapped in the wind. The white stripes around the borders and the white fist in the center of each clearly defined the political allegiances of the mass of people. This core group was made up of several hundred men and women, though an unusual percentage of them were rough-cut young men who might have been bused in from Naples's seedy Forcella market district, where drug dealers, thieves, pimps, and assassins gathered to prey on tourists and locals alike. *Marco Guappo's realm*, Natale reflected.

But before the thought could take full form, a second wave of protesters advanced, and he saw banners and signs demanding that NATO get out of Italy, that the United States military get out of NATO. These people began to mix in with the crowd, jostling and shouting, fanning the flames.

Natale's Mercedes inched along in the traffic, barely moving. As they neared the gates, the crowd spilled across the road to completely block them. A large banner was flaunted in front of the windshield: NATO OUT OF NAPLES, NATO OUT OF THE HEART OF ITALY: LONG LIVE THE FIGHTING FASCIST PARTY! People were chanting slogans. They seemed to have singled out Natale's car. They were shouting obscenities, making coarse gestures toward the four passengers.

Peter leaned on the horn and tried to inch the car forward, but the crush forced him to either stop completely or run the protesters down.

Judith wondered aloud if the protest was in response to the shooting or if it had been orchestrated in advance.

"I believe the *shooting* was orchestrated in advance," Natale said. "Which means this is a staged event."

"The question is, who's doing the staging?" Judith said angrily.

Tony One speculated as to just how long it would be until the chaos unraveled into a full-on riot, and as if in response to the question, the crowd began to crush in on them again.

Natale had his left hand on his gun now, inside the door pouch and out of sight. He steered with his right. He felt a lurch of claustrophobic panic as he tried to see out. The car was locked between walls of arms and legs. The seamy group spat curses through the rolled-up windows. A Neapolitan tough wearing a smile of evil glee slapped his palm on the window near Peter's face, almost hard enough to crack the glass, then spat onto the window directly in front of him. Without thinking, Natale let his temper flare, and he reached to open the car door.

That was all it took.

Suddenly the mob was on them, jeering, and a new hate-crazed face pressed into Peter's window. Natale regained his common sense and quickly relocked the door. He kept his gun hidden but ready, and he prayed he wouldn't have to use it. His heart was pounding from the oppressive closeness of the throng.

The protestors jostled one another to get a look at the people inside the car, and he heard the word spreading through the crowd: *Americans.* Allies of the man who had just killed their leader. Peter forced an expression of stoic indifference to his face and gazed blindly ahead, not making contact with any of the violent eyes. He glanced quickly sideways, saw a nerve jumping in Judith's cheek, something he had never seen before, then he took a swift look in the rearview mirror and saw the SISMI men, both holding their firearms hidden, ready to shoot their way out if they had to.

Peter felt the car rock, heard one of the SISMI men curse. He felt his blood rushing. The people were working themselves up to fever pitch. The car was rocking harder now, from side to side as more and more people joined in the sport. Then suddenly Natale felt the right-hand wheels leave the ground! The car was tipping over, tipping—but suddenly it rocked back and thudded into place.

The people drew back almost in a single motion, and Peter realized in that moment that a volley of rifle fire had ripped through the air. Then another volley sounded. Facial expressions changed. The mob forgot about their four prisoners and refocused on their own survival.

The nerve-grating sound of Klaxons filled the air. Peter could hear engines revving, then their car was inching forward again as the crowd began to separate, people began to run.

Six Italian Army jeeps roared into the clearing left by the locust-swarm of people. Each carried a half dozen uniformed soldiers brandishing rifles, some still firing above the people's heads. Some protestors stood their ground, their faces even more sullen with hatred as they watched the Jeeps move in to either side of the brown Mercedes.

Two Jeeps led the way. The soldiers still swept the crowd with their rifles, though they had stopped firing. Natale followed close behind.

They were stopped at the guarded gates, and the sergeant in charge asked what had happened. Natale explained. The SISMI men showed their credentials, and the gate guards leaned on their machine guns, curious, listening, also wanting to hear about the incident outside. Grim-faced, already calling up reinforcements on their hand-held radios in case the crowd tried to break through the gates, they finally let the Mercedes through.

Peter steered toward a field being used as a massive parking lot. There were crowds here too, but they were of a different sort. American and Italian military families were scattered beside the runways and were relishing picnic lunches on several wide lawns, all of them seemingly oblivious to the angry crowd outside the gate.

Several rows of near-filled bleachers had been set up for the spectators, and a central podium was bedecked with EU, Italian, NATO, and Allied flags. There, several NATO dignitaries, their aides, attendants, and guards sat watching the action in the air as several small planes displayed acrobatics. These dignitaries were ready to make the required speeches during the lapses between the air spectaculars. Natale craned his neck, trying to see Frost and Hammond among then. He thought he caught a glimpse of Frost's silver hair.

An announcer stood at a microphone, and words came through huge speakers around the grounds, traveling on a sort of reverberating echo. Natale heard enough to know that the announcer was cautioning the crowd not to leave just now and reassuring them that the MPs would have the demonstrations outside the gates well contained by the time the show was over.

Natale pulled the car to a stop in the row of vehicles, and the SISMI men leaped out. He and Judith stayed at a distance, while the two strode to the podium, flashed credentials at the guards, then touched the leg of an Italian MP who was sitting at the podium's edge, his gun out and ready. The man frowned and climbed down off the side of the podium. The three men spoke swiftly, then the MP returned to his post, and the SISMI men returned to the car.

"What's up?" Natale asked.

"All the action is outside the gates so far. They've been watching everything. They've checked the bleachers for bombs, you name it. Haven't found a thing."

Natale glanced back at the podium. He saw a stir of excitement buzz through the small group.

Judith shielded her eyes and pointed to the sky. "Look, Peter. The Diavoli Rossi has taken off." Italy's crack flying team was slated to perform in tandem with its US counterpart, the Blue Angels. This rare show was intended as a salute to the solidarity of the United States and Italian military forces: something to counter the growing anti-American sentiment and boost military morale.

Tony One was grim-faced. "I agree with the MPs that we don't want to panic the crowd," he said. "But the situation outside is bad. I think we need to break this whole thing up."

Natale was silent. He had never felt like such a complete failure as he did in that moment. He didn't know where to turn, what to look for, what to do.

He started to turn toward the podium. He still wanted to see if Hammond and Frost were seated with the other dignitaries. But just as he started to turn, people surged to their feet, the crowd began to roar, arms shot up to point overhead. He shielded his eyes from the sun and stared upward into the bleached hot sky.

The Diavoli Rossi—Italy's Red Devils, the top-drawer flying squadron beloved by the Italian people with far more devotion than Americans had ever shown their Blue Angels—were coming in low over the airfield, exhaust from their jet engines smoking over the high masts of radio towers. People shouted their enthusiasm and delight as the six A-10 Thunderbolts swept the length of the field, then sailed into the distance in a precise triangular formation.

Natale was stopped short by their majesty as they broke formation sharply, then climbed at a steep angle into the sky. They disappeared into a prism of sunlight, so he dropped his hand and scanned the crowd again. Nothing seemed amiss, though he could see serious-faced men in NATO uniform moving about, walking through the bleachers, stopping now and again to ask questions. All wore expressions of discrete determination, and he knew they were MPs.

Peter's eyes suddenly fixed on one man. A hand shielded the man's eyes against the sun and at the same time partially hid his thick features. Natale felt his eyes narrow, felt his muscles wrap tight.

The man stared at the sky, then dropped his hand and turned slightly as if he'd felt Natale's stare. It was Marco Guappo.

Guappo searched the crowd for a moment, and Peter made certain that there were people between them hiding him from Marco's predatory eyes. Guappo apparently decided he had no reason to be concerned. He turned his face upward again and stared hungrily at the sky.

Natale touched Judith's arm, directed her gaze in Marco's direction, and said, "Look who's here. Beside the bleachers."

Judith shook her head in amazement. "Is that Marco?"

Natale nodded. "The very man we wanted to see."

She and Natale exchanged a look. This was no coincidence. They began to press through the crowd toward where Guappo still stood, oblivious to their movement.

The Italian jets were back, and now the American Blue Angels roared in to join them, six in each team, twelve flashing silver birds flying high in a breathtaking maneuver that was first a hexagon, then opened into a massive double U-formation.

Natale glanced up, wanting to watch the rare symmetry, but he had work to do, and he immediately looked back to the earth. Excusing himself, he shoved past a woman with two children in tow, then looked up again as the jets swept around and came in low, buzzed the airfield, again angled upward, there to loop into circles and crosses and yet more hexagons, leaving feathery silver trails of smoke in the brilliant blue sky. The crowd cheered, their excitement filled the air, martial music played in the background.

Natale got elbowed sideways by the excited crowd and momentarily lost sight of the Mafia thug. Then again he spied him. He touched Judith's arm to direct her. "Come on," he said. He shoved his way through a press of people, all of them vying for the best viewing spots. Judith moved in his wake.

The jets came in again like shards of quicksilver against pale sky-blue, their formation precise. They made another sweep of the field, came back, and repeated their hexagons and U-formation as the crowd roared and milled about beneath them.

Marco was weaving through the crowd and toward the parking lot. Two men had joined him, and Natale slowed down to watch. At the car park they began sprinting toward a familiar black VW van—the same van he'd been dragged into only a few days ago.

Anger surged up in him, and he moved purposefully toward them.

Marco slid inside the rear of the van, threw out several blankets, and then jumped down. He was carrying something large and cylindrical.

Natale hid behind a truck and watched. Judith was so close beside him that he could feel her breathing. Marco reappeared, still holding the heavy cylinder—and suddenly Natale realized what it was.

He grabbed Judith's arm. "He's holding a surface-to-air missile! He's going to take out one of the jets!"

"Let's go! He's getting ready to fire!"

"Hold it! He might turn that thing on us instead, if he sees us coming. He could wipe out half this crowd."

Judith shuddered and stopped short.

"We'll have to blindside him. Come on. The vehicles will hide us until we're almost to him, then we'll rush him."

Judith nodded, and they started forward, hunched down so they could weave between cars.

Marco was still frozen, still aiming at the sky.

Three fighters peeled off the formation and went into a spectacular series of victory rolls. Every spectator was on his feet and cheering as the pilots executed the brilliant yet dangerous maneuvers. Then all three planes were rolling over and over, simultaneously, toward the earth. The crowd shouted its approval, then oohed and aahed, and the planes pulled out of the maneuver at the very last moment and shot back into the sky.

Three Blue Angels appeared on the other side of the field, more shards of quicksilver, more spectacular symmetry, and the crowd was on its feet again. The American Blue Angels flew symmetrically between the Diavoli Rossi, and now there were twelve planes in the formation again, a double vision of glorious precision, a tribute to technology and the men who handled it in union with other free nations to assure the freedom of the entire world.

Marco edged forward. His two accomplices stood back, waiting. It was obvious they still hadn't spotted Natale and Judith, who were several cars away, still moving carefully toward them.

Peter saw Guappo brace himself as three of the Italian jets peeled off the formation and went into another spectacular series of victory rolls. Three Blue Angels flew circumference. Every spectator was on his feet and cheering again.

And then the three Blue Angels jets also shot toward the earth in their own victory rolls, as the Italian pilots pulled out of their maneuvers and shot back to the sky like an erupting fountain, in a display brilliant as fireworks. It had the crowd screaming and roaring as never before.

At that instant, with Natale only one short car length away, the Mafioso pulled the trigger. The surface-to-air missile exploded out of its cylinder just as Peter dived, knocking Marco aside. But he was too late. The trajectory of the heat-seeking missile was visible from its smoking tail, and it was heading straight toward two planes, an American jet spinning toward earth, an Italian jet spinning back up out of its roll.

If the missile hit one it would demolish both, and suddenly Natale realized what Guappo was doing. He planned to kick off a massive anti-American campaign that would rid the Mafia of NATO and its peripheral intelligence apparatus once and for all by blaming the American flyers for the death of an Italian Air Force hero.

He pinned Marco down at a neck-breaking angle. Judith had her gun on his two accomplices. And in that instant the missile slammed into the wing of the Italian jet. The fighter shuddered and angled outward to break formation, coming so close to the American jet that for an instant Natale thought the planes were going to collide.

Guappo jerked out of Natale's hold and rolled sideways. His eyes narrowed, and for an instant Natale could see the awful, hideous wasteland wherein such acts were fomented. But then Peter had him again, and Marco was struggling, trying to force him far enough back so that he could break free. Natale stayed close, his gun aimed at the thug's heart as he tried to decide whether or not to pull the trigger.

Natale kept the gun pressed against Guappo's chest, glanced at Judith, then tried to look up all at the same time, so he partly lost track of what happened next. But he did know that the Italian plane seemed to hang suspended for the space of an instant, then plummeted out of control toward the earth.

People screamed and ran for cover as the Thunderbolt slammed into the far side of the field with a fiery roar that deluged the crowd, almost burst Natale's eardrums. Great black clouds roiled upward from the site of the crash, then shooting, searing flames.

Marco Guappo recoiled, struggled again to break free. Natale grabbed the man's throat with his free hand, so tight that the killer's dark eyes bulged.

He saw that Judith still held her gun on Guappo's two accomplices, both young Neapolitan thugs whom he didn't recognize. Now everything seemed to fall into slow motion. The crowd was stricken silent for a rushing instant, then a volley of screams, wails, and cries rent the air. Upon it came the louder sound of Klaxons, then a siren, then the sound of the announcer's reverberating voice from the loudspeakers—drowned by the roar of the crowd.

Natale felt Marco struggling again, writhing out from under him. He looked down into eyes black with hatred, and suddenly he was tired, so very tired of this endless battle against destruction. He brought his fist up, braced it, and with one granite motion slammed his clenched hand into Marco's jaw so hard that he knocked him out cold.

Peter climbed to his feet and reaimed his gun, but Judith seemed to have the other two men under control. He glanced around. Everything had occurred so swiftly that most shocked spectators were still in place, but now the crowd began screaming en masse, many of them pointing toward the sky again.

The American plane was in trouble too. The Italian jet had apparently collided with its wing after all and knocked it out of control. It was shuddering, moving too slowly. The pilot struggled with it, but it was too late.

The crowd rushed backward, some of them surging into the edges of the parking area where Natale and Judith held the three men captive. The plane plunged toward earth, now a horrendous fireball where a blink before had been a majestic silver bird. The fireball streaked across the sky, leaving a comet's tail of thunderous black smoke, then crashed like a meteor into the nearby sea.

Natale, stricken motionless, felt like someone had just poured battery acid down his throat. He looked sideways at Judith, whose lips were pursed into a stubborn expression. The two terrorists were apparently taking her seriously. They stood frozen, their backs to her, their hands high on the side of the van now.

Then Judith lifted her chin, indicating that Natale should look upward. He did, puzzled, and saw a tiny parachute, then another, floating to earth above the trees at the far side of the airfield. Judith offered him a fleeting smile, then refocused her attention on her two captives.

Both pilots had managed to eject!

But it was too soon to relax. The crowd was screaming, realization suddenly setting in, and not everyone had seen the pilots floating gently to earth behind the trees.

There was a vast drowning sea of shrieks, people in anguish, people fleeing from the crackling, spreading flames as the fire from the first crash began to lick across the field. They were heading for their cars now, forming a human wave.

Natale was unsure what to do. He looked at one of the terrorists, saw a lick of glee as he turned his head and stared lustfully at the roaring flames of the downed jet. Natale stepped toward him, brought his hand across the man's jaw in a karate chop that knocked him cold, then moved toward the other man, who cowered, then began to plead.

Natale felt the press of the crowd. He lifted Marco by the belt and tossed him into the back of the van. Then he tossed in the second unconscious man and turned to Judith.

"What do you want to do with him?" he asked, indicating the remaining thug.

"Look in the van for rope."

He found various lengths, one he suspected might be the rope that had tied him up a few short days ago. He tied the hands of Marco and his unconscious friend. Then he stepped out and bound the remaining terrorist and tossed him into the back of the van too, like a dead-weight side of beef.

He could hear people talking as they milled toward their cars. Someone said the radio towers were on fire, someone said that several spectators had been burned. The crowd outside the gate had been contained. It was possible to drive away. Now cars jostled for position in the line of vehicles that led toward the gate.

Natale took the keys from Marco's pocket. Now he and Judith climbed into the van. He started the engine and tried to back out. The crowd hysteria had brought the noise to a violent, impenetrable roar. He waited patiently while several cars filled with families, children, and old people forced their way past him. Then he angled the van around and also got in the long line that was inching toward freedom. He wanted to go back, get the SISMI men, find the MPs, and turn these thugs over. He was grindingly exhausted.

But somewhere back in the crowd was Frost, and with him was Hammond. And if Hammond spotted him, Natale was going to be the one leaving the air show in cuffs, Guappo and his thugs would be freed, and the whole thing would turn to ashes.

No, he and Judith were still on their own. And they would be until they had this straightened out, because Peter knew with absolute certainty that today's carnage was only one very small part of what these people—Hammond among them—had planned for the world. Whatever else happened, he had to at least do his best to stop them.

37

Naples

Bertinelli Field was still a beehive of activity. Thick traffic inched toward the exit, smoke roiled up from the far side of the airfield, armed soldiers elbowed their way through the milling crowd and toward the area from which the missile had been launched. The launching device was still there, abandoned amid the swirling throng of cars and people. The MPs would find it sooner or later.

Natale figured they'd probably trace it back to their own ill-guarded arsenals, though they'd never be able to determine who took it. He edged the black VW between a rusting Toyota and a red Fiat Uno and turned toward the highway. The din of Klaxons and sirens followed them away from the scene of the tragedy.

Judith climbed into the back to check on their prisoners. She'd found a roll of adhesive tape and scissors in a kit in the glove compartment. Now she taped their mouths, tightened their ropes securely, then climbed back to sit beside Natale again, a frown stenciled into her face as they passed the guards at the gate. In her hand was a telephone token; as they moved away from the airfield, she scanned the slowly passing terrain, looking for a pay phone.

They had reached the outskirts of the city before the traffic began to thin out. Finally they found a phone, and Natale called Karl Dietrich. Marco Guappo was still wanted for the Berlin brothel murders. Whatever else happened, they could at least hold him for that, though it might prove impossible to extradite him under Italian law.

"Karl," Peter said, "it's about Kaleidoscope. I've just captured Marco Guappo and two of his hired guns. Got any ideas what I should do with them?"

Dietrich emitted a salty epithet, then demanded that Natale bring them to his offices immediately.

Natale grinned all the way back to the van. That was exactly what he'd wanted to hear.

There was no point in taking Marco to the Neapolitan police. Vincente Guappo would have him out inside of an hour, then the Neapolitan Camorra would unleash their pack of killers on Natale and Judith—unless certain corrupted police nailed them first. Nor was there any point in taking him to the CIA's Naples station. Hammond would soon be raging through the place, trying to chop Natale off at the knees. Besides, Peter owed the Germans. He'd brought them into a dirty operation, and now they deserved a share of the wrap-up, assuming there was going to be one.

Judith remained stoically silent as they sped through the city. Natale spent the time fighting with Naples's relentless traffic and reflecting on all that had happened since he'd instigated the probe called Kaleidoscope. It felt good to turn the tables on Marco Guappo, to have the vicious thug in the back of the van, bound and gagged just as Peter had been a few short days ago.

They reached the Via Crispi and turned right. He slowed down and headed for a four-story concrete office building conveniently near the German consulate.

The day was dying. Evening gold reflected in the blind-eyed windows, though several squares of glass on the second floor showed artificial light through Venetian blinds.

There was little sign of security, but as Natale slowed down and started to pull over to the curb in front of the gated sidewalk, an armed guard stepped from behind the concrete fence and used his rifle to motion them into the tree-sheltered driveway.

Two more guards appeared on either side of the van, arms drawn and aimed at Natale, their faces set in stone. They walked the vehicle into a dark garage attached to a small one-story concrete building, then shut the doors and vanished.

Peter and Judith were left alone in uncomfortable darkness. He could hear Marco and his men now, awake and muttering through the tape.

Natale turned on the headlights. They were trapped inside a large empty cubicle. He looked up. Cameras, probably infrared, scanned back and forth, back and forth, missing nothing. Tiny turret-slits showed gun barrels poking through, aimed at the van from several angles.

A burst of light blinded Peter as enormous overhead strobes came on. Dietrich's voice came through a loudspeaker. *"Herr* Natale?"

"It's me. What is this?"

"Who is with you?"

"Judith Davies. From Moscow station."

"Ah, yes, hello, Ms. Davies. And where are your prisoners?"

"In the back of the van, for pete's sake. What's going on?"

Dietrich laughed. "You didn't tell me you'd be driving a black van. Can't be too careful these days, my friend. Please to climb out, then remove your prisoners so we can be sure of the circumstance."

Natale was irritated, but at the same time he understood the precautions. This was Naples, after all. Half the law enforcement and intelligence operatives had themselves barricaded against the rest these days, and he had forgotten to tell Dietrich that he'd be driving Marco's van.

He and Judith climbed out, then dragged the three bound men from the back and dropped them like sacks of potatoes on the concrete floor. Only then did Dietrich appear through a door with several more armed guards. The guards lifted the three terrorists and dragged them roughly off.

Natale, Judith, and Dietrich followed into a large room with metal folding chairs, metal desks and tables, and high brilliant lights that were fortunately turned off now. Natale was just getting his full sight back from the blinding strobes.

The guards took Guappo's accomplices to holding cells, leaving Marco behind.

Natale reached out and tore the tape from the assassin's mouth. His arms and feet remained bound.

Marco's mud-colored eyes ticked over every movement. The hatred he emitted was thick and rancid, almost a literal stench. But there was something else in his eyes too, a sickness creeping into him. Natale recognized the furtive looks, the slick sweat that appeared on his forehead. With mixed emotions, he realized that

Guappo was yet another soldier in the growing army of heroin addicts.

One part of him was sickened by the realization, but his compassionate side was swiftly buried beneath his practical nature. This interrogation was going to be easy. Marco was just stepping into the first agony of heroin withdrawal, and within the hour he'd be groveling and begging and selling out anybody, doing anything so long as it would get the Octopus's poisonous powder back into his bloodstream. Natale would soon own Marco mind, body, and soul—if he wanted to.

He pulled up a folding chair and leaned in toward Guappo, who had been seated on an identical chair. The tape recorder beside Dietrich was turned on. Dietrich and Judith sat back, watching and listening.

Natale fixed Marco with an icy stare. "OK, Guappo. You want to tell us what's going on before you get sick, or you want to wait until you're heaving all over the place and scratching your skin off? It's your call."

Marco sneered at him, though there was also a tiny lick of fear in his eyes.

"Let's start by getting acquainted. You remember who I am?"

Marco spat out his name and added a few scathing words about Americans.

"That's right, I'm an American," Natale said in a friendly tone of voice. "And these are my partners, Judith Davies and Karl Dietrich."

Marco's surly eyes moved contemptuously across the German, then focused on Judith and stopped there. Surprise flicked for an instant. Then he looked down at the floor.

Natale noted the reaction. "I see you know Ms. Davies. Why don't we start with her? Maybe you saw her in the garden at Hotel de Mer before you shot Rudy Brandenburg. You want to tell me about that?"

Marco was silent.

"You may be on your home turf," Natale said, "but the United States still has a law that allows us to kidnap drug lords. You and your father are internationally known heroin traffickers,

Marco. Why don't I fire up a company jet, and we'll haul you over to Langley and see how tough you are when you're looking at life behind bars."

Marco sneered again, but he spoke. "You're the one who'd end up behind bars, you fool. You think we don't have your people in hand?"

"Not my people. Not ever my people." He wanted to slam his fist into the man's smirking face. He controlled himself and gestured to Dietrich, who took over.

Dietrich got nowhere. He turned Marco over to Judith, who tried a more persuasive tactic, asking polite questions about his name, age, why he'd been at the air show.

Marco was beginning to look sallow. His eyes were set deep in their sockets, and he had started scratching his chin against his shoulder, rubbing it raw.

Natale could see something subcutaneous happening with the man, a sort of itchiness that went through to his bones. Natale watched him carefully. The killer was on the verge of cracking, simply because his body was starting to fall apart.

Judith said, "Any help you give us will make things easier on you."

Guappo's face suddenly collapsed into a rabid snarl. He called Judith a list of vile names, then muttered, "I see why Hammond said get rid of you. You are nothing but trouble to any man. You American women are worthless *vacci*, a herd of meddlesome cows who have never learned your place. I had a contract on you, you crone. I should have killed you! But you, you—" He collapsed into an unintelligible stream of venomous Italian.

Judith paled at the vehemence of his hatred.

Natale stepped in. "What do you mean, you 'had a contract' on her? When were you going to kill her?"

Marco's crafty eyes shifted to Natale. "Get me some *cinniri*. I'm getting sick."

"You're about to get dead. Tell me. What did you mean?"

Marco coiled forward as a stomach spasm wracked his body, then his eyes were suddenly frightened, pleading, and he began to talk in a faltering, pain-filled voice.

"They told me in Berlin . . . watch Rudy . . . can't you get me some *cinniri?* I can't talk . . . you've gotta help me . . ." He vented a stream of obscenities and then doubled forward, his stomach spasming again.

"Talk, and fast. Then we'll get you straightened out."

Marco talked, though at times he disintegrated again into unintelligible venom. Occasionally he stopped to plead for a heroin fix, for anything to dissolve the agony that was beginning to saturate his body and soul. He talked about the leak in Kaleidoscope, about Lepkov ordering him to kill the brothel owners and whoever else might be informing on the Berlin end of the heroin/armaments pipeline. He talked about the Sicilians, how they'd moved in on the action in Naples, how they'd humiliated the Guappo family by reducing them to vassals.

He talked about his rage at being forced into the lodge. He talked about the night he and his paramilitary cadre broke into the NATO arsenals and stole several surface-to-air missiles. He talked about the plans and the launching of the missile.

He talked—irrationally—about the Black Brigade, about his years of working under Lepkov. But most of all, threaded throughout everything, he talked about death and pain and destruction.

As Peter listened, he added what he knew to the circuitous words and more or less put things together. After they'd turned Marco over to the guards, he turned to Judith and Dietrich and began to summarize Marco's confession for them as he saw it.

Hammond had ordered the hit on Rudy. He'd lost control of the young man and realized that Rudy was about to betray him. When Rudy approached Judith in the garden at Hotel de Mer, Marco reported the breach of security to the prince.

Veresi immediately contacted Hammond in Langley. Hammond ordered Marco to kill Judith too—especially Judith—because Rudy had talked privately to her. But there was also the problem of Peter Natale. As soon as Marco dealt with Judith, he was to return to Naples and get rid of Peter too.

Marco had connections at the airlines. He learned Judith's flight itinerary. He purchased a ticket, flew from Nice to Milano ahead of her as a precaution against being recognized.

He planned to board her flight in Milano and quietly inject her with cyanide while she was resting. But by the time he boarded, Judith was gone. She never returned to her assigned seat. He had flown all the way to Moscow and back for nothing. Upon his return, he searched everywhere for her, but she had vanished.

Judith was smiling as Natale recapped the story.

Peter frowned. "I don't really see anything amusing about a contract on your life."

"I'm smiling about the way God does things," she said. "You can't believe how confused I was. But I knew, absolutely and without doubt, that I had to get off that plane. It was as if some invisible hand had lifted me up by the nape of the neck and set me off on a quest. I thought I was jumping ship on you and Frost. Which I guess I did, in a way. But most of all, all the time, God was saving my life."

Natale thought about that. He wanted it to be true. The enormity of the situation was far beyond human resources, and if ever they needed divine intervention it was now.

He had a small beeper on his belt that he'd worn in case something urgent came up and Frost or Jeremy Ward had to contact him. Now, suddenly, it sounded. He checked the number, then asked Dietrich for a phone. A portable was brought to him, and he dialed Naples station.

Jeremy Ward answered and immediately told him not to worry, that Frost and Hammond hadn't arrived yet. "Frost phoned. There was some trouble at the air show," he said.

"No kidding."

"You were there?"

"You don't want to know. Look, Jer, I really don't want to get you involved in any more of this. You know enough to go down with me as it is, if Hammond gets his way."

"I told you when you phoned last night, I'm one hundred percent on your side."

"Yes, but that won't do me any good if you're out of the picture. Believe me. Hammond is going to be lopping off heads when he arrives, and the less you know the better off you'll be. So—why did you beep me?"

"Carlo phoned a few minutes ago. Said he was getting ready to board the Gulfstream en route to Monte Carlo. He said he was meeting with Prince Dante di Veresi tomorrow afternoon. He seemed to think you might want to join the party. In fact, he said you wouldn't want to miss it."

Natale felt his heart skip a beat, then pound like crazy. "Did he leave a phone number?"

"He said he'd be in a private suite at Hotel de Mer after seven tonight—wait, I have the number here somewhere."

"Never mind. I know it by heart. And Jeremy?"

"Yeah?"

"You didn't hear from me, you didn't get a message from Carlo. Believe me, don't say a word to Hammond about anything. Judith and I may soon need a friendly face who is still in the picture."

There was a long silence, then Ward said, "I guess that makes a certain amount of sense. Just let me know if you need anything. And Peter?"

"Yeah?"

"We'll figure out a way to keep Hammond busy while he's here. What really worries me is Carlo. Just how much do you trust him?"

"Enough."

"Wish I could say the same. Take care of yourself, pal, whatever you do. You wouldn't be the first man to be set up by the Mafia."

38

Monte Carlo

Peter and Judith took a commercial flight to Nice, arrived at midnight, rented a car, and drove a few miles down the Corniche to Beaulieu-sur-Mer, where they rented rooms in a seaside hotel and caught a few hours of much-needed rest. The next morning, Natale contacted Carlo Ricaso, and they drove on down the coast to Monte Carlo.

Now it was almost 2:00 P.M. Peter, Judith, and Carlo sat in a huge room on the third floor of Hotel de Mer. The gilded furniture was bright green and gold-embroidered silk, spread across a pale-green Turkish carpet. The high, vaulted ceiling was inlaid with one of the cloud-and-nymph-strewn Olympian frescoes that seemed to span the various European eras. It was a cream-and-pastel mixture that softened the decor of the room.

The belle epoque finery of three windowless walls ensconced them in an array of marble arches, plaster palms, and inlaid pillars. This had once been a private dining room where the elite of the Blue Coast met to literally consume their wealth. Now it was the security chamber from which a few hand-picked, hard-eyed experts oversaw the high rollers who made bets of $100,000 and up in the *salons prives* of the Casino de Mer. The entire fourth wall was a grid of monitoring screens linked to cameras in strategic places throughout all the private salons. There were also several two-way mirrors that looked into an adjacent barroom, remnants from the pretechnical era.

Silver chafing dishes and other remnants of an elegant brunch sat nearby on a linen-clad pushcart.

Over lunch, Carlo had explained that he and Cesare had purchased Hotel de Mer several months before. He also told them about *don* Cesare's seizure.

"I don't want the job," he said with regard to his inherited position. "But I can't just walk away. While I'm sorting things out, I might as well do some housecleaning."

The various salons in the casino had gradually become riddled with thieves and con men during *don* Cesare's reign, he explained. "The old man was getting too paranoid. He lived on suspicion and didn't see what was happening right under his nose."

Natale knew that the casino had also been *don* Cesare's chief European money laundry even before he'd purchased it, though he was careful not to mention that fact. He was playing it by ear, and Judith was following his lead. Every time they tried to pry details from Carlo as to why they'd been invited, he smiled mysteriously and said, "A little surprise. You'll see."

Judith privately offered Peter her own theory of what was happening. In that scheme of things, Peter's kidnapping had led Carlo to uncover the fact that the prince had double-crossed the Ricasos in a big way by kidnapping Luciano, then using him as a bargaining chip against Volante Chicarelli. The Mafia always paid back a double cross. Always. Apparently Carlo was going to cut Peter and Judith in on some revenge, if they wanted a share.

The security experts were on leave with pay. Carlo explained that the casino's "bank" had been swallowed down a trapdoor, then passed along a conveyer belt to the main vault, which had been locked down. The vault was visible on one of the color monitors. It was a steel crypt with counting machines, stainless steel shelves, racks and bays filled with stacks of every denomination of money, every color and size of gaming token.

Carlo had more or less kept the conversation light, but now he checked his watch and finally got to the point.

"I have a little job for you to do. Come on over here." He nodded toward the comfortable gray leather chairs in front of the monitors and console.

Natale raised his eyebrows, Judith looked annoyed, but they both moved to the console.

Carlo stepped up beside Natale, his eyes keenly focused on the various glowing screens. "Take a look at these."

He indicated an especially interesting bank of monitors, which showed the Rose Salon. The roulette, blackjack, baccarat, and chemin de fer tables were covered with dust covers. The croupiers had been given time off with pay while Carlo had the books audited, interrogated employees, and otherwise weeded out the thieves.

The pale glow of the next monitor showed the vault with its cameras and electronic security.

Next came an opulent suite that Carlo explained was the manager's office, where credit was dispersed and decisions were made with regard to when to change croupiers or eject gamblers, and how to best eliminate cheats or other thugs from the private salons. It was empty. The manager had been dismissed for laundering money not sanctioned by the Ricasos.

The last five monitors showed different angles of a dimly lit barroom adjacent to the Rose Salon. There, a lean and solitary bartender dressed in a starched black-and-white uniform polished already gleaming glasses. The barroom was decorated in rose plush, the bar itself was curved teakwood. Across from it, along the wall, were perhaps a dozen rose-plush booths with banquette seats, and a half dozen small tables were arranged throughout the room.

"I'm meeting Veresi in the bar," Carlo said. "You are going to cover me." He stepped to a desk, opened a large drawer, and pulled out two 9mm high-power automatics with extra clips, which he handed to Natale and Judith. Then he indicated a small door almost hidden by an ornate alcove. "That door opens into the left side of the barroom. The bar is only twenty or so steps from here. You're going to be watching me on the monitors. Come in if you have to or when it's time. Otherwise leave me alone."

"When it's time?" Natale asked.

"You'll know, *amico*. Trust your gut instinct."

Natale turned a wary eye on the console. It featured every form of electronic surveillance technology yet devised by man, all of it incorporated into a bank of buttons and dials and earphones and lenses, enough security to protect the continent's gold reserves.

However, it took Carlo only a few minutes to show them the basics: how to switch viewing angles from one part of the barroom to the other, how to use the zoom lenses. He ran them through a short test, and Natale scanned the barroom, then zoomed in on the barman. The camera picked up the hairs in the man's eyebrow, the pores in his face, the deep frown lines between his brows.

The intercom buzzed. Carlo picked it up, listened, then hung up and said, "The prince is on his way in. I want everything down on tape." He double-checked the video-recorder controls to make sure they were turned on, then moved toward the leather-padded door.

Peter saw the door shut behind him, then turned to the monitors. The first showed Carlo walking down a short hallway, wearing a secretive smile. The smile disturbed Natale. He remembered Ward's warning about being set up.

"Look." Judith pointed at another monitor. It was the barroom. He saw a door opening, saw Carlo entering the dimly lit room, the bartender looking up now and nodding a greeting. On the console, the reel-to-reel audio backups and videotapes rolled smoothly.

They put on their earphones. Peter heard the muted sound of Carlo's footsteps, heard a squeak as the barman polished a glass. He and Judith shot each other a surprised look. Both the video and audio were of excellent quality. "You could hear a pin drop at a hundred feet," Natale said.

Judith nudged him. "Look!" She pointed again.

The main entrance to the barroom was a double-wide, leather-studded swinging door, opening toward the bar. As the door swung fully open, Natale could see the outlines of two figures—one tall, one short—against the brighter light of the hallway. Then the doors swung shut, equalizing the light, and he saw the prince and Bob Hammond standing side by side.

Peter groaned. "Oh man, oh man, I don't believe it. Carlo set us up."

Judith was watching carefully. "No, Peter. Wait a minute. Let's see what happens."

Veresi stepped toward Carlo with a theatrical flourish, arched his dark eyebrows imperiously, and started to shake Carlo's hand. Carlo haughtily tilted his head and extended his right hand, straight out, palm down. A huge gold ring shone in the light.

Natale was puzzled for a moment.

The prince's face clotted with quickly suppressed anger. Veresi steeled himself, then made a semi-bow and lightly kissed Carlo's ring—the required greeting of the Mafia vassal to the capo-Mafia.

Natale glanced at Judith. "Sheesh."

"Yes," Judith said. She was laughing.

The prince was wearing a black tailored suit and tie, a white-on-white silk shirt. The age lines in his face were more pronounced in the monitor, his dyed black hair seemed even thinner. His sin-black goatee and mustache were Mephistophelian, and Peter still believed it was a deliberate effect.

He paid only momentary attention to the prince, however. His interest quickly shifted to Hammond. The prince was now introducing him to Carlo.

"This is my colleague, Robert Hammond," Veresi said. "As I mentioned, he is the CIA's director of operations."

"I know," Carlo said.

The prince looked from one to the other. "Yes. Well, I think you'll be interested in what he has to say."

Hammond nodded to Carlo, though he made no suggestion of either shaking his hand or kissing his ring. He said, "I just heard about your uncle yesterday. I'd like to extend my sympathy."

Carlo nodded curtly and fixed Hammond with a cold, appraising stare.

Hammond ignored the challenge and moved farther into the room with an easy, comfortable gait. He stopped before he reached the bar and stood expectantly, as if wondering where to sit down. His gray trousers were sharply creased, his suit jacket was expensive and well-cut, his white shirt was spotless. Hammond was still the very picture of what every top-level government administrator should be. There was a slightly superior expression on his face as he stood looking at Carlo.

Carlo gestured toward a table with three chairs around it. "Why don't we get comfortable?"

Natale noted with satisfaction that Carlo positioned the prince and Hammond so that two of the cameras had excellent angles on their faces. He and Judith kicked back and watched every move.

The barman came to the table.

Carlo said to his guests, "Something to drink?"

The prince ordered a vermouth over ice, Hammond ordered coffee. When the bartender had retreated back to the bar, Carlo said, "So what can I do for you, friends of my friends?" He was still playing the role of capo-Mafia to the hilt.

Veresi and Hammond glanced at each other, then the prince spoke. "We are grateful to you for seeing us, *don* Carlo. I understand that you must be very busy right now. But Mr. Hammond and I have problems that might affect your family, and we wanted to straighten things out."

"I'm listening."

The prince nodded politely. He said, "First I must bring up a small problem in order to clear the air. My guards tell me you personally freed Luciano Chicarelli and the CIA man, Natale, from my guest rooms the other night."

"Yeah." Carlo's eyes narrowed evilly. "I wondered if you'd get around to explaining that."

"It was a mistake, a fool's error," the prince said. "I hope you'll understand—"

"Try me."

Veresi nodded again, and this time there was a feigned apology in the motion. "You have no daughters," he said, gesturing theatrically. "A pity. If you did, you'd understand my position so much better. As it is, I'm forced to rely on your considerable knowledge of the ways of the world, on your vow to honor the needs of a fellow member of the Caput Mundi, and on your reputation as a compassionate man."

"Get to the point," Carlo said.

The prince said nothing as the barman started to serve the drinks. Carlo stopped him with a nod that indicated he should leave the room. The man did—in a hurry.

"Very well. Luciano Chicarelli wanted to marry my daughter, Gianalisa. I believe you knew that. But my daughter—she is a beauty and has captured men's attention since she was a very young girl. But she is not normal, you see. The tragedy of her mother's suicide—surely you know that story, I am told the whole of Palermo repeats and embellishes it—"

Carlo nodded.

"Her mother's death damaged her deeply. She has been in and out of institutions. At times I have sent her to private schools. Now she has problems with the heroin. It is so easy to obtain in Sicily these days—"

Carlo's eyes narrowed dangerously.

The prince fell silent, apparently realizing the accusation in what he was saying. He began again from a different angle.

"You surely understand that such a girl cannot be a wife to any man. But Luciano refused to leave Gia alone. And so I—a desperate father with only his daughter's honor in mind—I am afraid I made a foolish decision to kidnap Luciano and keep him away from her, one way or another.

"I have since learned that certain people misconstrued my action and used the event to try to breed enmity between me and your uncle. These people actually tried to make it seem as if I was trying to interfere with Volante Chicarelli's bid for the EU presidency. But I assure you . . . uh . . . *don* Carlo, your uncle knew my true motives. I had spoken with him—"

Carlo was waving his hand back and forth, as if dispelling smoke. "So you kidnapped Luciano to break up a love affair?"

"To protect my daughter, *don* Carlo. A foolish move by a desperate old man, and one I deeply regret. I fear it may cause ill feelings between us, though I pray not—"

"Wonder who he prays to," Judith said, watching the prince keenly through the monitor's eye.

"Nobody I know."

The prince started talking again. "I understand you were personally responsible for admitting my daughter to a drug clinic outside Palermo," he said to Carlo. "I wish to offer my profound gratitude."

"Don't mention it."

Natale caught a trace of sarcasm in the voice.

"And what about Peter Natale?" Carlo asked. "Were you protecting your daughter from him too?"

Veresi was silent for a moment, caught off guard, and then he pasted a pensive expression on his face. "Had we known you were his protector, we would have come to you right away to ask you to resolve the problem."

"What kind of problem?" Carlo's eyes glittered evilly.

"Mr. Natale has been causing us a great deal of trouble. We hadn't realized he was your friend until you—well, I suppose you think you rescued him, though in truth we would have soon let him go."

Hammond spoke up. "As you probably know, Carlo, I ultimately approve and administer all of Peter Natale's operations. I get the summaries of all his targets and goals.

"Your uncle and I were friends, Carlo—though, of course, that fact was kept secret, even from you. He confided in me recently that he was concerned about the hold Peter seemed to have on you.

"Now I realize that Peter pretends to treat you as an equal, but when he's with fellow agents he expresses a great deal of contempt for you—brags about how he's going to bring you down. Frankly, he recently started an all-out move to directly target your family enterprises—at the same time conning you into thinking that his friendship was genuine. But you have my assurance that the Agency still values our alliance with your family and intends to honor its reciprocal commitments."

"Just what alliance is that?" Carlo asked.

The prince interrupted. "You are the new *capo-di-tutti-capi* of all of Sicily, *don* Carlo. As such, you will automatically inherit your uncle's old seat in the Caput Mundi. It would be my honor to arrange the ceremony as soon as you're ready."

Carlo's face grew stony. "My uncle isn't dead yet. We'll talk about it when he is."

"But you don't understand. There are certain . . . uh . . . business matters that he was committed to, and which you will certainly want to honor as well—"

"Yeah?"

"There is the matter of the political future of our great country, *don* Carlo. Your uncle and I were sponsoring certain sympathetic people for office. Certain funds were to be disbursed today, and I'm afraid certain political offices hang in the balance—"

"Look—" Carlo shifted, leaned forward, and peered at the prince "—don't finesse me, OK? I know how you used my uncle. I know the truth about Luciano. So you want something from me, lay your cards out on the table and stop insulting my intelligence, *capiche?*"

Veresi looked at the floor.

Hammond cleared his throat and took over. "What Dante is trying to say is that we had a good thing going with *don* Cesare, and we'd like to continue the status quo."

Carlo's dark eyes glittered as he fixed them, now, on Hammond. "You going to tell me what's going on, or you going to try to con me too?"

Judith, watching through the monitor, smiled. "He does a fair imitation of his uncle, doesn't he?"

"Mafia blood will tell," Natale agreed.

Hammond was talking. "I'd like to clear the air here. I realize you inherited your position rather suddenly, and you must have a lot of loose ends lying around. Some of them happen to tie into my and the prince's business, that's all."

"What business is that?"

Hammond leaned forward in a persuasive manner. "To begin with, I want to warn you up front. Peter Natale is going down for mishandling a case in Berlin. I have men combing Naples for him at this very moment, and I'll be flying back to handle his arrest. He leaked information and caused a major crisis between us and the German intelligence agency. I don't want to see any of his trouble rub off on you, so I'm giving you fair warning as to where this thing is going with him.

"Second, his self-righteous bimbo of a girlfriend is going down with him. Judith Davies. I understand you know her. I'd stay well clear of her too, were I you."

Judith's eyes shot fire. *"Bimbo!"*

Natale grinned at her, then nodded his head back at the monitors.

"We've never met," Hammond said, "because my position requires a good deal of delicacy with regard to these matters. But believe me when I say that your uncle and I go all the way back to the KINTEX days, back to the Soviet black market when your uncle used Berlin station's resources to ship stolen cars and other contraband into East Germany, then on to Russia. Yuri Lepkov, your uncle's liaison in Berlin, is in fact working with me and has been for a couple of decades.

"In other words, I'm your partner in a lot of very lucrative businesses, Carlo, and I doubt if you want to walk away from the amount of money your uncle, Lepkov, and I have been making together—let alone from the other advantages of doing business with me. And if you think Peter Natale could do you some good, you're not only deceived but you're still playing in the little leagues."

"I'm still listening," Carlo said. "So far all I hear is smoke and promises."

Hammond leaned forward once more. "We have certain assets in the hidden chambers of the casino's vault."

Carlo leaned forward too, his face flooded with interest. "The gold?"

Hammond looked relieved. "It's ours. *Don* Cesare was laundering it for us, a little here, a little there. It's a share of the Red Gold from the Moscow Central Bank vault, and it has a very distinctive chemical signature. That's why we've been feeding it into the banking system slowly along with the massive casino assets. That's one reason I was anxious to talk to you. Whatever you do, don't unload that gold into the system all at once. You'll trigger an avalanche of international spying agencies, all descending on you at once."

"What's the vigorish on the gold?" Carlo used the American slang term for the Mafia's percentage.

"*Don* Cesare was taking twenty-five percent off the top for laundering it. We'd like to continue that arrangement."

"How much gold are we talking about altogether?"

"You're holding two billion in metal, another hundred million in coins. That's a lot of money for you."

The prince sat up straighter. "But *don* Cesare was more concerned about the way we were spending it than in earning his percentage."

"*Some* of it," Hammond countered, his lip curling into an involuntary snarl. "We're only spending some of it."

Veresi was wearing a diabolical smile. "We've been using the laundered money to fund a sort of reptile fund to finance politicians, judges, and other members of the European Union who have political allegiances to the Black Nobility. Once we have all our people in place, we'll exercise the same amount of control over the EU that we presently have over the Italian government—"

Carlo interrupted. "That *I* have over the Italian government. Last time I checked, you and your Fascists were still depending on our people to pull most of the levers."

"Yes, well, we've pretty much been working together since there are so many mutual advantages," the prince said, clearly intimidated. "It would be best for us to continue as before."

Carlo leaned back, appraised the prince and Hammond, then said, "How much of the gold belongs to Yuri Lepkov?"

"Uh—some of it," the prince said.

Hammond was still seemingly relaxed, composed. He said, "His end got spread around. He's not as politically involved as we are."

"I'm cutting my losses with Lepkov," Carlo said. He scowled at Hammond. "Your Peter Natale pretty much wrecked that pipeline. Even though Marco Guappo took out the informants at the Berlin brothel, his rampage at the NATO air show was a piece of work, let me tell you. They nailed him, and I hear he's talking."

Hammond cursed.

"Yeah," Carlo said. "Just how much does he know?"

"Not enough to know he's dead," Hammond snarled. "I have friends in SISMI who are going to hang him in his cell tonight. That should cut off that end of it."

"I hear he ratted you out for ordering the hit on the EIA man—your wife's cousin. What was his name?"

"Rudy Brandenburg. Marco did the hit. There was never any direct communication between us, no way he can tie it to me."

"But you're going to have trouble just because of his accusations," Carlo said. "He's also blaming you and Lepkov for ordering the fiasco at the base yesterday."

"Like I said, I'm taking care of him tonight. The transcripts and tapes of his so-called confession are going to disappear in a fire, and he's going to hang himself. Period. End of problem."

"What about Lepkov? I hear the Germans are close to nailing him."

"I wanted to talk to you about that. I hear you have some people in Berlin who do certain work. I can't go to any of the people I knew through the CIA, and Marco and his thugs are obviously otherwise detained. I'd like to personally pay the tab to get him taken out," Hammond said. He might have been discussing stock options.

Natale's eyes went wide. He turned to look at Judith. She also seemed stunned.

At that moment Carlo turned to the camera, looked squarely at Peter through the monitor, and said, "How much do I have to hand you guys, anyway? Come on out."

Natale emitted a harsh laugh. He was on his feet already, his gun out. He pushed through the private door with Judith right behind him, sprinted into the barroom, and stopped short, his gun trained on Hammond, who stared at him, astonished. Judith covered the prince.

It took the two men a moment to realize what had happened. Then Hammond turned to Carlo. "You've got to be crazy. You—you—"

"I've been running the security video recorders," Carlo said easily. "We've got you cold."

"But *you're* on the tapes too! You—you—"

It was the first time Natale had ever seen Hammond sputter, the first time he'd ever seen him lose control.

"So what?" Carlo shrugged.

"But—you've implicated yourself in everything. If we go down, you go down! You're committing suicide—"

"Wrong. *Don* Cesare is implicated. You just admitted on tape that I didn't know a thing about any of it."

"But—you'll lose the gold, all that money—"

Carlo's grin was wolfish. "You oughta take a look at the money in my vault. I won't miss a single gram of your gold." Now he turned to Peter and Judith—still holding their guns on Hammond and Veresi—reached into his pocket, and brought out two small pairs of steel handcuffs. He tossed them to Natale.

"We'll put them on the Gulfstream to Naples," he said, "then put them on a US military transport. Matter of fact, I had considered putting a couple of bullets into their heads and just keeping the gold. But I decided I owe you."

"What about the gold?" Judith asked.

"That goes back to the Russian people, I guess. I hear they can use it. Now, my car is waiting. I got a couple of guards to keep you company all the way to Naples. The Gulfstream is at the airport, gassed up and ready to fly. Get these *scassapaghieri* out of here. It makes me sick to look at them."

Judith took a pair of handcuffs from Peter and moved toward Hammond as Natale aimed his gun dead at the man, covering him. "Time's up, Hammond. Your setup didn't work."

His frigid gaze swept past her and fixed on Natale. "You're stupid, Peter. You always were. You think that putting me away is going to change anything?"

"Yeah," Natale said, "I actually do. If we can get rid of you and enough others like you, maybe things will actually change."

Judith hesitated, holding the cuffs, tilting her head in curiosity as she looked back and forth from Hammond to Natale.

Hammond said, "You don't see it yet, but you will. The US government is so riddled with internal corruption that our country is going to collapse from within, Peter. It's happening, believe me. It's a global playing field now, and if you want to make a difference you have to learn a new game. Listen to me—you're making a major mistake. Carlo is the one who's setting us both up. Believe me, what you're doing here isn't the way."

Now Natale hesitated, his mind racing. Jeremy Ward's warning about the Mafia's setting him up came back, and he was suddenly unsure of himself.

"Peter, this isn't what it looks like," Hammond pressed. "You're about to mess up the biggest probe the CIA has ever managed to put together into EU politics. It's the fascist influence, Peter. We have to stop it, and we can't fight another war. That would bankrupt what's left of our country's economy. We've got to stop it another way this time. You don't understand all the variables at play here. You take me in and you're stepping square into the enemy's hands."

Natale thought about that. In this wilderness of mirrors, who ever knew the whole truth? What if Hammond *was* working against Veresi and Lepkov? What if the CIA *had* wormed its way into the highest echelons of the neo-fascist labyrinths in an attempt to forestall a repeat of the last fascist-Nazi stranglehold on Europe that had culminated in World War Two?

And how much did Peter really know about Carlo's business anyway? Carlo told him what he wanted him to know, period. Was he playing into the Mafia's hands? If he exposed Hammond, was he really thwarting a massive probe into EU corruption? How much was he willing to risk on Carlo's word?

On the other hand, he had just heard Hammond soliciting a hit on Yuri Lepkov. There was that. But certain misguided people in the CIA had always turned to assassination as a means of getting things done. And sometimes with the best of motives.

"Think about it," Hammond was saying. "We all have to do a lot of things we don't like in order to get the job done."

Judith gave him a scathing look. "You're nuts." She stepped forward to put on the cuffs.

Natale held up a hand. "Wait." He needed a moment to think, in order to be absolutely sure. "If that's true, why were you trying to set me up?"

"To get you out of the way for a while," Hammond said easily. "You got started on the wrong track, and I couldn't seem to stop you. For the past six months, everything I was trying to get done seemed to run into a brick wall you'd put up. Take Kaleidoscope. I almost had Lepkov set up to work for us, and then you and your German buddies stepped in and threw the game. I just wanted you out of the way for a while, Peter. I wouldn't have pressed charges. I just needed some extra playing space."

"Don't listen to him," Judith said.

Natale looked at her, almost not seeing her. "I have to be sure." He glanced at Carlo. "This whole thing is too easy, too pat."

Carlo uttered an obscenity but stood back, watching.

"Think about it," Hammond said again. "Look at your own situation. Some CIA cowboy could have called the game on you by showing your link-up to the Ricasos at any time. A kilo of heroin planted in your villa, a tip on one of your meetings with Carlo. What would it have looked like to people who didn't know the truth?"

He spread his hands, his face softening. "That's where I am right now, Peter. I let Carlo lead me into this. Believe me, he set this meeting up. I was just following his lead to see what I could learn—"

Carlo spat out another obscenity, then turned to Peter. "You going to listen to this garbage?"

Natale shook his head. "I can't make a mistake here, Carlo. Too much is riding on this."

"You saying you don't trust me?" Carlo's voice was icy.

"I'm saying you may not know everything that was happening between your uncle and these people. Maybe you missed something. I can't be wrong about this." He turned to Hammond. "What about Rudy Brandenberg? Guappo says you ordered the hit. Why?"

"He was a junkie, Peter. He knew too much. You know how these things go."

Peter's face set, hard. "And the prince here? Did you manage to turn him into a CIA informant?"

"I was working on it," Hammond said. "Your continued interference made things a great deal more difficult."

Veresi was staring in disbelief at Hammond. Now a hellish fire licked into his eyes. "You have betrayed us all." A hollow, supernatural quality seemed to have entered his voice. "You have no idea of the power of the forces you are dealing with."

Hammond looked as if something had him by the throat. He seemed to be telegraphing a hidden message as he looked at the prince. "Look, Dante, try to understand what's happening here." His eyes shifted back and forth from Veresi to Natale. Then to the prince he said, "It's not too late for you to come over to our side. My people can make you a good deal."

The prince was stiff with rage. "You dare lie to the Prince of Lies?"

Natale laughed mirthlessly at the indecision on Hammond's face. The DO was obviously trying to find a way to placate Veresi while continuing to lie to Peter. And in that instant Peter was finally certain of the truth.

"Cuff him, Judith. I don't care what else this snake was doing—he's on the wrong side if he can sacrifice some misguided kid who got hooked on drugs."

Judith nodded, a look of relief flooding her face, and moved to obey.

Hammond wilted, his body language passive, accepting. Then, just as she reached out to put on the cuffs, he lunged, his arms knocking the cuffs away. A gun appeared in his hand, and he gripped Judith in a stranglehold, then maneuvered her in front of him.

Natale froze. His gun was still aimed at Hammond, but there was no way he could nail the man without jeopardizing Judith. He felt a simultaneous flood of shame for his momentary gullibility that had led to this impasse and a flood of rage at the thought of Judith's being hurt. In that moment, he would easily have shot and killed Hammond—except for Judith.

The DO wore a frigid smile. His blue eyes took on a dead quality, and Natale knew the man had sold his soul.

They stared at each other above Judith's head, both with guns leveled.

Natale felt a seething white-hot hatred for all that Hammond symbolized. "Let her go," he said through clenched teeth.

"After you drop the gun. Carlo—" his voice was cordial, almost friendly "—why don't we go on down and open the vault? A couple of my men are waiting outside—they've already taken care of your guards. We'll be taking as much as your Gulfstream can carry."

He maneuvered Judith so that she was still in front of him, then indicated with the pistol that Peter and Carlo should precede him out the doorway and toward the vault. Veresi brought up the rear.

The hallway was sterile, windowless, with aging white-tiled walls and security cameras set at intervals. The cameras, Peter knew, silently tracked the motion of five people moving toward their destiny, three of them at gunpoint.

But the cameras' eyes were dead, empty, and no one was in the security room to witness the carnage that he sensed was about to take place in this makeshift death chamber.

Natale and Carlo came to a stop where the hall dead-ended before a circular door of reinforced stainless steel set into the concrete wall. Some eight feet high, it had a large metal wheel where a doorknob would ordinarily be.

Peter glanced over his shoulder to see Hammond still shoving the gun muzzle deep into Judith's side. She looked defiant and angry. Veresi stood behind them, an odd expression on his ratlike face.

"Open the vault, Carlo," Hammond ordered. "Or I'll shoot her."

"So shoot her." Carlo caught Natale's eye, and Peter knew the Mafioso was stalling, trying to find an opening that allowed for counterattack. "What is she to me?"

"Forget her then. I'll shoot you first. In the kneecap. Maybe both kneecaps. It might be interesting to see how well you'll cope when you're crippled for life." Hammond's voice was reptilian. "Open the vault!"

Carlo's shoulders sagged in resignation. He spun the wheel. Forward, back, forward again. The tumblers clicked with well-oiled precision. He hesitated only a moment, then shrugged. "It's only money. Take what you want."

The door swung open, two tons of dead weight on pneumatic hinges that slowly revealed the lighted vault Natale had seen earlier on the monitors.

"Move!" The DO shoved them through the door, then followed with Judith still at gunpoint.

The door stood open behind them, and the prince followed them in.

The air inside was musty, stale. Ventilation was poor. But Natale reflected that it didn't matter anyway. They weren't going to live long enough to suffocate, even if they were left here. Hammond would see to that.

The room was small—perhaps twenty by thirty feet—and the walls were stacked high with money bins and steel racks. A large iron safe took up the far end, where it had been deposited by conveyor belt. This was the casino's sealed bank, removed from the cashier's cage when Carlo put the casino in mothballs.

Natale glanced about. The small, neat bins held money of every color and denomination—deutsch marks, lire, pesos, gold rubles, pounds sterling, dollars, ecus in both gold coin and paper. Here were millions in cash, ready to be paid out for equal value in chips. The chips themselves were held in other racks, neatly wrapped in color-coded paper imprinted with the crest of the Hotel de Mer.

Above the bins, ceiling-high racks held bulk money that was baled in two-by-two-foot packages, shrink-wrapped and tied with twine. Peter knew this was almost certainly dirty money, accumulated from a thousand places around the globe, deposited here to be gradually fed into the casino's bank deposits or fed across the gaming tables to pay off corrupted politicians and judges, bent police officials, hired assassins, and more.

Natale had never before seen so much money. But there was no pleasure in being in the midst of such treasure. Rather, he felt as though he were in a crypt. A coldness permeated his soul, and a cloying presence filled the room like an invisible mist, almost smothering him.

In spite of his claustrophobia, he continued to scrutinize the vault. He saw none of the Red Gold he presumed Hammond was after.

Veresi suddenly muttered a scathing curse.

Natale, surprised, glanced back at the small, poisonous man who stood just inside the doorway. The prince seemed obsessively oblivious to everyone but Hammond. He was staring hotly at the DO.

Hammond apparently knew what was bothering the man. He shot the prince a contemptuous look. "Come on, Dante. Get over it. I'm not really teaming up with the enemy to do you in. All that was just a power play that didn't work."

"If you have betrayed me, you have betrayed the Black Nobility," Veresi said between clenched teeth.

The DO snorted. "You're nuts, with all your Black Nobility incantations and mumbo-jumbo. Can't you see I was just trying to lie our way out when I said I was working against you?"

"I can no longer trust you," Veresi said. His feet were still planted firmly, and he was glaring icily at Hammond. "It's your fault that we are in this situation."

"OK, so it's my fault. You can chain me in one of your dungeons and whip me, or whatever it is you do in your little horror chambers. But right now we've got work to do." He refocused on Carlo and snarled, "Open the other safe."

Carlo inhaled deeply, and Natale could see he was doing everything possible to contain his temper. Tension tingled through the room.

But then the Mafioso brought himself under control with visible effort. Resignedly he slid aside a rack of crates, disclosing yet another, smaller, door cut into the stone wall. It was barely large enough to accomodate a man. Carlo fiddled with a tumbler, spinning it as he fed in the combination. Slowly the door swung open.

The room was pitch black. Only a small triangle of dim light from the vault leaked inward to reveal a stone floor. Carlo stepped in and flicked a light switch. The room burst into burnished brilliance as the light fell upon stacks and heaps of gold bars and coins, filling the bins and racks of this vault within a vault.

"How many forklifts did you bring to carry this stuff?" Carlo gibed. There was a primal challenge in his eyes.

"Keep going and shut up," Hammond said.

Carlo's muscles coiled, and Natale thought he was going to react. He knew that Hammond sensed it too, for the man's trigger finger tensed. Peter felt cold sweat break out as he watched the scene and waited for the eruption.

But the Sicilian brought himself under control, again with visible effort, and Hammond forced the three of them all the way to the end of the small vault.

He nodded toward a narrow steel closet. "Open it," he snapped.

Carlo grinned coldly. "You sure know your way around here. Did *don* Cesare give you the guided tour?"

"Several times. Open the safe and shut up."

Carlo's fist bunched, but he got past that too and obeyed.

The door slid open, and Natale caught his breath. Here were small compartments on one side, cubicles on the other. Inside the cubicles were plastic-wrapped kilos of heroin, perhaps a hundred in all and each worth ten times its weight in gold. Now he understood. Hammond planned to take the most easily moved goods and leave the rest.

As if to validate his assumption, the DO carefully used his free hand to open a drawer. He withdrew a blue velvet bag, opened it, and peered in, still keeping one eye on his captives.

Peter watched, his eyes ticking over every motion, looking for an opportunity to make his move. He caught a glimpse of glittering gemstones inside the opened bag. Cut diamonds. Yet another light-weight way to move vast amounts of capital through a black economy.

Hammond caressed the velvet bag, and a lustful look briefly crossed his face. Then his expression went blank, and he rammed the gun barrel into Judith again.

She winced but bit her lip and remained angrily silent.

"Make yourself useful," Hammond ordered snidely. He indicated with the gun that she should remove the remaining half dozen blue velvet bags from the safe.

Judith began to place each sack on an adjoining table. She shot Natale a look of cold, suppressed fury.

The prince was still seething. He approached Hammond and tilted his head back to face the man. "I demand to know more about this CIA probe into the affairs of my organization."

Hammond dismissed him with a contemptuous brush of his free hand. "You've got to be crazy to go off on that tangent right now. Why can't you get it through your thick, perverted skull that I didn't betray you? I only said that to throw these fools off balance."

Veresi's eyes narrowed. "I think you plan to betray us all."

Hammond sent him a disgusted glare, then turned to watch Judith remove the last blue velvet bag. He gestured again with the pistol. "Get the heroin too."

Judith's jaw went steely, and her eyes flashed blue fire. "I refuse to even touch it."

"Why does this have to be so difficult?" Hammond sounded wounded. "Just stack it on the floor. Then you and I and the prince can tote it up to my car."

Judith stared at him. "What happens to Peter and Carlo?"

Hammond smiled. "The same thing that's going to happen to you if you don't shut up and get to work."

Veresi muttered another curse.

Hammond half turned. His eyes slitted as he focused on the prince. "You know, Dante, you're beginning to get on my nerves. If—"

Without warning Judith wheeled, then slammed into Hammond so that air burst from his lungs and he reeled backward.

Peter flew into action.

But Hammond recoiled with a speed that startled him. The DO backhanded Judith. She fell, catching herself on the side of a money bin as Natale lunged. He took a flying dive into Hammond, knocking the DO to one side, and yanked out the .38 semiautomatic he'd hidden beneath his armpit. As Hammond came up, Peter got off one shot, but the room was small, the angle was wrong.

And Hammond was coming at him now, coming and coming, and his finger was tight against his own trigger, and Natale was staring into eternity. He got off another shot. It went wide, and Hammond was still coming, an evil grin on his face now, and Natale realized that the DO was going to especially enjoy administering his death.

But in that split second of terror, Peter glimpsed what was happening behind Hammond. Judith, in a seeming tantrum of fury, was kicking at the base of the high money bins. Just as Hammond's eyes filled with the cold certainty of Peter's death, he understood what she was doing and threw himself aside.

A final kick destabilized the partitions holding the gold ingots. The heavy bars broke loose and avalanched down.

Hammond jerked at the sudden noise, startled. His shot went wide and into the gold that spilled toward him, hundreds and thousands of pounds of gold, to bury him, inundate him, from the hips down.

The prince leaped backward to flee. Carlo seized his arm and brought him up short.

A gold bar thudded into Natale's side. He winced and recoiled as another slid from a near empty shelf and glanced off his instep.

And then the turmoil was over, as quickly as it had begun, and he was standing, still holding his .38. The small room was filled with settling dust. Judith stood to one side, a satisfied look on her face and her eyes hard as blue steel. Carlo was standing between the prince and the door, and he looked stunned. Veresi stood uncertain, like a trapped animal trying to figure out which way to run.

Natale looked down on Hammond. *"Cherchez la cash."*

"Get me out of here!" There was pain in Hammond's voice, but he was still defiant.

"You're crazy. You want me to free you so you can try to kill me again?"

"My arm's broken—I can feel it. My legs are numb. Get me out of here."

Natale's head tilted, and his eyes narrowed. "You know, I'll never understand how people like you do it. I mean, how many blown agents have gone to their graves because of you?"

Hammond's eyes iced over.

"How does it happen? How can a man end up like you?"

There was growing fury in Hammond's eyes. "Get me out of here, and I'll tell you everything. I can still be useful to the Agency. I still know what the Black Nobility is really doing. I know where the bodies are buried—"

A pistol cracked, and Hammond's head jerked as a bullet took him in the side of his skull.

Natale spun to see Veresi standing with a coldly superior expression on his face. The gun in his hand was still aimed at Hammond as he savored what he had done.

Carlo seemed suddenly to realize what had happened. He tackled the prince and sent him sprawling, then pinned him to the floor. "You're nuts. You're absolutely crazy. We had him. Why did you have to shoot him?" He stripped away Veresi's gun and threw it.

"He did it because Hammond was going to talk," Judith said.

Natale kept his eyes on the prince. There was a look of absolute enslavement to evil in the man's eyes that permeated all the way through his body and well into his shriveled soul.

356

Cherchez la cash . . .

Natale thought about the prince. Then he thought about Carlo. About Judith. About Hammond, dead at his feet. He thought wryly about the gold and about the men who believed that if only they could get their hands on enough money—no matter what that money cost them in return—the money would make them free.

Carlo locked the vault. Then he, Judith, and Peter started back up the hall toward the security room, prodding the prince along in front of them. Halfway there, Carlo stopped, put a hand on Peter's shoulder, and leveled a certain look at him, snapping his growing black mood. "I want this shoved under the table, *capiche?*"

Natale nodded.

"I don't want it to shut down the casino—that the CIA's top spy was killed here. Understand?"

"No problem. The CIA isn't going to want this one advertised." He nodded toward Veresi. "What about him?"

"I'll handle it."

"I don't want him dumped in pieces in a hog pen, Carlo. That's not the way."

Carlo shrugged. "We can lock him up for kidnapping Luciano. Tell the world he's crazy. I own a couple of judges—we can do it quietly, put him in a private cell at Uccardione where he'll never see the light of day again."

"What about Jacovetti?"

"That faction is down for the count, one way or another. It's just a matter of how I decide to do it."

Natale nodded again. He had decided he'd have to stay out of this end of the problem, as long as it was taken care of. "And Volante Chicarelli? Is he still slated to be the next EU president?"

Carlo thought about that before he answered. "I really don't know, *paisano.* My instinct tells me to cut him loose. But *don* Cesare had him on the hook for an awful long time. Chances are if I cut him loose someone else is just going to reel him in. I gotta think that over before I decide what's best."

"Best for your family or best for the human race?" Judith asked gently. She had been quiet since Hammond's death—almost in shock.

Carlo leveled another of his long, penetrating looks at her. He finally said, "I have to decide what's best for me, Judith. And yes, for the Ricaso fammly. Things aren't quite so clear-cut from where I sit anymore."

"They're clear to me," Natale said. "Clearer than anything has been for a very long time. Don't let the power destroy you, Carlo. It's a dark power, and it's going to try to swallow your soul."

"I'll keep that in mind, *paisano*." He nodded toward the security room door down the hall. "The Gulfstream is still waiting to fly you back to Naples." Then he glanced back toward the vault where they had left Hammond's body entrapped by heaps of gold. "I'll get a couple of my best men to find out where Hammond's thugs have put my security guards. Then I'll have them come back and take that pile of garbage out of my vault—before it stinks up the whole hotel."

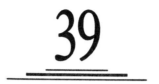

39

Naples/the Côte d'Azur

Natale, Judith, and Frost flew to Langley in a private CIA jet with Hammond's body in the baggage compartment in a body bag.

The director had been Hammond's ally, and they knew he was probably just as dirty as Hammond had been, although in a different way. They carefully patched their story together during the trip, then when they faced the director they told him about Hammond's link with the Red Gold. They told him how he'd been unmasked when Carlo Ricaso took over the Sicilian Mafia. They even told him about the prince and about the way Carlo was handling the situation with regard to him and the Fascists.

The director seemed relieved at the spin they had decided to put on the story, and he ordered up commendations for each of them, which all three quickly declined. He fed a story to the papers that the DO had been murdered during a trip to Naples. Hammond was buried with honors, and the news media played the European anti-American sentiment to the hilt for a few days. Then other global events usurped the story, and the incident quietly died down.

They were in and out of Langley in three days. Judith flew back to Moscow, Natale returned to Naples station.

He caught up on his paperwork, but the chore left him feeling futile and empty. He had tried once again to convince Judith to leave Moscow station and return to Naples. She told him she'd think about it. He asked her again to marry him. She told him she was confused, too much had happened, she'd have to think about that too.

Now when he thought about Judith, there was the taste of gunmetal at the back of his mouth and a tightness in his chest, so he did his best not to think of her.

His other work had more or less dried up. No matter. He wasn't ready to step fully back into the fray and take on other caseloads, but at the same time he was irritable around the office and needed something to do. Jeremy Ward, who was usually a friend, got on his nerves with his constant fretting about small, administrative problems.

Finally Natale accepted the fact that he was fed up. He took some time off. He gave his cleaning woman two weeks off with pay and shut himself away in his small villa perched atop a magnificent cliff above the ocean north of Naples. He spent long hours gazing out to sea from the small deck. He caught up on his mail, did sit-ups and squats and ran for five miles every day. He cleaned the house till it gleamed, cooked great pots of pasta, and experimented with different sauces. He climbed down the rock steps to swim in the nearby ocean and lie in the sun until he was golden bronze.

He thought about what had happened, thought about the corruption in the Agency, and tried to decide whether or not he was going to leave the CIA. And he thought most of all about Judith, about her new spiritual commitment, and whether or not he could ever fit into her world again. He thought about his own spirituality and wondered where he was going, whether or not his life mattered. The more he thought, the emptier he became.

Finally, on the fifth day, he awakened in the morning and knew he had to get away. He made a phone call to see if the villa above Nice had been rerented—it hadn't—and he made a two-week reservation. He packed a bag, phoned Naples station and told Ward where he was going, then caught the first flight back to the Naples-Côte d'Azur airport.

This was where the whirlwind had started, and here he would rest from the aftermath. And here, in every room of the small house, he would think about Judith and try to understand what this feeling of total desolation was, what part she played in his life, and how he could get over her.

The second day there he drove his rented car into Nice and bought the Rome and Palermo papers. Then he read about the aftermath of the scandals, about the new round of Mafia arrests—Carlo cleaning house—and about the purges within the European Union's burgeoning government. Lepkov had been arrested. Veresi, jailed for kidnapping, and Hammond were being pawed over by the tabloids and the legitimate papers alike.

But it was as if these things had nothing to do with him, as if they were happening on another planet. He hated these details of shipwrecked lives. The moral poverty just made him feel more disconnected, emptier.

By the third day he found himself sitting on the balcony for half the morning, staring out to sea just as he had in Naples. He realized with surprise that he was homesick, something he hadn't been in quite a while. His father had died when Natale was in the navy, but his mother was still living, remarried to a retired doctor and happily ensconced in a small seaside house in a little town north of Boston.

Natale phoned her—he'd not called for a month or more—and learned they were planning a vacation to Tahiti. They'd be leaving within the week, so his idea to visit the States fell through.

The next afternoon he drove down the coast and had lunch in the dining room at Hotel de Mer. Through the tall arched windows, he glimpsed a small blonde woman walking gracefully along a garden path, and he thought for an instant it was Judith. Then she turned slightly, and he saw her unfamiliar face.

Back in Nice again, he broke down and phoned Moscow station. They were sorry, they said, but Ms. Davies had resigned her position and was on her way back to the States.

Sick at heart, he phoned Frost, who was filling in at Rome until Tyler could be permanently replaced.

"Peter. I've been wondering how you were doing."

"I'm fine. Just need a little space right now."

"I have some good news."

"I could stand some good news."

"They've recovered at least two billion more in gold bars. Lepkov had it stashed in the Central Bank in Brussels. Europol has arrested several bank executives and a vice president for complicity in fraud. The gold is being returned to Russia, along with the gold in the casino vault—to pay for some of this winter's food supply for the starving masses."

"Excellent. If they keep looking, they have a good shot at recovering most of the rest."

Frost chatted for a moment. It was unlike him to engage in small talk, but Natale knew he was concerned. Gianalisa was getting her first weekend free from the clinic, and Luciano was picking her up, he said. He had heard that Gianalisa was a totally different person when her body was free of chemical poison. Luciano was getting straightened around, Volante was talking about retiring from politics.

Peter waited until Frost paused, then he finally asked, "Any news of Judith?"

"She didn't phone you?"

Natale didn't say anything. His throat suddenly ached too much to talk.

Frost sounded worried now. "She's resigned from Moscow station, Peter. She said she was going to take it easy for a month or so, then she'd let me know what she's going to do."

"You think she might come back to Italy?" Natale felt a sudden small surge of hope.

"Most likely not."

He cut the conversation short, then walked down to the town and ate dinner at a small restaurant. Afterward he walked along the beach. Finally he climbed back up to the villa and sat on the deck, looking out over the sea and thinking about life and his own spirituality and what it all meant. No matter what he had accomplished, he knew he wanted something more, a great deal more. And whatever it was, he knew he wanted it with Judith.

He thought about her. He wasn't going to change her. He knew that now. The question was, could he accept her as she was, impulsive, rebellious, obsessed with her crusade against evil? He thought he could, but it would take a lot of adjustment. His preconceived ideas about what he wanted his wife to be would have to go out the window.

He slept for a half hour, then awakened to the hot sun. The house seemed empty and desolate. He went outside, then began to walk and think. He had to decide what he was going to do.

He was walking along the cliff side when she came, and he didn't see or hear her drive up. He just walked into the small, sunny living room, and there she was, sitting in his chair, paging through the back issues of *L'Ora* he'd dropped on the floor.

She was wearing baggy white cotton slacks, an oversized white blouse with denim piping and blue-and-white checkered trim. Her face was scrubbed clean, and she looked young and very old, all at the same time.

"Ward told me you came back here," she said, as he walked in. "I wanted to see how you were doing."

"I'm OK, Judith. How are you?"

"I'm fine too. Still just a little confused about everything."

He hesitated, afraid of himself now because he wanted to go to her, wanted to hold her and stroke her hair and tell her how much he loved her. It was like an ache in his chest. At the same time he was afraid that if he moved she might see the need in his eyes. He didn't want her to know about it. If she saw how desperate he was, she might get up and leave.

She smiled. "You look worried."

"Always." He went over and sat down in a chair across from her.

There was a long, uneasy silence. Natale tried to figure out how to defuse the uneasiness. He wanted her comfortable. He wanted her to stay.

Judith smiled again. She looked around the living room. "It's just like we left it, but cleaner."

"Yes. I think they planted some new flowerbeds out back."

"Will you stay here long?"

He looked away from her. "Maybe. I'm taking it a day at a time."

"Peter, I've been thinking about us, and—"

He had to stop her. He couldn't bear to hear what she was going to say. "Look, Judith, it's OK. I understand."

"No, you're not listening. That's one of our problems, Peter. You never really listen to me."

He wondered if that were true.

"I've learned something, Peter."

He looked at the floor.

"We always start from the wrong place. That's why it doesn't work."

He looked up at her, puzzled.

"Don't you understand that I love you?"

He was surprised. And very pleased. And embarrassed too, because he didn't know what to say.

"You were right when you told me we had to seize the moment—that the world would never be an ideal place. But we're never going anywhere with this unless we're both straightened out spiritually. I can't fill the empty place in you that's reserved for God, nor can you for me. Until that's resolved, it's just not going to work."

"I've been thinking about that," Peter said. He saw tears suddenly well up in her eyes.

He stepped to the end table and pulled a tissue from a box, then leaned forward and dabbed at a tear that had spilled over and was running slowly down her cheek. Then he pulled her to him and held her gently.

At first she was rigid. Then he felt her begin to melt into his arms, and then she was crying, and it was all coming out, the pain, the fear, the emptiness.

"Peter," she sobbed. "I need to—"

"Shhh. I know."

Even more gently he drew her down till they were both kneeling on the carpet beside the sofa. He had one arm around her still, and her arms made a cradle for her head. She began to sob. He shut his eyes and bowed his head.

Their prayers were silent, separate, but after a moment Judith's sobs were stilled, and a great, gentle Presence seemed to fill the room.

She lifted her head and looked at him. Her face was radiant, peaceful, as if a fountain of joy had bubbled up in her. Her eyes were luminous, and the sense of confidence and holy peace that emanated from her nearly took his breath away.

He drew her up, then led her to the deck to look out over the blue sea.

"I love you," she said after a moment. "I get really tangled up about it, but I do. That's what I wanted to tell you." She paused. "I need you, Peter. But it's a question of trust. I mean, I find I don't fully trust God Himself. That's why I have to be on top of everything. Maybe that's why I can't fully trust you either, though I want to."

Natale chuckled. "I guess that leaves me in good company."

"Yes, but why can't I get past it?"

"You will." He stroked her cheek.

She was thinking hard. "So what now? Where do we begin?"

"I think it's about time for you to marry me." He took her hand and held it. "We could drive down to the church in Monte Carlo tomorrow morning."

Judith hesitated for so long that he was suddenly afraid she would say no.

But finally she nodded and smiled. "Yes, Peter. I do love you, and I want to share the rest of my life with you, whatever that entails. Yes, let's get married."

He held her tighter. "And I love you," he said. "So much that I can barely stand it sometimes." He could smell the perfume of her shampoo, and he knew he had never meant the words so much in his life.

They stood then, arm in arm, and looked out to the horizon. The sun was going down over the coastline. The waters were azure, tinted gold. This day was ending. But Peter knew, as he stood there, that he was looking at the beginning of a whole new way of life.